Carole Matthews is the internationally bestselling author of six other outstandingly successful novels. Her unique sense of humour has won her legions of fans and critical acclaim. *A Compromising Position* and *A Minor Indiscretion* were both Top 5 *Sunday Times* bestsellers. *For Better, For Worse* is being made into a Hollywood movie and was selected by one of America's top TV book clubs as their book of the month. Carole has presented on television and radio and when she is not writing novels and television scripts she manages to find time to trek in the Himalayas, rollerblade in Central Park and snooze in her garden shed in Milton Keynes.

For more information about Carole Matthews and her novels, and to read an exclusive short story by Carole, visit her website at: www.carolematthews.co.uk

'A feel-good tale . . . fun and thoroughly escapist'
Marie Claire

'Hilarious . . . Saucy, but nice'   *Express*

'Will have you giggling from the start . . . hilarious'
OK! magazine

'You'll love this!'   *Essentials*

'Funny, pacy and heart-warming'   *U* magazine

'An amusing romantic romp'   *Books* magazine

'She's good'   *Bookseller*

The Sweetest Taboo

Carole Matthews

First published in 2003
by HEADLINE BOOK PUBLISHING

First published in paperback in 2004
by HEADLINE BOOK PUBLISHING

10 9 8 7 6 5 4 3 2 1

ISBN 0 7472 6770 7

Typeset in Times by
Letterpart Limited, Reigate, Surrey

Printed and bound in Great Britain by
Mackays of Chatham plc, Chatham, Kent

Papers and cover board used by Headline are natural, recyclable
products made from wood grown in sustainable forests. The
manufacturing processes conform to the environmental
regulations of the country of origin.

HEADLINE BOOK PUBLISHING
A division of Hodder Headline
338 Euston Road
LONDON NW1 3BH

www.headline.co.uk
www.hodderheadline.com

To Lee 'Who's the daddy?' Brooks
Who will be cruelly disappointed yet again . . .

Chapter One

I can tell you exactly when I fell in love. The exact place. The exact minute. The London Book Fair. Here. *Now.* Let me quickly check my watch so that I will remember it for ever – 3.45 p.m. I have no idea who he is – yet – nor that he's about to turn my life upside down, but already I'm bitten, smitten. He looks at me again and smiles, and my insides flood with a tingling warmth that I haven't felt for a very long time. I also have pins and needles in my feet, but that's more to do with uncomfortable shoes and the first glimmer of a bunion than Cupid's deadly aim.

'We need someone gorgeous,' he tells me, and I realise that I'm staring.

He has an American accent that I can't place. East Coast, West Coast – I'm hopeless, they all sound the same to me. Drawly and sexy. And they all make me go weak at the knees. I adore American men. At sixth-form college my sociology teacher was from Charleston and I couldn't wait for each week's lesson to roll round. I never learned a thing about sociology – to this day I know absolutely nothing about the demographic breakdown of the population of the UK or the moral economy of trade or the effects of a cybersociety on the community . . . but I loved every minute of the classes. He could have been talking about the joys of collecting postage stamps and I, for one, would have remained utterly enthralled.

'It'll take about five minutes. No more,' the All-American man is saying to me now. 'Can you spare the time?'

I want to tell him that if he asked me nicely I could

1

probably spare the rest of my life, but only manage to stammer out, 'Y-Yes.' If he's called Chuck or Bud or Richie, I am well and truly done for.

Reaching out, he takes my elbow and guides me towards him. I gape round – having failed in the mouth-closing area – looking for approval from Nigel, the manager of the book stand where I'm supposed to be helping out. But he is busy talking numbers to a bookshop owner in a corduroy jacket the colour of a stagnant pond and no one else is the slightest bit interested in what I'm doing.

What I am doing is some temporary work for Bindlatters Books, publishers of a highly dubious range of Technicolor horror books for the 'youff' market that seem to involve more blood than your average abattoir sees in a week and lots of heads being ripped off.

Working for a book publisher may sound interesting – I can just hear myself dropping it into the conversation at dinner parties – but what I'm actually doing is wearing a red polyester uniform and attempting to give out leaflets to people who don't want to take them. They have probably had enough leaflets thrust upon them in the last few days to last a lifetime – although they may not have had ones like ours that are adorned with severed heads.

'Publisher?' my American asks as he eases me through a crush of people.

I guess it's a reasonable assumption to make at a book fair. Would that I could claim such a lofty position. I could pretend, but what would that achieve? But maybe I don't need to admit that my knowledge of books extends to buying the battered copies that have done the rounds of charity shops to fill my long and lonely nights. I am an aficionado of dog-eared Danielle Steel. 'No.' How can I make this sound riveting? I have no idea. I'm not that inventive – at least not at short notice. 'I'm Chief Leaflet Giver-Outer.'

He tries to look impressed as if I've just told him I'm Chancellor of the Exchequer.

'It's a temporary position.' Oh dear. I sound dreadfully bitter.

The London Book Fair is held in Olympia and it takes me forever to get here every morning – as I live in Battersea on the wrong side of the river. But it's only for a week. I have to keep reminding myself of that fact. However, what happens at the end of the week could well be worse. A big fat nothing is currently looming large on the horizon of my life.

I glance at my inadequate official badge. It doesn't bear my name – Sadie Nelson – or any of the other details that single me out from A.N. Other. Just the name of my stand. I guess the people who generally perform this thankless task don't hang around long enough to warrant having a printed name badge. 'Dogsbody' would have been an appropriate title, but they didn't have a badge that said that either.

'I'm Gil,' this gorgeous American says over his shoulder. 'Gil McGann.'

'Publisher?'

'No.'

'Agent?' There are a lot of those about here this week too. They're the ones who look like they don't go out in the sun very often.

'No.' He gives a dismissive shake of his head and takes a firmer grip of my arm as we thread our way through the oncoming throng. 'I'm a Hollywood film producer.'

Yes, and I'm Halle Berry.

'I've just bought a great book,' he continues. '*The One That Got Away.* A romantic comedy – funny as hell. I beat Bob to it.' He looks at me as if I should be bowled over.

'Bob?'

'Bob Redford.'

'Ah.' That's Robert to mere mortals, I'd like to point out.

'I'm here to do smiley things with the author.'

Oh good. So let me just get this clear: I'm standing here in a red polyester uniform, which as well as making me look like I'm having an afternoon off from Butlins, is designed specifically to fit someone shorter, fatter and forty years older than me, talking to a gorgeous Hollywood film producer about his latest movie acquisition. On the plus side, I'm having a good hair day. If he doesn't look at me anywhere below my neck he might not realise that I'm wearing leftover stock from when C & A went bust. And despite not asking my name, he told me I was gorgeous. Any minute now my alarm clock is going to go off and I'm not going to be able to decide whether this was a dream or a nightmare. Currently, it could go either way.

We squeeze through the crowd and onto another exhibition stand which is a hundred times bigger and swankier than Bindlatters Books' one. It is hung with huge posters of trendy books, some of which I've even heard of, but haven't read because they haven't hit the Skid Row of the charity shops yet. There is a group of people drinking champagne in the corner and laughing loudly. A stainless-steel table with a smear-free glass top has been arranged at one side and there is a crackle of anticipation in the few people, looking decidedly like fellow minions, who are milling around.

Gil stands next to me, but doesn't let go of my arm. I'm not complaining. I have goose-pimples all over me and yet I'm not the slightest bit cold. In fact, you could probably grill hamburgers on my cheeks.

'I hope you don't think this is too much of an imposition?'

'Not at all.' My hormones are nudging me to do my most winning smile. I can't – my feet are hurting too much from standing in one spot all day in high heels. Now I know why exhibition displays are called 'stands'. My lips stretch tightly across my teeth and from somewhere in the depths of my reserves, I send a tired smile back at him. 'Though you haven't actually told me what you want me to do.'

'Damn,' Gil says. 'Sorry. We need you to pose with Elise Neils.' He gives a nod of his head towards a mass of blonde curls surrounded by smooth, be-suited men. 'Feign adoring fan for some press photos – if you wouldn't mind.'

'Oh.' I suppose it could have been worse. It could have involved me perched on a stand giving out leaflets.

This, apart from my current pleasant interlude, has been

the job from hell. But beggars can't be choosers and I very nearly was a beggar before this rather dubious 'opportunity' with Bindlatters knocked.

I used to work in the City – great job, great flat, great car – until due to economic downturn, world recession, plummeting share prices blah, blah, blah, I found myself severely and swiftly surplus to requirements. First the job went, then the car, then the flat, then the fair-weather friends and, accompanying each, a slice of my self-confidence. I had slogged my guts and my liver out for that company – late nights, short lunch-hours, a social life that revolved around entertaining customers with copious amounts of vodka – and it chopped my heart into little pieces to be told to clear my desk and never again darken the door of Allen-Jones Holdings by someone I had considered a good mate.

I vowed never to work in the City again. Panic set in when I realised no one in the City actually wanted me to anyway. 'Recruitment freeze' was the most common term I heard. 'We'd love to employ someone of your calibre, but . . .' Then I found that recruitment freezes were not confined to my chosen industry alone.

Since then I've scrabbled around with a variety of part-time, poorly paid jobs that have barely provided enough to pay my share of the rent on the slightly scrubby flat in Battersea my lovely, lovely friend Alice has very kindly let me squeeze into with her – even though she knows I'm a credit risk. My savings are dwindling at an alarming rate.

I look back at Gil. And, for once, I don't know what to say to this man. I'm not normally known for my reticence, but all my words suddenly seem to have dried up. Perhaps it's being surrounded by a surfeit of them in all these worthy tomes that's making me feel inadequate.

'Here she is,' Gil lowers his head to mine and whispers close and in a faintly reverent manner right next to my ear. The goose-pimples go into overdrive.

The lucky author, who has had half of Hollywood chasing her – including Bob – is a bit too young and a bit too gorgeous for her own good and I could scratch her eyes out already. I wonder how far Gil McGann's 'being smiley' extends?

Elise Neils is oh-so hip and oh-so tiny and bears the confident air of someone who is used to being pampered. Sliding behind her special desk as if she's done it a thousand times before, she beams a practised beam at her waiting audience. She looks like a complete cow. I want a job that's glamorous, I think, shortly before I'm manhandled away from Gil by a publicity-type woman with trendy horn-rimmed glasses and am plonked next to Elise Neils in order to look adoring.

'Hi,' she says. Actually, she seems quite nice but I'm already determined that I won't like her. She takes up her pen and poses in a suitably authorish way, whilst I bend over and looking subservient and as if my life would improve 1000 per cent if she would deign to scribble in her book for me. A poster declaring: *THE ONE THAT GOT AWAY!* overshadows us both. We both grin like mad at a bevy of flashing cameras. This may be a regular thing for Elise Neils, but if this is to be my only fifteen minutes of fame, I'm going to make damn sure that I mug up to it!

The cameras go click-click-click as we turn our heads to and fro, inducing wedding photo-style smiles, and by the time we've finished I've decided that I don't want to be a celebrity after all.

'Thanks,' Ms Hot Author says to me and benevolently pats my arm with her oh-so tiny hand. She slides out from behind her table and sashays off in the direction of the champagne followed by a horde of devoted men.

I stand abandoned and look round for Gil. He is waiting there, thumbing through a book – the only male in the vicinity with his tongue still in his mouth. Gratefully, I wander back towards him.

'Thanks,' he says. 'You were wonderful.'

I'm not sure if he's being sincere or pulling my leg, but I grin thankfully anyway.

He nods over towards the scrum for champagne, where our future Booker Prize winner gives him the glad eye, but he is completely oblivious. 'Shall we join the crush?'

'I'd better get back,' I say with a flash of unbridled loyalty that surprises even me. What am I thinking of? Champagne with a Hollywood producer or giving out leaflets on an exhibition stand for less than a fiver an hour, and I choose the latter? I am clearly sickening for something. Or mad.

'I'll walk you back,' Gil says. 'Give me a moment.' And he strolls to the side of the stand to gather some bits and pieces. It gives me time for a more thorough appraisal. And already I'm regretting my decision to hotfoot it back to Bindlatters Books.

Gil is tall and slender and is wearing a suit that looks like it has been squashed into a suitcase on a transatlantic flight and worn on an exhibition stand for too many days. I don't think he's a natural suit-wearer. He isn't glowing with a typical Hollywood tan either and I thought everyone over there was a slave to the sun. Perhaps he spends too much time inside watching movies – I don't know. It sort of suits him, though; he'd look funny if he was tanned. He's boyish in a craggy way and I'm not certain how old he is, but I would suspect that he's still this side of 'life begins at . . .' He has a cute smile and enough charisma to make sure that most women are giving him a second glance. It's certainly working for me.

Gil comes back bearing a raincoat, because as usual this week it has been raining persistently in London, a folded copy of *The Times* and a hardback copy of *The One That Got Away*. He waves it at me. I daren't tell him that I'll read it in about five years' time when it has done the rounds of several offices, all the sex scenes will bear unsightly, unidentifiable stains and it'll probably have a few crucial pages missing. I hate it when that happens – but then it isn't the most irritating thing about being financially embarrassed. Having a cupboard that contains nothing but Ambrosia Creamed Rice and an out-of-date tin of pilchards is much, much worse. Believe me, I know.

He hands me the copy of *The One That Got Away*. 'For you.'

'Thanks.' I feel a flush of deep gratitude until I see a picture of the lovely, lucky and probably fabulously wealthy Elise Neils on the back.

He takes my arm again and we head back towards what I have lovingly come to know as 'my stand'. There are a thousand questions I should be fitting into the next two minutes and I can't think of any of them. This could be my big chance – for what, I'm not sure. But I do know that I am blowing it, like you wouldn't believe.

'Well,' he says.

Nigel is at the front of the stand giving me what I can only describe as 'a look'.

Gil and I sort of hover, looking and not looking at each other at the same time.

Nigel makes a point of checking his watch.

'My hotel does great afternoon tea,' Gil says suddenly. 'Very quaint. Very English.'

'Nice,' I say because my brilliant, sparkling wit can't come up with anything better.

'I think I'll head that way.'

'Sensible idea.'

'What time do you get off?'

'Me?' There appear to be no film stars or flighty young authors around. He nods. I have several thousand more flyers to get rid of before I'm done. Perhaps I could dump them in a wastepaper bin somewhere. 'About an hour.'

'Come to my hotel, Ms Chief Leaflet Giver-Outer. Join me for afternoon tea.'

'Oh.' I couldn't tell you when I last had afternoon tea. In fact, I don't know if I ever have. Isn't it only tourists and blue-rinsed old ladies that do afternoon tea? 'Okay.'

Gil takes a business card out of a silver holder, scribbles on the back and hands it to me. And it does, indeed, say GIL MCGANN, PRODUCER in big, bold letters. 'It's not far. I hope you can come.'

'I will,' I say before my brain has time to compute this and decide that one of us is barking mad.

'See you later.' And he walks off into the crush of publishers and agents while I stand and contemplate the fact that I have just agreed to go to the hotel of a man who hasn't even asked my name and, although he could have his pick of flighty, flirty young authors to get 'smiley' with, clearly has a fetish for women in red polyester uniforms. I watch him until he disappears, running my fingers round the sharp edges of his card.

Nigel sidles towards me. 'Leaflets,' he says, handing me another interminable pile.

'Leaflets,' I echo. And the earth rushes up to meet me with 'bump' written all over it.

Chapter Two

Gil flopped onto his bed. His room had cost some extortionate amount of money for what was little more than a broom cupboard. A broom cupboard in the attic. He guessed it was supposed to be cutesy, with original beams and steeply sloping ceilings – and more disconcerting, steeply sloping floors – but he kind of preferred rooms that you could stand up in. He'd end up with a hunch back if he stayed here more than a week – already his neck was developing a painful crick. Moving round invariably meant stubbing your toe on heavy mahogany furniture. There was no gym in the hotel and it had rained so much that jogging was out of the question. Jet lag weighed heavy in his unexercised bones. Next time he would stay at The Hempel and be damned.

Lying down was the easier option and Gil stretched out and enjoyed it briefly. Then, he tensed up again. What was he thinking of? There were a million and one things that he ought to be doing while he was in Town other than hitting on strange women. While he was here it had been his intention to schmooze some up-and-coming British writers. There were very few studios making classy romantic comedies these days, and Gil thought it was about time they had some competition. Tonight had been lined up to do some flesh-pressing. What had happened to his brain that it had been swayed so easily by a hot lady in a dreadful suit? As if his life wasn't complicated enough.

Gil couldn't do relaxing, it was too much of a waste of time. He got up and switched on his laptop. The time difference here was a pain. When he was raring to go, everyone in LA was still curled up in bed – or out at parties. He tapped in his password. The first message was from Georgina, under the heading of *Urgent*.

Gil groaned to himself. Nothing Georgina ever did was urgent. Not in the real world. He clicked the message open. *Call me!* It said. *Now!*

Gil glanced at his watch. Now would not be a good time to call Georgina. He wasn't even sure she would understand that the rest of the world didn't operate on 'Georgina Time'. She'd probably just broken a nail or something equally earth-shattering.

He clicked through the rest of the messages – mainly moans and groans from the studios regarding his latest projects – and dispatched his replies with professional ease. At least email never slept. Gil ran his hands over his face. A shave was definitely in order. His entire 'casual' wardrobe of one sweater and one pair of jeans was spread out on the back of a chintzy armchair and he wished he had thought to pack more clothes for socialising, but then he hadn't bargained on being blown away by a beautiful blonde. How long had it been since he had felt like this? Certainly not since he'd married Georgina, that's for sure.

The digital display of his bedside alarm blinked lazily at him. Gil worried at his thumbnail. Perhaps he'd better call Georgina. Just in case it was, for once, an emergency. There was always that horrible element of doubt with Gina, that some day she might even follow through with one of her many threats. Looking at the phone, he wondered where she was right now. Maybe he should leave it as long as he could.

Gil headed towards the shower, hoping that more water would come out of it than last time. He needed to freshen up and fast. Try to make a silk purse out of a sow's ear. For some ludicrous reason he wanted it to go right with this woman.

He also needed to do something about the situation with Georgina, but that was going to take some diplomatic handling. And he was fully aware that he had been putting it off for far too long.

11

Chapter Three

Mr Hollywood Movie Tycoon could just want casual sex – I fully appreciate that. And maybe it is easier to impress one of the more lowly administrative staff by saying you're a film producer rather than a flighty young author, who might well yawn and think, Not another one! I have no friends here at the Book Fair to discuss this with and I can't ring Alice as she has a real job and is busy, busy, busy 24/7. I also can't ring her because I know she would tell me that I'm being a total wimp.

I'm glad to be leaving the frantic crush of this conference behind. Only one more day to go. It's great if you're really involved in these things but if you're on the periphery of them, doing sundry unseen tasks to keep the whole thing rolling, then it's a bit of a drag. When I was a whizzy City-type, just a few short months ago, I used to love conferences. They took me all over the world – to Paris, Prague and Preston – although I could take or leave the actual work bit. I know it's not original or even unusual to meet one's lover at a conference. Aren't they always very little to do with work and more to do with leaving responsibility or the bosom of one's stifling familial duties behind and going mad for a while by embarking on a period of anonymous sex in an anonymous hotel room with a stranger from a rival company who you're quite sure you'll never see again? (Until the next conference.) I am, of course, talking about other people – not me. I was always purely an observer of these sexual shenanigans.

This is because I don't understand the concept of casual sex. Why would you want to get your bits and pieces out for a total stranger? Particularly one with a bigger turnover than you. I am into commitment and love and loyalty in a big way and Mr Gil McGann, film producer, is going to be cruelly disappointed if he thinks English girls are easy. Well, this one anyway. I can't vouch for my friends. They all seem to be able to bonk anything that breathes. Or am I just being fussy? It is a criticism that has been levelled at me in the past. Some of my friends have boyfriends *and* girlfriends. What's that all about? A fashion thing? Sexual greed? I don't understand it at all. Or is it just easier to date someone whose nail varnish you can share?

Anyway, I have more immediate problems. Thankfully, Bindlatters Books have supplied me with a locker so that I won't have to turn up at Gil's hotel sporting the red ensemble – although I realise that this may be the only thing about me that he found highly desirable. Oh dear. My confidence is at a rather low ebb.

I came to work wearing black boot-cut trousers and heeled boots from the days when I could afford to splash out on Russell & Bromley ones. On the downside, I am also wearing a cropped T-shirt bearing an embroidered Betty Boo and the caption *Diamonds are a Girl's Best Friend!* Alice brought it back for me from Universal Studios on her summer holiday to California last year – her final extravagance before she became a burdened home-owner. It seems a bit naff wearing a Universal Studios T-shirt to have afternoon tea with a man who might well work there in a serious capacity instead of just paying up to go in the theme park and experience a multitude of different ways of getting wet and sick.

I look in my purse. It contains three pounds and fifty pence and a credit card I keep threatening to cut up. Taking Gil's business card from my polyester pocket, I turn it over in my hand. The Townham Hotel. He's right – it isn't too far from here. My stomach has a shiver of indecision. But, hey, who's in charge here? Me or my digestive system? This is the only excitement I've had in days, weeks, months! It's another thing I can drop casually into dinner-party conversations for years to come. Ha! I may not be trendy enough to have a girlfriend – or desirable enough to have a boyfriend – but this must earn me at least a few 'cool' points. Better than discussing yet another crappy failed interview at House of Pizza.

I obviously come across as way too desperate. Before my last interview, I swotted up on all the different types of pizza the restaurant served and tried to dazzle them with my stunning array of knowledge by quoting special offers and making reference to the recent television campaign featuring the 'thick and crusty'. The manager was dumbfounded and clearly could not cope with the competition as he promised to let me know that afternoon if I'd got the job, but never did. He probably thought I was a mole from Head Office. He was as thick and crusty as his bloody pizza. Next time, I'm going to stick on some fake acne and snarl a lot – I'd be hired in a flash.

Throwing on an elderly Karen Millen version of an Afghan coat that has seen better days, I shoot out of the conference centre and grab a Tube to South Kensington, squashing in with delegates talking in la-di-dah tones about the kind of authors you see all the time on *Lorraine*. The Tube takes an age to chug anywhere from this part of the Underground, which means that every day we all have to suffer the same smelly, dread-locked busker singing old Simon and Garfunkel hits very badly. Nevertheless, in true British fashion, we all cough up our obligatory fifty pence before we are allowed to shuffle off at South Ken station.

The Townham Hotel is just round the corner from here, but before I head there, I dodge between the rows of speeding traffic and cross the road to a little boutique that does great clothes at knock down – and possibly 'knock off' – prices. When I say boutique, it's more of an upmarket charity shop. This is what I'm reduced to, not only for my books but for all my clothing needs too. I rush in and rummage like a woman possessed through the rows and rows of crushed blouses. Got it! For twenty-two quid I become the proud owner of a black lacy top with bell-bottom sleeves and a neckline that does nothing to hide the fact that I'm a girl. Ha! Down with red polyester!

I apologise to my credit card and give it a grateful kiss before battering it again and rush into a cubicle at the back the size of a broom cupboard and change out of my Betty Boo, which gets stuffed unceremoniously in my handbag. I clip my hair up and decide that I look a bit fab – well, better than in my Butlins Redcoat uniform. I'm not sure that the twenty-two-quid top will survive the rigours of Alice's washing machine but it will do for now. I just wish I had some blusher with me. I positively bloom behind a carefully applied barrier of Raspberry Whisper.

Chapter Four

The Townham is posh. Not as posh as the Ritz, say, but Victoria Beckham lower-case posh. I feel ridiculously nervous and lurk outside in the pouring rain for a moment, thinking that this could be bordering on insanity.

Before I'm completely drowned, I decide that I don't care if it is or not. This could be my big chance. Gil the film producer may offer me a part in his latest movie. Why not? Some very famous actress was discovered whilst waiting tables in Los Angeles. I can't remember who, because I know diddly-squat about Hollywood – but it was someone really, really famous.

Here I go. Deep breath, shoulders back, head up. This isn't do or die, but it's do or go home and eat last night's leftover risotto and moan to Alice that nothing exciting ever happens to me.

The receptionist gives me a really haughty look when I ask for Mr McGann. Ha! I bet he hasn't asked her to have afternoon tea with him even though she's weaving a navy-blue polyester uniform.

'Mr McGann *ees* in the loonge,' she says in the barely intelligible foreign accent that everyone who works in London hotels has these days. And when I look, Mr McGann is indeed in the lounge. He's in front of a roaring log fire, sprawled out on a big squashy sofa, *The Times* discarded on his lap. The suit has gone and he's wearing jeans and some preppy, hand-knit sweater that probably cost about a million quid and came from Fred Segal or somewhere; the only thing I do know about

Hollywood is that Fred Segal is a trendy shop because *Glamour* magazine says Madonna and Calista Flockhart shop there. How much more trendy do you want?

Gil's also fast asleep, but I'm quite pleased because at least he's not snoring – something that I always find very offputting in a man. His fringe has flopped over his eyes and I want to reach out and smooth it away from his brow and I'm suddenly seized by this overwhelming feeling of love and warmth. If I was a bit older, I'd call it a hot flush, but unfortunately I can't dismiss it so easily. I look at this man I don't really know and yet I want to hold him. I've only felt like this once before – and then I had the excuse of being fifteen and very impressionable. Simon Le Bon was a bit of a looker in his day too.

I stand there and don't really know what to do. Gil looks so peaceful that I could stay and watch him for hours, but on the other hand, having summoned up the nerve to come here, I'd really like him to be awake to acknowledge the fact.

The room is dark and mellow; the only light is from the flickering fire and a scattering of table lamps. There are a couple of nut-brown chesterfields and some squishy sofas too. The night has closed in, encouraged by the pouring rain. It's no wonder he's nodded off.

My dilemma is solved by two loud German business-men who come crashing into the lounge like an advance from the Panzer division, speaking in *Achtung!* voices. They carry big brandy balloons and march across the lounge to a far-flung chesterfield as if they are invading Poland. Gil's eyes shoot open and once they have stopped rotating in surprise they focus on me. A smile spreads across his face.

'Hi,' I say.

'Hey.' He swings his legs off the sofa and stands to greet me, even though he still looks a bit dazed. His fingers fold round mine and they're warm from the heat of the fire. 'I must have dozed off,' he says.

'Jet lag,' I advise as if I know about these things.

'I guess so.' Gil sits down again and pats the sofa next to

17

him. 'Join me. I've ordered afternoon tea, I just need to let Justine know when we're ready.'

Gil nods at Justine – the girl in the navy polyester, who has appeared and is watching us like a hawk – and she smiles brightly at him, exactly the way she didn't smile at me.

Slithering out of my damp, doggy coat, I throw it at the corner of the shaggy hearthrug, which probably resembles one of its long-lost friends, and sit down at the far end of the sofa. I always find it a nightmare sitting on a sofa with a stranger. I'm never quite sure of the etiquette of correct distance. Too close and you end up sliding down the middle of the cushions. Too far to one end and you look standoffish. I try to position myself centrally in the cushion, which I'm sure gives off its own message.

'Well,' Gil turns and appraises me. 'You look different.' By that, I hope he means better. His eyes linger on my cleavage.

'I don't think those uniforms were designed by Armani,' I joke awkwardly.

'No,' he laughs. 'Probably not.'

Justine brings in the tray of tea – eyes and smile fixed on Gil. I think if she could have slammed my end of the tray down she would have. I give her my best fluttery-eyed, sugar-sweet grin and she stomps off back to her perch.

There is a bottle of champagne on the tray and no sign of a teapot. 'I thought we'd do afternoon tea without the tea part.' Gil pours me a glass of champagne. 'To tell you the truth, I'm not that fond of tea. I'm more of a coffee person.'

I wonder if this is his only dark secret. I hate this part of meeting people – the part where you think they're potentially a fab human being and then you find out they've more skeletons hiding in their cupboard than a Christopher Lee film and all manner of undesirable habits. I also hate the fact that I always live in hope of being wrong. Gil lifts his glass.

'What are we celebrating?' I ask. '*The One That Got Away?*'

Gil shakes his head. 'I think Ms Neils has had enough glasses raised to her.' He clinks his glass against mine. 'Maybe we should toast the one that *didn't* get away?'

I assume he means me, but I'm not 100 per cent sure.

'I'm only here for one more night,' Gil says, and he gazes at me in a very twinkly way. 'I'd like to spend it with you.'

I nearly spit out my champagne. Blimey, this is a bit quick. We haven't even got as far as the smoked-salmon sandwiches and the iced fancies! Are all American men such fast movers? I manage to swallow my fizz instead of spraying it all over the place, but it goes down the wrong hole and I start to cough.

'Oh hell,' Gil says. 'I didn't mean it like that.' He pats me with an exuberant amount of force on my back. The Germans glare over their brandy at us. Gil and I start to laugh and before he beats me to death, I get him to stop pounding my vertebrae into submission.

'I'm fine. I'm fine,' I say. We fall back onto the sofa, slinking down, giggling, and I forget all about the territorial occupation of cushions; we put our heads together like a couple of naughty school-kids.

'Shall I start again?' Gil asks finally.

I wipe the tears from below my ears, hoping that my mascara is still in the place it should be. 'I think you'd better.'

'This is my last night in London. I am supposed to be going to a book signing with Elise. I'd rather spend the evening having dinner with you.'

He's choosing me over the cute, successful author! 'Won't she be mad?'

'I have just agreed to pay her an awful lot of money, so I think she'll cut me some slack.'

'We haven't eaten our sandwiches yet.'

'These wouldn't feed a Cockney sparrow,' he says in a Dick Van Dyke accent.

Why am I thinking up excuses for him to ditch me?

'Do you have other plans?' he asks.

'Yes.' I twiddle the stem of my champagne flûte. 'I'm

supposed to be eating last night's risotto with my flatmate.'

'Would he mind if you skipped it?'

'She,' I correct. 'No. But I'd better phone her.'

'I'll call Elise too.'

'Let's do it.' And with a nod, we both produce mobile phones and punch in numbers.

Alice's phone clicks straight to answering machine and I leave a garbled message while trying to keep one ear on Gil's conversation. He tells Elise that he's unavailable, but I notice that he doesn't explain why. Small point, but I wonder if it's pertinent. We both end our calls and then look at each other, vaguely embarrassed.

The Germans seem to take the hint that this is becoming a private party and leave. Gil stands up and throws another log on the fire and we listen to it crackle and hiss in protest for a while.

'I don't normally do this sort of thing,' Gil admits.

'Me neither.'

'Dating is a pretty weird business in California.'

'I think it's pretty weird in London too.'

'You're not in a permanent relationship?'

'Me?' I shake my head. 'No.' Would I be here if I was? I want to say that I've given up on men, but really I think they've given up on me. I have had three full-time, bona-fide, paid-up boyfriends in living memory, all of whom I adored and all of whom left me for someone bubblier and with bouncier breasts. It's given me some sort of complex.

I do dating occasionally, usually when one of my friends forces me to, but I find the whole thing traumatic. At eighteen the will-he-ring?/won't-he-ring? thing is part of the deal. At thirty-two I feel that I've grown out of it. I don't want to play dating games. I don't want to spend nights in loud wine bars with people that I don't give a toss about. I don't want seven men on the go at once. I want relationships. Sensible, grown-up ones. Preferably involving two people who care for each other. I don't want posturing and playing cool and keeping my options open. I don't want to pretend that I'm something that I'm not. I try very hard not to do manipulation or deceit. I run all my relationships with a view that honesty is generally the best policy. You'd think that men would like that, but they don't. Generally, they can't cope with it at all.

'You?'

'No,' Gil says. And I notice that there is no telltale white band round his finger from having hastily stashed his wedding ring away. Years of conference-going has made me suspicious. I have been approached by more married men whose wives don't understand them than I care to remember.

'I didn't really need you to pose with Elise,' Gil says suddenly with a nervous smile. 'I'd watched you for most of this week and didn't know how else to talk to you. Is that a terrible confession?'

'No.' It's a pretty amazing one though. I'd imagined Hollywood producers being used to having a string of obliging starlets hanging on their arm, not having insecurities about chatting up someone like little old me.

'For someone who professes not to be interested in giving leaflets out,' he continues with a smile, 'you were doing it with a certain amount of fervour.'

'Needs must,' I say. 'I'm at the stage where I treat every job as if it might be my last.' I pull my knees up towards me and let myself sink into the sofa in an attempt to convince my body I'm not as weary as I feel. 'I was a City trader, but the world of financial high-flyers decided they could manage without me.' I fiddle with my champagne glass to avoid eye-contact. 'I went from a ten-year career plan governed with the aid of a very pushy life coach, to not knowing what I'm going to be doing next week.'

Gil shrugs. 'The movie business is like that all the time. One day you're hot, the next you're not. You have to roll with the good times and try not to take it too personally when you're as popular as a fart in a spacesuit. Successes are quickly forgotten. Failure tends to hang around.'

'Like a fart in a spacesuit.'

Gil laughs. 'Exactly.'

'Have you produced anything I'd have heard of?' I venture. I like to think I'm a bit of a film buff – as long as it's something you can watch on Sky Home Box Office. By the time I get back from work most evenings, it's all I can do to sit upright and watch television. If he does deep and meaningful movies I won't have a clue.

'Maybe.' Gil reels off a list of films that were all major blockbusters over here as well as in the States – *Funny Bones, Teenage Dreamboat, Frankie and Sally, One Hot Night, Remembering Maude, Could It Be Magic?*

Oh good grief. He *is* a film producer. A hit factory. This is a man who does, indeed, know Bob on first-name terms. And it may well show an inherent lack of trust in men, but I was convinced he was going to turn out to be a fraud. I don't even want to examine how I came to this conclusion. I may still pop down to Blockbusters to check out the credits on the DVD covers just to make sure he's listed.

'I loved *One Hot Night*,' I say and blush over the implications of the title.

'You did?' He too flushes. 'It's my own personal favourite.'

'I'm very impressed.'

'I have to confess,' Gil says, 'I kinda hoped you would be.'

'I have my own confession to make,' I say. 'I spent twenty-two pounds I don't have on this top in an effort to impress you.'

'It worked,' Gil says. 'You look very lovely.'

'Thanks.'

He sighs. 'Why didn't we meet up earlier?'

I don't know the answer to this. We are too comfortable too quickly, and already I'm dreading the time when he'll have to go. Then I wonder if we'd met earlier whether it would, in fact, have made things better or worse.

'How can I feel like this?' Gil says. 'I don't even know your name.'

And if it's a line, I am falling for it. 'Sadie,' I oblige. 'Sadie Nelson.' And, at this moment, it's about the only thing that I am certain of.

Chapter Five

Why do nights whizz by so quickly when you don't want them to? Is it a rule of the universe rather like Mad Murphy's Law – which decrees that toast with jam on it will always fall face down, particularly if the bearer is wearing white or expensive clothing? Why couldn't the hours drag by like they do when you're sitting in a dentist's waiting room? Time, as they say, does fly when you're having fun. Even if you happen to be having it while you're in the land of Nod.

We didn't make dinner – or the bedroom, for that matter. We sat chatting for hours and then the next thing, without even realising it, we'd fallen asleep. I'm surprised Justine didn't come and prod us both awake. When we did wake, it was because we were both freezing cold as the fire in the Townham's lounge had long since died. I'd like to think it was romantic that we'd cuddled up together like children and slept soundly – although several of my limbs are starting to regret it – but part of me feels that I would have liked to stay awake all night and talked. That's the unacceptable face of getting older – the mind is still very willing, but the body is a right old party-pooper. Too many early nights in bed with nothing but ye olde battered paperbacks for company have made my party animal cells go all dormant.

'Hi, Sleepyhead,' Gil says, and I think that he's a fine one to talk.

And while I'm pleased that the 'bedroom situation' wasn't raised, I realise that the chance for carnal knowledge has passed and with that comes a certain amount of sadness. Not to mention downright sexual frustration. The Queen is having jubilees more often than I'm having sex – though I do have to admit that some of it is down to a certain reluctance on my part.

'Hi,' I say, even though my tongue is fuzzed up to the roof of my mouth. 'Ooo.' Bits of me are hurting and I don't dare to think what my hair looks like.

Gil takes my hand. 'I have to go,' he says. 'I need to call a cab, otherwise I'm going to miss my plane.'

I can't think of anything to say. No, that's wrong. I can think of too many things to say.

'I wish I could take a later flight.' He genuinely looks troubled. 'I have work and stuff. I need to get back.'

It would only be delaying the inevitable. 'That's okay,' I say. 'I have to go to work too.' The whole world of leaflet-giving-out could crumble if I'm not at my post by nine.

'I'll be in London again,' Gil says. 'Soon. I usually come over to the screenings in September.'

September? That's months away. Seven months away, to be exact. That's not soon.

'Great,' I say.

'You do want to see me again?' Gil asks. 'You do want to stay in touch?'

'Yes. Of course.'

'Do you have email?'

I can nick one of Alice's spare addresses. She's a good pal. She'll realise that this is a worthy cause. 'Yes. No. Not really. But I can get it sorted.'

'You still have my business card?'

I nod.

'It has my phone number and my email address on it.'

I nod again. This is too rushed, too hurried, too important.

'Come to my room,' Gil says.

'I . . . we . . .'

'No,' Gil says. 'Wait here. I'll be five minutes. Three.' Then he kisses me soundly and rushes out, ordering a taxi and sprinting up the stairs without pausing.

I want to cry, but tell myself, 'Don't make a scene!

24

You're made of sterner stuff than that. This man is nothing to you. You only met him yesterday. How can you be stupid enough to cry over him? This was a pleasant evening and you must enjoy it for that – even though there's a chance that you'll never, ever repeat it in your entire life.' Standing here mesmerised, tasting his kiss on my lips, I try to work out a game plan, but haven't succeeded by the time Gil returns.

He still looks like he's just woken up, but he's wearing his suit instead of his preppies and carrying a suitcase. 'The cab's here,' he says, and his voice is definitely tinged with disappointment and sadness and I don't know what else.

I grab the damp Afghan from the floor and throw it on and we both head outside.

It is a grey and drizzly London dawn. The sky is the colour of over-washed sheets. The sun, white and weak, is edging above the Tube station and looks as feeble as I feel. The Afghan is failing to keep me warm and I stamp my toes on the pavement in an effort to revive them.

Gil opens the cab door and throws his suitcase inside. 'Heathrow, please,' he says to the driver, who seems reluctant to put away his newspaper. Then Gil turns to me. 'This is it.'

'It's been nice to meet you,' I say.

'Nice?' Gil laughs in surprise. 'I hope that's traditional British reserve,' he says, 'because I think it's been a lot more than nice.'

'Very nice.' I can feel myself starting to cry. 'It was very nice.'

Gil wraps his arms round me. 'I guess "very nice" will have to do.' He kisses me again and this time it's warm and tender and very inappropriate for a cold, hard, city street. 'Don't go' rushes up and sticks in my throat.

Gil disentangles himself and holds me away from him. 'I don't want to remember you like this,' he says, 'looking sad and alone. And more than a little cold.'

'I'm fine.' I stamp my feet just to show how capable I am of creating my own warmth. 'Really I am.'

Gil brushes his lips against mine for a final time. 'I'll

call,' he promises as he gets into the back of the cab.

I hope to God that he does. 'Bye.' I put my fingers against the glass as he closes the door. The cab driver, oblivious to our plight, moves off into the first murmurings of rush-hour traffic.

'Bye,' Gil mouths back.

And they drive away, leaving me standing on the pavement, looking pathetically after them, any pretence of not crying long since abandoned. Gil's cab turns the corner and he is gone.

I find a manky tissue in my pocket and have a really good blub – just at the same time as Justine, the surly receptionist, is arriving for work. She smirks at me and it helps to bring my tears to a halt.

'He has gone? Yes?' she enquires.

'Yes.'

'Good ridd-*ance* to bad rubbeesh,' she declares loftily. 'Zees Americans, they like to loove 'em and leave 'em.'

Ha! So this means she's tried to chat him up and he wasn't the slightest bit interested.

'We've just got engaged,' I say, and take great delight in watching her chin hit the jolly old pavement. And before she can congratulate me, I stride off towards the Tube and my last day of giving leaflets out.

Good grief, what am I saying? Lack of quality sleep has clearly sent me quite bonkers. It's all very well playing the cocksure clown for a silly foreign bint, but back in reality, I know I may never see him again. The thought sends my mood plummeting to my Russell & Bromley boots. While Gil is heading swiftly back towards the California sunshine and the mad, bad, make-believe world of movies, here in my mundane little life in miserable little downcast London, it starts to rain.

If my life were a movie, the sun would be out, it would be full of love and laughter – and I'd get the guy. We'd walk off into the sunset arm-in-arm. And a Tom and Jerry cartoon-style ten-ton weight would drop on the head of the bossy receptionist.

As it is, it's pouring down and I have no umbrella. I am

not getting the guy, I am just getting very wet. And I'm doing it without having brushed my teeth. I escape the downpour, dive into the Tube and realise that somewhere between the Townham and here I've lost my weekly pass and will have to buy another ticket. A heartfelt 'fuck' is not far from my lips. An absolutely perfect day for giving out leaflets, I think.

Chapter Six

Alice and I are sitting in the Wing-Wah Chinese Takeaway waiting for the owner, Li, to create some wonder in our lives via the medium of sweet and sour pork. This has been my 'local' for years, even though it's never been remotely near where I live. It just happens to be the best around for miles.

'Why look so glum, lady?' Li says, while putting our prawn crackers in a plastic bag.

'Man trouble,' Alice informs him. 'Her. Not me,' she expands with a flick of her hair in my direction.

'Thanks,' I say, uncertain that I want the world and, in particular, the queue in the Wing-Wah to share my romantic troubles.

'Confucius he say all men are total borrocks.'

Li was born in Bermondsey and has lived for the majority of his thirty-five years in South London. He has never been to China and knows bog all about Confucius. He does, however, do a mean crispy duck so we tolerate all his insane ramblings from his interpretation of the lesser-known sayings of Confucius to the sheer brilliance of Jackie Chan – who, I'm led to believe, does all his own stunts.

'We're giving this one the benefit of the doubt,' Alice says. 'He's a movie producer.'

While I quietly die of embarrassment, the rest of the queue nod their approval.

'And he didn't try to sleep with her on their first date.'

The queue nod again.

'They just fell asleep in each other's arms.'

All the faces in the queue melt into a warm smile. I smile tightly back.

'So,' Li shrugs. 'What problem?'

'He's in Los Angeles,' Alice continues.

There is a sympathetic 'awh' from the queue.

'So what? Air travel velly cheap.'

Cheap is a relative thing when you have no money. As it is, Alice is having to sub me this takeaway until my cheque from Bindlatters clears. What's more, having survived my stint at the London Book Fair, I am now a fully paid-up member of the ranks of the unemployed. It is notable that Li drives a top-of-the-range Mercedes: that adds up to a lot of prawn crackers.

As Li bags up our sweet and sour, I look at his Chinese horoscope clock. It is just after 9 p.m. in the Year of the Pig. This thing is desperately inaccurate. I don't think Li has the foggiest idea how to set it. When the rest of the world were celebrating the Year of the Tiger, Li's clock said Rat. Whatever year it is, Chinese or otherwise, I wonder where Gil is now. His plane was leaving at some ungodly hour and the flight's about eleven hours long. And they're what – eight hours, nine hours behind us? Or is it in front? I don't know. I wish I was more *au fait* with international time travel. I haven't a bloody clue where he is. I only know that it isn't here. My lip wobbles slightly.

'Sweet and sour poke. Plawn clackers. Egg Flied Lice. Two steam dumpling.'

Li is perfectly capable of pronouncing his 'r's – he only slips into this Chinese stuff for effect. Whenever we see him in the pub he talks in a broad 'Sarf' London accent and says 'gor blimey, mate' a lot.

'We're on,' Alice says and stands up to grab our goodies.

I'm not the slightest bit hungry although normally nothing affects my appetite. I wish I was one of those people who can't eat a thing when they're stressed. Me, I stuff it all in whatever my emotional climate.

'Good luck, love,' a builder-type bloke says to me from his seat by the window and gives me a thumbs-up.

'Cheers,' I say. I think I might need it. I'm sure that the

minute Gil hits home turf and is surrounded by slender, gorgeous movie stars in the ilk of Uma Thurman, Gwyneth Paltrow and Winona Ryder, he'll come to his senses. After all, what could he possibly see in me? I will be a forgotten memory quicker than you can say, 'Sadie *who*?' One day, when he's attending the première of *The One That Got Away*, he may spare a thought for the Leaflet-Giver-Outer who might have been. But, then again, he may not.

'Tell your friend to say hello to Jackie Chan,' Li shouts after us.

'Yeah, right.'

I plod out after Alice and she hands me the brown carrier bag while she shimmies into her shiny new Ford Fiesta, which I'm dead jealous of. I slide in next to her and look at all the bells and whistles and gadgets and I want a nice car again. I pine for the time when I had a CD player and air-con. Being a transport-reduced, underpaid, poverty-stricken person is pants.

Alice pulls out into the traffic and we head back to the flat. Every journey with my friend is a white-knuckle ride as she has a blatant disregard for the Highway Code. We are followed everywhere by the honking of horns and the screeching of tyres. Everyone is fair game and cyclists are a particular treat – especially those wearing Lycra shorts. It's like being in a real-life version of Gran Turismo. I hold the carrier bag a bit higher in an attempt to shield my eyes.

Quicker than any speed limit could possibly allow, we are at her flat. Alice has the top floor of an Edwardian conversion and she bought it in a rush due to spiralling property prices and all that guff. It looked great – on the surface – but beneath all that Farrow & Ball paint lurked a heap of unseen and extremely expensive dangers. That was the point at which I moved in. We are now at the stage of no ceilings, exposed wiring and two deckchairs in the lounge carefully arranged amidst the plaster dust.

Alice pushes the door open and kicks a dust-sheet out of the way. Jerry, who we like to call 'our builder' even though he never does anything we tell him, is not the world's tidiest worker.

'I'm starving,' she says.

'Mmm . . .'

'Oh come on, Sadie.' My friend nudges me encouragingly as she puts the takeaway in the oven with some plates to give it a blast. 'He might ring. Give the bloke a chance. He's probably still over the Atlantic enjoying the delights of British Airway's plastic food.'

'Yeah,' I say, and feel all sorry for myself. Alice doesn't have men worries in the traditional sense of the word. She never has to wonder whether 'he' will call – they always do. My friend has a queue of them waiting for her and normally has about three or four different offers to sift through on a Saturday night, depending how the mood takes her. I don't know how she does it, other than she is particularly gorgeous, nice-natured and fun to be with. But that generally isn't enough, is it? I think she must be heavily into kinky sex too, but I don't like to ask. They certainly don't fancy her for her driving skills.

I, on the other hand, have absolutely nothing to look forward to. The weekend is yawning vacantly ahead of me – *sans* troublesome invitation quandaries – and come Monday morning, I will have to steel myself to go out into the cruel world and look for menial work involving some form of ill-fitting uniform again.

I ferret around in the kitchen drawer until I find the chopsticks, while Alice dishes out, piling our plates with a mountain of monosodium glutamate. We struggle through the stacked tins of emulsion paint to the lounge, ready to settle ourselves for a debauched night of calories and cheesy telly.

'There's nothing on the box,' she moans, flicking through the channels.

This is not a good start.

'Video?'

'What have you got?' I bag my deckchair, make an attempt to sweep some plaster dust from the surface and sit down, although this isn't the most comfortable place to relax in as we have no carpet, no curtains, no cushions and one bare light bulb dangling from the ceiling.

Alice roots through her stash of video standbys. '*Chicken Run* or *Sleepless in Seattle*?'

'*Chicken Run.*' I don't think I could stand anything slushy. Particularly not Tom Hanks, who always does very good slush. I haven't seen *Chicken Run*, but I can't imagine there are any big sick-making love scenes or unrequited love in the plot. I think, basically, it's just about chickens. Pretty safe ground then. 'What's it about?'

'Battery hens who are desperate to escape the drudgery of their lives,' Alice informs me brightly.

Maybe still a bit too close for comfort.

Alice sticks the video in and comes to join me. As the titles roll, she sits down and glances over at the answerphone. 'Ooo,' she says.

Its little red light is winking joyously at us. Alice is one fabulous invitation short of a complete set this weekend, so it's probably some hopeful suitor coming in with a last-minute bid for her company.

'I wonder who it is?'

If I could tell her that I'd be able to give up my day job and spend my time predicting Lotto numbers.

Alice prods the machine with a well-practised blow from her big toe. It whirrs into life.

'Hi,' a disembodied voice says.

I sit bolt upright – or as bolt upright as it is possible to be in a deckchair. I'd know that sexy American accent anywhere.

'It's Gil,' I say.

'It's Gil,' the voice on the answerphone says.

'*It's Gil*,' Alice echoes in hushed tones.

'I know, I know.'

'I got back home safely.'

'He's back home,' my helpful friend tells me.

'I know that. Ssh!'

There is a bit of throat-clearing going on down the line. 'I'm missing you,' the answerphone continues.

Alice chews her lip, ecstatically. 'Oh my God! *He's missing you.*'

'Shut up, Al.'

'Well.' A little disappointed pause. 'I'll try to call you again over the weekend. Bye.'

And that's it. The machine peeps and farts and rewinds and if Alice wasn't here I'd listen to the message all over again. But I can't, because she *is* here and she'd think I was too sad for words.

'Well,' I say.

'Do you want to listen to it again?'

I put on a cool expression and shake my head. 'No.'

'Well, I do,' Alice says. She gives the machine another kick and we listen to Gil telling British Telecom that he misses me all over again.

'He sounds very keen,' she observes as she turns her attention to her sweet and sour pork.

So he does. As we settle down to watch *Chicken Run*, it gives me a warm glow – which has nothing to do with the fact that my plateful of noodles is burning my knees.

Chapter Seven

'So? How was sunny London?'

'Wet,' Gil replied. 'Very wet.' He was sitting in a battered trailer on the back lot of Paramount Studios grabbing a rushed lunch with his dear friend and confidant, Steve Bernard. Gil was weary with jet lag and his eyes felt like he had scratchy stubble on the inside of his eyelids as well as on his chin.

A woman with a bald, purple head and red eyes sat in the corner of the office talking into a cell phone with a broad Brooklyn accent complaining about her last Brazilian wax.

'Martian,' Steve said, flicking a thumb at her.

'I thought Martians were little green men.'

'Hey, this is Hollywood.' Steve shrugged. 'Martians can be any colour we like. Maybe the green ones clashed with the wallpaper.'

Gil helped himself to half a pastrami sub.

'Oh man, get your own sarnies!'

'No time,' Gil said. 'I've got a meeting with the execs in ten.'

'About this new book?'

'Yeah. *The One That Got Away.*'

'Lead?'

'Hugh's the obvious choice.'

'Hugh.' Steve pursed his lips with approval. 'Are you gonna shoot in London?'

Gil, mouth full, nodded. 'Mmm mmm.'

'Take me,' Steve said. 'Local knowledge. I know the places to go where it doesn't rain.'

'There aren't any.'

'They're well-kept secrets we don't reveal to American tourists or movie producers.' Steve looked wistful. 'I haven't been home for donkeys' years.'

'What the hell's a donkey's year?' Gil thought Steve was a Cockney, but was never quite sure what being a Cockney involved and didn't dare to ask. His friend was an ex-pat Brit who had moved out to LA when the British film industry went into terminal decline some time ago. Steve was an Art Director by trade, working on the latest – and eleventh – *Star Satellite* movie, one of the most successful and spectacular sci-fi shows of all time. Fittingly, the two men were surrounded at this moment by blueprints of fantastical buildings and star ships.

What *Star Satellite* lacked in story, plot or depth of characterisation was more than compensated for by fabulous sets, an excess of pyrotechnics, state-of-the-art special effects and very skimpy costumes. 'If you go home, you might not want to come back to this madhouse.'

'No choice,' Steve said. 'Can't sit pining in Pinewood Studios longing for the good old days. It's dead over there. I've got to be where the action is.'

'Does Sarah like it any better here?'

'Not so's you'd notice.' Steve leaned back. 'She figures that there are enough worries and dangers to bringing up children without choosing to live on one of the world's major earthquake fault lines.'

'She has a point.'

'Women always do,' Steve said. 'You need to come over to our place sometime. It's been too long.'

'Yeah, well, you know what it's like.'

'Yeah. You hate my kids.'

'I don't hate your kids. They're adorable. In a kid sort of way. I just can't relate to them.'

'You're not supposed to relate to them. They're kids.'

'Maybe we'll fix something up.' Gil hoped he didn't sound too elusive. He and kids didn't seem to mix. Like the woman with the bald, purple head, as far as he was concerned they were beings from another planet. The last time he'd taken Gina out there for a barbecue, one of the kids had put a hamburger on her chair which she'd duly sat on, ruining a seven-hundred-dollar pair of white linen pants. That was the sort of scar that stayed.

Gil brushed crumbs off a small white polystyrene building.

'If you're going to take my food from my mouth, man, at least don't sprinkle it all over the Arutigan Senate.'

Gil gave it an admiring glance. 'It looks good.'

'What do you expect from a genius?' Steve waved one of his fries at his masterpiece. 'It's in Stage ten, if you want to take a peep.'

'I might just do that.' Gil helped himself to a fry. Steve looked pained. 'I'm helping you out,' Gil said. 'Otherwise you'll get fat.'

'Yeah – and then what?' his friend asked. 'Renée Zellweger won't want to snog me. Big deal. I'm a happily married man for heaven's sake. I don't have to starve myself. Shapely men are good. It's shapely women this town can't handle. Californian birds are too skinny. No meat.'

'I met a nice woman in London.' Gil looked up to gauge Steve's reaction. 'Shapely,' he added.

Steve looked round. 'That was a bit stage right.'

Gil shrugged. 'It happens.'

His friend frowned. 'Not to you, it doesn't. You don't do meeting women. You have Georgina.'

'Well, I met a woman. Big deal.'

'And?'

'And, nothing.'

'Is she British?'

'Yes.'

'Good. Good. Good start. As you know I'm genetically biased towards British women. Are you going to see her again?'

'She lives in London.'

'This is the Golden Age of travel, mate. She could get a ticket for a few hundred bucks. She could be here tomorrow.'

Gil tried not to look worried.

Steve frowned. '*Is* she going to come out here?'

'I don't know,' Gil admitted. 'I just got back. I've called her already. Maybe we'll email for a while.'

'Oh boy!' Steve huffed. 'You really know how to take risks with relationships.'

'Well, I am twice-bitten. I need to take things slow.'

'And there is the small matter of Georgina.'

'Gina's cool.'

Steve snorted. 'Georgina's never cool. She is in permanent crisis mode. I don't know how you deal with it.'

'Someone has to.' Gil took another mouthful of sandwich. 'Anyway, I'd better shoot. Don't want to engender bad feeling with the suits by being late.'

'They'll keep you waiting for hours.'

'That's their prerogative.' Gil stood, ready to leave.

'You are the worst kind of commitment-phobe, Gil McGann,' Steve said.

'And how do you work that out?'

'Because you don't even realise you are one.'

'What a bunch of baloney,' Gil scoffed. 'I've been married twice – and look where that got me. I'm not a commitment-phobe. Maybe I'm just all commitmented-out.'

Steve grinned. 'Send your English Rose a ticket. Take a chance.'

Gil kissed Steve on top of the head. 'You are such an old romantic,' he said with a smile.

'And you're full of shit,' Steve barked.

Gil ducked out of the door before he could be drawn any further on the state of his love life, and as he did so, a bit of Arutigan Senate building whistled past his ear.

'Catch you later,' Gil said and strode out into the warm Californian sunshine.

He headed across the parking lot, past the swaying palm trees and towards the historical, sugar-pink stuccoed buildings that formed the studio offices. Gil felt the sun warm his bones. The brightness of the cloudless blue sky hurt his tired eyes and he slipped his sunglasses on.

He'd only been in Los Angeles for a few hours and already chilly London seemed a million miles away. He thought about Sadie Nelson freezing her butt off back home and wondered, not for the first time, if she would come out here if he sent her a plane ticket.

Chapter Eight

Barmaid. I am a barmaid. I have a fancy title like Liquid Refreshment Entertainment Officer or something. But I am, without shadow of a doubt, a barmaid. And I feel this is an all-time low for me. It's one of those trendy bars that has very loud music but no chairs and I think that should be scaring me.

I am part of a TEAM, so I'm told. And we all have to work like a TEAM. Which mainly seems to involve pooling our tips and not having any tea breaks. My uniform for this job is ludicrous and already I'm longing for the feel of red polyester again. The name of the bar is Floosies and I have a Lurex, spangly skirt that barely skims my bottom and a matching cropped top suitable for someone with infinitely smaller breasts than mine. I definitely feel like a Floosie. Or a complete idiot. It serves me right. I lied on my application form and somehow convinced the manager that I was twenty-five, when in fact I am on the slippery, Sanatogen-strewn slope on the far side of thirty. I feel twenty-five – some days – so is it such a huge lie?

When I arrived for my shift, it was apparent that everyone else had lied about their age too. Unlike me, they're all *under* twenty-five – by about ten years. Most of them are still enjoying puberty. They suit minuscule Lurex because they have no thighs and concave stomachs. I, as is natural for a person of my advancing years, have the softly rounded belly of someone who has enjoyed a lifelong attachment to all things chocolate, and burgeoning child-bearing hips. They have belly-rings, I am at the age where the only thing I want in my belly button is fluff. The men

39

don't wear anything on their top at all except a spangly bow tie – at least I have not stooped so low. But it is, I admit, a very small step.

I have never been so miserable. We are in a TEAM huddle prior to the commencement of the night's festivities and there is some sort of chirpy chanting going on which is making me too depressed for words. It comes to a conclusion with a joyful whoop and a punch of the air, by everyone except me – I jump into action about thirty seconds later. The other staff turn to look at me as if they suspect there is an 'old' person in their midst and already I am singled out by the manager as not a TEAM player. I try a weak smile and give my Lurex a tug to make it appear longer. I fail on both counts.

We are sent to our allotted stations. I am in the quiet 'chill-out' bar as I am a trainee TEAM member. How can I be thirty-two and still a trainee? When I was eighteen and trekking round the major cities of Europe in my gap year, I had a vision of how my life would be. And this definitely was not it.

By now I was going to have had my fabulous and fulfilling career, have sown my wild oats along the way, leaving a trail of broken-hearted men who were, of course, grateful to have known me and richer for the experience. I was now going to be entering enthusiastically into a new phase of my life involving a rather large, detached country cottage, several blonde angelic children and a blond angelic husband who earned pots of money but from a job which allowed him plenty of time at home to share child-rearing duties – which, naturally, he would do with aplomb and without complaint. We would still, after the children were in bed soundly asleep, be mad for it like rabbits.

I am assigned to a twenty-year-old boy, Olly, who is to show me the ropes. He has more hair-gel than is good for one person and puts his hands on my Lurex at every opportunity. I am going to punch him before the night is out. No one ever drinks out of glasses any more, so all we have to do is dole out bottles. I can read and the till adds everything up for me, so how hard can it be? The main problem is going to be staying awake until three o'clock in the morning when the rest of the world is in the land of Nod and my shift finally ends.

Before I give the impression that all is doom and gloom, there are some parts of my life that are going particularly well. One part of my life, actually. I have spoken to Gil – I always go just that little bit shivery and smile secretly in a very coy way when I say his name – several times since Friday and it is still only Tuesday. In between long, luscious transatlantic phone calls, we text and email each other and do all those sorts of high-tech things that lovers now do. And while it is very nice to have a 'status' boyfriend that I can drop into conversations – or at least begin to compete with my flatmate – in some ways I think it is the contrast between his high-flying, glamorous, warm-temperatured lifestyle that is making me so unhappy with my low-slung, tacky, freeze-your-arse-off excuse for existence.

The thing is that I'm frightened of losing him before I even get a chance to start. I have nothing to talk to him about. He rattles on about Brad and George and Russell – and I think we all know who they are. He has meetings and projects and power breakfasts at Nate & Al's and drinks at Château Marmont. I have my daily fight on the Underground and my daily fight to survive. I have nothing to impress him with. I feel I have to rehearse some funny lines to throw in, which is never a good sign. We can't even talk about the weather, because it's always bloody sunny out there!

Olly nudges me in the Lurex again and I sigh heavily. 'This should be a gentle introduction,' he says. And I look up and see about two hundred people stampeding towards the bar. 'You'll be in your stride by the time the rush starts.'

And I really have no idea whether he is joking or not.

Chapter Nine

Gil had taken a guest to dinner at Morton's. It was a huge, high-ceilinged restaurant that still managed somehow to be intimate. Everything was crisp and starched – the napkins, the tablecloths, the waiters. The lighting was subdued to a level that spoke of discretion, and tables were thoughtfully placed so that conversations from your neighbours couldn't easily be overheard. That was probably why it was one of the favoured haunts of the movers and shakers of the movie industry. Gil nodded to a few acquaintances as they took their tables.

The meeting today had gone great. The execs had been more than enthusiastic about *The One That Got Away*, which was more than unusual, and it looked like this project could move very quickly to a green light. The writer whom he'd approached to do the screenplay, Danny Ziemska, sat opposite Gil nervously fiddling with his fork. Ziemska was a seasoned scribe who had written and sold six scripts, which were all stuck in development hell; consequently, none of them had yet graced the silver screen. Maybe Gil would be able to change that for him? He sure hoped so. And so did Danny Ziemska.

At the moment, Ziemska was tossing out some ideas – formed entirely on the basis that he had absolutely no knowledge of the contents of the novel. However, that didn't stop him from sounding extremely convincing.

Gil felt weary down to his bones and he could blame only so much of it on his transatlantic jet-setting. It was becoming harder and harder to find projects that excited him, and the relentless battles and struggles were starting to deplete him rather than energise him. He hoped *The One That Got Away* would get him firing on all cylinders again. If you were a producer who didn't want the cut and thrust of steam-rollering a project through to a finished movie, then it was time to cut and run, buy the remote farmhouse in Austin, Texas and write that novel you'd always meant to start but never did.

There was a relentlessness itching round the collar of his shirt like ants. Perhaps he was starting his mid-life crisis. They were all the rage these days amongst his friends. It seemed to occur at the point where you realised you'd achieved everything you'd ever dreamed of and yet with that came the even more startling realisation that there was still something missing. A vital nerve synapse connection that failed to make the jump and kick-start the happiness feeling.

But what would make him happy? Would another job put the spark to his flame? Was this the work for which he was ideally suited? His father had been in the movie business – on the other side of the camera – and Gil had followed him into it without questioning whether there was anything more appropriate to his talents. Did he want to do something else? Be someone else? But wasn't that part of the point of Hollywood? Everyone here wanted to be someone else. All the waiters, bus boys and cab drivers wanted to be actors or writers. All the actors wanted to be directors. All the writers wanted to be producers. And what did the producers want to be? This particular producer wasn't really sure.

If a change of career wasn't the answer, what was? Would it be a life like his good friend Steve had? Would he be content to spend his days making models and then going home to play happy families with his wife and kids? Was that what was missing in Gil's life?

Gil downed his drink. He still had the wife, but they no longer made the pretence of playing happy families. He and Gina could never have considered bringing up kids together when his wife had always been harder work than any eight year old he'd ever known. Maybe having a

43

family would have helped her to settle down. Gil somehow doubted it. How could he have reached the tender age of thirty-eight, live in a place with the most agreeable climate in the world, have everything that money could buy and still not be able to say that he was truly, bone-deep happy? Perhaps he still had enough of a grip on reality – even after years of living in this materialistic Tinsel Town – to appreciate that happiness was indeed the one thing that money couldn't buy. If it was, why did he know so many damn miserable millionaires?

Gil looked up at the writer who was still in full flow, unaware that he had long lost Gil's attention. 'Do you have a family?' Gil asked.

Danny Ziemska stopped midstream and paused open-mouthed, clearly wondering whether the wrong answer would affect his future employment. 'Er . . .'

'It isn't a trick question,' Gil said. 'I'd like to know.'

'I have two children,' Ziemska said. 'A boy of four and an eighteen-month-old girl.'

'Do they make you happy?'

'Y-Yes,' Ziemska stammered. 'I guess so.'

'Great,' Gil said. 'That's great.'

'Do I get the job?' The writer was hesitant.

'Yeah,' Gil said. He pushed a copy of *The One That Got Away* towards him. 'Read the book and then let me know your ideas.'

Ziemska took the novel and stood up. 'I'll get my lawyer to contact you to set up a contract.'

'Yeah.' No transaction was ever complete unless a whole bunch of lawyers were involved. The waiter hovered and Gil pushed the check and a wad of bills towards him. He needed to be out of here now.

They walked towards the door – another new and wary relationship established. Gil smiled to himself. It made him think of Sadie and where she might be now. He'd been thinking about her a lot since he'd returned from London. Maybe too much.

The writer said his goodbyes and jumped into a cab. Gil's sleek black BMW arrived courtesy of the parking valet and, handing over a generous tip, Gil took his keys and slid into the driver's seat. He swung out of the restaurant car park and into Melrose Avenue, heading for Beverly Hills and the monstrous modernist glass and concrete construction that Gina had chosen and which he now called home.

He couldn't imagine Sadie choosing a place like that. She was too straightforward, too down-to-earth. That's what he liked about her the most. She had no airs and graces, no pretensions, no apparent collagen implants. She meant what she said and said what she meant – which was something that hadn't been a huge feature of his marriage to Georgina. Sadie was pinned securely to the earth, while Gina floated to and fro on the Southern California breeze, changing direction just as often. Suddenly he wanted to see Sadie again, see if the feelings he was having were real. Damn this time difference, this ocean between them. Why on earth couldn't he have fallen in love with someone from Hollywood? Gil straightened himself in the driving seat. What was he thinking! Fallen in love?

Chapter Ten

It's just after four in the morning. I have feet the size of an elephant. They are throbbing and purple and I've no idea how they are going to resume their normal size before I'm due on my shift tomorrow night. Not even in my wildest dreams will I be able to get my poor, battered tootsies anywhere near my shoes at the moment.

I'm sitting in a deckchair in the bombsite that we call Alice's lounge with my trousers rolled up to my knees and my feet in the washing-up bowl full of cold water. I can't decide whether it is heaven or hell. It is, at least, bringing some feeling back to them – even if that feeling is pain. All I am short of is a knotted hanky plonked on my head and the picture would be complete. I am very glad that Alice is fast asleep and can't see me. My friend looks cool at all times – even in her cartoon nightdress – whereas I do not.

I sink back into the deckchair and close my eyes. There must be an easier way to earn a living than this. I've got to get my life back on track, and if I wasn't so exhausted by the process of trying to earn enough to put food in my mouth than I could possibly contemplate a major career change. How did I ever manage to hold down a responsible, well-paid job when I can't even cope with standing up behind a bar for eight hours? I'm just going to sit here for another five minutes and then head for my bed – and hopefully dream of Gil.

There is an alarm going off in my head and I've no idea where I am. Oh shit, my feet are in a bowl of cold water. Arrgh! I've remembered the pain. What's that bloody ringing? It's the phone. Good grief, what time is it? It's still pitch black outside. I fall off my deckchair and lurch for the phone before it wakes Alice. The bowl tips over and the water winds its way round the dust sheets and seeps in between the floorboards. I stub my toe on Jerry's Black & Decker sander.

'Bugger.' This had better not be someone selling double glazing or bloody UPVC conservatories. I snatch up the phone.

'Hi.' It's Gil's voice and I sink to the floor.

'Hi,' I say and all my anger floods out of me just like the water in the washing-up bowl.

'How are you?'

'Shit,' I say. 'Very shit. I have a crap job, a crap life and I'm living in the DIY section of Homebase.'

Gil laughs and I can't help but smile too.

'How are you?' I ask.

'Missing you.'

That's me gone to pieces again and suddenly all the pain in my feet dissipates in a warm rush of something nice. My eyes can't work out what it says on my watch – there's just a milky blur where the numbers should be. Then I remember I've fallen asleep with my contact lenses in and they're probably round the back of my eyes somewhere, puncturing my brain – again. I made a bad job of stifling a yawn. 'What time is it?'

'Time you came to visit me,' Gil says, and this time he doesn't laugh.

'Yeah, right,' I say. 'I'll get Harold to fire up the Lear jet.'

'I'm serious.'

'So am I.' I giggle.

'Will you come?'

'Gil, how can I? I am what is commonly known as financially embarrassed. I'm being paid below the minimum wage and I owe everyone else. It'll take me months to save up.'

'I'll arrange it,' he says. I wish I could see his face because he sounds as if there is no smile in his voice at all.

47

'You can pick up the ticket from the airport.'

'I can't do that!' I lean back against Alice's still unpacked tea chests.

'Why not? You said you were having a terrible time. You could be on a plane tomorrow night.'

'You are definitely from Planet La-la.' My feet are getting cold and I wrap them in one of Jerry's dust sheets – which aren't dusty because Jerry hasn't yet done anything workmanlike enough to produce dust. 'Real people don't just jump on planes willy-nilly. We think about it for months. Shop around. Complain that we're being ripped off. And then, and only then, after weeks of deliberation do we finally get round to booking a ticket. Even when I had the money to, I wouldn't have dreamed of flying off at a moment's notice. Real people don't do spontaneity.'

'Maybe you should try it.'

'I have a job.'

'You're working in a bar,' Gil points out.

'I can't let them down. Tonight was my first night. I'm part of a TEAM.' Although there wasn't much TEAM work going on when dear Olly slipped off to the Gents for a sneaky fag and left me to face a bar full of thirsty and increasingly aggressive ravers all by myself.

'You have a very misplaced sense of loyalty.'

I sigh. He may well be right.

'Don't you want to come?'

'Of course I do. It isn't that.'

'Then what is it?'

'I don't know.' And I'm not really sure why I'm not jumping at the chance. Is it because I'm as pasty as a milk bottle and I couldn't face putting my unfit body into a bikini until I've had at least half a dozen sunbed sessions and twenty hours of remedial therapy with a personal trainer? I can't remember when I last saw the sun or the inside of a gym. What if I got out there and Gil discovered I wasn't the wonderful woman he seems to have decided I am? I'd only have to stand next to one of those toned, tanned, salad-eating, stick-thin women and the game would be up. What if he realised within five minutes that I was really just a milk-bottle blimp with a rapidly decaying brain and wanted me to go straight home again?

'Am I rushing you?' Gil says into the space my whirring cogs are creating.

'Yes. Well, no. Why the sudden urge?'

There is a big transatlantic pause. 'I haven't felt like this for a long time,' he says. 'I want to see if what I feel is real.'

Ah! See? So he *does* want to check out whether I'm a milk-bottle blimp.

'Give me three reasons why you can't come here tonight.'

'Er . . .'

'And they need to be very good reasons – not bullshit about spontaneity.'

'Er . . .' I can't do this to order. I am a sleep-deprived person.

'I'll email you the details later, but a ticket will be waiting for you at Heathrow tonight. I promise,' Gil says decisively. 'I hope you'll be there too.'

'I . . . er . . .'

And without even saying goodbye, Gil hangs up. Ooo. Now what?

Alice and I are sitting on the deckchairs having a wholesome and nutritious breakfast – a nourishing bowl of Coco Pops and that other well-known delicacy, strawberry Pop Tarts. Alice is booted and suited and ready for work. If I came across her all power-dressed like that, I certainly wouldn't mess with her. I, on the other hand, have reverted to dressing-gown slob mode. We're watching GMTV, but not giving it our full attention.

'Tonight?' Alice asks.

'That's what he said.' I have a spoonful of chocolate milk and pretend that all this glugging in my stomach is down to my dubious diet.

'Impulsive.' Alice nods in a way that indicates she's impressed, and it takes quite a lot to impress Alice. 'I like that in a man.'

49

I give her my best worried look. 'He's paying.'

'Even better,' my flatmate says. 'Does he have a brother?'

'I don't know what to do.'

'Why?' Alice starts on the Pop Tarts.

'I don't want to appear desperate.'

'You are desperate.'

'I know, but I don't want him to think I am.'

'So what if he does.' My friend gives a careless shrug because, let's face it, it's not her life we're discussing. 'What have you got to lose?'

'I don't know that either.' I stare out of the dirt-streaked window into the pewter-coloured day looking in vain for inspiration. 'Except that it could all go horribly wrong.'

'I love your positive attitude,' my friend notes. 'Anyway, if it did at least you'd know. He could turn out to be a complete coke-head. It would stop you pining your life away for him.'

'Mmm.' I hadn't even considered that Gil might be a coke-head. That's a very positive thought, Alice! 'How would you feel about me going?'

'Great,' she says. 'I could get a lodger who actually pays me rent.'

'Thanks.' I try not to be hurt. 'My bed isn't even cold before you've got someone else in it.'

Alice folds her arms and stares at me in a very fierce way. 'Sadie, you are such a sad sack.'

'And this I don't know?'

She trundles on without acknowledging my inferiority complex. 'Life has been poohing on you from a great height for months now and finally you meet this absolutely Fandabbydozy bloke – this Hollywood producer-type hunky-chunky man who wants to whisk you away to a better life. This could be a turning point and you're behaving as if he's asked you to saw your left foot off for him. I don't understand you. I'd have my bikini and my fake tan packed and be humming old Beach Boys' hits in the Departure Lounge at Heathrow before this guy could change his mind.'

I bite the end of my spoon, nervously. 'Do you think he will change his mind?'

'You are so pathetic.' Alice crunches into her Pop Tart with a certain amount of venom. 'Why are you even hesitating?'

'Because this sort of thing only happens in the movies.'

'He is in the movies. He's Californian. It's accepted fact that they all have a very weird view of the world. Too much sun,' she says by way of explanation. 'It changes your concept of reality. This could just be an everyday thing for him and here you are making a great big deal out of it.'

'So you think I should go?'

'Grr . . .' Alice bounces over to my deckchair and I duck because I think she is going to hit me. Instead, she leans over and kisses me. 'I love you. You are my best friend. And when I get home from work, I don't want to see you here,' she says. 'Do this, Sadie. Do this and be damned. If you don't, you'll be damned anyway.'

Damn. I don't want to be damned. I *am* making a big deal out of it. It is a big decision. I help myself to the last Pop Tart in the hope that it will help me to make it.

Chapter Eleven

Gil sat outside the dingy, impersonal building set back on a corner of Sunset Boulevard waiting for Georgina and nibbling away the skin at the side of his thumbnail.

This was terrifying. He looked up at the sky for no other reason than he wasn't sure what else to do. There weren't even any jet vapour trails he could lock onto. If Sadie had picked up the ticket, she should be on her way by now, but he hadn't heard anything from her. He hoped there hadn't been any problem or that she'd had a last-minute change of heart. For whatever reason, it had been very important to him that she come out here.

The plain black door opened and a straggle of people wandered out, blinking as the sunshine hit them in the fraction of a second before the sunglasses reflex kicked in. A less than discreet row of limousines waited along the side street and the household names who owned them scuttled into the backs of them, shading their faces, hoping not to be seen. Gina, dressed from head-to-toe in white and carrying a silver vanity case, came out last. She waved at him and tottered across the parking lot on yet another pair of impossibly sexy five-inch stilettos from Diavolina.

'Hi,' she said as she slid into the BMW, air-kissed him on both cheeks and threw the case into the back seat.

'Hi,' Gil said. 'How did the meeting go?'

Gina lit a cigarette and blew the smoke out of the window. A dozen gold bangles jangled on her wrists and her cigarette bore the imprint of her full lips. It looked like blood. 'I don't go to AA because I'm an alcoholic,' she snapped. 'I don't have a drink problem.'

'You're strictly a wheatgrass only girl – these days.'

'I go because it's a great place to network. Do you know who goes to this class?'

'Yes, I do,' Gil said. 'I just saw some of them scuttle out. It's nothing to be proud of, Georgina. And it isn't a "class". People are trying to straighten out their lives.'

Gina stared out of the window. 'You called because you wanted to talk to me,' she said. 'If I'd known it was going to be a lecture, I'd have declined.'

'Do you want to go for a coffee?'

'No,' Gina said, rearranging her diamonds on her fingers. 'I'm detoxing – I can drink only lemon juice and maple syrup. Besides, I'm busy. I have an artwork booked for this afternoon.'

'You have a dog to do.'

Gina glared at him. 'You always reduce things to their most base level, Gil.' She fluffed up her hair. 'But, yes, I have "a dog to do". You can drive me there if you like.'

'Thanks.' Gil pulled out of the car park.

Georgina was on her seventh career reincarnation in as many years, still seeking the Nirvana of a job she enjoyed for more than seven weeks – or even seven days in some cases. She had lasted as a holistic manicurist for less than seven hours – which was a personal best – after she had tried to persuade her clients that it was all down to the toxic effects of nail varnish that the ozone layer was being slowly but surely destroyed. Now she was working as a Creative Canine Stylist, transforming the pooches of the rich and famous into more than just a fur-baby. Who, after all, wants to be seen out and about with a little cute 'ums who isn't completely colour co-ordinated. Easter was fast approaching and everyone wanted their pet suitably painted. Some of the pet owners with more money than sense were going for simple stencilled egg or rabbit designs, while those awash with cash were going the whole hog and having their pooch dyed in a variety of pastel shades with matching painted claws for the occasion. In a town where money was no object, the cost was astronomical. At least it kept Gina in wheatgrass and maple syrup. The rest of her expenditure still came from Gil's checking account. 'Where are you heading to?'

'Bel Air,' Gina said and relaxed back into her seat.

That was great. Exactly in the opposite direction to where he wanted to be heading. With a sigh, Gil swung out onto West Sunset Boulevard trying to take some solace in the fact that this was one of his favourite areas in town. Even now he still got a thrill driving through it. Though it was hip, happening and very LA today, there was still a feeling of how it must have been years ago when it was just a dirt track that linked the old studio lots to the stars' homes in the Hollywood Hills – except then they didn't have to hose down the sidewalks every morning to move on the homeless. Its twenty-six wide, curving miles were littered with legendary Hollywood landmarks – Gower Gulch where hopeful actors would gather for ten-dollar-a-day jobs in low-budget Westerns, the Trocadero nightclub that once had Nat 'King' Cole as its resident pianist, the Viper Room where the young actor River Phoenix died tragically after a cocktail of drugs, the Rainbow Grill where Marilyn Monroe met Joe DiMaggio on a blind date, and the sleazy by-the-hour motels of the east end of the boulevard, the area where the ladies of the night occasionally play host to reckless British movie stars.

'So . . .' Gina said into his reminiscing. Not only was it his favourite part of town it was his favourite avoidance technique. A walk down the Memory Lane of Hollywood's finest hour was always better than a real-life confrontation. 'What do you want to talk to me about?'

Gil could feel himself grip the steering-wheel tighter. There was only one way of saying this. He took a deep breath. 'I want a divorce.'

Gina spun round. 'You want a divorce? Just like that?'

'It's been overdue for a long time.'

'I don't want a divorce.'

'Life isn't always about what you want, Gina.'

'Everyone in Hollywood is divorced.' She fluffed her hair. 'I don't want to run with the crowd.'

Gil focused on the road. They were following a film

crew on the back of a trailer who were following another trailer with a boy band lip-synching away. Even driving along the street, it was impossible to get away from the movie business.

'You left me for the pool man.' Gil turned to look at her. 'Two years ago.'

'He wasn't the pool man,' Gina said. 'He was an actor. A very good one.'

Not good enough to be able to give up working as a pool man, Gil thought sourly.

'You could have given him a job.'

'Why would I want to give a job to a man who was sleeping with my wife?'

'You always think of yourself first,' Gina complained.

Gil overtook the film trailer. The guys singing as if their lives depended on it were all blond and tanned and impossibly young. Maybe they were a real boy band or maybe they were actors pretending to be. They probably all had day jobs as pool men.

The scruffy drag of Sunset Strip disappeared as they hit the boundary of Beverly Hills, and the dust and garbage on the sidewalks gave way to palm trees and manicured lawns.

Gina's lip still stuck out obdurately. 'Why so sudden, all this talk of divorce?'

'You're living with someone else,' Gil pointed out. He also wanted to point out that after two years of separation, talking of divorce wasn't sudden. The affair with the pool man/actor hadn't lasted. Gina had soon realised that despite her protestations, Kurt was better at dealing with chemical levels and leaf blockages and whatever pool stuff pool men did, than he was at acting. The only great act he had managed to do was convincing Gina otherwise – however briefly.

'What does Noah think?' Gil went on. 'Doesn't he want you to get divorced?'

Gina concentrated hard on the palm trees standing to attention at the side of the road as if she'd never seen them before.

His wife was now living with an aging British rock star – Noah Bender. Gil didn't know if Bender was his real name – or even Noah, for that matter – or whether it was a summation of his proclivity for dressing up on stage in leather garter belts and going on benders. Noah was five feet, three inches without his heeled boots and his concealed lifts. He had dyed blond hair with a mullet cut and skin so tanned that it would have made great shoe leather. He and Gina had met at a Narcotics Anonymous meeting, so maybe Gina was right about the networking thing. When Noah was sober he adored Gina. When he wasn't, he couldn't remember exactly which particular tall, leggy blonde he was supposed to go home with. But then after all the drugs that had gone up one rather large nose into one rather small brain, Noah Bender couldn't even be relied upon to remember the lyrics of his greatest hit song – the royalties of which had bought him his Beverly Hills home. It was the main reason he had stopped touring and had hung up his mascara and whip in sunny LA. That and the tax breaks. He was a neighbour of Jack Nicholson. He also had Kurt the Actor as his pool man – although Gil didn't think that Noah knew that.

'I'm happy as I am.' Her tight, pinched mouth didn't exactly scream inner serenity or contentment. 'Noah appreciates my need for security.'

'Get security with him,' Gil suggested in as reasonable a tone as he could manage. 'Divorce me. Marry him.'

'Noah's a free spirit,' Gina said. 'I respect that. He doesn't want to be tied down by the convention of marriage.'

'There's nothing conventional about our marriage,' Gil said.

'Then why do you want to end it?' Gina flicked her cigarette butt out of the window, ignoring the fact that it was likely to earn her a ticket in this town for constituting a fire risk. She turned towards him, squeezing her breasts together with her arms to enhance them further than they had already been enhanced. Gil knew Gina's breasts weren't her own, because he had paid for that too. He'd liked them a lot better when they were natural. Some sort of gold Chinese symbol nestled in her ample cleavage.

For some reason and in spite of the air-conditioning pumping away for all its worth, Gil's palms were clammy. 'I think it's time to move on.'

Gina let her cleavage sag. 'You've met someone else.'

'That has nothing to do with this.'

'Who is she?'

'No one. I met her when I was in London.'

'And she's no one?' Gina pursed her scarlet lips. 'I bet she'd like to know that.'

'She is someone,' Gil capitulated. 'Someone very special.'

'And how are you going to have a relationship with her in London? You can't even make it home to Beverly Hills most nights.'

'She's coming here.' He glanced over at Gina, who took in this information with a flinch. 'Tonight,' Gil added, hoping he was right.

'We're nearly here,' Gina said unnecessarily. 'Make a right here. We're heading for Bellagio Road.'

Obediently, Gil swung the BMW into the narrow winding row dotted with barely visible multi-million-dollar homes, secreted behind tall hedges and security gates and monitored by twenty-four-hour CCTV. Billionaires Row.

They wound higher into the hills.

'It's here,' Gina said and Gil stopped at the electric security gates and waited while Gina gave her name to the little black speaker box on the wall.

The gate swung open soundlessly and Gil drove up the sweeping driveway to a château-style house that looked as if a tornado had blown it here, perfectly intact, all the way from France. Gil stopped at the door, just as a liveried butler came and opened it. Three boisterous little Bichon Frises bounded out, nearly knocking the butler off his feet and barking as if they were bulldogs rather than irritating little balls of fuzz. They were currently lemon with pink ears instead of the customary white, but no doubt Gina would soon change all that.

His wife reached into the back of the car for her vanity case full of doggie dyes.

'Don't you want me to be happy?' Gil said.

'I want nothing more.' Picking up her case, she got out of the car. She shut the door and looked in through the window. 'But how can you be happy if I'm unhappy?' Then Gina moved away towards the house, her 'enthusiastic' smile fixed firmly in place.

Gil opened the door and started to follow her. The Bichon Frises nipped at his ankles. For fluffy white poodles they were ferocious little bastards. 'Why does my seeing another woman make you unhappy?'

'You are my husband, Gil.' Gina smiled at him – her 'genuine' look fell into place. 'I still love you.'

And with that she disappeared into the cavernous house. The dogs yapped and snapped some more.

'Oh fuck,' Gil said as he kicked them away. The butler gave him a sympathetic look. He whistled to them and with a modicum of persuasion from the sole of his Patrick Cox loafers they left Gil alone and scampered after Gina into the house as fast as their little yellow legs could go.

Gil got back in the car and headed off towards the Universal Studios lot where he had an important meeting for which he was going to be inexcusably late. He was all wound up and there was a sour swirling in his stomach. Reaching into the glove box he popped another Alka-Mint antacid tablet which he seemed to be eating like candy these days. But at least it was the only drugs habit he was cultivating.

This situation couldn't go on. He really had to do something about Gina. The worst of it was that he couldn't be entirely sure whether he wanted Sadie here because she happened to be the most fabulous and natural person he had met in a long time – he was absolutely sure that her breasts would be 100 per cent pure flesh – or because he wanted to confront Gina with the fact that there was life after her.

How had he managed to get himself in this situation? He was perfectly capable of manhandling multi-million-dollar movies into life. He had enough box-office hits under his belt to prove that. He could deal with petulant stars, petulant directors and petulant studio heads. And yet his petulant wife stamped all over him in her stilettos. His love life was like a low-budget B movie, going straight to DVD oblivion. There was only one thing for it – he needed very urgently to consult the only person he knew who had any handle on women at all.

He punched Steve's number into his cell phone. It went straight to voicemail. Perhaps it was just as well. The fact that he had a slightly insane, married man with two children as his own personal Agony Aunt was something that worried Gil immensely.

Chapter Twelve

Los Angeles from the air looks as if someone has upended several hundred of those fruit machines with forty different colours of flashing lights and laid them out end to end. You can tell that it is a place that positively teems with life before the pilot has even thought about lowering his undercarriage.

On the ground it's equally manic. I've just queued up for over an hour to get out of the customs hall because I arrived behind a jumbo jet load of tiny, chattering people from the Philippines whom the authorities clearly weren't very keen to let in. Perhaps it was because they were all bearing suitcases large enough to pack Grandma and several other relatives in. The noise is like a million parrots being battered to death. To entertain itself, my face has steadily eaten all my make-up and I'm quietly desiccating from the inside out. I push and shove my way outside, but that isn't much better. LAX is like Heathrow Airport on steroids – all careering courtesy buses, Terminator-type taxi drivers and honking horns. After an eleven-hour flight, I am in no fit state to cope with this assault on my nerves. It's getting on for midnight local time, which means it is some ungodly hour in the morning for me and my body clock.

Gil said 'come' and, lo and behold, I'm here. And at this moment, I am wondering exactly where he is. I tried to call him to let him know that I was brave enough to take up his offer of a plane ticket, but he wasn't there. I've left a message on his answerphone, but you would have thought that he'd be around to collect me. He was the one who booked the bloody ticket – he should know when my plane was due to touch down. And I kind of expected him to be waiting here with open arms and transport – not necessarily a dashing white charger, but maybe a top-of-the-range Sports Utility Vehicle.

I'm feeling vaguely numb. This is the start of a new life for me and I feel I should have done it with considerably more planning aforethought than this – but then I probably would have talked myself out of it too.

I phone Gil's number, but my stupid mobile doesn't work over here. Alice did try to warn me about this but I was in too much of a rush to leave our green and pleasant land to listen to a technical download on the merits of Tri-band phones. I have an old, knacky phone that has seen a lot of action in the bottom of my handbag and has served me quite well, despite the fact that its battery wears out at an alarming rate. This means, of course, that it is something else to which I have a completely misguided loyalty. I feel like throwing it in the rubbish bin now. Bollocks. Bollocks! And this is probably a bad time to admit it, but I have absolutely no idea where Gil lives, other than in the Hollywood Hills. But where the hell is that? It could be the size of Luton for all I know. Los Angeles is ten times bigger than London, and London is not to be scoffed at, size-wise. I know this useless fact because I read it in the in-flight magazine. Now I'm wishing I hadn't.

I have no American coins and I didn't see any sign of a payphone. I could sit here for a while and just hope that Gil turns up, but the police here look terribly mean and moody and I don't think they'd take kindly to me loitering here for too long. It would be better, even with my meagre resources, for me to book into a hotel for the night and then find out where the hell the Gil the Elusive is tomorrow morning, when I've had a good night's sleep and don't look and smell like someone who has wandered off the set of *Dawn of the Living Dead*.

Shit. This is not how I imagined my first night in LA. Not at all. In my fantasy it involved chilled champagne, a warm bubble bath with some frangipani-scented muscle rub or some such, cool sheets and a hot man. Still, I might be on for the bubble bath if I can find a hotel room that won't bankrupt me.

Chapter Thirteen

Gil was in a panic. He jumped into the BMW, smoothing down his wet hair with his free hand. His plan had been to arrive home early, fix the house up a little – to make up for his housekeeper Maria's inadequacies in that direction – relax by the pool with a cool drink and generally be in a great frame of mind ready to go and collect Sadie from the airport. Instead, due to a rash of unscheduled meetings, he'd barely managed to get back to his house in time for a quick shower and shave. All he had eaten was his finger-nails. Two more Alka-Mints would have to do for dinner. Again. It was no wonder that Maria never thought to put any food in the refrigerator. One day he must get round to firing Maria, but she was nice – reliable if inefficient – had a huge family and depended on the money. Being unable to let go of women seemed to be a recurring pattern in his life.

Now he was all kind of hyper and he didn't know if it was anxiety or excitement. Sadie's plane would be landing shortly and he'd need to get a move on if he was going to get to LAX in time.

Gil eased the BMW into gear and began to back out of his driveway, foot flat to the floor in the time-honoured style of movie car chases – just as a large black Jeep Cherokee screeched into the driveway; its driver also had their foot flat to the floor in the time-honoured style of movie car chases. The resulting crash was spectacular. Gil catapulted forward over the wheel, sounding his own car horn and inflating the airbag in his face.

'Oh man,' he said, checking his neck for whiplash

injuries as he got out of the car, untangling himself from the sagging balloon on his lap. There was only one person who could cause this much damage on his own driveway.

The front of the Jeep Cherokee was smoking gently. He opened the door and Gina, doing a great impression of a rag doll, flopped out. Her face was smeared with lipstick, her sunglasses were skew-whiff and she clutched a bottle of vodka in her hand which could never be considered a great omen. At the very least, it showed that she'd remembered little from her AA meeting – save the contact numbers of a few minor stars.

'I thought you were sober now?' Gil caught the vodka bottle as she let it drop. Gina was always sober – in between drinks. Most days even her wheatgrass juice was spiked. 'What are you doing here? You shouldn't be driving when you're drunk.'

An incoherent stream of invective came from somewhere in the scarlet mess that was her mouth. Her eyes rolled alarmingly.

'Oh jeeze.' Gil shook his head. He put his arms round Gina and heaved her out of the car where she promptly knocked them both into a heap in the driveway, the dead weight of his wife falling squarely on top of him.

Gina started to cry. 'I love you, Gil,' she muttered an inch from his face. He managed to dodge the string of dribble that followed the statement.

'You have a very strange way of showing it,' he said, and set about trying to push Gina off him.

She wailed louder. 'Noah doesn't love me.'

'Yes, he does,' Gil said. 'You've just had another fight.' He managed to hoist Gina to her knees.

'This is different.'

'No, it isn't.' Except that this one came complete with extraordinarily bad timing. 'I need to get you inside before the security patrol swing by and think I'm trying to murder you.' It was a tempting thought. She was wearing a white Lycra ensemble that did nothing to cover her toned, tanned body. 'Do you think you could show a little more co-operation and a little less flesh?'

'I don't think you love me any more.'

'I don't, honey,' Gil said, abandoning all attempts at decorum and heaving Gina over his shoulder. He would have to do some working out with the Fire Department if Gina was going to keep having these hysterical episodes. 'I care for you. Very much. In a past tense sort of way.'

'No one loves me.'

'They do,' Gil insisted. It was just that he'd be hard-pressed to give her a list at the moment. And that was the problem. Gina had no one else to turn to when things went ass-upwards, which they frequently did. She had very few friends and they all seemed to mysteriously fade into the background whenever there was a crisis. Perhaps it was because the crises were so very regular. So, Gil was always the one that she ran to. Much as it pained him to admit it, the running to bit sometimes involved going straight to his bedroom. Gina called it her comfort sex. She said she needed other men for excitement and adventure, but she always came back to him for warmth and tenderness. Gil never knew whether he should view this as a compliment or not.

It was a long driveway and when they reached the steps to the house, Gil was grateful to lower her from his shoulder. 'Put one foot in front of the other,' he instructed as he helped her towards the house while Gina tried to co-ordinate her Jell-O legs. Gil checked his watch. He should be long gone now if he was going to make the airport in time. 'Come on,' he said, and he dragged his limp wife the last hundred yards to the house.

'What's the hurry?' she slurred.

'I have to go to the airport.'

Gina stopped dead and looked up. 'Airport?' She sounded surprisingly coherent.

'Sadie's arriving.' He looked at his watch, more for show than the fact he needed to check the time again. 'Now.'

'I'm going to throw up,' Gina said, flopping again.

'Shit.' Gil dragged her to the nearest bathroom and without ceremony pushed her inside. 'You do what you have to do while I prepare the guest bedroom.'

Gina's head snapped up again. Her voice sharpened. 'Guest bedroom?'

'Sadie's arriving. Now,' he reiterated. 'I guess she'll expect to be the one in my bed.'

'Does she know about us?'

'Gina, there isn't an us. We haven't been in a relationship for two years.'

'We're married.'

'What the fuck does that matter?' Gil wanted to bang his head against the white Italian tiles that Gina had insisted on importing from Tuscany. 'You live with another guy.'

'You're jealous of Noah?'

'No, of course I'm not. But just because we aren't divorced, it doesn't mean that we're still married.' He was sure that was logical somewhere, but his head was starting to spin just as surely as if he'd drunk as much as Gina. 'This has to end. You can't keep coming back to me.'

Gina slumped by the toilet. 'Thanks for kicking me when I'm down.'

'Noah will be here tomorrow.' When he's sobered up too, Gil added silently. 'And you'll be back together before you know it.'

Gina sniffed and looked pathetic. 'He's sleeping with someone else. A twenty-year-old UCLA student called Tyler.'

'And you have Kurt, the pool man,' Gil reminded her. 'And very occasionally me. I'd say you were about quits.'

Gina made a sound that indicated imminent barfing. It was time for him to see to the guest room. The minute any one vomited in the vicinity, he had a dreadful, uncontrollable urge to join in. 'I'll be back in a minute,' Gil said and shot out of the bathroom towards the brief sanctuary offered by the call of household duties.

The guest bedroom was perfectly tidy. It always was. Maria seemed to take an inordinate amount of pride in its preparation – perhaps she had been a girl-scout in a former life. Or maybe Gina kept her on a secret payroll. There might be nothing edible in the fridge but there was always somewhere for unexpected guests – i.e. Gina – to rest their head.

Gil lay down on the bed, enjoying a moment's respite. How was he going to make Gina see that this situation couldn't continue? With Sadie here in person for a few weeks, maybe she'd finally take the hint that he was moving on with his life. After studying the ceiling fan for a few minutes, Gil got up and closed the drapes. Gina should be finished by now. It should be safe to go back into the bathroom.

But it wasn't. When he pushed the door open, Gina lay sprawled on the floor. Next to her was a bottle of pills, its white and possibly lethal contents spread out in front of her.

'Oh no, Gina,' he said. 'Not pills again.' He picked up the bottle and scanned the label. Usual stuff. Prescription sleeping pills. Gil massaged his temples. It had been a long time since Gina had gone down this route. Since the one time that he hadn't come home in time and crying wolf had nearly landed her in a funeral parlour. He thought that after that, she'd learned to have a less fickle attitude towards life.

He knelt down next to her and shook her.

'What?' Gina mumbled.

'Did you take any of these?'

Gina lolled against him.

'Tell me, Gina. Did you?' He counted the pills. There were supposed to be twenty and it pretty much looked like there were twenty on the floor. 'Tell me or I'll have to call 911.'

'I didn't take any,' she mumbled. Her eyes fixed on his and they were clear, unclouded by drugs. 'But I thought about it.'

'One day,' Gil said, 'you won't have to kill yourself. I'll be quite happy to do it for you.'

Gina sobbed. 'You don't mean that.'

Gil caved. 'No,' he said. 'You're right. I don't.'

From the depths of her despair, somehow Gina still managed a seductive smile.

'This is ridiculous.' Gil heaved Gina to her feet.

Gina touched her head gingerly and leaned against him. 'I feel kinda funny,' she said.

'Let's get you settled and then I can go to the airport.'

'You're still going to the airport?' Gina said. 'You're *leaving* me?'

'I have to. Sadie's arriving. You know that.' And Sadie would be wondering where the hell he'd got to. It wasn't a great start to their relationship, but he'd make it up to her.

Gil led Gina to the guest bedroom as if this hadn't been her home and she had never really moved out. Without protest, she slipped out of her white Lycra nonsense and slid, naked, between the sheets. When she wasn't being a complete pain in the ass she was still a very beautiful woman. Her face looked pale against the white pillow.

'Okay?' he said and stroked a strand of blonde hair from her face.

Gina nodded.

Maybe he should simply clear out, buy himself a beach house in Santa Monica and let Gina stay here. She'd chosen everything here and he'd never really liked any of it. It was all chrome and glass and hard-edged. A lot better to look at than it was to live in.

'Go to sleep,' Gil said as if he were speaking to a five year old.

'Don't leave me,' she begged. Her eyes filled with tears. 'I don't want to be alone.'

'I won't be long. You'll hardly notice that I'm gone,' Gil said, and eased himself away from her. 'Close your eyes.'

Gina snuggled down under the covers and obediently closed her eyes. Leaving when she was like this was hard. She was so weak and vulnerable. It tore Gil's heart apart.

Tiptoeing out of the room, he glanced at his watch again. Nightmare. He should have left an hour ago. He could call the airport while he was on his way and let Sadie know what had happened. Surely she'd understand.

He closed the front door quietly behind him and with a brief glance at the damage Gina had done to his car, he manoeuvred round the wreck of her Jeep and headed off towards Santa Monica Boulevard and the airport. There should be very little traffic on the road at this time of night, and with a bit of judicious speeding he could be there in half an hour. He could only hope that Sadie was still there too. Where else would she go?

Chapter Fourteen

I'm still wandering round LAX, nursing my abandonment like Linus's grubby security blanket. Heaving my case along the ground, I wish that I'd taken time to oil its wheels which are currently stuck on not-wheel. Oh, for some well-aimed WD-40. But I didn't have time to do anything. It was sheer good luck rather than good management that I even remembered to bring my pants. I just rushed headlong out of my old, crappy life into this new one – which is starting off in a rather crappy manner, it has to be said. I console myself with the fact that it would have been worse if I'd arrived in this brave new world knickerless.

The first cab driver that I give the glad eye to gives me the finger for reasons that elude me. Tentatively, I wave at the next one and he stops dead in front of me, even though I'm nowhere near the taxi rank. Is this a good sign? The driver gets out, yanks my case from me and stuffs it in a boot that appears to be already full of tools and ropes and dirty oil cans. I'm not sure that I want my case in among that lot. Too late. And equally too late, it is not until I'm ensconced in the back seat that I realise he's Armenian and is still romantically attached to his native tongue.

I know that he's Armenian, because when I say, 'Could you please take me to a nice, comfortable but affordably inexpensive hotel as near as possible to Hollywood Hills,' my driver grunts in return and says, 'Armenian.'

Call me peculiar, but I haven't been to America before and I sort of expected everyone to speak American not Armenian. So, in true British style when in strange and foreign lands, I then shout, 'Hotel!'

The Armenian grunts louder.

'Hotel.'

'Grunt?'

'Hotel! Hotel!'

'Grunt? Grunt?'

This continues until we are waved out of the road by an irate traffic cop and a voice crackles over the radio – a voice that mercifully speaks the Queen's English. The Armenian hands me the radio microphone.

'Hi,' I say. 'Can you tell me where there's a decent, cheap hotel in Hollywood?'

'In Hollywood?' There is a disbelieving laugh at the end of the static.

'Well, as near as possible.' The woman rips off an address, then shouts at the Armenian in what I presume is Armenian. He hands me the map and sets off at breakneck speed, while I try to peel myself out of the fur fabric seats and work out which way up the map is.

After a frenzy of bouncing along a motorway/highway/ freeway – I don't know what defines one from the other – that has seven weaving lanes of traffic, the hotel that I am deposited at feels like an oasis of calm. It is two streets down from Rodeo Drive, Shoppers' Heaven, so as swanky as you can get on a budget and somewhere in the vicinity of The Missing Boyfriend, I think. I curse Gil silently for leaving me to my own devices on my first night, when it is becoming clear to me that my devices are not really up to much.

I explain to the mad and grumbling Armenian in a variety of sign-language, shouting that I'd like him to heave my case out of the boot while I go and check whether they actually have a room available. And, believe me, I could weep with relief when Mary Ann, the lovely, neatly coiffured and manicured receptionist, tells me that I can bag the last one and at a price that is only marginally outside my reach. I hand over my credit card and go back out onto the deserted street – just in time to see the Armenian and my case driving away into the wide blue yonder.

Now I could really weep and not with blessed relief. But I don't, I stiffen my British upper lip and soldier on. All my life may have been packed into there, but it didn't really amount to much and I'm hoping that I remembered to renew my travel insurance policy when it expired three weeks ago. I plod back inside. Because anything more than plodding is now beyond me.

'Do you have luggage?' Mary Ann asks on my return.

'I did,' I say, but haven't the strength to explain further and, instead, with my most world-weary smile, take the key and head towards my room. How wrong I was to think that my man and this city would be ready and waiting to embrace me. If nothing else, the hot bath is still on the agenda.

The stairs are my last barricade to sanctuary. I climb them, unlock the door to my room and once inside, lean against it – glad that my trials and tribulations are over at last. My head hurts, so I decide against the light – not that I can find the switch anyway – and opt instead to fumble my way straight to the bathroom. If I lie on the bed first I'll never get up.

I do manage to find the bathroom light and my heart sinks to my very tired knees when I see that I have the wild-eyed stare of a woman completely out of her own time zone. There isn't a humungous bath after all, but a rather clinical and cold-looking shower cubicle which is not the fantasy my aching limbs and my cheese-smelling feet had entertained. My heart sinks a bit further when I look in the mirror and a large, naked and very sleepy man appears behind me.

'What the—?' he says, scratching his testicles.

'What the—?' I echo, wishing he wouldn't.

'Get the hell out of my room before I call the cops.'

'*Your* room?' I look at my key. Right room, right key. By this time a very bemused woman with a skew-whiff wig and a pink negligée has joined him. 'Sorry. Sorry,' I say, backing out, inching past them. Luckily, they are so sleepy that they've having trouble focusing.

When I get out of the room, I hear them double lock and

bolt the door. Quite right too. I clonk downstairs to Reception.

'There are two people asleep – two people who *were* asleep – in my room.'

'Oh my,' says Mary Ann, hand to mouth. 'Maybe we haven't got a room left.' She taps furiously at her computer and then gives me a horrified look. 'You're right,' she says. 'Mr and Mrs Lubisky are booked into 109.'

I doubt the Lubiskys will ever risk staying here again.

'We haven't got a room,' Mary Ann says.

This is truly the final straw.

She smiles sympathetically at me. 'But then your credit card company has refused authorisation.'

No. *This* is the final straw. Even my favourite piece of plastic has deserted me. At this point, all my brave stoicism departs. I lie down on the floor in Reception and cry. Big, loud crying.

'Hush, hush,' says Mary Ann and I don't think it's because I'm causing a scene in her nice, calm Reception. She rushes from behind her desk and helps me up, ushering me to a convenient plush velvet sofa. When I wail louder, she rushes off and brings back a cup of lukewarm water with milk in it and a tea bag.

'Oh my, oh my,' she says again. 'This will make you feel better.' She plonks down the tea and rushes off again to bring me a plate of chocolate chip cookies. Now that *is* making me feel better. I can feel an involuntary smile tease my lips.

Mary Ann sits down beside me, patting my hand while I tell her my sorry tale and regain my equilibrium with the aid of biscuits which Mary Ann bakes herself and brings in for the hotel guests because she's clearly that kind of person. She obviously takes after whoever the American version of Florence Nightingale is. I give Gil an extra bit of stick in the course of my regaling because – let's face it – this really is his fault. And despite it being two o'clock in the morning, Mary Ann hands over the Reception phone and I fish his number from my handbag which has thankfully escaped Armenian hospitality and call him. The phone goes straight to voicemail and I leave a tearful message telling him where I am.

'You lie down here, dear,' Mary Ann says and she somehow produces a chenille throw from somewhere and covers me as if I'm her favourite child. For the first time in a long time, I want to suck my thumb. 'I'll wake you as soon as the other guests start to appear.'

Gratefully, I lie down. At least Mary Ann hasn't abandoned me in my hour of need. Where can Gil be? Surely he can't just have forgotten I was arriving today? This does not bode well for future convivial relationships. I toss and turn a bit, trying to make myself comfy. Mary Ann gives me a sweet, sympathetic look. Though how on earth she thinks I'm going to sleep cramped up on the sofa, with my mind buzzing like this, heaven only knows. I can quite honestly say that's the last thing I remember.

Chapter Fifteen

LA was enjoying an unseasonably hot spell for this time of year. Even at this time of night, you could feel the pressure of warm air on your skin. Gil liked to think that the ambient temperature was responsible for the tiny beads of perspiration that had dampened his forehead, but it wasn't.

Screeching the car to a halt at LAX, he left it by the kerb next to a hundred signs telling him not to. He would risk whatever wrath parking control could throw at him – it would probably be less damaging than Sadie's wrath. Racing inside the airport terminal, he hurried to the arrivals area – but there were no disarmingly attractive, disgruntled British blondes waiting there.

This was disastrous. What would she think of him? He had dragged her halfway round the world only to leave her waiting at the airport. It was like being jilted. But then maybe she had decided not to come at all and hadn't actually got on the plane. Gil punched her number into his cell phone, but it rang unanswered until the answerphone clicked in. Did that mean she was over here or still at home but in bed? Gil rubbed his hands over his eyes. Why was life so goddamn complicated?

Gil went over to the information desk. There had been no messages left for him. Nothing. And, of course, they couldn't do anything useful like let him know whether Sadie was actually on the flight.

He did a final lap of the terminal, but she definitely wasn't there. Sadie, like Elvis, had apparently left the building.

★ ★ ★

It took Gil two hours and fifty-six dollars to retrieve the BMW which was in the process of being towed away when he'd emerged from the airport terminal empty-handed. Both he and the car had suffered enough indignities for the night, so he had followed it to the pound on a courtesy bus and had quietly paid up. It seemed a bargain in the circumstances as a tow-away downtown would have cost three times the price. Nevertheless, the journey back to Beverly Hills was a sombre one. Somewhere in this sprawling city, Sadie could be searching for him. If only he knew where she might have gone.

There was a light on inside the house when he pulled into the driveway. Gil sighed. He didn't think he could face any more histrionics from Gina and hoped that she had calmed down and sobered up by now. His wife was sitting in the kitchen as he let himself in through the front door.

'Hi,' she said. She was sipping a cup of hot water and looking very sheepish.

'Hi,' Gil said. 'Feeling okay now?'

'Better,' she said. 'Thanks.'

'Noah will be back tomorrow.'

'Maybe,' Gina said. 'Or maybe not. Who wants to hang out with a thirty-four-year-old woman when every day there are bus loads of skinnier, prettier, more obliging females arriving to make their fortune? What man will continue to look at me when faced with that? Noah's only human.'

Gil didn't want to point out that Noah was not only human, but an aging rock star – which seemed to be a particularly fragile form of human.

'I need to be twenty-four max,' Gina complained. 'I hate getting old in this town.'

'Let me fix you some coffee.' Gil put his hand on her shoulder and she touched it tentatively, giving his fingers a squeeze.

'I don't need coffee,' she said. 'I need more bruising liposuction. Another little squirt of Botox here and there. A plump of collagen.'

Gil poured them both a coffee and sat down opposite

her. He didn't want the coffee – it tasted stewed and bitter. 'You look fine as you are.'

She had looked even better before she'd had everything enhanced. There was something intrinsically more attractive about women whose faces and breasts moved.

'You're a one-off in this place, Gil McGann.' Gina examined the coffee and pushed it away. She sighed wistfully. 'A lovely, reliable man with monogamous tendencies.'

Gil didn't remind her that she'd spent most of their married life pouring scorn on his loveliness, reliability and monogamy.

'Sadie's very lucky,' she said. Then a light clicked on in her brain. 'Where *is* Sadie?'

'I don't know,' Gil admitted. 'But wherever she is, it wasn't at the airport.'

Gina hung her head. 'This is all my fault.'

For once, Gil didn't feel like rushing in to correct her. It *was* her damn fault. He glanced hopefully at the answerphone. 'Any messages?'

'No.' Gina gave him a sympathetic look.

'I'm going to bed,' Gil said. 'I'm just about done in.'

'Thanks again, Gil,' his wife said. 'I didn't know where else to go.'

He was too tired to point out that she always came here, no matter what the crisis.

Gina toyed with her hair. She looked at him from beneath spiky, mascara lashes and it crossed Gil's mind that she had reapplied all her make-up as the lipstick smears and grey tracks of her tears had all disappeared. He would never understand women. Gina's life might be crumbling around her, but she was always concerned that her nails were well-manicured while it did.

'I'll see you in the morning,' she said.

'It is the morning,' Gil said and gratefully made his way towards his bed. This was definitely not how he had imagined Sadie's first night in LA.

Chapter Sixteen

I wake with loo-brush hair and dead badger's breath and I get up, ignoring my aching bones which have spent too many hours on a plane and on a couch. Creaking over to the reception desk, I give my throw back to Mary Ann who crinkles her eyes sympathetically.

'Thanks,' I croak.

'Room 111 has checked out,' she says in her sweet sing-song voice. 'You've got a half-hour before the cleaners arrive. Wanna use it to freshen up?'

'I'd love to,' I say. 'But could you please double-check there's no one in it? I don't think my heart could stand another shock like that.'

Mary Ann smiles. 'Sure, honey.'

'No messages?'

Mary Ann shakes her head. 'Why don't you call him again?'

And even though I'm not in the mood to speak to Gil, I really have no choice. There could be a perfectly feasible explanation for why he forgot to come and collect me when I have given up everything I have ever known to be with him. I won't dwell on the fact that one of those things was dressing up in a Lurex costume to serve bottled beer to drunken yobbos. I am, after all, feeling very aggrieved.

Mary Ann roots behind her counter and produces a toothbrush. She gives me a little wave with it. I don't like to ask whether it is a new one or one from the lost property – at the moment I don't care. I just hope it didn't belong to someone who had mouth ulcers or herpes or a deadly disease. What can you catch from toothbrushes? I'll have to make sure that I run it under the hot tap.

I take it gratefully despite my doubts about its pedigree and go up to Room 111. Peeping round the door, I'm relieved to see that there aren't any residual occupants and go inside and crash out on the bed. What I wouldn't give for another couple of hours in here! But Mary Ann has been so kind already, that I move my bum and head into the bathroom to indulge in a short, but much-needed scrub. After that I hope I'll have found the strength to phone Gil.

Gil shot awake at the first hint of a ring. It had to be Sadie. He grabbed at the receiver. 'Hi,' he said.

'Were you sitting on it?' Sadie's flat British vowels were a joy to his ears.

'Yeah.' Gil swung his legs over the edge of the bed. 'I've been out of my mind. Where are you?'

Sadie reeled off the name of the hotel. 'Why weren't you at the airport?'

'I was.' Gil leaned back against his headboard, relieved that Sadie had turned up unharmed and in relatively good spirits. 'But I was hideously late and I guess by then you'd given up on me. I had an emergency.'

Gil rubbed his tired eyes like a bad actor doing a waking up scene. When he removed his curled-up fists, he felt his eyes catapult out on stalks and ping back into the sockets. 'Arrgh!'

'What's the matter?' Sadie said.

'Nothing. Nothing.' Gina was lying in bed next to him also trying to pull herself from sleep.

'Hi,' she said, inching towards him.

Gil clasped his hand over the mouthpiece. 'What are you *doing*?'

Gina smiled. 'Keeping you company.'

Gil jumped out of the bed, then realised he was stark naked and covered himself with the body of the phone. 'I don't need company!'

'You don't need what?' Sadie said.

'Nothing. Nothing.' Gil kept edging away from the bed. 'Stay exactly where you are,' he said. 'I'll be right with you,' Then he hung up the phone.

Gina rolled over seductively. 'Shall I stay exactly where I am too?'

'I want you out of here now, Gina. By the time I am showered and dressed, you need to be gone.'

'I can take a hint.' Gina pouted.

'You seem to have made a remarkable recovery,' Gil observed.

His wife looked completely unabashed.

'I won't let you spoil this for me.'

'I don't know what you mean.' She rolled over in the bed, exposing some more flesh. 'I want to meet Sexy Sadie.'

'All in good time,' he assured her. As soon as he'd managed to broach with Sadie the fact that he still had a wife. Gil scratched his head. All in good time. Now he wondered how he was going to get past Gina and into the bathroom without using the phone for camouflage.

Chapter Seventeen

Washed, scrubbed, but still wearing yesterday's underwear
– albeit inside out – I venture back down into the Reception of the hotel.

'He's on his way,' I say to Mary Ann and she looks so
pleased you'd think I told her that Gil had proposed rather
than just remembered that I exist.

'Do you think it will work out with him?' Mary Ann
squeezes my hand.

'I don't know,' I admit. 'I certainly hope so.'

Mary Ann tears a piece of paper from her jotter and
scribbles on it. 'Take this.' She pushes the paper towards
me. 'It's my daughter's address. She lives in Larchmont
Village.' I have no idea if this is good or bad. It could be
the LA equivalent of a sink estate. 'Daniella's looking for a
housemate. I think you two would get along fine.'

I take the piece of paper.

'Men are not reliable,' Mary Ann advises me in a
conspiratorial tone. I have managed to work this out for
myself, but her concern for me brings a lump to my throat.

'He seems very nice,' I say, for some reason rising to
Gil's defence. But then whenever you see mass murderers
being carted away on television news, the neighbours
always pop up to say what a nice man he was. You can't
trust anyone. Or do I watch too much cheap TV?

'If you get problems, call her. I'll tell her your name.'

'Thanks.'

'Do you have work?'

I think I'm going to adopt this woman as my new mum
– *mom*. 'No. Not yet.'

81

'I could maybe fix you up there too,' Mary Ann says with the contented nod of one of life's fixers. She scribbles on another piece of paper. 'A friend of mine runs this agency. She's looking for some help. One of her staff has sustained a fractured skull. Call her when you've settled in. Tell her Mary Ann recommended you.'

This woman should be on commission.

At that moment, Gil crashes through the doors at full speed.

I give him a little wave. 'Hi.'

He comes and crushes me with a bear hug, lifting my feet off the floor. 'I'm sorry,' he says. 'Really sorry.'

He doesn't know the half of it yet.

'Where's your bag?' Gil says, looking round for it.

'Gone,' I say. 'I got a taxi when I realised you weren't coming to the airport. The driver stole my case.'

'He stole your case?'

'Mary Ann let me sleep on the couch.'

'You slept on the couch?'

My new best friend and surrogate mother nods. 'He stole her credit card.'

'He stole your credit card?'

I nod in agreement. No point in admitting that the damn thing's gone *boing!* of its own accord.

'This is terrible,' Gil says. 'You should have called me as soon as you got here.'

'I did,' I say. 'I called from the hotel. My mobile doesn't work here. I left a message on your machine.'

'You did?' When I nod again, a dark and menacing frown crosses his brow. He leads me to the door.

'Wait.' I go and hug Mary Ann. 'You've been an angel.'

'It's been so nice to meet you,' she says. 'Call me.'

Gil and I head towards the door.

'You look after her,' Mary Ann warns.

There is a black BMW parked on the kerb and it shocks me because it suddenly brings home to me how little I know about this man. I didn't even know what car he drove and yet I've entrusted my life to him. Before I can voice my disquiet, Gil ushers me into it.

'How was your flight?' this stranger says.

'Long and full of screaming kids.' And then I remember that I didn't even have to pay for it. 'But fine. Fine. Thanks.'

'Good.'

This is hard. Gil still looks absolutely gorgeous. He hasn't gone bald, acquired a toupée or a bulbous nose since I last saw him. Things in my stomach are still going *wee-hee*! But it feels like we're different people on this side of the world. If you discount the crushing bear hug, we haven't touched either. Is that odd? Is it me or is it him?

'So what was the emergency?' I ask, settling into the plush leather.

'Emergency?'

'The one that left me stranded at the airport.'

'Oh, that emergency!' Gil focuses on the road. 'It was a friend,' he says. 'I had to help out.'

What about my emergency? I want to ask, but don't.

'I'll make it up to you,' Gil says. 'I promise.'

I try not to look too doubtful, but am sure I fail. I'm also trying not to be tense, but that's not going so well either. And it's a shame, because if I could force my shoulders down from my ears, then I'm sure I'd be delighting in my surroundings. On first impression, I think Los Angeles gets very bad press. I'd expected ghettos and shoot-outs and rundown housing estates – and I guess there's plenty of that too – but at the moment I seem to have landed in a little slice of paradise. The temperature is not too hot and not too cold, but just right. The streets are lined with palm trees that look exactly like the ones that lie flat to let Thunderbird 2 get off Tracey Island. And one thing is for certain: this is a million miles away from Battersea. It's clean for a start. When you live there, you sort of forget how disgusting and dirty London has become. The buildings here are painted enticing pastel shades and there are trees bearing lemons and oranges on the grass verges right by the roads – I'm resisting the urge to check that they're not plastic. The sky is so blue, it's heartbreaking. My only prior knowledge of Beverly Hills is that it's where the Beverly Hillbillies lived – Jed, Elly May, Jethro and Granny Clampett. I can see now why they loaded up the truck and moved to Beverly Hills. I can't believe that I'm going to live here too. I'm going to love it!

Gil pats my leg – really, he does – and I wonder where all the passion from the phone calls and emails and our one night in Town has gone. We're awkward with each other and I'm not sure why. For the moment I put it down to getting off to a bad start.

I once went on a blind date with a vegan, who didn't tell me he was a vegan until my rare sirloin steak arrived. You can't get off to a much worse start than that. He didn't say anything at all about meat being murder, but tried to avoid looking directly at the blood oozing all over my plate and stared at his tofu stir-fry pointedly throughout the meal. I choked down every dripping mouthful, even though I'd decided that I'd like to become a vegan too by the time I'd eaten half of it – the steak was so tasteless I should have eaten the polystyrene packing it came in instead. If only he'd told me when they brought the menu I would have pandered to his sensibilities, eschewed the steak and gone for mushroom tagliatelle or something. Needless to say, it wasn't destined to be a match made in heaven; it was only memorable because it was one of the most uncomfortable evenings I'd ever spent in the company of another human being. And I sort of feel like that now.

'Are you a vegan?'

Gil looks puzzled. 'No.'

Didn't think so.

'We'll go back to my house,' he says and does a U-turn complete with screeching wheels which is just *so* American. 'You can freshen up.'

I don't really like to tell him that – apart from a change of clothes – this is about as fresh as I get.

We head off into Beverly Drive where the palm trees become taller and close together, the grass is so lush it just invites you to roll in it and there is no LITTER anywhere! I try to remember when I was last in a street without litter.

Every home is begging to have a movie star living in it. They have quaint porches and leaded windows and elaborate sprinkler systems which twist and turn as they water the lawns as if they're dancing in time to some silent music. Never before have I found the process of lawn maintenance so marvellous. There are thatched roofs and Spanish haciendas and one that looks like the original Gingerbread house. Lavish mansions are ten a penny. It's like a real estate theme park for the incredibly rich. Real people cannot live in these houses.

We pull up outside a huge glass and concrete place that looks like posh Council offices. There is a Jeep with a wrecked bumper bar in the block-paved drive. Gil frowns.

'Is this your house?'

'Er . . .' Gil says. There is something like fear in his eyes. Maybe this isn't his house, he's just going to pretend that it is. 'Yes, it is my house.'

'Wow.' I like concrete and glass – in moderation. But I guess this looks more like a movie producer's home than your average house. What would I know? It's hard and urban and seems out of place here.

'Do you like it?'

'Well . . . yes.'

'I don't,' Gil says.

'Then why do you live here?'

'I'm beginning to wonder that,' he says enigmatically. He turns to me and appears to look at me for the first time. 'I think we'll take you shopping.'

'Now?'

'You have nothing to change into,' he says. 'I'll take you to Rodeo Drive.'

'They won't be open yet, will they?'

Gil checks his watch. What I want is a sit-down and a nice cup of tea – but that is so British I can't even bring myself to say it. The last meal I had was a plastic tray full of squashed rubber spirals that were supposed to be pasta. I could do with some brekkie – hot waffles, cinnamon toast, pancakes dripping with maple syrup. These are the things I'm fantasising about.

'I don't have any money to go to Rodeo Drive with,' I say. Has Gil forgotten the fact that I don't have any money at all? How embarrassing would it be to get your card bounced in Armani?

'My treat,' he says. 'It's the least I can do.'

I hope he's not going to be the type of guy who tries to buy himself out of 'situations'. I hate that. Although at this particular moment I'm prepared to be bought.

'Can't we go into the house for a short while?'

Gil chews his lip. 'The Pest Control man is still there.'

'You have pests?'

Gil pulls away from the house. 'Only one,' he says. 'But it's a very large one.'

Chapter Eighteen

Rodeo Drive is sparkly in the morning sun. No wonder this is called the Golden Triangle. The shops are all glitzy and gaudy, glittering walls of glass, all dressed up in gold. And they are all closed. Only the street cleaners grace the pavements.

Every shop is a fat fashion magazine name: Prada, Escada, Versace, Gucci, Armani, Tiffany. It's like reading a litany. I don't do this type of shopping. Even when I had money, I didn't go this mad. I was, after all, a girl about town with a mortgage. Now I need the American equivalent of Matalan. In passing, we look in one jeweller's window and there are dress rings the size of chandeliers and gold rope necklaces that would be sufficient to hold a cruise ship in harbour. Do people really wear this sort of thing? It's all top-of-the-range, one-of-a-kind stuff, a lavish showcase with a capital L. Excess on a scale that I never knew existed. I can't cope with this opulence on an empty stomach. We find a small deli and coffee-house that is cool and dark and we go inside.

The waitress shows us to a quiet booth and Gil sits down opposite me.

'Hi, how are you?' she drawls.

And I have to say that I'm really not all that sure. She hands us the menus and disappears. We both take a tense deep breath and then smile. 'This isn't how I thought it would be,' Gil says.

'Me neither.'

He takes my hand across the table. 'Let's get back on track,' he says and his eyes crinkle when he smiles.

87

'I'd like that.'

The waitress comes back and I order my pancakes. Gil does the same. For the first time since I arrived, I'm starting to relax.

'How long are you planning to stay?' Gil asks.

A big bubble of disquiet inflates in my brain.

'I could take a few days' vacation. Show you around,' he offers.

'That would be nice.' Is it at this point that I remind him that he sent me an open-ended ticket? I thought that was more or less the same as being one-way. I had rushed out here to be with him, not thinking that it was a temporary assignment, a holiday. I had been planning to stay indefinitely. I will now admit that I had heard the very faintest tinkle of wedding bells. Gil, on the other hand, looks worried that I might stay a fortnight. Clearly our communication has been somewhat transatlantically challenged.

The pancakes arrive. They are luscious, golden fluffy clouds piled high, smelling like heaven and joined by an angelic host of whipped cream, fresh blueberries and a lake of maple syrup. 'Oh yum.'

I can't eat a mouthful. How can I have got this so wrong? I thought he was gagging for me to be out here. What happened? Shit happened, that's what.

Gil tucks into his without hesitation. 'I'd like to see as much of you as possible while you're here.'

'That would be nice.' I need someone to whack me on the back of the head to jog my needle along the record. 'I could stay for a while,' I say with more confidence than I feel. 'If you wanted me to.' His fork has ground to an abrupt halt halfway to his mouth. 'I have the offer of a job.'

'Oh.' Gil looks like he might cough up his pancakes. 'What sort of job?'

'At an agency,' I say, wishing that I had looked at the scrap of paper that Mary Ann kindly gave me so that I could tell him what type of agency.

'That would be nice,' he says. Good grief, now he's doing it!

We both stare at our food.

'The weather's great here.' British stock conversation in times of crisis.

'Yeah. It's not normally so hot right now.' Gil is trying to look enthusiastic about his subject. 'We get less than fifteen inches of rain each year.'

'Wow.' I try to look equally riveted. 'We get that in London every day.'

'I know,' Gil says.

I push my pancakes to one side. The sweet smell is making me feel sick. Gil pushes his plate next to mine.

'Let's go shopping,' I say and I'm out of the booth before he can argue.

Chapter Nineteen

We arrive back at Gil's house and the wrecked Jeep of the Pest Control man is still there. Gil blanches slightly when he sees it. There is definitely more to this Pest Control man business than meets the eye.

After a moment's hesitation, Gil swings into the drive and stops the car. 'I have something to tell you.'

I have been steeling myself for this. 'Do you want me to go home?'

'No. No!' Gil looks horrified. 'Why ever would you think that?'

I shrug. My emotions are far too complex to put into words.

'It's more complicated than that,' Gil says, rubbing at his chin. I want to rub at his chin for him. Preferably with my lips. He looks very desirable when he's anxious. 'You know that I helped out a friend last night?'

I nod.

'Well, that friend is still here.'

'Is that a problem?' I'm not sure that I'd be so cagey if I was taking Gil back to meet Alice.

'She can be very difficult.'

She? 'So can I.'

Gil laughs nervously.

'She's the Pest Control man?' You can't pull the wool over this girl's eyes.

'Yes,' he says although it clearly pains him to.

I put on my jaunty face. 'Let's go and meet her then.'

Gil's Pest Control man is tall, slender and blonde. She's

wearing white Lycra and full war-paint. Not the usual outfit for exterminating cockroaches, I wouldn't have thought – but then this is LA. I wonder at what point Gil would have expected me to twig that he was telling porky pies.

Gil is shuffling from foot to foot. We are standing in a magnificent glass atrium and he's behaving as if it isn't his house at all. The Pest Control man is sitting watching morning television with her feet curled up against her on the sofa. I'm laden down with bags from some of the trendiest – and most expensive – shops in the world. It felt so great going into Dior in yesterday's airline-crumpled outfit – *not*. I didn't have the bravado to pass it off as the latest London trend and shrunk under the scrutiny of their haughty, borderline anorexic sales staff. I feel like I'm in *Pretty Woman*. Gil is Richard Gere and I'm the scruffy hooker with a heart. Even though I managed to downgrade Gil to some of the area's more downmarket shops – Gap, Banana Republic, Morgan – I am now the proud owner of two thousand dollars' worth of clothes – none of which I really wanted. I have pants that I could live off for a week. I drop the bags on the floor. The Pest Control man spins round.

'Hi,' she squeals and stands up. She has an awful lot of leg. When the Pest Control man bends over to turn off the television, her bottom is a small, underripe apricot and she's wearing Capri pants that are so tight I don't know how she managed to sit down in them. They are definite SRO's – Standing Room Only. They also show that she's wearing no underwear even though she probably hasn't had it stolen. To continue the fruit theme, her chest sticks out like two very firm cantaloupe melons. It is gravity defying. The only other chest I have ever seen like this is Barbie's. Like the smiley author and the French receptionist, I hate this woman already. The concept of sisterhood is currently eluding me big time.

She saunters over to us, licking yoghurt from her fingers. 'You must be Sadie!'

'Yes,' I say.

She holds out her yoghurty, sticky hand. 'Gina,' she says, grasping mine. Her eyes scan me like one of those metal detectors they use at airports to find hidden manicure scissors and tweezers that might come in useful for terrified passengers during terrorist attacks. She is clearly taking in my visible panty line, lack of melonious chest and bottom like a bagful of walnuts. I knew I would hate this bloody place the minute I arrived.

I have a quick scan of myself. I probably do look a bit like a Bosnian refugee. 'I had my clothes stolen,' I say in my defence.

'Oh.' She takes in the shopping bags and scowls at Gil. 'Well, it sure looks like you've been having fun replacing them.' The labels get another examination. 'I don't know that Gil has room in his closet. But I can always move some of my clothes.'

The Pest Control man flutters her eyelashes. None of us speak.

'You are staying here?' she asks.

'No,' I say, to which they both look suitably stunned. I have to say that I'm a bit stunned myself. 'I have a place organised.'

'Oh,' Gina says, faintly bemused. And I notch up one tiny little victory even though it feels very hollow.

'You must stay here,' Gil says, ignoring me completely and looking directly at the other contender. 'I invited you.' I was beginning to think he'd forgotten. 'Gina will be leaving very soon.'

'Well, you know what they say,' I quip. 'Two's company, three's a crowd.'

'In LA they say two's company, three is a lot of fun.' She gives me a sultry and very superior look.

'I like my own space,' I say. On yes. This from the woman who's been living in her friend's deckchair for the last three months.

'Come on,' Gina says, whipping some of my carriers bags. 'I'll show you the guest room. Gil, honey, fix us all a nice cool drink.'

Without protest, Gil disappears into the kitchen.

Gina totters along in front of me while I trail behind wishing my bottom wiggled more. We enter a bedroom that is the size of Alice's entire flat. It has one wall made completely of glass and it overlooks a swimming pool that looks like something out of a David Hockney painting. Beyond that are yet more palm trees and the Hollywood Hills. I would like to stay here very much.

I lay my new clothes down on the bed. I'd really like to follow them and have some more zzzs – jet lag is making my eyeballs as heavy as marbles. Perhaps I'll feel better when I've changed. But there's no way I'm going to get undressed in front of this stick insect.

Then I realise, if I am going to hang around, it would be worthwhile getting on more amenable terms with Gina. She may not be my idea of friendship material, but she is quite obviously going to make sure she stays part of Gil's life.

I'll try the friendly tack. Something innocuous. 'So how do you know Gil?' I ask.

Gina opens one of my designer bags – a tiny little carrier from Saks Fifth Avenue that contains an even tinier lacy thong. She looks at it with disdain and then up at me without altering her expression.

'Didn't he tell you?' The disdain changes to a faintly demonic grin. 'I'm his wife.'

Chapter Twenty

'You told her *what*?' Gil said. He wanted to bang his head against the refrigerator door and he would have done if it hadn't cost so damn much. Things hadn't got off to a great start with Sadie; now they were going from bad to worse.

'Only what you hadn't,' Gina snapped back.

'You are not my wife,' Gil insisted.

'Show her the divorce papers.'

'She'll wonder what in hell's name she's come to. Let's return to sanity,' Gil pleaded. 'Go back to Noah.'

'I can't.'

'Have you called him?'

'Of course I have. He doesn't want me back.' Gina stifled a sob. 'And now you don't want me.'

'Gina.' Gil spoke quietly and reasonably. 'Sadie is important to me. This relationship is important to me. Don't spoil it by turning into Elizabeth Taylor.'

Gina pouted. 'She had to find out sometime.'

'Yes, she did. But not right now.'

Gina sidled up to him and slid her arms round his waist. 'Why can't we all stay here together? I won't be in the way.'

'We want some privacy to get to know each other. I'll call Noah,' Gil offered. 'I'll have a drink with him.'

'He doesn't drink,' Gina pointed out.

'Can't you move into his pool house?'

'You want your wife living in a pool house?'

'I'll buy you your own house. Anything.'

Gina looked thoughtful. 'Where?'

'Anywhere. Have this house.'

'Isn't it a little small?'

'It has six bedrooms. There are six bathrooms. You should know, you chose it. How many of the damn things do you want?'

'There's no need to get cranky.' Gina checked her watch. 'I have a doggie to do.' She grabbed her bag and car keys. 'Catch you later.' She blew a kiss to Gil as she skipped out.

'Move out!' Gil shouted after her.

'A few days, Gil,' she shouted back. 'You can't deny me that.'

Gil sighed. The main problem was that he seemed unable to deny Gina anything.

Chapter Twenty-One

Welcome to Tinsel Town, where everything is fake. Especially the people. I fit in very well. I'm wearing DKNY embroidered jeans and an Armani T-shirt that cost over two hundred dollars and I don't have a brass razoo to my name. I do look very cool though and more than a match for Gil's wife. I wish. Being a complete coward, I haven't dared to venture out of the bedroom to find out exactly what the situation here is because I don't think that I want to know. I just know that I have to get out fast. Oh, won't I have a lot of fun recounting all this down the pub? Alice will laugh her socks off.

This is madness. I pull out the two crumpled notes that Mary Ann gave me and try to decipher her writing. Job first, then accommodation when I'm sure I've got something to pay for it with? I dial the number from the bedside phone, not caring that I'm abusing my host's hospitality now that I know he's a lying bastard.

'Cunning Stunts.'

'I beg your pardon?'

'Cunning Stunts,' the voice says again. 'For all your stuntwork requirements.'

'Oh,' I say. I did wonder. 'Can I speak to Bay Cavendish please?' I hope that's the right name. Mary Ann may be a wonderful woman, but she is not a student of calligraphy.

'One moment.' Much muttering. 'I'm afraid she's busy right now.'

'Oh. Her friend Mary Ann told me to call,' I say. 'My name's Sadie Nelson. I've just arrived from London and I'm looking for some work.'

Message relayed. 'Come on down. Bay will see you right away.'

'Oh good.'

'Where are you coming from?'

I have absolutely no idea. 'Beverly Hills?'

'We're on Wilshire Boulevard.' The woman rips off the address, rattling on about boulevards and cross streets, midtown, uptown, downtown, while I frantically try to remember the directions and search in vain for a pen.

'Thanks,' I say. 'I'll be there in a little while.'

With a little flutter of panic I hang up. Gil stands at the doorway. 'Where?'

'Job interview,' I say, standing up and smoothing down my new jeans.

'You look great,' he says.

'Thanks. I'll pay you back.' What with I'm not quite sure, but I'm becoming a master of the grand gesture.

Gil shakes his head. 'It doesn't matter. Money I have plenty of.'

'You seem to have quite a few women on the go too,' I observe in a surprisingly calm way when I really want to hit him round the head with my shoe.

'That is just *so* not true,' Gil says. 'What can I say? Gina is not my wife.' He sits down on the bed. 'Not in the real sense of the word.'

'Why didn't you tell me?'

'She left me two years ago for the pool man.' Gil attempts a laugh. 'Now she lives with an aging rock star. They fight. She drinks, takes pills and turns up on my doorstep.' He looks as weary as I feel. 'I know I should, but I can't turn her away. I'm the only one who looks out for her. She'd be a mess without me and I can't have that on my conscience.'

I sit down next to him. 'Bollocks,' I say with a heavy sigh. I don't know about the Golden Triangle, I seem to have walked straight into an *eternal* triangle.

'This is simply very bad timing,' Gil says with a sanguine air that I don't share. 'Bear with me,' he begs.

'I think you need to sort this out with her,' I say.

'Stay here while I do.'

I get the feeling that he won't be able to pluck up the courage unless I'm around, but I'm not prepared to be used as a battering ram. 'I can't sleep in the next room to your wife,' I say. 'It might be very LA, but I can't get my head round it at all.'

I realise this is tantamount to saying, 'It's me or her!' But that's how I feel and, at the moment, it doesn't look like it's me who's winning. 'I need to get to my job interview,' I say.

'I'll take you.'

'I can walk.' My legs have forgotten what it's like to move.

'No one walks in LA,' Gil says. 'You'll get arrested. If you want to walk we can go to a gym.'

'Okay,' I say. I can't fight. I'm a defeated little mess. My Prince Charming has toad-like tendencies as all of them have. When will I learn that all is not what it seems? And if there's any place I should be more aware of that than usual, it's here.

Chapter Twenty-Two

Bay Cavendish, owner of Cunning Stunts and Double Take talent agencies, is in fact plain old Barbara Cavendish from Essex. She may have dropped her boring name for a more glamorous pseudonym, but her accent is pure white-stiletto country. The adage 'you can take the girl out of the council house, but you can't take the council house out of the girl' has never been more true.

'Hello, duck,' she says, shaking my hand. 'Mary Ann said you need a job.'

'I do.'

Bay is of indeterminate age – fifty going on thirty, buxom and bottle blonde. If there was ever anything that made me wish I was a brunette it's coming to LA. Brown hair appears to be in very short supply. Bay could be Jackie Collins's other more portly sister. It doesn't seem to matter to her that the 1980s have long since gone – she's wearing leopardskin Lycra leg-warmers and a black chiffon shirt that shows her bra.

'Can you start now?'

'That's my interview?'

'We don't stand on ceremony here,' Bay says. 'Mary Ann reckons you're okay and I can pay you cash under the table.'

What more can one want in an employee? From the outside the office is a chic black-glass affair, tiered like child's building blocks. Bay's agency has the top floor with views over a major traffic intersection on Wilshire Boulevard. The inside is less prepossessing: a jumble of grey desks, piles of portfolios and a spider plant in a state of near-death.

'Exactly what does the job entail?'

'Min looks after Cunning Stunts.' Bay nods at a pretty Chinese girl, who smiles at me. 'We provide stunt actors for action movies – people who are prepared to throw themselves off tall buildings in order to get paid.' Bay looks as if she's bemused by the idea. 'Anything that involves danger and daring. You'd run Double Take. Anyone who needs a bottom or boobs comes to us – Julia, Gwyneth, Cameron. Although I think J-Lo does her own bottom.'

It's an interesting thought.

'We also do famous lookalikes. Brad, Bill – Clinton,' she adds so that I'm in no doubt.

I can't think of any other Bills. 'Bob?' I say to show that I'm hip and up with the Hollywood lingo.

'Bob who?'

'Redford.'

'Not much call for him. Bit old now.' Bay pulls a disappointed face. 'Fergie's always popular. Irish girl, Bernadette, who lives on La Brea. Very good value. Posh voice and everything. She can do fat Fergie or thin Fergie.'

I don't want to know how. I don't even want to know how the real Fergie does it.

'Bernadette did a book launch last week. Couldn't tell the difference. Quite at home with the champagne and canapés. I'd rather do that than have someone set fire to me for a living,' Bay observes.

'What happened to the last girl?' I enquire. 'Mary Ann said she'd fractured her skull. Did she go out on a stunt job?'

'No, no, no. We're strictly admin,' Bay assures me. 'She tripped over a computer cable. She's suing me, the cow.' Bay claps her hands. 'Well, are you going to join us?'

I laugh. 'I'd love to.'

'Great,' Bay says, slapping me on the back. 'Min, get the kettle on and then show Sadie the ropes.'

A wave of delirium sweeps over me. I can't believe this. One day in LA and already I've lost a boyfriend and gained several designer outfits and a new job. All I need

100

now is somewhere to live and some money.

'We'll have a lot of fun,' Bay promises.

And I'm sure that we will. I'm just glad that I'm not the one who has to answer the phone and say 'Cunning Stunts' with a straight face.

Chapter Twenty-Three

'Please don't do this,' Gil says as he drives me to Daniella's house. Daniella Silverstone is Mary Ann's daughter and my new landlady for the foreseeable future. Gil doesn't need to drive me. I could throw a stone out of my office window and hit Daniella's house. But guilt is written large on his face.

'I have to.' I'm clutching my collection of designer carriers, like an upmarket bag lady. 'I can't share a house with your wife.'

'She isn't my wife.'

She certainly acts like it.

'Gina isn't my type of person,' I say, which is the most tactful I can manage for 'Gina is a manipulative bitch'.

'She isn't my type of person either,' Gil insists.

We pull up outside Daniella's house. She lives in a small one-storey home in a quiet back street in Larchmont Village. It has a tidy patch of lawn, a front porch with lots of planted terracotta pots and a smart SUV in the drive. This is more my size of house. More bijou, less hotel. You could fit the whole thing into Gil's atrium. I've only spoken briefly to Daniella on the phone, but I'm hoping that she's as nice as her mother.

'Let me come in with you,' Gil says. He is looking agonised.

'No.' I shake my head. 'I'll be fine.'

'This will only be for a few days,' he promises. 'Gina will go back to Noah and she'll be off our backs.'

And onto her own back. Thinking catty thoughts always

makes me feel better. I will, of course, believe this when I see it.

'I bought you a new cell phone.' He hands it over to me. 'It has my numbers programmed in.'

He presses a few buttons to demonstrate and a string of different numbers pop up. Six different office, home, mobile, health club etc., etc. I'll never keep track of him.

'You must stop buying me things, Gil.'

'It's the least I can do.'

It's the most irritating thing you can do, I think. But wisely say nothing. Mind you, I do have a slight cash-flow situation. 'I need to ask you a favour.' It pains me to do this, but I'm getting very good at pride swallowing.

'Anything,' Gil says – which I think is a very rash statement given our current predicament.

'I need a loan,' I say. 'Until I can get myself sorted out.' I may have struggled through my first afternoon with Double Take, but I won't get paid until the end of the week and I don't suppose Daniella will take kindly to an IOU. 'Can you lend me a few hundred dollars? I think Daniella will want a deposit from me.'

'It's yours,' Gil says as he pulls out his wallet and peels off a thousand dollars.

'I don't need all this.'

'Have it.' Gil presses the money into my palm. 'Keep it as a contingency fund.'

I take the money. Even though it feels awful, I have no choice and I remind myself that it's a temporary measure. 'I'll pay you back.'

'You don't have to,' he says. 'It's only money.'

Spoken in the typical blasé way of someone who has some. It's true that money isn't everything, but it's an awful lot more when you haven't got any. And besides, it isn't Gil's money I want, it's his time, his attention and half of his double bed. It's not his money, nor his wife in the spare room. I wanted a one-woman man. Is that too difficult to ask for?

'I'll have another talk with Gina tonight,' he says.

Apparently.

'I'll sort this out.'

Methinks that if he hasn't managed to sort it out in two years, I'm best not to hold my breath. And I thought it was supposed to be women who were complicated.

'I'd better go and get settled in,' I say, and wonder whether I should have marked this all down as a bad job and got on the next plane home.

'Can I see you later?' Gil asks as if I haven't come all this way just to see him.

'I'm tired,' I say. Too tired to face Gina again is what I really mean.

'There's a restaurant just around the corner,' he says. 'A small Greek place. Very good food. You'll like it. Let's have dinner if nothing else.'

It seems as if nothing else is very much on the menu.

'That's fine,' I say and we look at each other for a bit. We haven't had a kiss or anything yet and the longer we leave it, the harder it seems to get to bridge the gap between our lips.

Gil appears as if he might be considering giving it a go and then changes his mind. Is this reticent creature the same man as the one who was mad for me and declaring undying love on our one night in London? It certainly looks like it.

Chapter Twenty-Four

Gil and Steve were sitting in the Arutigan Senate – a massive plywood construction in Sound Stage ten – perched on two packing cases and drinking machine coffee. The set was nearing completion and a painter 'marbled' the pillars to the constant sound of hammering from the carpenter laying a cardboard 'slate' floor.

'It sounds like you're making a complete bollocks of this, mate,' Steve commented after due consideration. 'If you don't mind me saying.'

'That's why I came to you for advice,' Gil said. 'I knew you'd be constructive.'

'Well, what do you expect?' Steve said. 'She's dropped everything . . .'

'She has dropped nothing,' Gil interrupted.

'She has flown all the way over here,' Steve corrected, 'just to be with you and she turns up to find you still shacked up with your mad not quite ex-wife.'

'Don't you start.' Gil was exasperated. Why could no one understand his situation? Why couldn't *he* understand his situation? 'I am not shacked up with her. I'm helping her out in a crisis.'

'Gina has a crisis every other day and twice on Sundays,' Steve pointed out. 'And you're always there to bail her out.'

'I can't help it,' Gil said. 'I feel responsible for her.'

'Just as well,' his friend observed. 'She doesn't seem to feel very responsible for herself.'

'She may be a little unstable,' Gil agreed.

'That's like saying Julia Roberts is a little gorgeous.'

'I'm frightened that she'll do something stupid if I point-blank tell her to leave.'

'So in the meantime you are doing something stupid instead and jeopardising a potentially rewarding, not to mention lustful relationship with the best thing that's happened to you in a long time.' Steve gave Gil a knowing glance. 'There are some quotes in there, you know.'

'You think I'm being stupid?'

'Just a tad,' Steve said.

Gil stared at the pillars. On the screen this would look like a million dollars' worth of inter-galactic real estate. People in cinema seats all over the world would gasp when they saw it. In reality it was nothing but some lumps of wood and cardboard with a fancy paint job. Nothing was what it seemed in this town. 'I don't know what's wrong with me.' Gil shook his head.

'I know what's wrong with you.' Steve wagged his finger. 'She isn't mad enough for you.'

'That's nonsense.'

'It's not,' Steve said. 'You're used to women who are bonkers. The more bonkers the better. You've only got to look at your sad, mad, ex-wife.'

'Gina's not mad.'

'She's got that stiff, news-anchor hair.' Steve nodded decisively. 'Hair that doesn't move scares me. It should scare you.'

Gil tutted. 'This is all you look for in a woman? Floppy hair?'

'Sadie's probably just too normal,' his friend said, ignoring him. 'English women are like that. Down to earth. It's all the rain. It keeps them soggy and consequently very grounded.' Steve was warming to his theme. 'Californian women dry out and float off. Air heads. Believe me, Sadie will want nothing more kinky than to give you regular helpings of Shepherd's Pie and Spotted Dick.'

Gil looked alarmed. 'I don't think I want Spotted Dick.'

'It's a pudding,' Steve explained. 'A proper pudding. With currants in it.'

'I definitely don't want it.' Gil shuddered. 'Is this why

British cuisine is so popular?'

'Don't knock it. A plain old-fashioned girl would do you the world of good.'

'Firstly, Sadie isn't plain. She's gorgeous. And secondly, she isn't old-fashioned.'

'Even better.' Steve shrugged. 'So what's your problem?'

Gil's shoulders sagged. 'I don't know.'

'I do.'

'I'm beginning to wish I hadn't asked now.'

'You're too good-looking for your own good,' Steve continued, unthwarted. 'You are your own worst enemy. It's meant that you can spend your life having gratuitous sex with a bevy of young, willing Botoxed women – while the rest of us have to do it once a month while the kids are on a sleep-over. Don't you ever get fed up of meaningless sex?' Steve slapped his forehead in disbelief. 'What am I saying?'

Both men laughed. But the truth was that Gil was heartily sick of meaningless one-night stands. He did it more because it was what was expected of him, rather than for any real enjoyment. How tragic was it to admit that?

They watched the painter put the final touches to a flimsy makebelieve pillar that looked as if it was supporting an equally makebelieve solid marble ceiling. She stepped back to admire her work and they gave her a round of applause.

'Tell me,' Steve continued in a more serious tone, 'when did you last have a real relationship?'

'With Gina?'

'No. *Real* real,' Steve stressed. 'Your wife – and I use the term loosely – she had a dozen different men while you were married – and never failed to tell you all about it. I think this has left you with a deep-seated fear of becoming involved again.'

It was something his shrink told him regularly. So regularly that Gil had stopped going to him. Nor did it help that his first wife had left him for an actor ten years younger than her. It had given him a pathological fear of all tall, blond males with high cheekbones and chiselled jaws. And a fear of being hurt again.

'It could be the male menopause,' Gil said. 'It's a very real phenomenon.'

'You're too young.'

'I'm beginning to question everything in my life.'

'How old are you?'

'Thirty-eight.'

Steve took a sharp intake of breath. 'You're right. That *is* a bad age to be in this town. The movie business is filled with people who never get past thirty-five. Some of them start counting backwards. At least mentally.'

Gina's fears were justified in some ways – as a guy, the older you got the younger the arm candy had to be. Gil felt his bones weighed down with weariness. 'Don't you ever get tired of this industry?'

'Mate,' Steve said, 'yesterday I took a piss with a one-eyed, ten-foot pink beetle with eight arms. He had no idea which of them was his own. The guy took five minutes to find his todger. How can you get tired of that?'

'There are days when I don't know what I want,' Gil admitted. 'But you . . .' he shrugged, 'you don't buy into the whole thing.'

'That's how I keep sane. Otherwise you start to think that it matters. And it doesn't. It's an illusion, just like that pretty pillar.'

His friend had it nailed, but it was so difficult to remember when you'd been steeped in the industry as long as Gil had. None of it mattered – they weren't curing cancer, they weren't saving lives, they were entertaining people and sometimes not very well. It wouldn't do to voice that thought too loudly or too often. In a town with a population of nearly ten million, he could count his friends on one hand and he didn't even need to use all the fingers. Steve was the only person he could entirely trust to confide in – and wasn't that a very sad way to live?

'You've spent too long here.' Steve spoke into his thoughts. 'This is the most fickle of fickle places. Every-one is waiting for the bigger, better deal. Sometimes you have to bite the bullet and decide that nothing else is ever going to be any better.'

Gil chewed his lip. 'Like Sadie?'

'Only you can tell that.' He patted Gil's knee and then stood up and stretched. 'Don't leave it too long though,' he advised. 'Or someone else might realise that she's a hot property too.'

Chapter Twenty-Five

'If there's one thing more irritating than sitting on the end of an automated phone service,' I say with feeling, 'it's finding out that your dream boyfriend already has a wife.'

'Tell me about it,' Daniella says, taking a contemplative glug of wine. 'It sucks.'

She has opened a bottle of Californian grape juice of impressive vintage and a packet of Doritos to celebrate my arrival and my status as new housemate. Already we have been friends for twenty years.

Daniella dips her Dorito into her wine before eating it. 'Gina sounds nuts.'

'Not so nuts. She's managed to get her husband exactly where she wants him.'

Daniella goes all dreamy. 'Really Gil's like Mr Rochester in *Jane Eyre*. He has a sad, mad wife tucked away in the attic.'

'Guest bedroom.'

'How romantic.'

'Not for poor old Jane Eyre,' I remind her.

'Of course,' Daniella says.

My bags have been unloaded into Daniella's spare room, which is very nice, very Shaker, with a patchwork quilt on the bed. It even has its own en-suite bathroom. And no en-suite wife.

My new friend examined, minutely, the contents of all my carriers and judged me to be suitable lodger material. The deal was done. I feel that my American 'adventure' is starting to take a turn for the better. Daniella reluctantly hands me the bowl of Doritos.

'I'm on a Doritos-only diet.' Daniella examines her rounded belly. 'I don't think it works.'

'How long do you stay on it?'

'Your entire life, I think.'

'It doesn't sound very healthy.'

'Who cares about health when you're stick thin?'

Daniella is not stick thin, despite her obvious desire to be. The girl has a long way to go. She is small, slightly pudgy and has strong, dark eyebrows that frame dazzling, deep-blue eyes. Her nose is extraordinarily cute and child-sized, and the thought occurs to me that it might not be her own. She takes the Doritos back before I have the chance to eat any.

'My own Mr Rochester still lives with his wife too,' she says with a sigh. 'He's a mad movie mogul. I was young and silly. He spends his days surrounded by beautiful, long-legged creatures who will do anything to get a part in a movie. And I mean anything,' she adds with an air of disgust. 'He told me I could be a movie star and that I meant the world to him. I couldn't believe that he loved me even though I had Donald Duck syndrome.'

I throw her a questioning look.

'Short fat legs, waddly ass,' she explains. 'Turns out I was right. He didn't love me at all.' She chain-eats Doritos. 'Long-legged creatures don't get attached,' she says. 'They just move onto the next sucker. I proved a little harder to detach.'

She holds up a framed photograph of a little girl who looks about ten years old. 'Alexis,' she says. 'My daughter. And Mr Rochester's.'

I take the photograph. Alexis is a mini-Daniella – small, rounded with puppy-fat and inherited genes. Her dark hair falls in long lazy curls to her waist and she has her mother's button nose – and I feel mean for thinking that Daniella had parted with good money to have hers surgically adjusted. I guess not everyone in Hollywood worships at the altar of cosmetic surgery.

'She's adorable,' I say, and suddenly it hurts that I am older than Daniella and have no picture of a daughter to show in return.

'He never sees her,' she says, returning the photograph to fit in the shiny gap made by an absence of dust. 'On my bad days I call him the Sperm Donor – but not in front of Alexis. When I like him, he's affectionately known as the Mad Movie Mogul.'

Maybe she sees my eyebrows raise.

'No names,' she adds. 'He's a big cheese in this town. One of the movers and shakers. Alexis is our little secret.' There is a hint of bitterness, laced with regret in her voice. 'To make sure I keep it that way, he pays for all this.' She gestures to encompass the house. 'All of it. And I take it. It helps to remind him that we exist.'

'Do you still see him?'

She shakes her head. 'Rarely.'

'But you still love him?'

Daniella laughs without humour. 'Love is an illusion in this town. Everyone wants something and they only love you for as long as you'll give it. Remember that.' She stands up and pours us some more wine. It is going down far too well. 'This is a definite DNRR – Do Not Resuscitate Romance. I am not under any circumstances to restart the heart of this dead relationship. If I show any sign of weakness, stop me,' she instructs me. 'This is one that must die.'

If it hasn't died after ten years of neglect, it must be a tenacious little bugger. Like the spider plant at Double Take. 'I think Gil is a Mad Movie Mogul in training,' I confess.

'You are doing the right thing,' she says. 'Believe me. Play hard to get.'

'I can't play games, Daniella. I'm not that sort of person. What you see is what you get.'

'Then you'll be eaten alive here.'

It's not a great thought to relish – the fact that *I* could be the relish.

'You're seeing Gil for dinner, right?'

I nod.

'Be late.'

'I'm never late.'

112

'Try it,' Daniella cajoles. 'See what happens.'

The door bell rings and it's Mary Ann with Alexis and I'm saved from admitting that I can't wait to see Gil this evening. I was actually planning to be early. How naïve can I be?

Mary Ann hugs me, while Alexis shyly eyes me with interest.

'Thanks, Mary Ann,' I say gratefully. 'I really don't know what I'd have done without you.'

She shrugs. 'My daughter calls me meddlesome.'

'That is *so* not true.' Daniella kisses her warmly. 'I love you interfering in *other* people's lives.'

'Alexis,' Mary Ann says, 'say hi to Sadie. She's come all the way from England.'

'Hi,' Alexis says. 'Do you know the Queen?'

'Not very well,' I admit.

'Oh,' she says, indicating that I'm clearly a disappointment to her. 'Would you like to see my collection of Barbies?'

'I try to discourage her,' Daniella says, 'but she takes after her mother. Anything pink and glittery and she's gone.'

'I'd love to,' I say and with a wave to Mary Ann, I'm led away wishing that I could remember the days when all my problems were pink and glittery.

Chapter Twenty-Six

'Just another chapter, Aunt Sadie.' Alexis has already adopted me as a surrogate relative.

'No. I haven't got time. I have to meet Gil.'

She has clearly practised her beguiling pout for a long time, but I try to harden my heart against it.

'I'll read you some more tomorrow night,' I promise.

She smiles a smile that says, 'Sucker!'

I close Lemony Snicket's tale of *The Vile Village* in the most decisive way I can manage. I can't believe this, but I'm going to be late. Not intentionally and fashionably late, but late because I'm reading a bedtime story to my new and devoted friend, Alexis.

'Have you got children?' She slides out of bed and plods after me towards the bathroom.

'No,' I admit, deciding I haven't got time to force the persistent Ms Silverstone Junior back into her own room. Clearly my bedtime reading skills are lacking. Shouldn't she be flaked out by now?

'Why not?'

I disappear into the bathroom, closely followed by Alexis.

'Why not, Aunt Sadie?'

'I haven't found the right man yet,' I tell her.

'Oh.' She thinks about this for a minute. 'Is Gil going to be the right man?'

'I'm not sure, sweetheart. I don't know him very well yet.' I'm having to run round the bathroom like a thing possessed in a frantic attempt to tart myself up, all under the watchful eye of my miniature critic.

'Oh,' she says. Then: 'You'd better get a move on,' she observes, 'otherwise you'll be a grandma before you've been a mommy.'

What a disturbing thought – even more disturbing that it's been brought to me courtesy of the twisted wisdom of a ten year old.

'You could have a little girl just like me,' she says brightly, twirling around in a space that isn't big enough for twirling. I nearly poke my own eye out with my mascara, which is not the look I'm trying to achieve.

'Yes.'

She leans on the sink next to me and hands me my lipstick. 'Don't you want your own baby to love?'

Alexis stops me mid-lippy application. 'Yes,' I say with a sigh that sounds just a little too sad. 'I would like that.'

'I'll find you a Barbie to play with,' she offers. 'That way you can have some fun while you decide if you like Gil.'

Alexis trots out of the bathroom, looking very chipper for someone who's supposed to be sleepy. I stare at my reflection in the mirror – the overly bright pink lips, the painted cheeks and the eyelashes like Daisy the Cow and wonder how only Alexis has ever managed to see through the façade to the person beneath it who wants to be a mother.

Alexis returns with a doll sporting sturdy wings which she lovingly entrusts to my care. 'This is Angel Heartstring Barbie,' she declares. 'You can pretend she's your baby.'

'Thank you.' I give the doll a kiss on the nose and something about it does pull at my heartstrings. I wonder for all my declarations of being honest and straightforward if I haven't been pretending for far too long.

Chapter Twenty-Seven

Before I finally left the house, I had a ten-minute discussion with Daniella, who tried to dissuade me from walking to the restaurant in the interests of my personal security, even though it's in the very next street, and that made me even more late.

Now I'm sitting in Zorba's, breathless with anticipation and from doing a speedwalk in three-inch heels. And, guess what? Gil isn't here. Even though I am late, he is later. I wonder what the psychology of that is.

The restaurant is small and chic with enough naff Greek taverna touches to make it accessible. It's busy, but not bustling. Most of the tables are taken up by couples holding hands and talking in hushed tones. One table of businessmen by the window punctuate the atmosphere with raucous laughter. There are olives on the table and I amuse myself by spearing a few to show that I'm unconcerned about being here alone.

The waiter comes over and he is tall with floppy, brown hair and the sort of chiselled, square-jawed look that is very common among MTA's – Model Turned Actor. I'm delighted that I've learned something useful in my first afternoon as a talent agent.

'Hi,' he says in chirpy American style. 'I'm Tavis and I'm your server for this evening.'

And I know that I'm in America and there are an awful lot of people here who have American accents, but it just works for me and my knees go all sort of silly. I can never understand why Americans seem to like Brits so much – we're rude and surly and very grey. Here everyone is as sunny and bright as the weather.

'I have a message for you,' Tavis says, still sounding as if I've just told him he's won the Lotto. 'Mr McGann says that he's running late and he'll be here in five. He tried to call your cell, but it's turned off.'

'Oh,' I say, rummaging to find my mobile phone. 'I'd better have a drink then.'

'What will it be?'

'Wine. White. Please.'

The lovely Tavis disappears and it gives me time to rearrange my hair and my thoughts. This isn't quite how my fairytale was supposed to work out, but back here in reality I'm glad that I've moved in with Daniella. She's a great person and I think we'll have a lot of fun and I don't feel compromised by being there. I don't owe anyone anything except Gil – and that's only money, as he says.

Tavis reappears with my wine and a wide smile. I wish waiters were as handsome and as friendly in the UK. What do we do with our handsome men? Are they all locked away in cupboards somewhere? I can't think of the last time I saw anyone completely gorgeous or even just mildly shaggable walking down the street.

'Thank you,' I say.

He lingers. 'You're from England, right?'

'Yes,' I say. 'How did you guess?'

'I have an ear for accents,' he tells me and I forget that Americans don't do irony. 'I'm an actor,' he continues. 'I like to specialise in English accents.'

I don't dare ask why.

'Hello,' he says, sounding rather like Prince Charles. 'How are you this evening? Isn't the weather fine for this time of year?'

I crack up, but in fairness he's quite good. Clearly, it isn't only Gwyneth Paltrow and Renée Zellweger who can do passable Brit.

'Very funny,' I say.

He looks crushed. 'It isn't supposed to be funny.'

'Oh.' I bite my lip. 'I suppose it sounds funny to hear someone imitating us.'

117

He looks mollified.

'I promise not to do my New York accent for you,' I say. 'It's a killer.'

'What are you doing in LA? Vacation or business?'

Tricky. What *am* I doing here? 'Well,' I say, still trying to formulate an answer, 'I came out here to be with someone I met in London. But it doesn't seem to be working out.'

'That's the guy you're waiting for?'

'Mmm.' I nod. 'His name's Gil McGann.'

Tavis's eyebrows shoot up and his eyes do a Jim Carrey pop. '*The* Gil McGann?'

'I don't know.' Damn, I need to know more about the movie industry.

'He's one of the best producers in the business.'

'Is he?' Tavis looks at me as if I'm from a different planet. Which I think in some ways I am. 'I know that he's produced some well-known stuff,' I say, trying to rescue myself.

There is a small, but perceptible shake of the head.

'Have you done anything with him?' I have no idea what the correct terminology is.

'Would I still be waiting table, if I had?' he says with a laugh. 'If I could get Gil McGann to notice me, it would be my dream come true.'

It would also be *my* dream come true, I think ruefully, but say instead, 'Have you been an actor for long?'

'I used to be a model,' he says. See, I'm not *that* ignorant! 'I've done some commercials. Juicy Jack?' he says, looking hopeful.

'I don't think we had that in England.'

'No,' Tavis says with regret. 'Maybe not. I have a part in *Happiness Hospital*. Dr Robert Carrington.'

I try not to look too blank.

'That's where I use my English accent. My character's an aristocratic heart surgeon.'

'Great.'

'Well, yeah,' he says. 'Except I got killed in a car wreck last week. Nurse Cathy had dumped me.'

'Oh. Too bad.'

'It happens.' Tavis shrugs. His shoulders sag a little more. 'Frequently.'

'She doesn't know what she's missing,' I offer and he laughs.

'Sometimes they resurrect characters who have died and hope the viewers don't notice. Just because I'm dead, it doesn't mean I'm buried yet. I was very popular.'

'Well, I hope you don't stay dead for long.'

'I'd better get back to work,' he says. 'The guys here hire me again every time I get screen dumped or die. I don't like to take advantage. It's been nice meeting you.'

'Yes,' I say. 'Likewise.'

Tavis walks away. He has a very small, neat bottom. Not that I'm looking. But I can just imagine him in hip-hugging Calvin Kleins strutting his stuff in *Vogue* and I have to say that it brings an involuntary smile to my lips.

'Hey,' Gil says when he eventually arrives and kisses me on the cheek. Cheek! He's shown to the table by a woman who is no one's idea of a Greek mother. Although she's pushing sixty, she's sleek, slim and styled. No Mediterranean bottom, bristly moustache or skin like a leather handbag in evidence here. 'I'm sorry I'm late.'

'Problems with Mrs McGann?' I know that I sound bitter and twisted, but I don't care. I'm fuelled by a rapidly dwindling bottle of wine and half an hour of sitting on my own. I wonder what Gina would say if Gil left *her* sitting on her tod for that long? I know that he left me a message, but I don't really want to see the good side of him at the moment.

'No.' Gil takes my hand. 'Work.'

He orders a bottle of wine and out of the corner of my eye I see that Tavis is busy, but he's gawping in our direction and I can't tell if he's looking at me or hoping to get a glimpse of *the* Gil McGann.

'I've been meeting with a director about *The One That Got Away*. I'm keen for him to do it, but he doesn't seem to share my enthusiasm. Anyway,' he says, taking a sip of the wine that's been poured for him and nodding in approval, 'let's not talk about that now. I want to know how you're settling in and I want to assure you that I will sort this out. It will be my utmost priority.' He reaches out and takes both of my hands in his. 'Gina is not going to be a problem. I want this to work between us, and I hope you feel the same too.'

His fingers are strong, warm and comforting and his blue eyes are dazzling in the candlelight. There is a fairly revolting wine bottle on the table overflowing with a dozen different colours of wax and it's melting, slowly but surely – just as I am. I'm gradually being transported away from Battersea and the greasy Labour government and the rain. I feel the tension ease from my shoulders. At this very moment I could quite believe anything Gil tells me.

Chapter Twenty-Eight

There was a huge white stretch limo with blacked-out windows in Gil's driveway when he arrived home and Noah Bender was weaving his way very unsteadily towards it with a large joint hanging from his lips and a bottle of Jack Daniel's in his hand. Gil parked the car and hurried over to catch him before he disappeared.

'Hey, Noah!' Gil shouted.

'Gil, my man,' Noah called back.

Gil smiled to himself. Noah Bender was a raddled old drunk, but there was a certain roguish charm about him that meant you couldn't help but like him.

'You've been to see Gina?' Gil sounded too hopeful even to his own ears.

'That is one hell of a stubborn bitch.' Noah waved his bottle in the direction of the house. He grabbed hold of Gil's jacket and leaned against him. Gil reeled as the smell of stale booze and soft drugs wafted towards him. Noah narrowed his eyes and tried to focus on Gil. 'Get her to come back to me,' he begged. 'I can't talk to her.'

'I can talk to her,' Gil said, 'but I don't think she listens any more.'

'I love her,' Noah said, sounding as if he was about to sob. 'Your wife is my world.'

Gil didn't have the strength to point out – again – that Gina being his wife was a mere technicality.

'If she doesn't come back to me I don't know what I'll do.' Noah swayed unhappily in front of him. It occurred to Gil that it didn't matter how rich or famous you were, it didn't mean that you had a better handle on life. If anything, it was often infinitely worse.

'Why not come back tomorrow when you're more . . . less . . . when you're feeling better,' he settled on.

Noah peered at him through his halo of smoke, only one eye left open as a slit. 'I'm going to go and get seriously blind drunk.'

Gil didn't think he exactly had twenty-twenty vision as it was.

'Take it easy,' he suggested. 'Go home. Get some sleep. Alone.' Then he helped Noah to find his thirty-foot car which appeared to have a disco going on in the back seat. 'Everything will seem better in the morning.'

'I love you, man,' Noah said. 'I wish you were a bird and then I'd marry you.'

A light bulb went on in Gil's brain. 'Have you asked Gina to marry you?'

'No, man.' Noah appeared to have sobered up several degrees. 'Too heavy.'

'It would work,' Gil said, realising that he sounded too desperate.

'I'll sleep on it,' Noah said, easing himself into his car.

'You can't keep running round with teenage blondes.'

Noah looked horrified. 'I can't?'

'It messes up Gina's head.' Gil leaned on the car roof. 'She needs security.'

'She has you for that,' Noah said and with a wink, he closed the door.

Gil watched as the car rolled down the drive and made its way towards the Hollywood Hills before going inside.

Gina was stretched out on one of the white leather sofas, watching *Jackass* on TV. Some 'jackass' had smeared his naked body with honey and was heading for a swarming beehive marked, for the hard of understanding, with the word BEES. There was a bottle of vodka on the table and six full shot glasses lined up. She was drinking one after the other and laughing at the antics on the screen. Gil watched her for a moment, unobserved, and wondered how long she could keep this up. In some ways she and Noah were well suited and in other ways they seemed to bring out the worst in each other. Neither could embrace the concepts of sobriety or monogamy.

'Hi,' Gil said, taking off his jacket and throwing it over the nearest sofa.

'Good dinner?' Gina asked, glancing up from the TV.

'Yeah.' He sat down next to her and gave a pointed look at the shot glasses.

Even more pointedly she picked one up and drank it down in one. 'Join me?' she said.

Gil shook his head. 'No. I'm too tired.' He watched the honey-coated man get hideously stung while the audience and his cohorts roared with laughter. Perhaps he was getting old – he didn't seem to understand much of what was going on around him these days. The programme played away with all the excitement of wallpaper before his eyes. 'Gina,' he said, 'I think we need to talk.'

'I hate it when you start sentences like that,' she said without looking at him. 'It means you're about to turn into my father.'

'This is for your own good.'

Gina snapped off the TV. 'You *are* my father.'

'I saw Noah,' Gil explained. 'In the driveway.'

'Did you have a cosy chat?' Gina huffed. 'You guys are always like brothers.'

Gil couldn't see the familial devotion himself – it was just that things were an awful lot easier for him when Gina and Noah were seeing eye-to-eye and Noah was, on the whole, a much more reasonable person than his wife.

'He said he wants you back, but you aren't interested.'

Gina stared at the wall.

'Gina,' Gil said. 'You can't stay here for ever.'

'This is about her, isn't it – Sadie?' His wife curled herself up into a ball. 'You want me out because she's here.'

'It isn't about Sadie,' Gil said. 'Not entirely. It's about me. I need space. Privacy. I need closure on our marriage.' Gil rubbed his hands across his eyes. I need peace, he thought. He'd had a long day and an equally long evening trying to woo a lovely lady and, at the moment, they both seemed like a lot of hard work. Except that wasn't really fair on Sadie. She'd come a long way and given up a lot to be here with him. And she wasn't here with him – Gina was, which was unfair on both of them. 'If you were free, perhaps Noah would propose.'

'Have you talked to him about this?' Gina turned round to glare at him.

'Not in as many words,' Gil admitted. But I am very hopeful, he added to himself. 'I know how much he wants you back.'

'Noah wants me back only on his terms,' Gina stated.

'Which are?'

'I don't want to be having this discussion with you, Gil,' she said firmly.

'I don't want you to be living in my house,' Gil said, 'but you are and I need to find a way for this to work for all of us.'

'This is not your house,' Gina pointed out. 'It is *our* home.'

Clearly ownership wasn't dictated by the person who paid all the bills.

'I chose it. I remodelled it.'

Not strictly true, Gil thought. Against his will, Gina had brought in some hot, homosexual and extortionate designer – because she believed gay guys had better taste in furnishings. He had ripped out all of the original Art Deco features and had replaced them with steel and glass 'statements' and then because the interior no longer suited the exterior, that was remodelled too. The designer wasn't content until the building's former glory had been completely eradicated and it resembled nothing more aesthetically pleasing than a concrete cage. Gil hated it. All of it.

'You can have it,' Gil said. 'I don't want to live here any more. *I'll* move out.'

A look of panic crossed Gina's beautiful features. 'You can't do that.'

'Why? If you like it so much, you stay. I'll go.'

Gina came over to him and snuggled against him. 'The reason I want to be here is because you are.'

'If that's how you feel, why did you leave me in the first place?'

'You're too normal, Gil,' she sighed.

He didn't think it was one of the more usual grounds for divorce. 'Too normal?'

'You're upright. You never let your hair down.'

If he continued to let his wife rule his life, he soon wouldn't have any hair left to let down.

Gina wrapped her arms round him and Gil eased himself away.

'I may be too normal for you, Gina, but I may be perfectly fine for someone else.'

'This is back to that Sadie, isn't it?'

They could spend all night going round in circles and Gina would never see his point of view. It hadn't really mattered before because it had never really impinged on his life – other than on his wallet. Gil laid his head back on the sofa that he didn't like either and closed his eyes.

Gina leaned closer to him. He could smell the scent of her perfume, a heavy and oppressive cloud that enveloped her. She twined her fingers through his hair. 'Spend the night with me,' she whispered. 'I know how to relax you.'

That was certainly true. The only thing that had kept them together for so long was the fact that they had great making-up sex. 'I don't think that's a good idea,' Gil said.

He felt Gina stiffen. She wasn't the only thing that was stiffening and right now he didn't want her to know that. He hadn't got laid for months and he wanted Sadie. He wanted to lie with her and make love with her. Instead he had come to a harpy of a wife and a sterile box that he laughingly thought of as home. What was he doing with his life?

Gil stood up. 'Talk to Noah in the morning,' he said. 'We need to sort this out.'

Gina picked up the vodka bottle, poured herself six more shots and fixed Gil with a glare that was as steady as her hand. 'I'll think about it,' she said.

Chapter Twenty-Nine

I had a fantastic evening with Gil – marred only by the fact that I can't take him back to my new home and I won't go to his. We had a passionate good-night kiss in the BMW and then chastely went our separate ways. Daniella's advice to play hard to get might be sound, but it is rather difficult to put into practice. All I wanted to do was fall into bed with him. Alexis had left me another Barbie – Ballet Star Barbie – on my pillow to keep me company. Which was so sweet, but somehow it wasn't the same.

I did, however, get a great night's sleep and now feel up to spitting in the eye of jet lag. I root in my designer carrier bags and find something suitable to wear for my first proper day at Double Take – though I realise that whatever I wear, I will look underdressed next to Bay's leopardskin Lycra.

Daniella is sitting at the kitchen table, tapping away at a fairly battered-looking laptop when I finally make it to the kitchen. It's a gloriously sunny room which overlooks a small patch of garden filled with the sort of stuff we consider houseplants. She takes off her glasses and studies me. 'Good night?'

'Great,' I say.

'Trainee Mad Movie Mogul?'

'Good,' I say.

'What did he say about you being late?'

I grimace. 'He was even later.'

'Hmm.' She chews a pencil. 'Not good.'

'He said it was work.'

'Don't they all?' She gives an unconvinced tut. 'You were back early.'

'I was tired.'

She leans on her hand and examines me closely. 'He didn't invite you back to his place for coffee?'

'No. A bit of rampant snogging in the BMW love-bus and thank you and good night.'

'Hmm,' Daniella says.

'It was like being fifteen again,' I note. 'In a very depressing way.' I wouldn't mind being fifteen again if it meant I could regain slim hips, the ability to eat anything and the chance to live my life over with the knowledge I have now. If it means just snogging in cars then you can keep it. I wouldn't be that age again for the world.

'Help yourself to fruit and cereal. There's a disgusting range of kiddie crap if you can stomach eating something called Berry Berry Kix.' She points to the appropriate cupboard. 'Or if you want to be super-hip, try the Kashi GoLean.'

'What?'

'It's very trendy.'

I find the packet and examine it suspiciously. 'How can cereal be trendy?'

'It's full of protein and high in fibre.'

'Does it taste all right?'

'Who cares? It is *the* thing to eat. I am the Queen of breakfast cereal, take it as gospel.'

I'm backed into a corner now, so I pour out some Kashi GoLean and opt for some back-up fruit too – figuring that if it's grown here on the premises, it's going to be better than stuff that's been halfway round the world in a refrigerated container and then sweated on Sainsbury's shelves in a plastic carton for a few days.

Daniella resumes tapping.

'What are you doing?'

'Trying to buy my freedom from the Mad Movie Mogul.' She stops again. 'I'm a scriptwriter.'

'Really? Anything I'd know?'

'No. I've never sold a script,' she admits. 'Although I have come very close a few times. I've only been doing it for ten years.' She gives me a bright, theatrical smile.

'Sometimes it can take fifteen years to become an overnight success.'

'Can't 3Ms help you?'

'I wouldn't ask,' Daniella says with a flick of her hair. 'He pays me enough that I don't have to lap dance, do phone sex or wait table to make ends meet while I'm waiting for my big break – a lot of people aren't so lucky.' She gives me a rueful smile. 'I have, however, done my share of dead-end jobs.'

That I can empathise with.

'I might whinge about him – occasionally – but he does good by us,' she continued. 'By the way, Sadie, I wouldn't want that repeated. He'll think I'm getting soft.'

'My lips are sealed.'

'If I showed this to him, he'd buy it. Right off. Because it was me. I'd get a huge cheque and then he'd add it to the pile of scripts at the bottom of his office closet never to come out again. But that's not what I want. I would actually like to someone to think that I've got enough talent to do this.'

'Good for you,' I say.

'Yeah.' She gives a resigned shrug of her shoulders. 'Like everyone in this town, I'm hoping to make it big one day so that I can tell someone else to stick it.'

'Is the script nearly finished?'

'Not far off,' she answers. 'It depends how much I get side-tracked by the gym. We must sign you up too.'

'I need to get some money behind me first.'

'Then you'll be too old to do your crunches.'

'I'd better go,' I say. 'I'm not sure how long it will take me to walk.'

'You can't do this,' Daniella says. 'You'll wear out your legs. You need wheels.'

'I like walking.'

'It's not good for your image.'

'I don't have an image.'

'Everyone will think you're an eccentric Brit.'

'There's nothing eccentric about using shank's pony to get around.'

'I have no idea what that means.'

'It's a quaint old British saying for walking.'

'Well, walking isn't quaint in LA. It's insanity.'

'You were just telling me I need more exercise.'

'Walking doesn't count,' she insists. 'I'll swing by your office at the end of the day and take you to a car lot. The only thing you can buy round here are Mercedes. On your budget we need to go outta the Beverly Hills area.'

'On my budget we need to go to "Outta" Mongolia. They'll have to be giving them away.'

'We can see what miracles our feminine charm will work.'

'I think mine has gone into semi-retirement.' I stuff an orange into my handbag for lunch. 'I need to give you some money for groceries too.'

'I'm cool,' Daniella says.

I kiss her on the cheek. 'You are a great mate,' I say. 'I can't thank you enough.'

'Do one thing for me.'

'Anything.'

'Take a can of Mace with you,' she says. 'In case you get mugged.'

Outside it is another day of blue skies, white fluffy clouds and seventy degrees and I realise that you could never wake up here and blame your bad temper on the weather.

Larchmont Village looks like a little slice of Surrey that has been carefully extracted and set down in among the thrusting suburbs of Los Angeles. Guildford, CA. It is a cool, green oasis in a traffic-choked town. I don't know why Daniella is so worried. I can't imagine gangs of Yardies running riot here. Long, leafy avenues of mature trees run from Daniella's house all the way to Wilshire Boulevard and I reckon it will take me about fifteen minutes to walk to the office if I stride out. The houses are large stockbroker-belt types with beautifully manicured lawns. Above the hum of the rush-hour cars, there is the early morning chorus of birdsong and squirrels scamper across the grass dodging the lazy whirring sprinklers. I feel

129

my lungs open and my spirits lift. This is a darn sight better than doing battle on the Tube every day.

I up my step, enjoying stretching my legs. And with my newfound energy, I resolve to be kinder to Gil. I still want to be with him, but without the complications; I've decided that I'm not going to put any pressure on him and I'm going to have a great time here whether I'm with him or not.

My sunny mood lasts all morning, despite the fact the phone rings again the minute I put it down. So far, I've been asked to find a Barbra Streisand for a cocktail party, a Cindy Crawford for a swimwear launch, Marlon Brando as the Godfather for a private birthday bash and a firm, young bottom to fill in for Cameron Diaz's. I would have thought she had a perfectly firm and young one of her own. Perhaps she's just not keen to share it with the movie-going public? Every single person – without fail – told me they loved my accent and I've received one proposal of marriage. Not bad for my first day's work.

Gil has called three times and left messages on the whizzy new mobile he gave me. I know it's him because he's the only person who has my number. I'm not being cool by failing to return his calls – I simply haven't had the time. There is a little envelope symbol flashing at me too, but I haven't got an instruction book, nor have I the time to sit and fathom out how it works.

Bay has been fantastic. Both she and Min have made me feel right at home and Bay even found a Union Jack that she had left over from the Queen's Golden Jubilee which she had draped over the front of the filing cabinets. I have my own desk – my own little space in LA – and I'm as pleased as Punch. The only cloud on the horizon is that I have no idea how much I'm going to be paid yet and whether it will cover my increasing overheads.

The buzzer on the office front door rings and we all glance up. This is the first caller we've had all morning. Bay answers and invites our guest in. A few minutes later a face pops round the door. Despite only being in LA for five minutes, it's a face that I recognise. Who said this was an anonymous place?

'Hello,' I say in surprise. 'What brings you here?'

'Hi.' Tavis looks equally surprised. 'I didn't know that you worked here.'

'New girl,' I admit. 'First day.'

Min claps her hands to her mouth. 'It's Doctor Robert,' she squeals.

Tavis flushes slightly.

'You're my favourite character,' she gushes. 'Are you really dead?'

''Fraid so.' Tavis looks fairly pissed off about it. 'That's why I'm here. I've come to register with Double Take.'

'My department,' I say with a ridiculous rush of pride. Although I can't say that at the moment Tavis bears a striking resemblance to anyone. A less pouffy or soulful Joseph Fiennes at a pinch, but not close enough to fool his great-aunt. 'Do you have a portfolio?' I say, trying to sound as professional as possible.

'I do.' Tavis clears his throat and looks anxiously round the office. He pulls the bag he has over his shoulder closer to him.

'May I see it?'

'Oh.' He opens the bag and pulls out a neatly typed resumé which I take and examine. I've never heard of any of these commercials or programmes, but he has quite a long list, so I try to nod knowledgeably. Tavis is fidgeting uncomfortably. 'These are my pictures.'

They are in a brown folder and without thinking I open it on the desk. My face goes the colour of tomato ketchup. The folder is full of pictures of Tavis in various states of undress – mainly completely undressed. I slam the folder shut. 'Fine,' I say tightly. 'Fine.'

'I thought I could do some work as butt double or underwear modelling.'

'Y-Yes,' I stammer. 'That's what I thought too. I'll keep you on file.'

'Great,' Tavis says. 'I heard this is a good agency.'

'Oh yes,' I say, trying to get my mouth to form coherent

sentences. 'If anyone wants a bottom I'm your man . . . woman.' Grief, I'm a blithering idiot. 'You have a very nice bottom,' I add, just to compound my humiliation.

Tavis has the grace to smile. Min has hidden under her desk which barely disguises her snigger. For a small and very pretty person she has a very witchy laugh. Bay is licking her lips lasciviously behind him.

'That's a professional assessment,' I tell him hastily.

'Thank you,' he says. 'That means a lot to me.'

'Well . . .' I cough, hoping that he takes the hint that I'm really, really busy. I can't wait to get to the file to have another peek at his bum. I pick up and put down other folders to show that I'm frantic.

Tavis turns to go and I feel my breath release. He changes his mind and I inhale sharply. 'Would you like to have lunch with me?'

'Me?'

Bay and Min dissolve into fits of unconcealed laughter. They will pay for this later.

'I can't,' I say. 'I'm very busy. This is my first day.'

'Go on, honey,' Bay says in estuary English. 'You need a break. I'm not a complete slave-driver.'

'It looks like you have a lunch date,' Tavis says and I hate how quickly he has regained his cool when I most definitely have not.

'Thanks.' I shoot a glance at Bay which she ignores and grab my jumper. Technically, this could be considered work, I suppose. From my vast knowledge of the London Book Fair, I'm sure agents are supposed to schmooze their clients. I stuff my mobile into the depths of my handbag. Gil will think I've disappeared off the face of the earth. If I get a minute I must try to call him.

132

Chapter Thirty

Gil tapped in the number of Sadie's cell phone for what felt like the seventeenth time. This was meant to make it easier for him to reach her, but it would sort of help, he guessed, if she answered it. For once, he had good news to impart and he couldn't wait to talk to her.

'Answer it, goddamn.' Gil shook the phone. But the phone steadfastly remained unanswered. He tossed it into his pocket. Maybe he'd call by her office later and give her the glad tidings of great joy.

He was due at a meeting with an exec from Universal Studios and he didn't want to be late. It was going to take him twenty minutes to get up to the studios – but then it was a standing joke that everywhere in LA was twenty minutes away. Gathering his script and papers together, Gil decided to take one last look to make sure that he wasn't hallucinating. He walked down to the guest bedroom and sure enough, the closets were still flung open and they were still devoid of every single scrap of Gina's not inconsiderable wardrobe. She'd gone. There was no note, no message, no goodbye. All that was left was a trace of make-up on the white linen sheets. It could only mean one thing. She'd finally seen sense and gone back to Noah. Gil felt as if his heart had wings – not dinky little Cupid wings, but great big Boeing 747 ones. This was fantastic. More than fantastic. It meant that Sadie could move out of her rented room and back into his arms. Things were finally going his way. He felt so optimistic today, he was sure that he could swing a deal with the studio for *The One That Got Away*.

He closed the closet doors with a small thrill of glee. Today was the beginning of the rest of his life. He was going to contact his lawyer, get the divorce moving, pay Gina off and then get on with the equally important business of making things right with Sadie.

As he headed towards the door, the sun was shining through the atrium, picking out the sparkly bits in the black granite floor. It looked like the pavement on the Hollywood walk of fame, and for the first time Gil didn't feel as if he was living in a fish bowl.

He flicked down the automatic hood on the BMW, enjoying the warmth on his face. Life was good. Life was very good. He was going to cook dinner for Sadie. He'd go to Bristol Farms and buy all the stuff himself. This would be the whole nine yards – sumptuous food, soft lights, champagne, something sexy on the CD-player. They could start over again on the right foot. And he wanted to do that more than anything.

Chapter Thirty-One

Tavis drives one of those big bus-type cars – the sort that you see in road movies or films like *American Graffiti*. It's an ancient, rusting, turquoise-coloured thing the size of a small boat and I think I'd like a car just like his. We lurch and wallow into a parking space on the main street in Larchmont Village and he feeds a meter.

You could live and die in this tiny street without ever needing to go anywhere else. It has banks, bistros, boutiques, antiques emporiums, ice-cream parlours, shoe shops and hairdressing salons and you would never go short of coffee. But the best thing of all is the view. The big, bold white HOLLYWOOD sign gazes benevolently down over the entire street from its lofty hill and makes me feel like I've really arrived.

Tavis has brought me to Zorba's for lunch. He insisted it was going to be his treat and, when I agreed, insisted that also it had to be Zorba's because he doesn't have to pay here.

The restaurant looks as if it has a much livelier atmosphere at lunchtime and the tables on the pavement are mostly full. Its patrons are made up of men in beige linen suits and trendy shades who all appear to be eating salad without coercion. This is truly a long way from home. When did you last see a British man eating salad without the lure of some form of sexual deviancy as a bribe? The women are all immaculately made-up and sip at glasses of water through scarlet lips. As we approach I'm really quite pleased that my luggage was stolen and that my wardrobe is now packing a wide selection of designer labels – I'm not sure that I would have been at home here in last season's Matalan and charity-shop finds.

The reason it's so busy, Tavis tells me, is because a bus runs down here in the lunch-hour from Paramount Studios – so these are all movie folk apparently. Everyone has mobile phones clamped to their ears and they all look very spruced up. Tavis, although he's sporting the relatively informal ensemble of a baseball cap and embroidered cargo pants, is still managing to turn heads. I don't know – maybe his look is supposed to be dressed-down movie star. He has the long rangy stride of a catwalk model and hips that are barely big enough to keep his pants up – hips that I would die for. It's very nice to be seen with someone so utterly gorgeous.

Tavis is hugged and kissed like a longlost son and we're seated at one of the few remaining tables, under a striped awning which protects us from the searing heat of the sun. My skin hasn't seen the sun for so long that I'll probably do a Count Dracula and shrivel up on the spot if any rays inadvertently hit me.

'Let me choose some of the house specials,' Tavis says and I nod – I have no idea what half of the dishes on the menu are anyway. I'm sitting here quietly toasting and am quite happy for him to take charge. In fact, it all feels rather nice. But then I wonder what I am actually doing here with Tavis. This is the sort of thing I should be doing with Gil – but where has he been when I've needed him? Absolutely bloody nowhere in sight, that's where.

'I didn't realise you'd only just arrived in LA,' Tavis says. He leans back on his chair looking much more relaxed than I am.

'Two days ago,' I admit. Although it already feels like half a lifetime in some ways.

'And you came here to be with Gil McGann?'

'That was the plan,' I say, and I wonder whether that's why Tavis is taking such an interest in me. Is it only because of who I know? More than likely. The thought makes me relax somehow, even though I should probably be pissed off. 'Only it's not quite working out like that.'

'Can I ask why?'

'I'd rather you didn't at the moment,' I say. 'It's complicated.'

Tavis grins. 'I love your accent.'

'Yours is very cute too.'

My newfound friend laughs. Our food arrives and Tavis spoons several delicious-looking dishes onto my plate. 'So how come you're working at Double Take?' he asks as he ladles.

'Sheer fluke,' I say. 'I think I'm going to enjoy it though.'

'Maybe you can put some work my way?'

'I'll certainly try.' If anyone rings up asking for a peachy male bum, I'll know exactly where to look.

'I owe my roommate so much rent.' Tavis shakes his head. 'We fund each other's "resting" periods,' he tells me. 'Luckily we've had very few times where we're both out of work.'

'That must be hell.'

Tavis gives me a slow smile. 'We manage to scratch by.'

'Is it a very precarious profession?'

'I think there are more of us waiting table than acting,' he says with a hint of irony.

'Have you been an actor for long?'

He sighs. 'Long enough to have been more successful by now, but not so long that I've been written off yet.' He pushes his food round his plate. 'I moved here five years ago,' he says, 'from New York. Along with thirty thousand other hopefuls.'

'That's a lot of hope.'

'Yeah,' he says. 'And there's thirty thousand more who leave here every year, their dreams in tatters.'

'Tough.' It makes my little problems look like chickfeed.

'Now you can see why I wouldn't mind being someone else's butt.'

'You have a very English sense of humour.'

'My grandparents were from Wales,' he informs me.

I don't like to point out that Wales isn't in England. But

if the President of the United States doesn't know that, why should anyone else just because his grandmother came from there?

'Maybe someone will be so impressed by how my butt performs, they might like to check out the rest of me?'

'I hope you get your big break,' I say and I mean it. Tavis is so laid back and unaffected and so *not* up his own butt, that he deserves to succeed.

'Thanks,' he said. 'I don't want to be Doctor Robert for the rest of my life.'

'Or death,' I note.

He chuckles.

'I'll try to introduce you to Gil,' I offer. 'Would that help?'

'Sure,' he says. 'That'll be great.'

'It's the least I can do after such a lovely lunch.'

Tavis fixes me with his eyes and it is truly mesmerising. I think he's been watching too many Clark Gable films. 'Sadie,' he says, 'you're a very nice person.'

'My mother tells me that all the time,' I quip. Actually she doesn't – my mother despairs of me.

'You're a dying breed,' he says.

'Yeah. Me and dishy hospital doctors.'

Dishy? Did I really just say dishy out loud? Not that Tavis seems to notice. He's probably more than used to women falling at his feet. He must be a crap actor, otherwise he'd have been snapped up ages ago.

The sun is warm on my neck and my eyes are starting to roll. I could quite happily stretch out here and have several winks.

'I'll get you back to the office,' Tavis says as he stands up and we walk back to his car. 'I hope things work out for you and Gil.'

'Me too,' I say, but for now it seems less important than it did. I'm just one person waiting for my big break, I don't have to compete with twenty-nine thousand nine hundred and ninety-nine others. I have only one rival.

Chapter Thirty-Two

Daniella collected me from the office and has driven me to Ralph's Wrecks – a beaten-up car lot in an area that's an awful lot scruffier than Rodeo Drive. It's one of those scary places that has wall-to-wall cars with strings of tinsel bunting draped over them. If there was a breeze, I guess they'd be fluttering. I think this is much cheaper and nastier than even Daniella had in mind.

'That one looks okay.' I point to my favourite rusty heap.

'You cannot be serious,' Daniella says as she looks at the range of cars in horror.

'Tavis told me it was a great place to buy a cheap car.'

'What is this guy? A starving actor?'

'Yes,' I say. 'Pretty much.' Although he'll probably never starve because the family who run Zorba's would never let him. If anything he's going to have to watch that he doesn't run to fat if he works there for too long.

'Come on,' I say. 'I may not be a starving actor, but I have the budget of one.'

'You cannot do this.'

'Fine.' I shrug. 'We can go home. I don't even want a car.'

'Don't be ridiculous,' she says as she climbs out of her shiny SUV.

'This will be an experience for you. You can write about it one day.'

'I don't do horror movies,' she says and she tiptoes across the dusty yard as if she's walking knee-deep in mud. 'I'm hyperventilating just looking at this.'

We pass something old and pink that is a convertible. It has *Grease* written all over it – in grease, probably. This is exactly the sort of car that one of the Pink Ladies would drive and I can see this is where Tavis bought his wheels from too.

A fat and slimy salesman comes out of the rundown prefabricated hut that fills the function of an office.

'You cannot buy a car from this man,' Daniella hisses under her breath.

'You like this one, ladies?' he smarms, pointing at the sexy little two-seater that probably once was smart. 'Try it for size.'

'I'm going to puke,' Daniella warns.

He opens the doors for us. I slide in, followed by Daniella who only takes her place in the passenger seat after she has examined it for deadly diseases. If she had some antiseptic wipes with her, she'd probably have given it a good going-over. This car may not be anywhere near as sleek as the sassy little Fiesta I left behind, but it makes up for its shortcomings by having heaps of character. If rust equals character.

The man, whom I assume to be Ralph of Ralph's Wrecks, hands me the keys. I start the engine and there is a lot of clattering and smoking. This does not sound like the sweetest automobile melody I've ever heard – as if I know what I'm looking for. I wish I'd had the sense to ask Tavis to come with me instead of Daniella. He would have known if it was a pup or not.

'I should have brought Tavis,' I say, thinking out loud.

'You're talking an awful lot about this man,' my friend remarks. 'You must have mentioned him a hundred times on the way over here.'

'I did not!'

'Tavis this . . . Tavis that . . . Tavis a-bit-of-the-other . . .'

'Huh!' I snort.

'Huh, indeed,' Daniella says. 'I know where he works, what he looks like and too much detail about his butt.'

I remain silent, in case anything else I say is taken down and used in evidence against me.

Daniella nudges me in the ribs.

'Ouch!' I mean.

'Is he very cute?'

I give a reluctant smile. 'Kind of.'

'Is that why you didn't think to bring Gil?'

'I don't think Gil would know about wrecked cars. He's not the sort.'

And this certainly is a wrecked car. One of Ralph's finest moments, I feel.

'This is utterly grotesque,' Daniella whispers.

'I'll take it,' I say, and count five hundred of my borrowed dollars into Ralph's sweating hand.

'I think walking may have been a better alternative to this,' Daniella says, curling her lip.

'It'll be fine,' I say. 'I feel like Olivia Newton-John.'

'You look more like a piece of trailer-trash who sleeps with her cousin.' She runs her finger over the plastic door panel and examines it for dirt. There is plenty.

'Alexis will love it.' I wiggle the steering wheel about. It groans in protest.

'That child has no taste. How can anyone with three Magic Jewel Barbies know class when she sees it?' she mutters. 'Sometimes I think that Alex is not my daughter.'

'How can you say that?' I beep the horn. It sounds like someone has stood on a duck's neck.

My friend wrinkles her dainty little nose. 'I think we ought to check the glove box thoroughly for suspicious white packages.'

Ralph pats the wing. 'Look after her,' he says with a smile. I'll swear I hear a bit drop off somewhere.

'I bet he treats his wife like this too,' Daniella says. She gets out of my new car and slams the door. Something else creaks. 'Jesus,' she mutters as she walks back to her SUV. 'Follow me. But not too closely.'

'I don't have any insurance.'

'Do you really think that matters?' Daniella asks as she gets into her car.

I putter out of the car lot behind her, chugging and

141

smoking, and I think the radio has more poke to it than the engine.

And suddenly I want to drive round to Tavis's house and show him my new wheels. He'll like it, I know he will. He'll think it's ridiculous and fun. And he'll think I've got a great bargain and an original car – not that I've been completely and utterly ripped off.

Chapter Thirty-Three

Tavis took off his baseball cap and threw it on the nearest chair, followed immediately by the rest of him.

'Hi, gorgeous.' His roommate, Joe Mavers, abandoned his typing and came over and kissed him affectionately on the cheek. 'Busy day at the office?'

'Hell,' Tavis said. 'I signed my ass away as a double.'

'For who – John Candy?'

'Yeah. Hilarious.'

'You'll get something soon.' Joe patted his shoulder sympathetically. 'You always do.'

'I wish I had your optimism,' Tavis admitted.

'If you lose that, my man, you might as well move back to Boise, Idaho and get a job pumping gas.'

Tavis shook his head. 'There are times when I think about it.'

'Yeah,' Joe said. 'And you'd die within a week.'

'That's why I never do it,' Tavis said.

Tavis and Joe went back a long way. They had both arrived in LA at the same time and had bowled up at the same Hollywood acting class. When, after a few months scraping a living, Joe had landed a plum role in a soap, they had wound up sharing the same top-floor apartment in a tidy and consequently expensive block on La Brea. Joe had helped Tavis a lot over the years. Many's the time he would have jacked it in and gone home – if not to Boise, Idaho, then back to his native New York – if it hadn't been for Joe's unceasing strength and support. It was like having a great older brother and a little bit more.

'Beer?' Joe asked, already on his way to the fridge. He

143

threw Tavis a bottle of ice-cold Bud. Tavis juggled it in his hands and then snapped off the top on the window ledge.

Joe was a 'character' actor – not classically handsome enough to play a leading man. He was also far too camp to play a leading man. Few actresses would be willing to work with a gay romantic hero. Rupert Everett might get away with it, but Joe wasn't nearly pretty enough for that. He was tall and blond, but despite hours in the gym, the sauna and as many hot tubs as he could find, he was still more than a little chubby.

Joe had left his own home in smalltown America when his effeminate ways and theatrical tendencies had made his folks uncomfortable and attracted the attention of too many prejudiced fists. In a land full of dirt-poor cattle farmers, Joe was never going to fit the mould. He had drifted through a variety of states working at menial jobs and dating menial men until he landed in LA. The hick accent had gone, groomed out through hours of practice, and he only lapsed back into it for effect when he was particularly drunk or stoned.

Tavis still had the support of his family – moral, spiritual and occasionally financial. His folks had always tried to understand his leanings, no matter how alien they were to them. Joe had no one. His two older brothers had ostracised him the minute he came out. His folks never called. Tavis was the nearest to family that Joe had.

Tavis took a refreshing slug of his beer. 'I met a great contact today,' he said.

'We all could do with a few more of those, darling.'

'She's Gil McGann's girlfriend.'

'Mmm . . .'

'A very fine lady,' Tavis said thoughtfully. 'Very fine.'

'I thought you'd given all that up?'

'I have. It's far too distracting. Nothing is going to matter in my life but my career.' Strong words and very easy to say, but then it was a long time since anyone of the opposite sex had stirred his interest.

'So what shall it be tonight, my friend?' Joe asked, resting his beer on what one day would undoubtedly be a paunch. 'The Viper Room? The Polo Lounge? The Sky Bar?'

'Or why don't we go to our acting class and be humiliated like we always do?'

'Good idea,' Joe said. 'Do you think your new friend can get you an introduction to the big cheese himself?'

'I hope so.' Tavis nodded in what he thought was a hopeful manner. But then, it wasn't so much who you knew in Hollywood, but who knew *you* – he was more than aware of that. Just as he was more than aware that Sadie's hair had smelled of vanilla.

Sometimes when you'd been kicked down so many times, it was very hard to make yourself stand up again. He tried to laugh about Doctor Robert getting bumped off and he tried even harder not to take it personally. *Happiness Hospital* was a crap programme with a crap script and a bunch of crap actors – but he had been good, given the material he had to work with. He was sure he'd been good. But he wasn't sure that simply being good enough or determined enough was ever going to get him where he wanted to be – and that was right at the top of the tree.

Chapter Thirty-Four

Gil wanted to sing. And dance. And maybe do a bit of shouting from the rooftops. But his housekeeper, Maria, would think he had lost his marbles. As far as he could tell, his marbles were exactly where they should be, but he did feel as if he had lost a tremendous weight – from around his neck and from around his heart. When he arrived home laden down with groceries there had been a certain amount of trepidation: perhaps he'd only imagined that Gina had gone, and she was, in fact, still firmly ensconced in his guest bedroom and his life. But, no, there was still a gap where his ex-wife used to be.

Now he was attacking a bunch of scallions and looking forward to seeing Sadie again. If only she would ring!

The meeting at Universal had gone great. The reluctant director he wanted for *The One That Got Away* had said yes. The scriptwriter was tapping away nicely and Gil was hoping against hope that the script would be delivered on time. They had a big-name actor lined up for the lead. Steve was keen to do the production design. Being a movie producer was a truly fabulous thing. Gil picked up his glass of fine Californian wine and took an appreciative sip. Gina had gone. Sadie was coming back. He had appointed a divorce lawyer. Everything in his world was lovely.

Maria was looking worried that he had taken over her kitchen. 'Here,' Gil said, pulling a fifty-dollar bill from his wallet. 'Take the night off. Go to the movies.'

Maria looked at him blankly.

'*Vaya a las peliculas*,' he said in loud and halting Spanish.

Maria brightened and took the money, tucking it into the depths of her uniform pocket. '*Si, Señor. Gracias.*' And she was out of the kitchen in a flash.

She probably wouldn't go to the movies, Gil thought. She'd just sit in her room watching *Jeopardy* and *The Weakest Link* and give the money to her wastrel son – but at least he had tried. And he and Sadie would have the place to themselves.

Dinner was going to be fabulous. He didn't cook very often, mainly due to lack of time, but he could rustle up a few signature dishes when required. And he was pulling all the stops out tonight with spaghetti vongole, his favourite dish of pasta with steamed clams. Not great for the breath, but weren't clams supposed to be an aphrodisiac – or was that oysters? Virtually the same thing, Gil decided. Both small and fishy. He rubbed his hands in satisfaction.

Just one last check on his *pièce de resistance*. Gil whipped off his apron – no need to scare the neighbours. Particularly when his neighbours were the sort of people who didn't even know where their own kitchens were.

He skipped out of the side door and through a passageway that led to the drive. And there it sat. All gleaming in the sinking evening sun. Gil felt a thrill of anticipation. Sadie would love this. The garage had delivered the small, sporty Mercedes this afternoon after a few frantic phone calls. It had a soft top, cream leather upholstery, sleek black lines and a big red bow tied around it. If her heart had been hardening towards him, this would surely melt it.

Chapter Thirty-Five

'Oh bollocks!' I press a few more keys on my snazzy new mobile and half of the messages disappear. 'I can't get this bloody thing to work!'

'Give me that,' Daniella instructs, and does the one-finger punch of an expert.

We are back at the ranch in Larchmont, lying on the sofa, feet up, drinking iced tea – a complete anathema to me, but when in Rome, etc. Alexis is home from school and is on the floor trying to persuade Super Gymnast Barbie to put her legs round her neck.

Daniella holds the phone to her ear. Her eyes widen. 'Gil says he loves you.'

'Does he?'

'No. But it's very similar. More gushy.'

'Gushy is good.'

She listens again. 'He says that Gina's gone.'

'Gone?' This certainly makes me sit up straight. 'Does he really say that?'

She nods.

'Gosh.' I have to admit I'm taken aback. 'He must have talked to her.'

'Either that or he's put an axe through her head and she's under the deck.'

'You write too many movies,' I say.

'Ssh,' Daniella instructs. 'He says to get a cab up to his house as soon as you can. He's going to make dinner. And he has a surprise for you.'

'Ha!' I say. 'And have I got a surprise for *him*!'

Delores – my new and faithful mode of transport –

148

behaved herself impeccably and peeped and farted all the way back here without breaking down once.

'He's more likely to have a heart attack if you turn up in that thing,' she warns. 'The LAPD will probably arrest you as a star stalker.'

'She's lovely,' I say defensively.

'Is it a car, Aunt Sadie?' Alexis asks.

'Yes,' I say. 'It's a very nice one. She's called Delores. She's a classic.'

'Museum piece,' Daniella mutters. 'Anyway,' she says, 'why are we talking about that piece of S.H.I.T., when the fact that the other piece of S.H.I.T., having moved her ass out, is much more interesting.'

'Mommy, that spells shit,' Alexis informs us brightly.

'Great,' Daniella says. 'There's nothing wrong with your spelling. I only wish your math was as good.'

I stand and stretch. 'I'd better get myself up there then.' What I really want is a long hot bath and an early night.

'Try to sound a little more enthusiastic,' Daniella says.

'I'm tired.' But if I'm truthful, I sort of wished that we were going to meet up at Zorba's again. I wanted to see Tavis and tell him about my car. He wouldn't think it was a heap. He'd like it – I know he would. I just hope Gil likes it too.

'It's a good job that Cinderella wasn't this reluctant to go to the ball,' Daniella remarks.

'No,' I say. 'Although she might have felt differently about kicking her shoes off if she'd known all along that Prince Charming was married.'

Chapter Thirty-Six

There is a slinky black car outside Gil's house and for a moment my heart stops and I think about turning round and going straight back home. And then I realise that home now means Daniella's house and not London, and the knot of my tension unravels slightly. If Gina is here, I'll just have to face her. Call on the fighting spirit that prevailed at Dunkirk and survived the rush-hour Tube every day.

I pull into the driveway with a few expressive farts from Delores and park as far away from the chic automobile as possible in case Delores decides to scratch its eyes out while I'm gone.

I smooth down my swishy chiffon skirt – these designer carrier bags are bottomless, I swear. The more outfits you pull out, the more keep appearing. Surely we didn't really buy all this stuff?

I'm feeling like I should have brought something to the party – wine, chocolate, flowers – but I have come empty-handed and am now even more self-conscious.

Shuffling from foot to foot, like some fidgety four year old, I ring the bell. Maria comes to the door immediately and shows me into the vast atrium, muttering incomprehensibly in Spanish as Gil comes to the door of the kitchen.

'Hey,' he says softly and pulls me to him.

Maria blends into the background.

'You look great,' Gil says with a most welcome sigh of admiration.

'Thanks.' Gil also looks good. He's wearing a baggy T-shirt and shorts. He's the first man I've seen in about twenty years who looks great in anything that stops mid-thigh. All the men at home have spaghetti legs with knobbly knees and pale blue dead-fish skin from lack of sun. Or is it just my ex-boyfriends who have been so afflicted? In contrast, Gil's legs are strong and tanned. It's suddenly got very warm in here.

'I'm glad you're here,' he says, and tugs me into the kitchen. Beautiful garlicy smells waft up from steaming pans. I'm glad I'm here too, now that I think of it. I might not have been jumping for joy earlier, but little bits of me are starting to bounce happily.

He hugs me close. 'You like your car?'

I smile. He must have seen me arrive in my old jalopy. 'Yeah,' I say. 'It will do for now.'

A look of disappointment crosses his face and I feel a pang of disloyalty towards Delores.

'It's fine,' I say, squeezing him.' It will get me from A to B. Just about.'

He still looks a bit put out.

'I'll pay you back, I promise. You can have a down payment as soon as I get paid.'

'It's a gift,' he says rather tightly.

'Don't be silly.' I give him a jocular punch on the arm and he looks at where I hit him. 'You wouldn't choose anything so tasteless!'

Gil disentangles himself from me, despite his initial enthusiasm, I'm sure he loathes Delores. I knew he would. Probably not LA enough for him.

'Shall we eat?' Gil says rather crisply.

I'm starving and could probably eat a scabby donkey. 'Mmm,' I say. 'It smells wonderful.'

'Spaghetti vongole,' he says proudly.

I don't know what a vongole is. Perhaps it is a scabby donkey. It sounds more like small rodent – a mole or vole. 'Oh.' California is doing its best to make me feel ignorant in the ways of food. There are always so many weird things on the menu. 'What does that involve?'

'Clams,' he says.

Bugger. Are they like mussels? I'm allergic to mussels.

151

'It's my speciality,' he says.

Bugger. It looks like I'm about to find out.

'So,' I perch on a kitchen stool. 'Where's Gina?'

Gil looks up from his preparations. 'Gone,' he says. 'Didn't you get my message?'

'Well, yes. Sort of.'

'She went this morning,' Gil continues. 'Noah came down last night, begged her to go home and this morning she'd gone. Along with all her clothes – which is definitely a first.'

My word. Maybe Daniella was right – she has got an axe in her head somewhere.

'I have started divorce proceedings.'

Ooo. This is news.

'And not before time,' he admits. And then Gil gives me a large glass of wine which I want to gulp straight down. 'I think we should celebrate,' he says.

'I'll be driving later.'

'I kinda hoped that you'd stay,' he says with an uncertain laugh. 'Didn't you bring your stuff?'

'What? All of it?'

'That was the idea.'

It may be your idea, pal. But it isn't mine!

'I want you to move in with me.'

'But I like being at Daniella's,' I say.

Gil frowns. 'You don't know her.'

'I don't know you.'

'But you came halfway round the world to be with me!'

I thought he'd conveniently forgotten that. 'I did,' I say calmly, and decide that I do need the wine – Delores probably has some sort of automatic homing device. She's that type of car. The wine goes down in one. 'And when I got here,' I remind him, 'I found a little more than I bargained for.'

'Gina,' he says.

I shrug and Gil walks over to the nearest kitchen cupboard and bangs his head slowly against it.

'I'm not saying I won't come back,' I point out before he

suffers brain damage. 'Just that I don't think we should rush it.'

Gil looks deflated. He's a man who's used to getting his own way. At work, at least. 'Whatever you say. I guess I have to earn back your trust.'

Just when I think he's being a shit-head, he turns round and comes out with something like that. And now I feel mean and ungrateful.

'Dinner looks lovely.' I get off my stool and tenderly kiss his cheek. He smells of cinnamon and spring onions.

The smile eases back to his lips, but I can tell that this is not going the way he planned it. 'It's just about ready,' he says.

I'm going to have to eat this vongole stuff come hell or bloody high water, I think, and suffer the consequences. Otherwise this entire night could turn out to be a complete disaster.

Chapter Thirty-Seven

Mary Ann came back from Alexis's bedroom. 'She's asleep,' she said as she sat down.

'What?' Daniella asked as she felt her mother's gaze fall on her as she sat typing at the kitchen table.

'You look all done in yourself.' Mary Ann picked up and shook out the newspaper.

'I'm fine,' Daniella said. She took off her glasses and rubbed her eyes.

'Why don't you give it a rest for tonight?' Mary Ann suggested. 'There's absolutely nothing on TV. We could sit and watch it together.'

'I have to go out,' Daniella said.

Mary Ann checked the clock. 'Now?'

'I have a writing class.'

Mary Ann studied her daughter. 'You're not going where I think you're going?'

'Mom,' Daniella said with weary exasperation.

'I don't want you to go down that road again.'

'Do you think I'm stupid?'

'When it comes to *that* man, then yes, I think you are.'

'You're my mother,' Daniella pointed out. 'You should support me.'

'Honey,' Mary Ann said, 'the world is full of married men who cheat.'

'I know,' Daniella retorted. 'My father was one of them.'

Mary Ann looked stung. 'Don't you think that's why I want better for you?'

Daniella picked up the scattered typed pages and tapped them into a tidy pile on the surface of the table.

Mary Ann came over and wrapped her arms round her daughter's shoulders. 'You're young. You're beautiful. You should find someone else.'

'Someone else with no wife?'

'There are nice men out there,' Mary Ann said.

'Well,' Daniella said, 'you and I don't seem to have much luck in finding them.' She stood up and stretched, disentangling herself from her mother. 'I won't be long.'

'I wish you wouldn't do this,' Mary Ann said with a sigh.

'I have to,' Daniella insisted. She kissed her mother on the cheek. 'I'll be back before you know it.' And she headed for the front door, ignoring the resigned shaking of her mom's head.

In a city that has more than its fair share of rich residents, Bel Air is considered the enclave of the super-duper-stellar rich. The evocative strip of Sunset Boulevard still cuts a swathe through the haves and the have-nots. The multi-million-dollar price tags guard the best views in the city. If you want the ultimate status symbol of someone who has made it mega-mega big in the entertainment business, this sleepy hillside community is where you must buy your real estate.

The first super-star mansion in the cool wooded canyon was built way back in Hollywood's golden years by Douglas Fairbanks and Mary Pickford, and everyone else who was anyone followed suit – Elvis Presley, Barbra Streisand, Lana Turner, Natalie Wood, Gene Kelly, Tom Jones, Elizabeth Taylor – they'd all lived in Bel-Air at one time, along with all the other great stars – too many to list. The Mad Movie Mogul was no exception.

Daniella parked outside the ten-foot-high security gates of his ostentatious house tucked away deep in the grounds of his heavily guarded estate and wound down her window. Even the air tasted of wealth. Her mother was right – this was madness. She should take her advice and move on. What good did it do her to come and sit on the outside of his world and look in? It just made her more hollow inside.

There was nothing to see for the casual visitor. Celebrities and Mad Movie Moguls who valued their privacy hid behind imposing walls, steel gates, security cameras and token bougainvillea hedges. It was a futile and depressing way to spend time. She didn't do it often – but more often than she should do after all this time.

Daniella had been inside the house just once and had toured through every room, remembering exactly the colour, texture and placing of the furnishings, lingering longer in some than others. She and the Mad Movie Mogul had been in the first flush of their affair. They had made love in the master bedroom – is that the sort of thing a man does if he adores his wife? Sleep with his girlfriend in the marital bed? She could picture it now, as clear as then. If Mrs Mad Movie Mogul had remodelled in the meantime she would have no way of knowing.

A breeze rustled stealthily through the tall trees. There was no party in progress tonight. No stream of white limos. No valet parking. No burly guards with black jackets, mirrored-sunglasses and walkie-talkies. No tinkling piano to tighten her insides. No sound of laughter drifting on the warm night air. No sign of frivolity from which, once again, she had been excluded. Those were the visits that hurt the most.

Tonight all was quiet in 3M Towers. Perhaps he was watching the rushes of his latest project in his private cinema. Perhaps he was enjoying a drink with his wife. The wife whom he had said he no longer loved. The wife with whom he no longer slept. But with whom he still remained, despite all these things. Maybe by breathing in the same patch of air, he would somehow sense she was there. Daniella closed her eyes, listening to herself breathing and imagining the rhythm of his.

She wound up the window. If she didn't move on soon, the Bel Air armed security patrol would be round and they would move her on. In an area where your neighbours included the likes of Nicolas Cage and Hugh Hefner, everyone who wasn't a resident was viewed as a potential stalker. And maybe they wouldn't be far wrong. What would it look like to the Mad Movie Mogul? Still, she knew she wasn't a stalker, a freak, an obsessive fan. Just an old flame, who had quietly guttered along for many years without ever quite managing to blow out the light. Part of her knew that he still thought about her. She knew that just as surely as she knew that someone, somewhere would be brave enough to take a risk on one of her growing pile of movie scripts.

Chapter Thirty-Eight

The spaghetti vongole was actually superb and I'm feeling very replete and not at all nauseous – for which I'm eternally grateful. Gil and I have moved into his cavernous lounge and are snuggled up on one of his white leather sofas which would easily seat an entire coachload of people. I wonder why anyone would ever want sofas so large. This is not a homely house. It's like . . . well, I don't really know. It's like nothing I've ever seen before and probably exactly like the sort of place a movie star would live in. You can hear the echo as we speak, our words bouncing back to us off the acres of bare white plaster walls. All the paintings are variations of great big blocks of primary colours that look like they've been knocked out by nursery-school pupils and I assume that makes them hip and extortionately expensive.

I'd like to be outside enjoying the warm night, but I expect that's a British thing. We don't care whether we get bitten to death by bitey things or battered by bad UV rays, we're just so desperate to be outside that we rush out whenever we can, because we're never quite sure when in the next decade we might see the next dry, sunny day. If you live somewhere that's dry and sunny for pretty much all of the time, it must cease to be an issue. We like to fry, Californians like to stay cool.

Despite all that, and I think it must be the several glasses of wine and the bursting stomach that are helping, I feel surprisingly mellow. My eyes and limbs are heavy, but not in a dead tired way and I lean against Gil and sigh.

'This is what our first night should have been like,' he says ruefully.

'I know,' I say, snuggling into him. 'Let's try and get back to that.'

I feel him nod and his lips toy with my hair. After a little persuasion, my shoulders give up their knots. Gil's lips follow the line of my neck, his breath hot in the air-conditioned room. His kisses travel softly and slowly along the line of my jaw and over my cheek, my eyelids, the tip of my nose. And I'm burning up even though my goose pimples have goose pimples. His lips find mine and he takes my wine glass and without breaking the kiss, he puts it down somewhere – less worried than I am about his white leather. Our arms fold round each other and I can feel his heart pounding through his T-shirt. Oh, how I have waited for this! His hands, hot and searching, cover my body and I'm definitely beginning to wish that I'd brought my toothbrush.

My fingers wander underneath his T-shirt, tentative, easing it from his body. It is so long since I've done this that my mouth has gone dry with anticipation. This boy has a fine set of abs and a toned chest as smooth as silk. Sometime in between being a hot-shot movie producer and his wife's keeper he clearly finds time to work out.

Over the gasps of our breath, there is a screeching of brakes and the headlights of a car illuminate the atrium, making the plants look like something out of *Jurassic Park*. Gil and I part and watch the lights, breathing heavily. There is a moment of quiet, followed immediately by the most almighty smash. Gil jumps up, pulling his T-shirt down and rushes to the door.

'Goddamn it, woman!' he shouts out into the night and shakes his fist for good measure.

I tug my clothing back to a more modest arrangement and follow him.

'She hit your goddamn car!' Gil is beside himself with rage and I'm not far behind either.

'Delores!' I cry. 'Not Delores!' And I rush out into the drive, pursued by Gil.

159

Gina is sitting in her new SUV, slumped over the steering-wheel. Steam is puffing from her engine. The lovely sleek black and shiny Mercedes now has a deep, crumpled 'V' in its boot.

'Jesus!' Gil says and rushes to snatch open Gina's door.

How has she managed to hit this car as well as Delores? I rush to see my baby and she is still parked unobtrusively in the corner of the drive, tucked under a large bougainvillea bush, rusting quietly but otherwise unscathed.

'Look what you've done to Sadie's car!' Gil yells. He is shaking Gina, but she is blissfully unaware of the fact.

'That's not my car,' I say quietly.

Gil spins round. 'What?'

'Delores is fine.'

'Who?'

'Delores. My car.' I'm aware that I'm swallowing most of my voice. 'She's fine.'

Gil follows my eyes and I see him recoil as his eyes rest on Delores's well-rounded, terracotta-spotted curves.

'Jesus,' he breathes.

'That's my car,' I reiterate, because he's suddenly gone very pale.

'*This* is your car,' he says, and points at the sleek, black, wrecked one. At the moment it looks in a rather worse state than Delores.

'It's not,' I insist. 'I don't know whose it is. I thought it was Gina's.'

'It's yours.' His voice is rising alarmingly. 'I bought it for you.' His hands look like they are shaking. 'That's why it's got a *fucking* big red bow on the front!'

Oh. I hadn't seen that. Even if I had, I wouldn't automatically have assumed it was for me. 'Don't shout at me,' I shout. 'I don't want a car with a *fucking* big red bow on the front!'

'I bought it for you!'

'I don't want it,' I shout louder. 'You can't buy me.'

'I'm not trying to buy you! I want you to be happy.'

'I *am* happy.' I'm still shouting and sound anything but. 'With Delores!'

160

'You can't drive round in that heap.'

'It's all I can afford.' Technically, I can't even afford Delores and it is Gil's money that paid for her, but at the moment I'm prepared to gloss over that fact.

'What do I have to do to say I'm sorry to you?' Gil is breathing heavily and not in the same passionate way he was a few minutes ago.

'Just that!' I can feel my nostrils flaring and it isn't attractive. 'Say you're sorry. Don't buy me things.'

Suddenly Gil is very quiet. 'It was done with the best intentions,' he says. 'I thought you'd like it.'

I want to cry. Why are we making such a mess of this? 'I do,' I say. 'Very much. The front is very nice.'

Our eyes take in the beautiful and extremely dented car. We both start to smile.

At that moment, Gina slides from the driver's seat and is loudly sick on the driveway.

'Oh fuck,' Gil mutters and we both hotfoot to where her inert form has landed.

Gil hoists her up.

'Sorry,' Gina mutters.

'Sorry?' Gil has gone white with anger. 'You have wrecked two cars in as many days, you stupid woman. I've had it with you, really I have. This is it.'

Gina slumps onto his shoulder and I go and bear the weight of her other arm and between us we drag her towards the house. For someone who looks as if nothing more solid than a lettuce leaf ever passes her lips, she weighs a ton. She is not a pretty sight either. The last time I saw her, the layer of foundation she was wearing was immaculately applied – now it's rubbed round her face in an Aunt Sally way. Her eyes are bloodshot slits and she has absolutely no control over her limbs.

We bounce her up the steps, a bit more vigorously than is strictly necessary in my view and when we get into the atrium, she throws up again.

'Maria! Maria!' Gil shouts. Gina groans. The sound is splitting my head, so heaven only knows what it's doing to hers.

The diminutive Mexican housekeeper appears. She is wearing a housecoat and rollers, which she is trying to hide under a chiffon scarf. She is also doing a very good impression of a headless chicken and is running round, crossing herself and wailing incomprehensible Spanish laments at the top of her voice. It's not really helping the proceedings.

Gina groans and barfs again.

'Get a bucket for Mrs McGann,' Gil instructs and we both exchange a glance after the word 'Mrs'.

Once we get Gina to the guest bedroom, Gil throws her onto the bed on her back. She lies there comatose.

'Maybe we ought to turn her onto her front,' I suggest. 'She may choke on her own vomit.'

'Good,' Gil snaps.

Maria appears with a bucket. It has a mop in it. 'What I wouldn't like to do with that,' he says, eyeing it and his wife malevolently.

'Is there anything else I can do?' I ask. Now I feel like a spare wotsit at a wedding. And I don't mean bridesmaid.

'No,' Gil says wearily. 'Maria will help me to clean her up.' He looks at me sadly. 'It won't be the first time.' He comes over and hugs me. 'Thanks.'

'I don't know what to do,' I say.

'Go and get ready for bed,' he tells me. 'I'll be through shortly. Maybe we can continue where we left off . . .' But I can tell from his eyes that it's a bit of bravado and he isn't at all hopeful.

'I think I'd better go.'

'Stay.'

'She needs you,' I say, shaking my head. I can't sleep with Gil in the room down the hall from his drunk and disorderly wife. It's unnatural. How can he not see that? He steps towards me and I step away. 'I'll call you in the morning.'

'Sadie . . .' his voice is hoarse. 'I don't want Gina to come between us.'

But that is exactly what she is doing. And I wonder how much of it is calculated. I take another step towards the door.

'Sadie . . .' He looks from me, to the comatose Gina, to Maria who is trying to make herself invisible. 'There are things I want to say.' He clears his throat. 'But now isn't the right time.'

'No,' I say. 'I'll call you tomorrow.' And I blow him a kiss before leaving.

In the driveway the wreck of the Mercedes glints in the moonlight. It is a beautiful warm night and I know that I've had too much to drink to be driving, but I've not had nearly as much as Gina, so I reckon I'll be okay.

I go over to Delores and pat her fender. 'We need to go home,' I say as I jump in and start the engine. 'I hope you know the way.'

Like the old trouper she is, the car creaks and groans out of the drive, the corsets of her suspension pinging with the effort.

'Well done for staying out of the heat, old girl,' I say. I plant a kiss on the steering-wheel. 'If only your owner were half as clever.'

Chapter Thirty-Nine

This may not be the most rational thing I've ever done, but I don't care. Right now I want someone to love Delores – and if I analyse it a bit closer I'd like someone to love me too. And if I can't have love, I'd at least like a bit of attention.

I know someone who would love this car as I do and I want him to see it. If I go back to Daniella's house now, everyone will be asleep and I'll be all alone and miserable. There's only one person I can turn to in my hour of need. I'll drive past Tavis's apartment – just the once – and if the light's still on, I'll risk it for a biscuit.

Scooting down Santa Monica Boulevard, I'm amazed that the traffic is so light. Rush-hour in London seems to last 24/7 and you can't go anywhere out of second gear. Delores's speed limitations are more to do with a self-governing engine: if you accelerate above thirty miles per hour, it sort of peters out. I enjoy the warm air on my face and the wind ruffling my hair, and spare a thought for my friend Alice back at home who will be somewhere shivering her bum off.

I turn into La Brea, cruising to find the right apartment block and when I find it, the light is indeed still on in Tavis's window. He is strolling backwards and forwards in front of it at a measured pace, holding what looks like a script. He's not wearing a shirt.

I park Delores and totter up to the door. Is it the done thing to turn up unannounced in LA? In London you'd be treated as a social pariah and probably stoned. Stoned as in having small rocks hurled at you, not as in high on drugs.

The label by the doorbell says *Mavers–Jones* and I give it a decisive press.

'Hi.' It's Tavis's disembodied voice coming from a little box on the wall.

'Er . . . hi,' I say, leaning close to it in a furtive manner. 'It's Sadie.'

'Wow,' Tavis crackles back at me. 'You're the last person I expected.'

'I'm sorry,' I say, Dutch courage seeping out of me. 'I know it's late. I have something I wanted to show you.'

'You wanna come up?' I hear the door buzzer sound.

'No.' I check to see that Delores is looking her best and wish that she hadn't mussed up my hair so much. 'I'd like you to come down.'

'Okay,' he says. 'Give me five.'

It takes him two and he steps out into the street, still not wearing a shirt – or shoes. He looks genuinely pleased to see me and you don't know how relieved I am.

I do a 'lovely assistant' pose and present Delores. 'Da, da!'

'Oh man!' Tavis coos, and without bothering to open the door, he jumps over into the driver's seat. 'This is so cool,' he says, fiddling with Delores's bells and whistles. 'Mmm mmm!' He gives Delores a hearty thump on her rump.

'I thought you'd like her,' I say proudly.

'What are you waiting for?' Tavis jerks his head. 'Get in.'

'Where are we going?'

'Does it matter?'

'It's late.'

'Where haven't you been yet?'

I shrug. 'I haven't been anywhere.'

'Then we must go and look at the moon over Venice Beach.'

'How long will it take?'

'Twenty minutes.'

'Okay.' I open the door and get in next to Tavis in the more traditional way. He's still not wearing a shirt. 'Won't you be cold?'

165

'You sound like my mom,' Tavis says.

'Sorry. In Britain you can't go to the beach without wearing an anorak. Even in summer.'

'Well, now you're in Cal-i-forn-i-a!' he shouts.

And I'm really quite glad that I am.

He grinds Delores into gear and grins at me as we pull away. Delores – the shameless flirt – purrs up to fifty without pause. Tavis clicks on the radio and the Beach Boys blare out. We fly down La Brea, then chew up the miles and spit them out on Venice Boulevard, singing *I wish they all could be California girls* at the top of our voices.

Twenty minutes later, we park up at the beach. Tavis comes round and helps me from the car. The night is as black as new tarmac and a big, shiny moon looks as if it has been hole-punched into the sky. I can hear the sea lapping at the sand, but can't see it.

'Come on,' Tavis says.

'Won't we get mugged or shot?' I'm nothing if not cautious.

'Not today,' he says. 'There may be a few homeless guys sleeping out, but that's all. You're safe with me.'

So I take off my shoes and we stroll out over the sand towards the Pacific Ocean. I try to remember when I last went to the seaside and fail. Long enough to have forgotten what it is like to taste salty sea air on my lips and feel the gritty sand work through my toes.

'Sit.' Tavis does just that and as he pats the sand next to him, I join him.

'I think this is the first time since I arrived in LA that I don't feel I'm running around like a loony,' I say with a hearty huff.

'You need to kick back and come down to our pace,' Tavis advises and I'm sure he's quite right. I feel like I've spent the last few months in one of those Dyson washing machines that twist both ways because for some reason it's better for clothes. I have to say it's not a great feeling for people.

166

He lies on the sand and I follow suit, trying to block out the thought that sand is nothing more than pretty coloured dirt and crushed-up shells. Is this a sign that I'm too stressed? I practise my yoga deep breathing, which is an effort because I haven't been anywhere near a class for months, and wiggle my toes into the damp layer beneath the top powdery stuff. Eventually I start to enjoy the rough texture of the sand and the coolness on my back. It feels so good, I could weep with weary joy. I'm probably still hideously jet-lagged.

Tavis turns towards me, drawing circles in the sand with his finger. 'Are you enjoying LA?' Moonlight does wonderful things to his bone structure. He's wearing cut-off combat trousers and a leather friendship thong is plaited round his ankle. Delores has given his hair a battering too.

'I don't know,' I say truthfully. 'It's not working out quite as I planned.' I give him a rueful smile.

'Don't talk about it if you don't want to,' Tavis says.

'I'd like to,' I admit. 'I have so many things going round in a loop in my head, I feel as if I'm going potty.'

'Potty is bad, right?'

'Potty's very bad.' I look up at the moon. The moon is responsible for all kinds of things – the pull of the tides, werewolves, irrational moods. But it just hangs there looking rather attractive and as if it isn't doing very much. Its lure has driven men crazy for centuries. I would like to be like the moon, but I'm probably more like the Tasmanian Devil from the Bugs Bunny cartoon – whirling about, muttering, cursing and grumbling and ultimately being outwitted by nothing more than a smartass rabbit.

'It's Gil,' I say, digging my toes a bit deeper. 'I really like him.' I give Tavis a look that says it's probably more. Why would I have dragged my arse all the way out here to LA otherwise? 'I want to be with him.'

'But?'

'He has a wife.'

Tavis raises an eyebrow.

'She's supposed to be long gone and shacked up with someone else, but I can't see much evidence of that.' I sigh

167

and several PSI of pressure drift up into the atmosphere. 'She seems very much still attached to Gil.'

'And what does Gil say?'

'That he's sorting it out. But it looks to me as if she has him exactly where she wants him.'

'And in the meantime?'

'I'm hanging round like a lemon.'

'These Hollywood wives can be very tenacious,' Tavis warns. 'She may not want him, but she may want to make damn sure that no one else gets him.'

'He didn't like Delores either,' I confess. 'He called her a heap.'

'The man clearly has no style.'

I don't tell him that Gil had just bought me a Mercedes and probably had every right to feel a bit piqued that I preferred my rusty old bone-shaker.

'I'm making him sound awful,' I say, feeling guilty. 'He's not. He's really nice.'

'I guess he must be if you're prepared to put up with all this.'

'I'd like you to meet him.'

Tavis brushes down his shorts. 'I'd like that too.'

'I suppose we'd better get back,' I say. 'I hope you don't mind me calling on you unexpectedly?'

'I'm glad you came by.' Tavis is smiling but he looks sad. I don't know what colour his eyes are, but they're glinting black in the night.

'I knew you'd understand,' I say. 'I don't know how, I just did.' I want to hug him or something, but have no idea how to cross the six inches of sand between us. 'Thanks.'

Tavis walks his fingers across towards mine and I meet them. We touch them together like a chaste kiss. Tavis takes my hands and pulls me to my feet and we stand so close that I can feel his body heat. He is one hot guy. And he's tall. Very tall. And all sort of skinny and muscly at the same time. It must be the last vestiges of alcohol kicking in because suddenly I feel all warm and swimmy and my legs don't want to stand up any more.

Tavis puts his hands on my shoulders and they scorch

my skin like the heat of the midday sun. He's so close that I can see a pulse beating steadily in his throat and when I look up towards him, his face is serious. He turns me away from the pull of the sea and the lure of the moon and back towards the car park. 'Come on,' Tavis says in a husky movie-star type voice that makes me shiver all over. 'Delores will be missing you.'

And I wonder if Gil is too.

Chapter Forty

Tavis stops outside his apartment building and turns towards me. He hands me back the keys to Delores.

'Thanks,' I say. 'It's been great.'

Tavis bites his lip. 'Come in for coffee.'

'I should get home. Daniella will be worried.' Like hell she will – she'll be fast asleep in the land of Nod thinking that I'm having a rampant night of unbridled lust with Gil. Little does she know! Still, it's a great excuse. I don't know if I want to get into all the complications that coffee might imply. I have definitely taken more pleasure than I should have done in watching Tavis drive my car back bare-chested and I don't want him to feel that I'm leading him on. He might be utterly bite-the-back-of-your-hand gorgeous, but I want an uncomplicated friendship with him. Is that ever possible with a man?

Anyway, Tavis is so heart-stoppingly handsome that he is totally out of my league. He's the sort of guy who will date long-legged models and up-and-coming actresses. Gil is more my type – a bit more bashed around the edges. Even though he's also the sort of guy who should probably be dating long-legged models, etc. Let's face it though – who would be happy sharing their hair gel with a man?

The strange, and nice thing, is that Tavis seems so unaware of his charisma. Maybe he's such a good actor that the whole thing is an illusion anyway.

'Big decision?' he teases. He can see I'm tempted. Tavis is such easy, laid-back company. Whenever I'm with Gil, I feel like I'm walking a tightrope.

'One quick drink won't hurt,' he says and jumps out of

Delores using the unconventional route.

'A quick one,' I agree.

'Wait there like a good girl,' he says to the car.

And, also like a good girl, I follow him up the stairs and into his building.

A tall, blond man is waiting at the door of the apartment to greet us and it takes me by surprise. 'Hey,' he says, clapping Tavis on the back as he approaches. 'Great car.'

'Delores,' Tavis informs him. 'This is her owner, Sadie.' As he eases me into the apartment, I notice that he exchanges a look with the man. 'Girlfriend of the great Gil McGann.'

The man bows in mock reverence. 'Respect,' he says.

I laugh. 'Sometime girlfriend,' I correct.

'Ah,' the man says. 'The course of true love never runs smoothly. At least not in Hollywood.'

'This is Joe Mavers,' Tavis says. 'My partner in crime.'

'Yes,' Joe says, hugging Tavis to him. 'This guy and I have been together for years. We've stuck it out through thick and thin, haven't we, darling?'

Tavis looks slightly bashful.

'Oh. That's nice.' This is a revelation. I had absolutely no idea that Tavis was gay. But it's quite clear from Joe's territorial manner that their partnership extends to more than mere crime.

Something inside me sags a little. What a bloody waste! I don't want to appear fickle, particularly considering my situation with Gil, but I did feel there was a bit of 'chemistry' going on back there at the beach. At the very least I thought Tavis was a red-blooded male. This is a bit like finding out that George Clooney or Russell Crowe is gay.

My judgement seems all to cock these days – no pun intended. But in some ways it feels nice to know that he was merely being understanding and protective and a good mate and not in any way trying to qualify for an inspection of the contents of my underwear.

'Coffee?' Tavis says and I realise I'm staring.

'Yes, please. That would be lovely.'

'I adore your accent,' Joe says and he shows me to the sofa and I sit down. I feel a bit of a twonk now. I've got loads of gay friends at home. Well, two – Crispin and Paul. And I guess Crispin's a bit of a gay name. But they both look really gay – if you know what I mean. There'd be no mistaking Crispin for someone who'd want to jump your bones. Or even potential boyfriend material. Is anyone in this town what they seem to be? Sometimes I feel very naïve in the ways of the world.

'Relax,' Joe says. 'You look very tense.'

I realise that my shoulders are scrunched up somewhere round my ears and the brief respite I had from my stress on the beach has somehow wandered away.

'Joe is in one our major soaps,' Tavis shouts from the kitchen area.

Joe tries to look modest and fails.

'Fantastic.' I'm really weary now and I shouldn't have come back here as I haven't the wherewithal to make small talk.

Tavis comes back into the room and gives me a steaming mug which has a cute pig on the front and the caption *Hamming it up*. He sits on the chair opposite me and I study him. He still doesn't look gay even though I now know that he is. Still, not all gay men walk around looking like the Village People. I'd hazard a guess that Joe is a few years older than him. Tavis's boyfriend is an attractive guy and I would have said he was quite rugged, but when I look more closely there's a softness to his features, matched by a softness round his middle. As soon as he opens his mouth, there's no doubting that Joe is as bent as a nine-bob note. He has a gentle, effeminate way of talking and he camps it up outrageously. I think he's someone who would be fun to have around. But try as I might I cannot find it in me to see these two as an item.

Joe stretches theatrically and makes a loud yawning noise. 'I'm going to leave you two sweet things,' he says. He comes over and kisses my cheek. 'I'll say goodbye for now, but you and Gil must come to dinner. I won't take no for an answer.'

172

'That would be very nice. Thank you.'

'Your accent kills me.' Joe hugs himself. He goes to Tavis and kisses his cheek too. I can feel myself blush and I look away to study the curtains which I have to say are a bit flowery for my taste. 'Not too late, Tav.' Joe wags his finger. 'We have sides to do.'

'I have it.' Tavis nods.

Joe blows me another kiss. 'See you again,' he says.

'I hope so.'

And when he leaves, the room seems suddenly quiet.

Tavis smiles at me over his coffee. 'He's the best,' he says with open admiration. 'I don't know where I'd be without him. Off my head. Up my own ass. I don't know.'

'He seems nice.' I'm not sure what else to say. Tavis is observing me intently. 'What are sides?'

'Oh.' He shrugs. 'Lines.' He picks up the script from the coffee-table next to him. 'I have an audition tomorrow morning. I need to go through them before then.'

'And I'm keeping you from them?' I put down my coffee. 'I feel terrible.'

'Sadie . . .' Tavis smiles at me and it is warm enough to melt an ice-lolly. 'I wouldn't have had it any other way. I've really enjoyed tonight. It's been a blast. I love Delores and . . .' he frowns as he glances at me, 'and . . . I think an awful lot of you too.'

'Thanks. You're a mate.'

'A mate?' he says it in Queen's English and laughs: 'I'm a mate.'

I throw a cushion at him. 'Stop taking the piss out of my accent!'

'Help me out,' Tavis says. 'This character is English. You could listen to my lines.'

I curl my feet up on the sofa and snuggle down into the corner. 'I'd love to.'

Tavis opens his script. His fingers and long and tapered. 'Are you sure you're not too tired?'

'No,' I say with a shake of my head. He is such a beautiful person, I could lie here and look at him for ever. 'What's it about?'

173

'It's about a man who is desperately in love with someone who doesn't even know he exists.'

'Ha!' I say. 'That I can relate to.'

'Me too,' Tavis says quietly. He wiggles about on the chair and jiggles his shoulders until he's comfortable. That boy still isn't wearing nearly enough clothes. Tavis looks nervous and he clears his throat. His eyes sparkle, animatedly. 'Here goes.'

His voice, strong and clear and very English, flows over me and all thoughts of sleep are forgotten.

Chapter Forty-One

'What the hell are you doing?'

Gil glanced up without breaking from his task.

Gina stood in the doorway, hands on her hips. She looked better than she did last night, but that wasn't saying a great deal.

He had his suitcases open on the bed and was stuffing clothes into them as fast as he could. 'I'm packing.'

'I can see that,' Gina said. 'What I want to know is why?'

'Why?' Gil wanted to beat his head against the wall. 'Do you remember what you did last night?'

A dark shadow crossed Gina's face and the pout on her lips transmogrified to a tight pucker. 'So, I got a little drunk.'

'You are ruining my relationship with Sadie,' he said. 'I want my life back, Gina. One that doesn't have you *crashing* into it. Literally.'

'Well, that's very nice.'

'It's how it has to be.' Gil slammed the lid shut on one case. This was easier than he'd thought. The only thing that was nipping at him was why he hadn't thought of it earlier. He glanced at the bed. Only one side was messed up and he hadn't slept a wink all night for thinking about Sadie and what they might have been doing if Gina hadn't been dead to the world and snoring in the guest bedroom.

'You can stay in the house,' he said, 'until we get the financial side of our divorce finalised.'

'Our *divorce*?'

'You can have the house if that's what you want. I don't

even like the goddamn thing.'

'Don't you want to know why I was upset last night?' his wife demanded.

'No,' Gil said. 'Because if I know, it will involve me and I don't want to be involved.'

Gina slithered down the door until she was sitting on the floor, long, shapely legs splayed in front of her. 'Noah asked me to marry him.'

Gil stopped mid-pack. 'He did?' He felt a rush of levity to his heart. 'That's great.' Gina didn't look like she thought it was great. 'Isn't it?'

'He asked me to sign a pre-nup.' Gina's face screwed up as she prepared to cry. 'Can you believe it?'

'And that's why you're upset?'

'Wouldn't you be?' she snapped.

Gil wished that he'd thought of getting Gina to sign a pre-nup. If she'd kicked up a fuss like this they might never have made it up the aisle and what a blessing that would have been. Clearly, Gina didn't see it in quite the same way.

'This is LA, Gina,' Gil said. 'Everyone signs pre-nups.'

'I don't,' Gina said.

'You'll get a fortune from me,' he pointed out. 'You'll be a wealthy woman.'

'How wealthy?' Gina wanted to know.

'Very,' Gil said. 'Enough to keep you happy.' But he wondered if any amount of money would ever keep Gina happy. 'Sign it. It's only sensible,' Gil tried to push the point home. 'Noah is worth millions. Millions and millions. He's had how many wives? Three? Four?' Maybe a few he's forgotten. 'He'd be working as a bus boy at Wolfgang Puck's if he hadn't got pre-nups.'

'Trust you to see it from his side.'

'Get a good lawyer. Negotiate yourself a great deal. Then kit yourself out with diamonds. Have them put in all of your nails or your teeth. Or both. You'll never spend your way to the bottom of Noah's money.'

Gina seemed to brighten slightly. 'You really think that's what I should do?'

176

'Of course.'

'You're not just saying that?'

Gil dropped a shirt in his case. It was one that he never wore and he had no idea why he might be packing it. 'Gina . . .'

She came across to him, wrapped her arms round him and with a breathy sigh said, 'Why did I ever leave you, Gil?'

'Because you thought I was a boring motherfucker,' he said. 'You told me so on many occasions.'

'That's my idea of a pet name,' Gina said. 'They're all words of love really.'

Yeah, right. 'Anyway,' Gil said. 'I'm outta here.'

'Where are you going?'

'To a hotel.'

'You can't live in a hotel,' she said. 'It's so . . . so . . . Howard Hughes.'

'I can't stay here with you,' he said. 'It's too cramped.' Which was a fine thing to say about a home with more rooms than you could shake a stick at.

'What about me?'

'You can do what you like. You're on your own, Gina.'

'Don't be like that, Gil,' she begged. 'I need you. I need you to be my best friend.'

'And I need you to be *my* best friend,' Gil said. 'I need you to stand on your own two feet. No drink. No drugs. No stupid threats.'

'You're right,' Gina said. 'You're absolutely right. You always are.'

Gil was stunned.

Gina held up her hands in surrender. 'I should go home to Noah and tell him yes. Right now.'

Yes! Gil felt like punching the air.

'You should stay here. This is your home. I won't hear any more talk of hotels. I must go right now.' Gina said, starting to fuss.

'I'm going to San Francisco,' Gil said. 'You have the weekend.'

'No. No,' Gina insisted. 'I'm out of your life right now.'

Gil moved towards her, but she held up her hands.

'Apologise to Sadie for me,' she said. 'Noah will pay for the damage to her car.'

So some things never change. She kissed Gil on the cheek distractedly. 'I love you,' Gina said. 'You're the best husband I ever had.' She lowered her eyes and took in the bed. 'I don't suppose we could have a last . . . for old times' sake?'

'I don't think so,' Gil said.

Gina shrugged. 'I must go and shower. Noah will wonder where I am.' And with that she strode out of the room.

Gil frowned. He was getting too old to deal with Gina. He spent his working days dealing with tetchy technical crews, diva directors, lachrymose leading ladies and libidinous leading men; he needed to come home to a wife who was sane, normal and not into severe substance abuse. Someone exactly like Sadie.

Gil glanced at his watch. She hadn't called and she said she would, but then again they hadn't parted on the greatest of terms. He wanted to send her a huge bunch of red roses to apologise, but would that be construed as buying her something? He punched in the number of her mobile. It was switched off. Typical. He called Daniella's number and Sadie's new friend answered it after a couple of rings.

'Daniella?' he said. 'Hi, it's Gil. Can I speak to Sadie, please?'

'Hi, Gil,' Daniella said. 'Sadie's not here. I thought she was with you.'

'With me?' Gil shook his head even though he was on the phone. 'She left here around ten.'

'Oh.' There was an uncomfortable pause.

Gil scratched his chin. 'And she didn't come home?'

He could hear the hesitation in Daniella's voice. 'Not as far as I'm aware.'

'If she turns up, could you ask her to call me?' Gil said.

'Sure,' Daniella said brightly, but he could tell she was worried.

Gil hung up. He should never have let Sadie drive away in that goddamn heap. He just hoped that she wasn't wrapped round a palm tree somewhere on Beverly Glen. And if she wasn't, then where the hell was she?

Chapter Forty-Two

'Wake up, Sleepyhead.' Tavis is sitting next to me. He's damp from the shower, his bare chest covered in perfect movie-style droplets of shimmering water. The only thing protecting his modesty – and mine – appears to be a very insubstantial white towel.

I try to open my eyes a little bit further but they just won't co-operate.

'Oh jeeze!' Tavis breathes. He drops down next to me and smoothes my fringe from my eyes, looking vaguely alarmed. 'What happened to you?'

'What?' I say. 'Where am I? What happened?'

'You're on my sofa,' Tavis says. 'You fell asleep. My rendition of thwarted lover apparently bored you to death.'

'Did it?' I have absolutely no recollection of this.

'You were gone within five minutes.' And he looks a little disappointed about this.

'Why didn't you wake me?'

'You looked like you needed the sleep,' he says.

I can't argue with that, I suppose.

'I don't know what the hell else happened,' Tavis says, shaking his head. 'But I hope it's not my fault. I'll get you a mirror.'

'What? What?' It feels like someone has glued my eyelashes together. Tavis patters out and comes back with a shaving mirror. I hold it up to my face. My eyes are red and swollen and almost closed. My face is covered in scarlet blotches, the like of which I haven't seen since Vincent Price in *The Masque of the Red Death*. I put down the mirror. 'Clams,' I say.

'Clams?'

'Spaghetti vongole. Gil's favourite.'

'This is an allergic reaction?'

'Looks like it.' I'm lucky I didn't get ana . . . anapha . . . anaphalact . . . whatever that thing is you get with peanuts. Instead I just have beef tomatoes where my eyes used to be and measles for blusher.

'Does it hurt?'

'Only when I laugh,' I say. We both giggle. 'So Doctor Robert, can you come back from the dead and tell me what I should do about it?' Now that I know it's there, my skin's starting to itch.

'I'll get dressed and take you to the drugstore. Let's see what they come up with. Are you going to work?'

'I can't let them down on my second day,' I say. 'I have to.' Besides, I can't afford not to work. The amount of money I owe Gil is racking up daily. And it's Friday, so I've only got to last until tonight.

'You look terrible,' Tavis says.

'Is that a professional opinion?'

'No,' he says, 'but this is.' Tavis sucks in breath in. 'Maybe I shouldn't be saying this, but I don't think you're destined to be with Gil.'

'What?' I feel stunned with shock. This is more than I can take with my eyes glued together.

'Some relationships are meant to be,' Tavis continues in a rush. 'The universe smiles on them. Everything goes right. You always have a great time. There are no obstacles in your way. The sun always shines.'

'Are you trying to tell me the universe is pissing on me?'

'I'm not saying that it's pissing on you. But maybe it's trying to tell you something.' He clears his throat and hesitates before he speaks. 'He might not be the right man for you, Sadie. There may be another reason why you're here.'

That sounds like Californian fuck-your-head-up stuff to me and I've never been one for self-help books. Oh, don't get me wrong. Like everyone else, I buy loads of them, but

I never read them and then they just help to make me feel guilty by sitting looking at me from the bookshelf, gathering dust. There are a lot of self-help books on Tavis and Joe's bookshelf and they don't have a speck of dust on them. Either one of them is a demon with a duster or they get an awful lot of usage.

I do not have a great knowledge of actors, never having met one before, but I understand that the general opinion of them is that they're not on this planet. Californian ones may be worse.

'I don't know what to say.'

'I shouldn't have raised it,' Tavis admits. 'I had it on my mind. I guess I'm just trying to help.'

'At the moment the most helpful thing you could do is find something to stop my eyeballs burning, Doctor Bob.'

'We have cucumber in the refrigerator,' Tavis says, standing up. 'I'll cut you some slices and you can give that a try while I get dressed.'

I give him a weak and feeble smile, which I hope will hurry him up.

'I could be wrong, Sadie,' he says.

'Yeah,' I agree. 'Very wrong.'

'He could be perfect for you.'

'Yeah.' I lie back and close my eyes.

Tavis takes the hint and pads out to the kitchen while I consider the things that are pissing on my relationship with Gil – such as his inability to get rid of his clinging wife and my allergy to small and otherwise inoffensive molluscs.

'Perfect,' I say to myself. 'But then again, I could be wrong too.'

Chapter Forty-Three

My day at Double Take is thankfully uneventful as I sit in the office with sunglasses on in the manner of people all over the world who are hoping not to be recognised. Bay and Min think it's very funny that Tavis had to lead me in like a blind person and, I must admit that apart from pouring a large amount of cold water – along the lines of the Pacific Ocean – on my relationship with Gil he has been most helpful and charming. You could almost believe that he was once a real doctor.

'Tavis was voted America's Sexiest Medic,' Min says approvingly as he leaves the office to rush off for his audition.

'Really?' I don't tell them that I know at first hand that he does have a rather good bedside manner. I do, however, remind myself not to keep falling asleep on sofas with strange men.

I book Tom Cruise, Tom Jones and a Tom Selleck lookalike for what must be a 'Tom' themed cocktail party on a yacht in Marina del Rey. I call Gil three times and he calls me back, but we never manage to talk once. Daniella calls and we arrange to meet in Larchmont for a coffee after I leave work. I wish Tavis would call and tell me how his audition went, but he doesn't and I don't like to call him even though I have his folder out on my desk with his mobile phone number on it circled in highlighter pen.

I book a Pamela Anderson lookalike lap dancer for a bachelor party and fake Fergie is delighted to get another airing. We have a Posh and Becks come into the office, but they look nothing like either of them. Even with my tomato eyes and fat arse, I look more like Posh Spice than she does. We don't sign them on. Bay doesn't think anyone here will have heard of them anyway. I take off my sunglasses at regular intervals and fill my eyes full of some anti-allergy drops that Tavis bought me at the chemist or whatever they call it here. I still haven't managed to get Tavis's bottom any work, even though I think it's the least I can do for him.

Bay and Min are so busy that we don't have time to chat, and they say they'll redress the balance by taking me on a girls' night out next week. When four o'clock comes round, Bay presses an envelope into my hand and as soon as she disappears, I check how much it is and am quite pleasantly surprised even though I've only been here two days and my eyes were only fully functional for one of them. It's hardly going to clear Third World debt, but it means I can give Daniella some of my rent.

At four-thirty a small, independent film company phone. Their leading man has gone all shy and won't get his togs off for the love scene. Apparently he has unexpectedly become afflicted with a pimply arse. It happens even to the best, I guess. Can I help? *Can I help!* I tell them I have America's Sexiest Medic on my books – not a pimple in sight – and rush Tavis's resumé round to them by courier.

By five o'clock Tavis's bottom has got a job lined up for tomorrow and I'm a happy, but still bloaty-eyed woman. Now I have a legitimate excuse to phone him, and as I bash in the number I wonder why I think I need one. He's not picking up, so I leave a message and take the details, ready to drop them into Zorba's for Tavis later. I leave dead on five.

I feel very LA, as I pull up in Larchmont Village at a parking meter. I could have walked here in ten minutes, but no, I have brought Delores with me, although she is being a bit more temperamental than when Tavis drove her. I feel like telling her that Tavis is gay and she's wasting her effort.

Daniella is sitting outside a trendy little coffee shop,

sipping from a monster-sized cardboard cup.

'Hey,' she says.

'Hey,' I say back, entering into the spirit. My friend and I do the air-kiss thing.

'Get a coffee and pull up a chair,' she instructs.

'What's that?' I point at her bucket of beverage.

'A tall, skim, de-caff, caramel macchiato.'

'Right.' How will I ever begin to understand the men when I can't even get a grip on the drinks?

'What's it like?'

'Good,' Daniella says. 'It's good.'

I make a mental note to get the smallest size they do, otherwise I'll spend the rest of the evening weeing. I go inside to get myself a whatever-it-was coffee. The giant bucket thing *is* the smallest one they do and once I've managed to plough my way through a truly bewildering choice of beverages without recognising anything, I've forgotten what Daniella said it was and decide on a boring old cappuccino – the first thing on the list – and rejoin Daniella in the beautiful blistering sunshine.

As soon as I'm settled, I take off my sunglasses and give her a flash.

'Oh my God,' Daniella says, taking in my red, screwed-up eyes. 'What happened?'

I do my 'clam allergy' routine and after much commiseration from my buddy, she looks at me over the top of her DKNY sunglasses and says, 'So where did you get to last night, girl?'

I sigh.

'Gil called first thing this morning,' she continues in a rather censorious tone. 'He sounded very anxious.'

I've consumed half of the bucket of coffee before it's even touched the sides. 'Gina turned up again. Drunk.' I take a moment to relive the events. 'I had to get out of there.'

Daniella looks duly sympathetic. 'And?'

'And then I went to show my car to Tavis.' This comes out in rather more of a rush than I anticipated.

'Tavis?'

185

'Mmm.'

'Was he impressed by you turning up – presumably unannounced – in the dead of night?'

'It wasn't that late.'

Daniella doesn't back down from her questioning look.

'We drove out to the beach.'

'Which beach?'

'Venice Beach.'

'You drove out to the beach with someone you didn't know?' Daniella takes off her sunglasses and peers at me. 'This isn't sleepy little London,' she says. 'This is LA. That's crazy.'

'I came to live out here with someone I didn't know . . .'

'And look where that's got you!'

'London doesn't have a beach,' I point out in an effort to use diversionary tactics. 'It isn't a situation that's previously arisen.'

'Did he hit on you?'

'Who?'

'*Tavis.*' Daniella mimics my accent. Very badly.

'No.'

Daniella snorts in disbelief.

'He's not that sort of man.'

'They're all that sort of man.'

'Not Tavis,' I say, and wonder why I sound so disappointed. 'I went back to his place for coffee.'

Daniella shakes her head in a very drama queen way and flings herself back in her seat. 'This just gets worse!'

'I met his partner,' I say calmly. 'Joe.'

'Partner? Joe?'

'Joe.'

'Joanne? Jolene? Josephine?'

'No. Joseph. Male Joe.'

'Oh.'

That's wiped the frown off my friend's face. 'Tavis is gay,' I confirm.

'Oh.'

'He's a really nice guy.' I glug some more of my bucket of coffee. 'I fell asleep on his sofa. He took me to the chemist to get me Rite Aid allergen relief eye-drops. They're for allergies caused by ragweed, pollen, grass, animal hair and dander.'

It didn't say anything about bastard little clams, but Tavis thought that it could well cover it.

'A guy who knows about eye-drops must be gay,' Daniella feels moved to inform me.

'He is.' I can feel that little saggy feeling again and try to ignore it.

'He is?'

I nod sadly. 'It's a hell of a waste though.' And I don't know if it's against client confidentiality or what, but I whip Tavis's file out of my chi-chi designer bag and plonk it on the table, flicking it open at a rather attractive photograph of a buck-naked Tavis.

'Ooo!' Daniella hurriedly puts her sunglasses back on for a better look. She points at Tavis's bottom. 'That's gay?'

'Yeah.'

'Goddamn it!' She holds the folder up to get better light and then shakes her head. 'It's Doctor Robert,' she says. Her mouth has dropped open. 'Doctor Robert's gay?'

'And from last week he's dead too.'

'Shit,' Daniella says and I'm not sure which revelation she's more pissed off about.

'He's an actor,' Daniella puffs, slapping the folder back down. 'They're all gay.'

'Isn't that a hideous stereotype?'

'Which in this case happens to be true?'

She has a point.

'I should have warned you,' Daniella says.

'I didn't need warning. He's just a friend.' I close the file before Daniella slavers on it. 'He works in the restaurant down the street.' I nod in the direction of Zorba's which is about three doors away. 'I got his backside a job this afternoon. Come with me while I tell him.'

Daniella slugs down her coffee. 'Drink up. Drink up,' she says.

'Why the rush?' I could spend another week getting to the bottom of this cup.

'We have work to do,' she says.

'What?'

'Some gay men are less gay than others.'

I can quite categorically state that I have absolutely no idea what that means.

Tavis is leaning on the bar flicking through a magazine, but comes over to us as soon as we enter Zorba's door. He lifts up my sunglasses. 'Ooo,' he says.

'They feel better,' I assure him. 'The eye-drops are doing a great job. Thanks for that . . . and for everything.'

'My pleasure,' Tavis says.

'It was fun.'

'Yeah,' he agreed. 'We should do it again.'

Daniella is staring at him in a very goo-goo, ga-ga way. I nudge her and she tries to look slightly less mad. 'This is Daniella. My new best friend and my landlady.'

'Hi,' Tavis says and he shakes her hand.

I'll swear Daniella hangs onto it for longer than necessary and flutters her eyelashes and goes all girly. This must be her way of checking out how gay he is. I nudge her again.

'Hi,' Daniella says as if she's out of breath.

'I have good news,' I announce and pull the necessary piece of paper out of my bag. 'I got your bum a job.'

'Great,' Tavis says and snatches the paper with glee.

'The leading man has got pimples on his. I told them you hadn't.'

Daniella has gone all dreamy again. I nudge her harder.

'This is great,' he says and kisses me affectionately on the cheek. 'Really great.'

Ooo. Ooo. That's made *me* go a bit dreamy. 'Well,' I say, 'it's hardly the leading role in *Four Weddings and a Funeral* the sequel, but it will keep the wolf from the door.' It's ridiculous but while I'm yabbering, I want to reach up and touch where Tavis kissed. I can still feel its warmth – and other bits of me appear to have gone quite hot too.

'One day as my agent and you got me a job,' Tavis is

clearly pleased. 'I have to phone Joe,' he says, and Daniella and I exchange a glance. 'He'll be delirious. I can pay him rent.' He rakes his hair and looks so excited that I get a rush too. It is a pretty decent pay cheque for what should be a few hours' work.

'Let me buy you ladies a drink,' he says. 'We need to celebrate.'

'White wine,' Daniella says without pause for thought.

I shrug. 'Same.'

Tavis ushers us outside into the sun again and seats us at a prime table under a striped umbrella. After a moment he brings us two very large glasses of chilled white wine, dripping with condensation.

'Thanks, Sadie,' he gushes as he places them in front of us. 'I appreciate this.'

'You're welcome,' I say. I lift my glass to him. 'I appreciate this.'

'To Tavis,' Daniella says and she's got that silly look again.

'To Tavis.' You can't say fairer than that.

'To me,' Tavis says and joins in the toast even though he hasn't got a glass.

Daniella and I throw back our wine in unison.

'Now I must phone Joe,' Tavis says. 'Excuse me, ladies.' And he disappears into the depths of the restaurant.

Daniella leans towards me. 'He was flirting with you.'

'No,' I say. 'I think that's just the way he is.'

'Gay,' she says as if to remind herself. She takes another sip of her wine and tuts. 'He doesn't know what he's missing,' she says in disgust.

I haven't really got an answer for that one. 'Maybe he tried it and decided he didn't like it,' I suggest.

'He didn't try it with *me*,' Daniella says. 'I would have convinced him.'

'Joe's really nice,' I say. 'They seem happy.'

Daniella groans miserably.

'Anyway,' I say brightly. 'What did you get up to last night?'

Daniella shrinks slightly. 'Nothing.'

It is the sort of 'nothing' that means 'something'.

'Nothing?'

Daniella, rather theatrically, checks for eavesdroppers. 'You mustn't tell a soul,' she says. 'Especially not my mother.' Then my friend lowers her voice to confessional level. 'I went and sat outside the house of the Mad Movie Mogul.'

My eyebrows rise in surprise.

'For an hour,' she adds.

'Bad,' I say.

'More than bad,' Daniella hisses. 'It's ridiculous. What would I do if he saw me? What would I say?' She looks up at me. 'Mary Ann would *kill* me if she knew.'

'I think *I* might kill you,' I say. 'You said this was a DNRR.'

'I can't help it.' Daniella's eyes fill with tears. 'It's like an obsession.' She dabs underneath her sunglasses with the back of her finger.

'Think of his wife. What has she done to deserve this?'

'She doesn't understand him.'

'Can you please say that again and try not to sound like a bad cliché.'

'He can't be happy with her,' Daniella says, but I'm not sure that she's aware that I'm listening. 'She's been his *only* wife. They've been married for over twenty-five years. How weird is that? She is fifty-four years old!'

'A lot of women are,' I point out.

'They're not married to Movie Moguls!' Daniella sniffs. This is clearly a subject that she's thought a lot about over the years. 'He's fifty-five,' she continues. '*I'm* nearly too old for him!'

'Perhaps he loves her?' I venture.

Daniella glares at me in disgust.

'Or maybe he's trying to be loyal?'

'Loyal?' Daniella looks at me as if it is an alien concept. 'Who cares about loyalty when you could be sleeping with a twenty-two-year-old babe with silicone breasts?'

'Would you really want to be with someone like that?'

'Yes,' she snaps. 'It's the way things are done here!

190

Don't you read Jackie Collins?'

I reach out and take Daniella's hand and give it a squeeze. 'I don't know what to say.'

A tear escapes from beneath her sunglasses and cuts a lonely track through her foundation. She wipes it away as it reaches her full red lips. 'I'll get over it,' she says.

But if she hasn't managed to shake these feelings in ten years, then I somehow doubt it.

Tavis comes back.

'Is Joe pleased?' I ask.

And he grins with such pure joy that it makes the strings round my heart tighten. 'Can I get you ladies anything else?'

'I think we might need some more wine.'

'Stay for dinner,' he says. 'On the house.'

'Thanks. That's sweet.'

'I'll bring you menus.' If he puts as much into his acting as he does waiting tables, the boy is sure to be a star.

'Tavis,' I say as he turns away. 'I hope it goes well tomorrow.'

'It will,' he says and he holds my eyes with his. 'This is the universe working for us, Sadie.'

I flush as he walks away.

'What did that mean?' Daniella misses nothing.

'I'm not really sure,' I lie.

She watches Tavis as he chats to other women while he seats them. And I admit to having a sneaky glance myself.

My friend is looking pained. 'That guy will make it big one day,' she says. She drains her glass. 'Are you absolutely sure he's gay?'

I nod.

'God, I hate this town,' she says.

Chapter Forty-Four

Gil and Steve were sitting on a low brick wall in Paramount's parking lot. All the cars had been moved out and a huge crew of technicians were in the process of flooding the area with water. Another crew painted the towering wall at one end with a pastel blue cloudless sky.

In this episode of *Star Satellite* the rescued Arutigan Emperor would crash down spectacularly into the sea, shortly before he emerged to save the earth. Et cetera. In reality the parking lot would become the Pacific Ocean and the flimsy fibreglass pod containing the hot and sweating character actor Billy Moreno squashed into a livid scarlet Alien suit would be hurled from a crane into a few feet of water. And once again the public would be blissfully unaware of the tricks of cinematic photography.

Gil could sympathise with the actor. It was a blistering hot day and both he and his friend Steve were sweating in Boss T-shirts as they sipped ice-cold sodas purloined from the mobile snack truck that was vital to keeping the crew happy.

Steve kept one eye on the proceedings as he talked. 'So Boomerang wife has bounced back for the final time?'

'I sincerely hope so,' Gil said.

'And now you can turn your full attention to the lovely Sadie?'

'I sincerely hope that too,' he agreed. There was much hustling and bustling as cars were moved out of the vicinity. 'You remember that show we worked on together – *Henry's Luck*?'

'The one where all the crew went down with salmonella

and the leading man got a black eye from fooling around with a basket ball?'

Gil nodded.

'The one where the leading lady got knocked up and spent every day honking with morning sickness?'

'The same one.'

'The one we filmed in the Mojave Desert where it rained every day for three weeks?' Steve pondered. 'And the Director was a raging drunk?'

'Mmm.'

'And the studio spent every day trying to pull the plug on us for going over budget?'

'Uh huh.' Gil sipped his drink.

'No,' Steve said. 'I don't remember that.'

'Well, I do,' Gil said. 'And currently I feel my relationship with Sadie is in a worse state than that picture was.'

'It was a huge box-office smash,' Steve recalled. 'The guy got the girl. Everyone forgot that the production was a bag of shite.'

'Nearly everyone,' Gil said.

'Sadie will too,' Steve assured him. 'You need to start over again.'

'Did you and Sarah start out like this?'

'No,' Steve said wistfully. 'We were love's young dream.'

'That was not the answer I was looking for.'

'Come out to the house this weekend,' Steve suggested. 'I'll incinerate some steak. We'll have too much beer and a few laughs. Let your old buddy charm her for you.'

'Tempting though it is,' Gil said, 'I can't. I have to go up to San Francisco. The writer's threatening to lie down in Lombard Street and let cars run over him.'

'That bad?'

'I guess.'

'This is not a good start,' Steve said. 'Your first weekend together. Your first Gina-less weekend and you're swanning off to San Francisco?'

'I'm not *swanning* anywhere. This is work – urgent work.'

'Take Sadie with you.'

'You know I can't do that.'

'Take a day off from being a movie producer for once in a while.'

'You know I can't do that either.'

'Priorities, mate,' Steve said. 'And may I suggest that yours are slightly skewed?'

'I don't know what you mean.'

'You're not trying to hide behind something else, now that Gina has conveniently disappeared?'

'No,' Gil said. 'I am *desperate* to see Sadie tonight. I've put off leaving until the morning especially. But she isn't around. I've been calling her all day, but she never has her damn cell phone on.'

'Turn up at her place unexpectedly,' Steve said. 'Women like that sort of thing.'

'It's not my style,' Gil said. 'I've spent too long with Gina. If you turn up unexpectedly, the surprise is usually on you.' Usually in the form of some other guy's ass bouncing up and down.

He didn't want to share the fact that Sadie, for whatever reason, hadn't been at home last night. Where had she gone to? As far as he was aware, she knew no one in this town. It was a horrible feeling when you were sure that you could fall head over heels in love with someone, if only you were sure that they wouldn't hurt you. He'd seen too many women who were happy to feign love for money, status and an easy life. But those weren't accusations he could currently lay at Sadie's door. She had been nothing but straight with him – so far.

His cell phone rang and he snapped it open, putting it to his ear in one practised move. 'Hi.' His face broke into a grin. Steve grinned back at him. '*It's Sadie,*' Gil mouthed silently.

Steve went all gooey. '*Sadie.*' He wrapped his arms round himself and turned his back to Gil, giving himself a mock passionate embrace and making slurpy kissing noises.

For someone who wanted to help, Steve was going the

wrong way about it. '*Man!*' Gil hissed, hand over the phone. But it was no good, Steve was too engrossed in snogging himself to care about his sensibilities.

'Where are you?' he said to Sadie. 'I'll be right there.'

He hung up. Steve stopped his one-man kissing demonstration. 'Good news?'

'I think so.'

'She's still in LA?'

'She's in Larchmont Village. In Zorba's.'

'Then run to her,' Steve said.

The Arutigan Emperor was remonstrating with the crew who were trying, unsuccessfully, to coerce him into his escape pod. The director looked as if he was moving in to strangle him. 'He'll never save the world at this rate,' Steve sighed. 'Time for me to make a sharp exit.'

'I can't blame him,' Gil said. 'Would you want to be dropped on your head in a flooded parking lot?'

'No, mate,' Steve said. 'But then I've no idea why anyone in their right mind would want to be an actor.'

'Kissing Julia Roberts,' they said together.

Gil stood up and stretched his legs. 'I'm not going to mess this up,' he said decisively.

'I'm pleased to hear it.' Steve patted him on the back.

Gil just hoped that he was right.

Chapter Forty-Five

'I think I'm drunk,' I say to Daniella.

'Me too,' Daniella agrees. 'But it feels kinda nice.' She pushes away her empty plate, which bears no trace of the moussaka it previously bore. 'Bang goes my Doritos diet,' she says, gently massaging her stomach. 'I need to thank Tavis and then I need to go. Alexis will be home from ballet class and as hungry as a horse.'

I think she has inherited her mother's constitution. The restaurant is becoming busy now with the evening crowd and all the outside tables are taken.

'Wait,' I say. 'Gil's on his way. He'll be five minutes. I'd like you to meet him.'

'I'd like to meet him, too,' Daniella says. 'As well as giving him the once-over, I might well be beating a path to his door with a script.'

'He's here,' I say as his car pulls up outside and Gil gets out. He's wearing a black T-shirt and black jeans and is looking pretty cool. I still get a thrill when I see him.

Daniella adjusts her sunglasses. 'Mmm, mmm,' she says approvingly. 'You are one lucky lady. He's young, good-looking and loaded.'

'Money isn't everything,' I say defensively.

'No?' Daniella tears her gaze from Gil and fixes me with it. 'There are certain things in life that are better when they're very rich,' she says. 'Coffee. Chocolate. And men.'

I laugh.

'I'm not joking,' she says. 'Poverty sucks. I've tried it.'

I still have a foot very much in that camp.

'Hey,' Gil says as he sees us. He kisses me on the cheek. 'I've missed you.'

Daniella is doing 'crumbling' behind him. 'This is Daniella,' I say. 'My new best friend.'

'Hey, Daniella.' Gil shakes her hand and slides into the seat next to me. 'Thanks for looking after Sadie for me.'

I'm not sure that I like that, but manage to keep the frown from my forehead. The only reason I'm at Daniella's house is because he's looking after Gina rather more than he is me. My friend might like her men rich, but I definitely prefer them attentive.

'I'm going to leave you love birds,' Daniella says. 'Are you coming home tonight?'

'No,' Gil says before 'yes' is out of my mouth. This time the frown wins. 'If that's okay with you,' he adds.

'I was going to get an early night.'

Clearly this idea is not very impressive. 'Late one last night?' he asks tightly.

'I'll catch you later,' Daniella says, wisely extricating herself from her seat. 'I won't wait up.' And she clip-clops out into the street in search of her car to drive the hundred yards to her home.

The silence hangs between Gil and me. 'So,' he says eventually, 'where did you get to after you left?'

Tavis comes to the table and I glance up at him.

'I was at Tavis's apartment,' I say. Gil follows my eyes. 'Tavis Jones. I'm his agent.' It seems sensible to fill him in quickly. 'At Double Take. He's an actor.'

'Oh.' Gil's look says 'isn't everyone in this town?'

'I took Delores to see him.'

'Isn't she great?' Tavis is looking uncomfortable.

'The car or Sadie?' Gil says.

'Can I get you a drink, Mr McGann?' Tavis says.

'I think we're just leaving.'

I gather my belongings. 'Hope it goes well for tomorrow,' I say. 'Call me and let me know.'

'Sure,' Tavis says. 'And thanks.'

'You're welcome. Thanks for dinner.'

I can see that Gil is getting impatient.

'Hope your eyes clear up,' Tavis calls after us as we start to leave.

I wave at Tavis as Gil steers me by the elbow towards the door. 'Your eyes?'

Out on the street, I dip my sunglasses. From Gil's reaction I can tell that they still look pretty bad. 'I'm allergic to something.'

'I hope it isn't me,' Gil says.

I daren't tell him that it's probably his spaghetti special. 'That's why I wanted an early night.'

'Come back to my place,' Gil begs. 'Gina has finally gone. We can have a quiet time together, just the two of us. You can rest your eyes. We can get to know each other again.'

Why am I hesitating?

'I'll cater to your every whim,' Gil promises.

'Now you're talking.' He puts his arm round me and we walk towards the car.

'What about Delores?' I ask. 'I can't leave her here all night.'

'If you're worried about someone stealing her,' Gil says with a cheeky smile, 'I really don't think you need to.'

I take a lingering look at my mechanical soulmate. 'Won't she get towed away?'

Gil glances at her too. 'We can live in hope.'

We head out of Larchmont and Gil takes me past the fancy wrought-iron gates of Paramount Studios on Melrose Avenue so that I can see where he is spending most of his working days. The pretty pink building is bounded by uniform lines of palm trees, and despite being the only studio left in Hollywood, it still has an air of glamour as movie studios should.

We head up to Gil's house along Melrose. This is more my sort of place than Rodeo Drive. The shops look sort of hip and avant-garde like London's King's Road with more sun and less attitude. Aladdin's caves of clothing to get your credit card pumping. It's where you'd go to get your belly button pierced if you were into pain in the name of fashion. When I've had several more pay days than I've currently enjoyed, I'm definitely going to have a retail therapy outing along here.

The soundtrack from *Notting Hill* is on the car stereo and I notice that Gil's musical taste revolves round British movies – *Sliding Doors, About A Boy, Bridget Jones's Diary*. And I wonder if he thinks of me when he plays them, but I don't like to ask. The air is heavy with the sweet scent of bougainvillea and the bite of car exhaust fumes, and I still have a feeling that I'm just on holiday here and that it isn't quite part of my life.

Gil turns to me and strokes my cheek. 'I want to put everything that's happened behind us,' he says softly. 'Start with a clean sheet.'

'Sounds good to me.' His lips are looking particularly kissable. And I think I just might stay the night after all. 'We can spend the weekend chilling out,' I suggest.

I'd like to see Venice Beach in the daylight and think it's probably not a good idea to mention that I've already seen it by moonlight. Hanging out on the sand at night with a guy doesn't conjure up a great picture – even if that guy happens to be gay. I think this is more information than Gil needs at the moment.

'Er . . .' Gil says. 'That might be a little difficult.'

I'm all ears.

'I have to fly to San Francisco in the morning.'

I can feel my face fall.

'I'll be back as soon as I can.'

'Which is when?'

'Maybe Sunday morning.'

That's not so bad.

'Or evening,' he admits. 'It's hard to tell. I have problems there.'

'You seem to have problems everywhere.' I think he can tell that I'm not best pleased.

'Be patient,' he says. 'Now that Gina's gone everything else is a walk in the park.'

We pull up outside his house. All the lights are on. 'Wow.' There is a white stretch limo the size of a small street of terraced houses taking up most of the drive. 'Whose is that car?'

'Oh no!' Gil exclaims. 'Oh no. Oh no.' And he's out of the car and racing to the front door before I get an answer.

'Gil.' I chase after him, wobbling slightly in my heels due to excessive Californian Chardonnay consumption.

Gil bursts through the door, followed shortly by me. He stops in his tracks at the entrance to the lounge and I don't and cannon into him.

'What the fuck are you doing?' Gil shouts.

I peer over Gil's shoulder and it seems quite obvious to me what the *fuck* they are doing.

A small, wrinkly man with long hair is lying on the floor in Gil's lounge. He is wearing Gil's cooking apron and Maria's yellow rubber gloves. He's also wearing stockings and suspenders and treacherously high heels which may well be his own. Even though my eyes are suffering a severe allergic reaction, they manage to open to astonishing widths. It looks like . . . my good God, it is . . . it's Noah Bender. England's answer to Rod Stewart. I have another look just to check. It's definitely him. Strange. I thought he was a lot taller than that.

'What am I doing?' Gina roars. 'What are *you* doing here?'

Gil's wife, on the other hand, appears to be wearing nothing but whipped cream on her chest with what seem to be strategically placed cocktail cherries. She is sitting astride Noah Bender and is brandishing a wooden spoon.

I don't really know where to look and almost wish that my eyes were still swollen shut.

'You said you were going to San Francisco!'

'I changed my mind,' Gil yells. 'I'm going in the morning. You said you were leaving!'

'I am,' she says. 'Noah came to collect me and we . . .' She looks down at the man underneath her.

'Hey, man,' Noah says and flicks a peace sign at us both.

'Get out,' Gil says. 'Get out now!'

'Goddamn it, Gil,' Gina says. 'You'd think you'd never seen a man in women's underwear before.'

200

'I haven't,' Gil said. 'Not Noah, anyway. And not in my own lounge.'

I can safely say that I haven't seen a man in women's underwear before. Not at such close proximity. It's not a pretty sight. The colour doesn't suit him at all.

'You're ruining my rug,' Gil complains.

'Your rug?' Gina is indignant with rage. 'You are always so uptight.' In Gina's position I think I would be a lot more embarrassed and a lot less put out. And to be fair to Gil, there does seem to be whipped cream all over it.

'Get me a towel,' she barks.

'I'll get you one.' I'm volunteering primarily because I'd like to be out of here.

'Thank you, Sadie,' Gina says.

I rush off to the nearest bathroom and grab a couple of towels. I'd heard about these Hollywood goings-on, but never thought that I would crash one of them. Noah Bender! The tabloids would pay a fortune for this.

When I get back to the lounge, Gil is standing as far away from Gina and Noah as possible, staring out of the window. Noah is sitting cross-legged on the sofa looking very drunk. I hand Gina the towel and she takes off her cherries and gives them to Noah, who duly eats them. Then she rubs herself down vigorously. She has a fantastic body, but I'm not sure that I want to be seeing so much of it.

'Hi,' Noah says to me plus peace sign.

'Hello,' I say. 'Nice to meet you. I'm a big fan. I love your music.'

'Cheers, darlin',' Noah says, looking very pleased with himself. His accent is sort of Brummie mid-Atlantic which you'd never guess from his songs.

Gina is throwing on her clothes.

'Shall I put the kettle on?' I venture.

'Great idea, darlin',' Noah says.

'No.' Gil snaps his head round. 'You will not put the kettle on. Noah and Gina are leaving.'

'Come on, Noah,' Gina says. 'Put this on.' And she throws him a voluminous coat that will certainly help to hide his dubious taste in lingerie.

Gina yanks her boyfriend towards the door while he's still dressing.

'You will be hearing from my lawyer,' Gil shouts after them.

Noah gives Gil the peace sign again and Gina gives him the finger.

The door bangs and the room is suddenly very quiet.

'Well,' I walk over to Gil. 'Another ordinary day in Hollywood.'

'I don't need any wisecracks right now,' he says.

Actually, I think that's exactly what we need.

Gil turns to me. 'I like your music?' he says. 'What was that about?'

'What did you want me to say to him? That I thought his knickers were a size too small?' I sink down onto one of the white sofas and then realise that I should have checked it for surplus cream first. 'Given the circumstances I think I coped admirably.'

Gil says nothing.

'How come *I'm* suddenly the baddie?'

Gil rubs his forehead as if he has a headache coming on. And who'd be surprised in the circumstances. 'I don't know,' he says, and comes over and flops down next to me. 'I'm sorry.'

'We seem to be saying it a lot.'

He takes my hand, but doesn't really look at me. 'I know.'

'It was pretty funny though,' I say. 'Once you get over the shock.'

'I don't think so,' Gil says quietly. 'How do you think I feel, knowing Gina prefers that to being with me?'

'There's no accounting for taste,' I quip lightly, but I can see his point. 'I wouldn't take it personally.'

'Is there any other way I can take it?'

'I gather you and Gina didn't . . .' I glance rather furtively at the rug.

'No,' Gil says, and I'm rather grateful for that.

Gil stands up. 'I'd better take you home.'

'Oh.' I shrug. 'I don't mind staying.' I rather had my heart set on it.

'I think I'd prefer to be alone,' he says.

'Oh. We don't have to . . .' My eyes wander to the rug again. 'We could just have a cuddle. You look like you need one.'

'I have an early start,' Gil says crisply. 'But thanks for the offer.'

'You're welcome.' I'm not really sure what else to say other than Gina is proving to be one of the most efficient contraceptives I've ever come across.

Chapter Forty-Six

I should ring Gil, but I'm sulking. And anyway, he's quite capable of ringing me and he hasn't. It's 9 a.m. and the sun is already competing with the air-conditioning in my bedroom. Alexis sneaked in beside me when I was still half-asleep and then fidgeted and kicked me for ten minutes until she was sure I was fully awake. We are now playing with a select few of her two dozen Barbie dolls – Barbie Birthday Wishes and Fairy of the Garden Barbie. I wonder if there is an Unlucky in Love Barbie.

'Hey.' Daniella comes in wearing a lurid silk kimono and a hangover face. She gives Alexis an exasperated look. 'What are you doing in here?'

'Aunt Sadie was lonely,' Alexis explains. How true.

'She's also very patient,' Daniella says. 'You wriggle like a worm.' Daniella grabs her daughter and tickles her until she's a shrieking heap.

'You should kick her out,' my friend says to me.

'She's fine,' I say. 'I really don't mind.' And a sudden pang makes me feel that I'd like my own daughter to rough and tumble with. What am I thinking of? I haven't yet snared a man and my womb seems to have gone into nesting mode.

Daniella hugs Alexis to her. 'How would you like to spend the weekend with Grandma?'

'Yeah!' Alexis is out of my bed and on her way to pack her overnight bag – fickle child that she is.

Daniella sits on the edge of my bed. 'I'm off to a scriptwriters' convention.'

'Oh,' I say. 'You never mentioned it.'

'It was fully booked,' she tells me. 'A place came up at the last minute.'

'That's great.'

'It will be useful for my career,' she agrees. 'I can make some contacts. I guess you'll be seeing Gil.'

'You guess wrong,' I say with a sigh. 'He's out of town. San Francisco.'

Daniella's face falls. 'Your first proper weekend in LA and you'll be all alone?'

'It doesn't matter,' I say. But inside me somewhere there's a little bit that thinks it does.

'I feel terrible,' my friend says.

'Don't. This is important to you.' I squeeze her hand. 'I'm not your responsibility and I can quite easily entertain myself.'

Daniella looks doubtful.

'Delores and I will hit the road,' I say.

'Are you sure?'

'Yes,' I assure her. 'I'll even remember to drive on the right side of the road.'

'That Gil,' Daniella says, 'he might be cute, but he sure is messing you around.'

'You don't know the half of it.' I sink back on my pillow.

'How did it go last night?' Daniella asks. 'I heard you come home.'

'Not good,' I admit. 'Not good at all.' Noah Bender in his stockings and suspenders appears in flashback behind my eyes. 'I'm not sure whether this relationship is ever going to get off the ground.'

'You should get your ass read,' Daniella tells me. She isn't laughing so I know that she's serious.

'I beg your pardon?' This has certainly got me off my pillow.

'You should get your ass read,' she repeats even more earnestly. 'Rumpology,' she goes on to enlighten me. 'A fanny-gram.' These words are still not making sense in my world. Daniella tuts. 'You get your butt inked up and sit on a piece of paper. Then you send it off for analysis. It will tell you all about your past.'

'I don't need my ass – arse – inked up to tell me about the past, that's for sure. All my arse says is too much cake!'

'It could tell you about your future.'

'I know about my future. My arse will get fatter, if I continue to eat too much cake.'

Daniella's mouth has tightened into a determined line. 'It could help you to find out why Gil won't commit.'

'You don't really believe this, do you?'

'Sly Stallone's mother does it, so how can it be fake?'

'Sylvester Stallone's mum reads bottoms?' I think I've heard it all now.

'A lot of people swear by it.'

A lot of people who live in California, I suspect.

'Think about it,' Daniella says as she stands up and leaves my room. 'It could be just what you need.'

I need another cup of tea, that's for sure. If the creases of my buttocks hold the key to my floundering relationship with Gil then the world – and this part of it in particular – is indeed a very strange place.

I get up and plod into the shower wondering what to do with a weekend that now stretches emptily ahead of me. Probably exactly the same thing I did with all my empty weekends back in London, but with more sun.

Aren't American showers wonderful? More water than Niagara Falls and all of it hot – much better than the three spluttery farts and a drip of lukewarm stuff that Alice's shower always managed to produce. All that talk of bottoms makes me think of Tavis. He'll be due on set soon and I wonder whether I should give him a call to wish him good luck. I know he hasn't got anything exciting as lines or the like, but I feel very nervous for him, like a parent sending her child off to the dentist unaccompanied. I think I will say hello, just to let him know that I'm rooting for him.

I pick up the phone as I rub myself down with a towel. Tavis answers after the first ring. 'Hi,' he says. It's a shame he's not got any lines, because he has a very sexy voice.

'Hello.' I'm sort of embarrassed to be ringing him now. 'It's Sadie.'

'Oh, hi!'

'I just thought I'd wish you well for today.'

'Gee thanks,' he says. 'I can't wait.'

'Well, that's all I wanted really,' I mumble. 'Good luck.'

'Wait,' he says. 'I guess you're busy?'

'No.' Chance would be a fine thing. 'Not very.'

'Have you been on a film set before?'

'Er . . . no.'

'I don't suppose you'd like to come with me?'

'Well, yes. I would.'

'I'll pick you up,' Tavis says. 'In a half hour. Be ready.'

'I will,' I promise. Tavis hangs up.

I fling my towel to the corner of the room and contemplate which designer carrier bag I'm going to raid first. What should I wear – casual or chic, casual/chic, chic/casual? Think back to documentaries about film-making. Don't they all wear baseball caps? I don't need to rummage in my bags to tell me I don't have one. This is ridiculous! I feel like I'm going on a date, when all I'm doing is accompanying one of my clients to a job of work. I must try and stay cool.

'Daniella! Daniella!' I shriek, doing my best impression of a cat with a scalded bum. 'I need help! Quick!' If at this moment she advises me to get my butt read to choose my ideal outfit I can tell that I'll be phoning up Sly Stallone's old mum in a trice.

Chapter Forty-Seven

Gil wasn't sure which of them he wanted to punch more – or first. He'd arrived on location in San Francisco to discover that a distraught writer was the least of his problems. And he'd arrived later than he wanted to because he had risen at dawn and moved lock, stock and barrel into the Beverly Hills Hotel.

Gil had decided at some time in the wee small hours of the night while alone in his bed, that he wasn't going to spend a minute longer in a place where Gina had twenty-four-hour access. As a precaution against his wife tracking him down he had – taking a tip from the more paranoid movie stars – checked into the hotel as Mr M. Mouse.

His key players – the director, the leading actor and the writer – were all lined up in front of him in a gigantic Home of the Stars trailer which was blocking out the sun on Montgomery Street. They were all squaring up to each other and he was trying very hard not to square up to them. The director was a talented maverick. The actor was a talented asshole. The writer was a talented recluse, asshole and maverick. Everyone was shouting and no one was listening. It was one of those moments when Gil seriously considered moving into real estate and he knew before the weekend was out he'd probably have cut his life short by two years.

'I am not saying this shit!' The actor managed to get a few decibels above the mêlée.

The movie was a big-action, big-budget show – the kind where the hero blasts his way out of burning buildings in nothing but a ripped vest and then winces when the heroine hugs him at the end.

The actor was in his ripped vest, fake blood streaming from various fake injuries, being careful not to smudge his fake dirt from his surgically sculpted cheeks. These were the type of injuries that Gil liked best – fake ones, Hollywood ones. Ones that would rub away at the end of the day. Not real-life ones that cut to the quick and stayed with you, chewing away at your insides for years.

'It's banal,' the actor raged. 'It's puerile.'

This was an actor who had become a household name by running around burning buildings in a vest whilst saying banal and puerile lines. This was an actor who was being paid ten million dollars to say only ten banal and puerile lines in the entire movie. For a million dollars a line, Gil would have said whatever the fuck anyone wanted. It would have been deemed unprofessional, but Gil was more than tempted to suggest that if he wanted something of more substance he ought to try *Hamlet* next time. Then he would get a lot more than ten fucking lines and a lot less than ten fucking million.

'It needs more sensitivity,' the actor insisted.

It just needed for them all to get back in their prams – an English phrase that Steve had taught him and for which he was extremely grateful – and get back to work, Gil thought. The movie was way over budget too and this morning, while he was moving into the cool, dark bungalow that would be his home for the foreseeable future, the studio had shut the production down. At this rate, the actor might not be required to say any more lines at all.

This was a hundred-million-dollar movie and so far they were twenty million dollars over the top with four weeks of filming left to run. It was not a good place to be. The action centred round a heist in the towering needle of the Trans-America Pyramid and they'd been allowed to close one of the access roads for two days while they shot the outside sequences. In a business that called itself 'the industry' there was often very little industrious going on that didn't involve the concerted eating of pastries and hamburgers. Now even that had ground to a halt and everyone was standing idle. The way the numbers were racking up, it would have been cheaper to fund a space programme.

Gil suspected that the actor was trying to prove he was more sensitive to get inside the pants of his leading lady. What the actor didn't know was that his love interest was – away from the celluloid screen – actually a die-hard lesbian, and while the sight of him rippling his muscles in a ripped vest might inspire most of the world's population of women to surging hormone levels, it was doing absolutely nothing to her.

The director decided it was his turn to shout. Gil needed this like a hole in the head. He didn't want to be here. He wanted to be back in LA with Sadie doing weekend stuff. But at least he knew that by Sunday when he flew out of here everyone would be placated. Ruffled feathers would be smoothed, cameras would be rolling and the writer would have written pages and pages of extraordinarily sensitive dialogue that would be left in a heap on the cutting-room floor.

If only he could be so confident and decisive in his personal life.

Chapter Forty-Eight

Tavis's bottom is a vast improvement on the leading man's – even though I could be accused of being ever so slightly biased. The leading man is sitting glowering moodily in the corner and he looks as if he might think so too.

We are on the massive Universal Studios set, cocooned in the square box of a vast Sound Stage just opposite the incongruously pink Back Lot Café – and deep in the heart of the cinematic make-believe.

Tavis, my client and my reason for being here, is writhing about on a fur rug with an extremely nubile young actress and he looks as if he's thoroughly enjoying it. That boy must be a very good actor.

He isn't the slightest bit embarrassed about the fact that we're in a studio the size of a small football stadium and there are about seventy people watching him romp around in the nip simulating a jolly good shag. I can't even contemplate making love to Gil with his ex-wife and his housekeeper in the same building, so what does that say about me?

This is supposed to be a steamy sex thriller – *Killers Always Come Twice* – and it certainly is very steamy at the moment and thrilling. I'm getting very hot under the collar and I'm not wearing a collar. Even the man next to me, who has been sitting reading his newspaper all morning, is peeping over the top for an eyeful. I wish I had something to peep over the top of too. I can hardly bear to watch, but perhaps that's because I'm enjoying it rather more than is good for me. I'm finding it very hard to keep an objective professional opinion. That is one hell of a cute butt.

'And cut!' the director shouts. I know he's the director because Tavis told me he was hot stuff. To me he looks about fourteen years old and totally incapable of directing a school play, let alone a movie. He's wearing a baseball cap back to front. Tavis and his friend stop in their tracks.

'Good job,' the director says.

The crew clap and I join in a bit too enthusiastically. Good grief, I need a drink and a lie down in a dark room.

Someone rushes up and hands Tavis a towel which he wraps deftly round his waist. The teenage director goes over and shakes his hand and then Tavis walks over to me. He's looking very pleased with himself.

'That was great,' I say and to my horror I sound all breathy and girly.

'Thanks,' Tavis says. His cheeks are flushed and his pupils dilated. His hair is even more messy than normal. 'The director was real pleased.' He winks at me. 'But then it's not hard to fake it with someone who looks like that.'

The tiny Oriental leading lady – similarly attired in a towel – waves at Tavis and he waves back.

'I wish all my women were as easy to please,' he laughs.

I laugh back, but I'm not sure why.

'I'll be back in five,' Tavis says and he wanders off, presumably to restore himself to his rightful clothing.

I stand there and look like a lemon while the crew move round and set up for another scene.

Eventually Tavis appears again amid much back-slapping and high-fiving and we are loaded into a stretch golf cart of all things and are driven away from the Sound Stage. I'm so excited I could bite my own legs off and it's very hard to stay looking cool. We head off down James Stewart Avenue between rows of low beige bungalows.

'Those used to be dressing-rooms for the stars,' he tells me. 'Now they're offices for writers and producers.'

Daniella would be in writer's heaven if she ever landed an office here. The stars, it appears, do their ablutions or whatever they do in glorified caravans nowadays.

We sail past a tour bus full of punters ogling a street set

where an episode of the *X-Files* is being filmed and I feel a frisson of glee that I have even one tiny toe in this world and I haven't had to stump up twenty dollars to get in here.

I think Tavis sees my joy because he turns to me and says, 'Do you need to get back?'

'No.' If only he knew. 'Not especially.'

'Hey, buddy,' Tavis says to the driver. 'Spare five minutes and take us on a tour.'

'Sure,' the man says and we whizz off through the narrow streets filled with bits of scenery and trucks and empty trailers.

We bump and joggle along and Tavis rests his arm across the back of the cart to steady himself. It does nothing to steady me. I know this sounds ridiculous, but he has such presence that he's making me all hot and cold and weird inside. And I know that he's not interested in me and I'm not interested in him either, but the fact that he is completely unaware of the effect that he might be having on me – *if* I were interested and *if* he were interested – is completely unnerving. I'm not even sure if that makes sense. Out of all the boyfriends I've had, I've never felt as comfortable as I do with someone who's gay. And is it simply because we can become mates with no agenda? Oh bollocks. I don't know. I'm just going to enjoy the ride.

'These are the metropolitan sets,' Tavis tells me. 'With a lick of paint they can be Rome, England, Boston or anywhere in the world that you want it to be any time. They use it for *Ally McBeal* and the Austin Powers movies.'

A line of 1960s cars makes his point.

'How come you know so much?'

'We shot *Happiness Hospital* here,' Tavis informs me. 'Over there.' And he gestures at a building that has a banner with *Happiness Hospital* strung up above the massive doors. A shadow crosses his face. 'I kinda miss it.'

I touch his arm. 'It won't be long before you get something else.'

He grins at me gratefully, and I hope that I'm right. I can see the attraction of losing yourself in a world that is both glamorous and not quite real. The sort of world that ordinary people don't really get to experience.

We take in the Bates Motel from *Psycho* – I can imagine Gina being quite at home here. Then the set for *The Best Little Whorehouse in Texas* – I'm not even going to comment on that one. We scoot through a Mexican pueblo complete with a fake flash flood, and the Wild West street where Tavis tells me *Alias Smith and Jones* and *The Virginian* were both filmed among a dozen other Westerns I've never heard of.

'They filmed all the cowboys against short, narrow doors to make them look bigger and bolder,' Tavis says. 'It's called false perspective.'

Another one of my illusions shattered. I feel as cheated as the day I found out that John Wayne was really called Marion. No wonder he walked like that.

From the Wild, Wild West we criss-cross the tried and tested route of the tour bus and end up in New England where we stop in a reconstruction of Amity Island and watch the tourists shriek as the fake shark from *Jaws* leaps out at the bus and squirts them all with water.

After Amity there's a huge concrete slab the size of an aircraft hangar. 'That's the largest backdrop in the world,' Tavis tells me, and he's so enthusiastic. 'It's where Jim Carrey reached the end of his world in *The Truman Show*.'

'I remember that.'

'See that tiny lake in front?' We pull up at another vantage point. 'That was the ocean for the splashdown of *Apollo 13*.'

'Really?' I'm grinning like the Cheshire Cat and Tavis beams back at me. And just for a moment, I feel very sad. Even this isn't how it should be. A boy and girl bouncing round in a buggy laughing as if they haven't a care in the world. But it's the wrong boy. Gil should be showing me this world. His world. Tavis is only an inch further in than I am. He is still lingering on the outskirts. Gil is right in the middle. The hub.

'OK?'

Perhaps he has seen my smile die. I nod.

214

'Nothing is ever quite what it seems here,' Tavis says, meeting my eyes. 'Remember that.'

And before I can say anything else, we jiggle away again to take in The Court of Miracles which was the set for the original *Hunchback of Notre Dame*, and a steamy, bone-strewn bit of *Jurassic Park* before the driver zips past the monstrosity of a car park that's disguised with painted trees and deposits us at the main gate. Tavis tips the man generously and we leave fantasy land behind and step out into the real world once more. Traffic whizzes past us.

We cross the road to the parking lot located outside of the inner sanctum and stand next to Tavis's heap of a car – complete with real rust and real worn tyres. I don't know what model it is, but it is in a marginally worse state than Delores. No wonder he has such an affinity for her. He opens the door and I get in.

'What does the rest of the weekend hold?' he asks as he pushes the gear stick into reverse with an alarming graunch.

'Not much,' I admit. 'Gil's away in San Francisco. Some problems with the movie he's working on. Daniella's gone to a scriptwriting convention.'

'Oh,' he says. 'Too bad.'

'I thought I might do sight-seeing and stuff,' I say, trying to sound as if I'm not pissed off.

'Alone?'

I nod. We pull away and head out on the Hollywood Freeway and down Vine Street towards Larchmont. The Eagles blast out from the radio and I lean back in the seat, letting the breeze cool me down. Tavis is deep in thought.

When we stop outside Daniella's house, Tavis turns to me. 'I have the weekend off – the first one in months. I'm heading out to visit with my parents,' he says. 'Why don't you come with me?'

It takes a moment to sink in.

'They live out in San Juan Capistrano. It's cute. We can drive out on the coast road and I'll show you some of the sights. We'll be back tomorrow.'

'Overnight?'

'You can pick up a few things.'

'Won't they mind?' You have to book in to see my parents about three months in advance, so that my mother has time to lay in stocks of apple pie and starch the sheets in the spare room so that they slice you in half when you lie in them.

'Why would they mind?'

'I don't know.' I shrug. 'What about Joe?'

'Joe's working,' Tavis says. 'Hey, two actors, both employed. Our luck could be changing!' He fixes me with imploring eyes. 'Come on,' he says. 'I can't leave you all alone on your first weekend in LA.'

The thought piques me that it didn't seem to bother Gil this much. And I hate to say this, but I'm sort of glad to have a break from him and his whining wife. I don't need Rumpology and Sly Stallone's mother to tell me that it doesn't bode well. I could sit around on said rump waiting for Gil to ring – or I could not.

'I'd love to come,' I say. 'Give me a few minutes to grab some stuff.' I jump out of the car. 'What shall I bring?'

'Whatever you normally wear to barbecue and laze round the pool.'

Oh, right. Clearly, Tavis has no idea what my life in London is like.

Chapter Forty-Nine

On Saturday in California people hang out at the beach – surfing, skating, cycling and any other activities that involve the wearing of skimpy, colour co-ordinated clothing. At home I would probably be wrapped up in my warmest coat, shoving a shopping trolley round Waitrose, looking for marked-down produce and snarling at any small children or doddery old people who got in my way. Stressed, *moi*? This is an infinitely more pleasurable way to spend the day.

'We'll take the scenic route,' my friend says and drives us out of LA, winding his way through a bunch of identical-looking streets flanked with Dunkin' Donuts, KFCs and McDonald's until we eventually pick up Route 1, the Pacific Coast Highway to San Juan Capistrano, and catch a glimpse of a glittering blue sea. In England we have the M1, the M6 and the M25. The Americans have the Pacific Coast Highway. No competition.

Tavis hangs his arm out of the side of the car and steers with one hand, which is just so American. Sunny surf music blares from the radio, accompanying us all along the route and, as Tavis sings along at the top of his voice, I sink back into the torn, worn vinyl of his car seats, realising that this is the happiest I've felt in a long time. Perhaps it's the sun. Perhaps it's the silly music. Perhaps it's the good company. Whatever it is, it's working in spades.

Tavis turns to me and gives me one of his movie star melt-your-drawers smiles. 'Okay?'

'Yes.' And this time I don't get the feeling that I'm

doing this with the wrong man.

We pass the flat golden sands of Huntingdon Beach that spawned the Beach Boys' *Surfin' USA*, the upmarket traffic jam of Laguna Beach and its multi-million-dollar beach-front properties, following the sweep of the Pacific Coast Highway up towards Dana Point, before turning away from the coast and climbing into the hills.

San Juan Capistrano is a sleepy little town that looks like a modern version of the Mexican pueblo we saw at Universal Studios and is about as different as it could be from the sprawling big city. It's probably what's known as a one-horse town. It might have only one horse, but it does, however, have several dozen art and craft shops.

'Let's stop in town before we get to my parents' house,' Tavis suggests. 'Once we get there, they'll never let us sneak away.'

And I like the idea of sneaking away with Tavis. We park outside a coffee shop that looks more like a brewery and stroll down the street. Along with all the art centres, there appears to be one bar and there's a wedding celebration in full swing. Several men who look like extras from *The Blues Brothers* are dancing up and down the pavement with all the style of Jake and Elmo.

'Ever come close to tying the knot?' Tavis asks.

'No.' Not even remotely close, I want to add miserably but restrain myself. 'You?' And then I realise it was a pretty stupid thing to say.

He laughs at the very idea. 'No.'

We stop at a cross walk and he takes my hand to stop me jay-walking. It's warm and strong. When the little white man appears on the sign, he tugs me across. On the opposite side of the street an Irish band with bodhran drums and penny whistles thumps out a few jigs. For a small town it certainly seems to kick some ass. We window shop in a very coupley way and buy a huge, colourful bunch of flowers for Tavis's mother before retiring to the coffee shop to sample their wares. And I try not to notice that Tavis is still holding my hand despite the fact we crossed the road aeons ago.

In the coffee shop, after trawling through another five hundred variations on America's favourite beverage, I plump for whatever it is Tavis orders – something involving chocolate chips and a mountain of whipped cream. At least I can blame the excess of calories on someone else. One day I will be grown up enough to make my own beverage choice, I'm sure, but now is not the time. I'm quite nervous about meeting his parents – probably because I hardly know Tavis and this seems like a very intimate thing to be doing. I only used to risk taking boyfriends home when I considered them 'serious' – mainly because my parents are extremely embarrassing. My father used to grill them about what they earned from the minute they walked through the door and my mother tried to feed them on the hour every hour. After taking three 'serious' boyfriends home and getting promptly dumped by them, I realised it was the quickest way to end a potential relationship, so stopped doing it. I have never met any of my exes' parents and I wonder idly if this is a London-thing or whether none of them ever viewed me as potential marriage material.

We sit on tall bar stools at a table in the window and watch the wedding guests conga down the street.

'What are your parents like?'

'Fine,' Tavis says. 'Middle-class, middle-aged worriers. You'll get grilled by my mother. She'll think we're getting married.'

'She will?' I'm so surprised that I misjudge my mouth and end up with whipped cream on my nose. Tavis takes a napkin and wipes it off for me. 'Doesn't she know about—'

'Gil?' he says. 'No.'

'I didn't mean Gil,' I say. 'What about your . . . your . . . lifestyle?'

'They tolerate it,' he laughs. 'But I guess every mother is secretly yearning to be a grandma.' He stirs his coffee thoughtfully. 'Except mine doesn't do it secretly. She keeps hoping that I'll have a sudden revelation and change my ways.'

I bet there are a few women out there who have felt like that. Particularly if he goes around doing that affectionate, hand-holding business.

'She'll probably be examining you to see if you've got good child-rearing hips.'

I give my ample rump a hearty smack. 'She won't be disappointed then.'

'But she will, won't she?' Tavis says sadly. 'A wife and children are definitely not on my shopping list.'

'No.' I dig further into my cream. 'But you shouldn't write it off entirely. One day you might . . .' How do I put this delicately? '. . . change your proclivities?'

Tavis laughs. 'I might,' he says, chuckling out loud. 'Come on. We'd better go before Mom sends out a search-party.'

We jump down from our stools and head out into the sunshine once again. Back at Tavis's car, he opens the door for me while I get in. He comes round and hops in next to me, eschewing the door as an optional extra. He puts the key in the ignition, but doesn't start the car; instead he turns to me and wearing his serious face, says, 'Sadie, I wanted to let you know that if I ever did change my . . . proclivities,' he smiles at the word, 'it would definitely be for someone like you.'

'Oh.' I'm not sure what the right response to that is. It makes me feel like scratching my head, for one thing. 'Thanks.'

'You're welcome.' Tavis grins at me and guns the clattery engine and we set off to do the parent thing – but not quite.

And I don't know whether I feel happy or sad that I'm exactly what Tavis would be looking for in a woman, if only he wasn't gay.

Chapter Fifty

'She is gorgeous!' Tavis's mother, Alma, peered out of the kitchen window, straining to get a better look at Sadie.

'Yes, she is,' Tavis agreed, stealing a tomato and getting a slap on his hand for his trouble.

'Wash your hands,' his mother said.

Tavis obliged whilst sneaking a look out of the window himself. He was glad that Sadie looked so relaxed. Ever since he'd met her she'd looked as stretched as an elastic band that was about to snap. And he was sure that hot shot Gil McGann was more than a little responsible.

Sadie was reclining on a sun-lounger by the pool, being plied with beer and entertained to the history of their town by his father, Carey. She was wearing cut-off shorts and a trendy tank, which despite their casual appearance bore some serious labels. Sadie might appear down-to-earth and a little down-at-heel, but she was obviously packing some serious cash from somewhere. Labels like that didn't come cheap. She looked very cool – or did he mean hot?

Tavis shook his head unconsciously. Women had meant nothing but trouble for him and that's why he'd decided to give them up a long time ago. Bizarrely, the less interested he was in them, the more interested they were in him. Go figure. Except for Sadie. She'd accepted straightaway that all he could offer her was friendship. But then she was probably so wrapped up in this Gil guy that it didn't matter to her whether he was available or not. Shame really. He had meant what he said to her in the car – though heaven only knows where it had popped out from. He hadn't intended to say anything at all. But it was true. If he ever did consider resuming relations with the opposite sex, then Sadie would be his first choice. He wondered if she'd feel the same.

Now that he met his mother's hygiene standards, she cut a piece of tomato and handed it to him. It was good to get home for the weekend. As his mother was quick to point out – it had been too long. But with acting class, waiting table at Zorba's, a constant round of auditions and the occasional acting job, he had very little time in life for anything else. He sometimes wondered why he'd chosen this path.

His parents' house was light and airy. A low-rise Mexican style – small but nicely proportioned. There was a square of shady garden at the front and a courtyard with a lap pool out back. His mother made ceramics, when she had the time – bright cheerful things that graced the white plaster walls.

'. . . And so English.' Alma continued to scrutinise the unannounced stranger. 'I love her accent, don't you?'

'Yes, I do, Mom.' And he did. In fact, there was quite a lot he liked about Sadie. She was funny and fresh and very un-LA.

'How long have you known her?'

'Not long,' he said vaguely. 'She works at an agency I use. She could be a useful contact. Her boyfriend is a hot shot producer.'

'Her *boyfriend*?'

'Yes.' Tavis smiled at the unconcealed look of disappointment on his mother's face.

'I wondered why you were suddenly bringing a girl home after all this time.'

'Well, now you know.' He didn't go on to tell his mother he thought Sadie was great company and that if any girl had made his head turn in recent history, it would be her. Some things were better kept to yourself. 'No new hat, I'm afraid.'

His mother smiled sadly, but there was a glimmer of hope in her eyes. 'Daddy likes her.'

'Uh huh?' he answered with as little conviction as

possible. His parents had been married for nearly forty years – a triumph by anyone's standards. The fact that they had been happy for the majority of it was somewhere approaching a miracle. They'd move out to San Juan two years ago when a bullet in his leg had encouraged Carey Jones to take early retirement from the New York Police Department. Now Carey worked part-time at the local train station and Alma worked in one of the many art stores that made up the town's pretty high street.

The fact that they were nearer to their youngest and flakiest son made them both very happy. What made them less happy was their conviction that said son never ate enough, never earned enough and never settled down enough. Their ideal would have been for him to work in a bank like his older brother and have two bonny children bouncing on his knee. They couldn't understand his life-style or that furthering his career meant more to him than any number of kids. It didn't stop them hoping that one day he would change.

'How's Joe?' his mother continued while washing salad.

'Good,' Tavis said. 'He would have come up, but he's working today.'

'In the bookstore?'

Joe had a part-time job in a trendy bookstore on the more salubrious part of Sunset Boulevard – Book Fever. Anyone who was anyone liked to be seen buying their literature there. It was run by two not-so-ex-hippies who, like Zorba's owners, were very tolerant of Joe's need to slip off to auditions. Even when he was in work, he carried on doing cover shifts for them when he could. Joe insisted he was being charitable by returning favours and that it kept him grounded in the real world. Tavis was in no doubt that Joe would have given up the real world in a second to go stellar, but he'd been around long enough to worry about it ever happening. Tavis was also convinced he just couldn't bear to miss out on the bookshop gossip. He also lived in hope that one day, when he was on shift, Steven Spielberg would feel the need to shop there.

'No, real work,' Tavis said now. 'Acting work.'

'Real work? Your daddy was a cop. That's real work.'

Tavis felt his jaw tighten. His daddy had spent his days fighting the good fight. Their son spent his days pretending to be someone else's ass. No one in their right mind would understand why he should want to do that for a living. There were some days when he didn't understand it himself. His mother caught his eye.

'That's good,' she said softly, realising that she'd trodden on his toes and on his dreams.

Yeah, and maybe when he was a big movie star, they'd finally get off his case. In the meantime, the less they knew, the less they had to worry about.

'I worry about you.'

Tavis smiled to himself. 'I worry that you worry,' he said. 'I'm fine. I had a great job today.' Though it was wise not to go into the details.

'This is a very strange life that you live. You need someone to support you.'

'I have someone to support me.'

'I meant a woman,' his mother said with a sigh. She cast a wistful glance towards Sadie, and Tavis smiled at her transparency.

His mother and father liked Joe well enough, but they weren't entirely approving. They seemed to think it was Joe who led him off the rails when what Joe actually did was love and support him unconditionally. There were too many weeks when Joe glossed over the fact that Tavis couldn't come up with the rent money. No one could have a better friend and one day he would pay it all back.

'Someone to nurture you,' she continued.

'Joe nurtures me.'

'He doesn't feed you properly – like a good woman would.'

'I work in a restaurant, Mom. I get all the moussaka and beer I need.'

'You *can't* get enough moussaka.' His mother poked him in the ribs. 'Look at you. You're all skin and bone.'

Tavis squeezed his mother round her ample waist. 'I'm a lean, mean love machine.'

'You're anorexic.'

'I'm fashionably thin.'

'You don't eat regularly.'

'I eat three square meals a day.'

Tavis's mother snorted with disbelief.

'Do you think Robert de Niro gets this from his mother?'

'Yes,' she said, then touched his arm. 'I only want what's best for you.'

Tavis kissed her lightly. 'I know.'

His mother straightened her apron. 'Go light the barbecue, son. I'm going to fatten you and that lovely young girl up with some prime rib.'

Chapter Fifty-One

What do women want? Mel Gibson went through an extraordinarily painful experience in order to find out in the film of the same title, but by the end of it, he – and I – were none the wiser. Except that what we women seem to want is 'it all'. I'm not even sure what 'it all' involves. I myself am thrashing around in the shallows of even getting the basics together.

Right at this moment I'm still rooted to the sunbed I've been lying on for the best part of the day watching Tavis's bronzed, toned and near-naked body as he swims effortlessly up and down his parents' pool.

'That happened in the last earthquake,' Alma says.

'Pardon?'

'The tiles,' she says, pointing at several large fissures in the terracotta tiles that surround the pool. 'We're lucky it didn't crack the pool.'

'Oh.'

'When that ground shakes, we know all about it!'

The earth moving is something I haven't experienced for a long time, but I don't feel this is the right time to share it. I push my sunglasses further up my nose. It brings a smile to my lips to think that Tavis's mother assumes I'm looking at the state of her flagstones rather than the powerful, graceful movements of her beautiful son. Perhaps she is aware that I'd be wasting my time. I console myself with the fact that there's no harm in looking.

So what do women want? And what does *this* woman in particular want? I sink back into my sunbed and follow the few wisps of hazy cloud that drift across the sky in the hope that they might ease some sensible thoughts into my brain. I'd forgotten how debilitating the sun can be to a body that's been starved of rays for too long. Even thinking is proving an effort. But this is the first time in longer than I care to remember that I've had the chance to simply lie and think. I've spent the last few months careering from one part of my life to the next.

'Careering' is a good place to start. Like the majority of women in the new millennium, I felt I was defined by the success of my career. I was reasonably happy on the treadmill of little black suits, bonuses and back-biting – until that treadmill was forcibly removed from me. Having thrown myself into a whirlwind of making ends meet, I no longer know whether I really and truly want to go back to long hours, missed lunches and stress-related insomnia in pursuit of a high salary. Instead I've been working long hours, missing lunches and having stress-related insomnia in a wide variety of menial roles that pay peanuts. What comes first – the chicken or the egg? What's the worst scenario – having bags of money but no time to enjoy it, or not having enough money to pay your bills and bags of time to dwell on it?

I'd built up a lovely barrier of capable career woman and was making a very good job of hiding behind it. Now that's been blasted into the water, I'm not sure I have the strength to rebuild it.

It's also been a long time since I've had strong family relationships, and being here with Tavis today makes me realise that I've been missing that too. My nice high wall seems to have had a lot of wobbly bricks in it for a lot longer than I thought. His parents nag him ceaselessly in the proud way that parents do and I've decided that I want children of my own that I can nag and be proud of.

It troubles me to think that I've reached the ripe old age of thirty-two and, whilst I've been kissed more than a few times, I've never yet had a proposal of marriage. Not a real one. The last – and only – person to ask me to marry them was John Finchley and he was sixteen and had been at the Strongbow Cider. It was at Erica Litherland's birthday party. I turned my back for ten minutes to contemplate his proposal and when I returned with my answer he was already snogging Geraldine Brownlow. The fact that I had decided I didn't want to marry the spotty and drunk John Finchley didn't stop the tears. It has been a recurring theme in my relationships ever since.

What's wrong with me? That's what I want to know. Why am I not marriage material? I haven't got bad breath or a hideous disfiguring disease. But nor do I have the talent for beguiling men. When I compare myself to Alice I definitely come up lacking. She's like a squirt of Raid – men fall like flies at her feet. I, on the other hand, seem to be just a squirt. Someone who, after an initial impact, disappears off into the atmosphere to be forgotten.

In my twenties I was very keen to settle down – before I had done anything remotely wild – get married and have children. I used to tell everyone this, including men whom I had only seen and ever did see, for one night. My friends – and my mother in particular – blamed my desperation for my marriage-free state. That was when I abandoned the idea altogether and convinced myself that what I secretly wanted was to be a self-sufficient career woman all along. As soon as I was self-sufficient and suitably and success-fully 'careered' and still no men came along, my friends – and my mother in particular – blamed my self-sufficient vibes for my continuing marriage-free state.

I'm useless at the political manoeuvring between the sexes. I have read all the books – *The Rules*, *Men are from Mars*, *Emotional Intimacy*, *The Surrendered Single* – basic-ally anything that would give me a clue about how to turn your average shag-monster into a sensible, caring husband. And what did I get out of them? Not a sausage, that's what. Mind you, I should have known better than to rely on a book which had the scary subtitle of *A Practical Guide to Attracting and Marrying the Man Who is Right for You*. That's an awful lot of promise for ten quid.

Someone told me that the bloke who wrote *Men are from Mars, Women are from Venus* had split up from his wife. If that's true, then it is an extremely depressing fact.

He must be a sensitive and caring individual and a millionaire to boot from telling everyone else how to become sensitive and caring individuals. If he can't cut it, what hope is there for the rest of us? Perhaps his wife was really pissed off that he could write bestselling books about it all, but like most blokes still wouldn't dream of putting out the bins without being asked a dozen times.

All these self-help books give such conflicting advice. If you follow *The Rules*, you don't let any sad sap, no matter how hard he begs, get the better of you. And never ever should you think about bringing up the 'm' word, other than for the purposes of pouring scorn on the poor idiots who indulge in it. For *The Surrendered Single*, playing hard to get is an anathema. She, conversely, smiles at all men however dubious-looking, and wears short skirts. She offers to clean his flat. After half a dozen dates, you should be flashing your ring finger.

Whenever I've played hard to get, the object of my coolness has just lost interest and gone chasing after some tart who's gagging for it. When I've appeared compliant and in need of a man, they've run in the opposite direction – usually after someone who doesn't give a shit about them. When I've just sat there and been me – veering between hard to get and needy – that's given them the collywobbles too. I am becoming *The Resigned Single*. I feel the nunnery beckon.

Take Gil. What does he see in Gina that I don't have – apart from the fact that all her body parts appear to be hardened up with silicone? Isn't a bit of healthy wobble more attractive than someone who is permanently scuttered or high? Gil's wife/ex-wife seems to play it all by her own rules and it works perfectly. Certainly for Gil – no matter how many times she changes them or how badly she behaves. Instead of treating her like a leper, maybe I should be asking her for lessons. I think what men want is an infinitely more taxing question.

In the olden days – I sound like my mother – men had to get married to have sex. No self-respecting woman would indulge in such things without a ring on her finger and no self-respecting man would marry a woman who did. Double standards I would say, but perhaps less complicated than some of the arrangements we have now. If a man can sleep with anyone he wants after a night down at the wine bar, then why should he commit to any of them? If a woman has half-a-dozen kids by a similar number of lovers, it's a bit tricky to then argue that all you've ever wanted to be is a one-man woman.

At this point in my thoughts, Tavis pulls himself out of the pool. He comes over and sits down on the sunbed next to me and grabs a towel. I try very hard to concentrate on his mother's broken terracotta tiles as he rubs himself down. He's even more attractive when he's damp than when he's dry. And it occurs to me that I've seen a lot more of Tavis naked, than I have of the absent man purporting to be my boyfriend.

His mother stands up. 'I'll fix something to eat.'

If we eat any more we'll all explode.

'Watch your skin, honey,' she says to me. 'Your cheeks are a little pink.'

I can't be entirely sure that this is down to sunburn. Alma goes into the house leaving us alone.

Tavis gazes at me. His eyes are very unnerving. They don't flicker at all. I get a very strange rush in places where I shouldn't be having strange rushes. 'You're looking very pensive,' he says.

'Yes. I'm thinking about my life and the mess I'm making of it,' I admit.

'Gil isn't making you happy.' And I'm not sure whether it's a statement or a question.

I try to smile. 'It's a bit hard when he's in San Francisco.'

'I think that's a suitable way of dodging the issue,' Tavis says with a smile.

I stretch out and avoid Tavis's eyes as well as the issue. 'Is there a code of dating conduct for gay men?'

Tavis looks slightly surprised that I've voiced this. 'I have absolutely no idea.'

'Oh.'

'Why do you ask?'

'I'm trying to think of a way to snare my man and I'm failing,' I say. 'I wondered if it was easier for gay men.' Presumably they at least have a clue about what the other one is thinking.

Tavis frowns. 'Is that what would make you happy? Snaring Gil?'

I'm not sure what would make me happy now. Perhaps it's because with every relationship I have I feel further away from the altar. It would be a comfort to know that I am at least still heading towards a happy union rather backing away from the church at an alarming rate.

'I don't know,' I admit. 'If I can still have dark and brooding thoughts whilst lying beneath a careless blue Californian sky, perhaps there's no hope for me.'

'Never give up on hope,' he says. 'It's all we have.'

'I hope one day – in the not too distant future – to fall in love with someone who loves me back.' I peer at him over my sunglasses. 'Is that too hopeful?'

'I think that's a great thing to hope for,' Tavis says with an enigmatic glance in my direction.

I think so too, but I'm going to have to do something about my selection process. To *The Surrendered Single* every man is to be viewed as potential husband material. Men should only be overlooked if they have two heads.

I have a habit of falling in love with the wrong types, but this time I've excelled myself. I am head-over-heels in love with a man who is still fixated by his wife/ex-wife. And if I wasn't very careful I could be performing similar acrobatics for a man who is gay. Tavis may not fit the criteria of being a two-headed male, but there are some definite compatibility shortcomings on his part. I could analyse this a million times, but it all comes down to the same thing – I'm not really giving myself a fighting chance.

Chapter Fifty-Two

'Ooo. Ooo. Ahh. Ahh.' I feel I must mention that this isn't being said with any form of passion. '*Aaahhhh . . .!*'

'Keep still,' Tavis instructs.

'It hurts. It's cold.'

My torturer stops and smiles at me. 'Which?'

I am determined not to smile back. 'Both.'

Tavis tips more calamine lotion onto his cotton wool and resumes dabbing with zeal.

'Ahh. Ahh. Ooo. Ooo.' Every bit of me that was exposed to the strong Californian sunshine is doing a passable impression of a par-boiled lobster. My nose looks like it has been slammed in a door. 'Ahh. Ahh!'

Tavis is frowning with concern, but is quite clearly trying not to laugh. 'This will hurt tomorrow.'

'It's hurting now!'

'I'm sorry,' he says. 'I should have given you some suntan lotion.'

'I was wearing suntan lotion.' Some pathetic little weedy factor only strong enough to keep out feeble British sun. This Californian bugger has fried all my skin off. I'm going all hot and cold.

'Are you going hot and cold?'

'No.'

'I don't want you to get sunstroke.'

Oh. That's what it is. And there was me thinking it was down to Tavis's stroke. I never guessed it would be so erotic, being rubbed all over with damp cotton wool. Or it would be if it didn't hurt so much.

'I might be a bit hot and cold,' I admit. I feel like

crying at my own stupidity. I can't even do sun-tanning right – and how hard can that be? I sniff miserably. I bet Gina's never roasted her own nose off. 'I'm going to be peeling for years.'

'No, you're not,' Tavis says. Doctor Robert stands back and admires his handiwork.

I look in the mirror and all I can see is one of those scary Aborigines all dolled up in full war paint. I've got pale pink chalky stripes all over me. 'Fuck!'

'It's not that bad,' Tavis assures me, but his face says that it is. He gives up the trying not to laugh option and chortles loudly. I know that chortle is not a word used often out of the world of the *Dandy* or the *Beano*. But that was a definite chortle.

'I'm such an idiot,' I say.

'It can happen to anyone.'

'Has it happened to you?'

'No.' Tavis gets a glare for his honesty. 'I've been lucky,' he adds quickly.

We're in the guest room of his parents' house and it isn't quite on the same lavish scale as Gil's myriad guest rooms. The bathroom is down the hall and there are two small beds, one either side of a rather dilapidated-looking chest of drawers. This fact is helping to keep my mind from some of my pain. Is this where we are sleeping? Together?

Tavis follows my gaze. 'I'll sleep on the sofa if you're not happy with sharing.'

'No. No,' I say, before my brain has time to think about the implications. 'I can be grown-up about this.'

Tavis chortles again. 'Are you sure you can resist the temptation?'

To what? 'I think so.' God, what if I fart or snore? Or both?

'I'll leave you for a while.' Tavis puts the lid back on his calamine lotion and heads for the door. 'To get yourself ready.'

For what?

'For bed,' Tavis says, even though I haven't spoken.

'Yes. Right.' I wonder if the after shampoo conditioner

I'm using that guarantees thickness is working on the right part of my body.

My room-mate departs with another chortle to himself and, gingerly, I peel off my clothes. Oh Lord. I look like a zebra that's been painted by some colour-blind, artistically challenged five year old. With a promise to have a proper wash in the morning, I slide into the cool sheets, every inch agony on my burning body.

I switch off the light and lie in the dark, trying not to move, fidget or itch. It's hot and I want to throw the sheets off, but I'm lying in the nip because I can't bear a T-shirt near me either. Oh bollocks! Why was I born so stupid? The air-conditioning unit is clattering away, humming at a soporific level. I'm just about to drop off, when the door creaks open and Tavis tiptoes in. I lie still but crack one eye open. He's stripped down to his boxers and it's a very unnerving sight. I screw my eyes up again. I'm not sure I can be grown-up about this after all. I wish Tavis was out of harm's way on the sofa, but it seems a little too late to voice this.

'Sadie?' Tavis whispers. 'Sadie, are you awake?'

I keep my mouth shut. Which is not something I do often enough. I can hear him pad towards my bed and I stay stock still.

'Sleep tight,' he says and plants a cool and tender kiss on my fevered forehead.

And I think that's possibly the one thing that will guarantee that I don't sleep a wink all night.

Chapter Fifty-Three

Gil threw his bags down on the bed and took time to survey his new home. No one could say that living at the Beverly Hills Hotel was slumming it, but it was certainly cramped compared to what he was used to. Cramped, however, was only a rich person's word for cosy. Two rooms instead of ten. And it was definitely all the better for being a Gina-free zone.

It was Sunday evening. Not as early as he'd planned, but not too late. The director, actor and writer hadn't, in the end, indulged in fisticuffs. The movie was shooting again. Crisis averted. At least this particular crisis.

Gil glanced at his watch. He'd planned a wonderful evening with Sadie. And there was only one thing missing. Sadie.

He hadn't found the time to call her until this afternoon – which was remiss of him and he wasn't sure why he'd hung out so long. But now he was sorry that he had. Her cell phone had steadfastly remained unanswered. He'd fixed to have a romantic dinner on the private terrace of the bungalow – flowers, candlelight, champagne on ice – the whole nine yards. But now he wondered whether he should cancel it. Gil tapped in her number again.

This time when it rang, a young girl answered. 'Hi.'

'Hi,' Gil said. 'Who's this?'

'Alexis. I'm ten,' she said.

'I'm Gil,' he responded.

'How old are you?'

'I'm thirty-eight.'

'That's old.'

'Yes.' He felt much older, but he wasn't about to explain why. 'Alexis, is Sadie there?'

'No.'

'Are you sure?'

'Yes.' Alexis sounded very sure.

'Do you know where she is?'

'With Tavis,' Alexis said.

Gil could feel the hairs on the back of his neck stand up. 'With Tavis?'

'Hmm, hmm.'

He was sure he should know who Tavis was.

'Would you like to speak to Magic Jewel Barbie instead?'

'I don't think so, honey.' Wait! Wasn't Tavis the far-too-handsome server at the restaurant? What was she doing with him? 'Do you know where she's gong?'

'They're away for the weekend. She left a note.'

This was not sounding good. 'What does it say?'

'It says . . .' Gil heard Alexis take a deep breath. '*Hi Daniella and Alexis. Hope you had a great time at your convention and at Grandma's house.*'

Gil could feel his patience ebbing away. There was another deep breath. 'Is Mommy there?'

'No,' Alexis said. 'Grandma is. Do you want to talk to Grandma?'

'No. No. Could you just cut to the important part?'

Alexis's fuse sounded shorter than his. 'This *is* the important part.' Another deep breath. '*I've gone away with Tavis. Back Sunday. Love you both. Sadie.*'

'Thank you,' Gil said.

'And she's put three kisses on the bottom.'

Gil wished that Sadie would put three kisses on his bottom.

'Can you take a message?'

'I'm not supposed to talk to strangers.'

'Isn't it a little late for that?'

'Barbie could take a message,' Alexis suggested.

'Fine,' Gil sighed. 'Does Barbie have a pencil?'

'Hmm, hmm,' Alexis said.

'Could you tell Sadie that I'm at the Beverly Hills Hotel and I want her to join me for dinner at eight o'clock?'

'Barbie says you're talking too quick.'

'Could you tell Barbie that I don't have all day?'

'Barbie's ten too,' Alexis informed him sharply. 'She's going as fast as she can.'

'Maybe you could get Sadie to call me?'

'Okay,' Alexis said. 'Bye.' And she hung up.

Gil sat on the corner of the bed, feeling dazed by this conversation. Why didn't he have the knack with women – of any age? He guessed that he should be pleased that Sadie hadn't just hung round in LA waiting for him to call, but he wasn't. The minute his back was turned his women always managed to find someone else to entertain them. He hoped that this time it was going to be different.

Gil surveyed his impersonal hotel room. So what to do now? He could unpack the parts of his life that he'd brought into their new homes. He could take a shower. He could read the guest information brochure. And then what? He could wait and see whether his date turned up.

Chapter Fifty-Four

'Hey.' Tavis gently shakes my shoulder.

I jump myself awake and quickly check my shoulder for dribble. No matter how hard I try, I forget that I have no need to impress Tavis at all.

'We're here,' my driver says with a grin.

And we are here. Back outside Daniella's house. We didn't get into genealogy, but Tavis's mother is definitely Italian or one of those Mediterranean races where they like to overfeed you. We both had a huge plate of spaghetti before we left and I've obviously slept like a baby all the way home. Who needs a Star Trek transporter-style machine when you have an Italian mother? It could also have been the two very large glasses of Chianti that helped.

The last thing I remember is the traffic lights in San Juan Capistrano. Which is just as well, as I didn't get a wink of sleep last night. Tavis's breathing was just too close and too disturbing to allow me to relax. Coupled with the fact that my skin was trying to melt itself off and failed. It's now retaliating by being extraordinarily painful. I'm sure I've got more pain receptors than most people, because no matter how much calamine lotion I've dotted all over myself, it still hurts like fuck. It serves me right if in years to come I end up looking like George Hamilton's Nana.

'I must have dozed off,' I say with typical British understatement. Bet I snored like a pig.

'You snored like a pig.'

Sometimes the truth hurts.

Before I have a chance to hit him, Alexis comes skipping out of the house. She's dressed from head-to-toe as a fluorescent pink fairy. It's an alarming sight, but Tavis looks completely unfazed.

'Hi,' Alexis says. 'Who are you?'

'Tavis.' He high-fives her. 'And you must be the Perfect Princess Barbie?'

Alexis beams, clearly impressed by this assessment. I do not want to know why Tavis is a Barbie expert.

'Cool,' Tavis says and the life-size Perfect Princess treats him to a brief run-through of her favourite ballet positions and then gives a cursory swish of her wand over Tavis's car. If she is her mother's daughter, she's probably hoping that it will change into a Porsche.

'Are you Sadie's new boyfriend?'

'Alexis!' I cry, not knowing where to start in explaining to a ten year old that it's perfectly acceptable to have men as friends. And just because you share a bedroom, it doesn't mean that you're in any way – whatsoever – romantically attached.

'No,' Tavis laughs. 'I'm not.'

She's not to be dissuaded from this line of interrogation. 'Do you want to be Sadie's boyfriend?'

'Alexis!' I splutter. The few bits of me that aren't burned to a crisp are going red. 'Tavis already has a boyfriend of his own.'

Oh my word, what am I saying? Tavis starts to guffaw. I wonder if he learns his wide range of laughing techniques from his acting class. He certainly has the right one for every occasion. This is a perfect sound to accompany me making an arse of myself.

Alexis looks at Tavis. 'Yeah, right.'

Tavis is shaking with mirth.

'Look, let's go inside,' I say, fumbling for the door handle.

Perfect Princess Barbie leans against the car. 'If Tavis isn't your boyfriend, can I talk about Gil then?'

'Gil?' I say. 'Gil? Of course, you can talk about him. Why?'

'He left a message,' Alexis says. She's wearing her best concentration face. 'He said you had to go to his hotel for dinner. Tonight.'

'Which hotel?'

'The Beverly Hills.'

Tavis looks impressed. 'When did he say this?'

'He called on your cell phone. It was on your bed.'

Bugger. I never remember to take that thing anywhere and when I do, I don't switch it on.

'I'd better call him.' I can hear the panic in my voice. I check my watch and can't believe the time.

'He said to be there at eight o'clock.' That means I've got exactly five minutes to get there. Alexis looks at her watch. It is a big pink daisy, but seems to work just as well. 'You don't have time,' she says.

'I'll take you straight up there,' Tavis says.

Bugger. Decisions. I can arrive on time and looking like a bag lady. Or be late and look like a zebra in a cocktail dress. Maybe it isn't such a difficult decision.

'Alexis?' I have to ask this. 'Are you sure you got the message right?'

'Hmm, hmm,' she says, not upset by the fact that I'm questioning her powers of memory.

'That's really very good.'

'I lie on the telephone for Mummy all the time,' she says brightly and does a fairy-type twirl.

Tavis and I exchange a smile.

'Where did you say Sadie had been?' Tavis asks his favourite fairy friend.

'I said she'd been away for the weekend with another man.'

Tavis's understanding of the little folk is obviously more advanced than mine. I have a protracted heart-sink moment. 'Oh good. Good girl.'

Tavis puts the car into gear, high-fives Alexis again and pulls away. He glances over at me. 'I think you'd better tell Gil that I've got a boyfriend too,' he advises. 'Very quickly.'

And I think it's probably a very good idea.

Chapter Fifty-Five

I think we are both a bit embarrassed as Tavis chugs up to the front of the Beverly Hills Hotel. It's an opulent oasis of palm trees and pink plaster the colour of one of those French Fondant Fancies that Mr Kipling does that never look quite real. A pretty pastel palace. Alexis would love it here.

Tavis glances over at me, so I try to look as if I'm chill about it.

'One day I'll come back in a Mercedes,' he says with a determined air. And I don't know if it's for my benefit or if he really means it.

The man in charge of valet parking tries his best not to look horrified as we cruise along to the expanse of red carpet that sweeps up to the entrance. Hasn't anyone ever told these people that red and pink are a no-no? I feel Tavis's car doesn't serve him well. It shudders to an ungainly halt. It may be reliable, but it looks like a wreck. Delores, on the other hand, is a wreck with attitude.

Tavis sighs enviously. 'That's some boyfriend you have, Sadie.'

'Is it?'

'Anyone who is anyone in the movie business hangs out here.'

'Do they?' He looks at me as if I'm mad not to know this.

'You'll be knee-deep in movie stars.'

'Will I?'

My friend gives me an exasperated look. Ooo. I get a little shiver of excitement. I've been in LA for days and days now and I've not had one single sighting of a real-live movie star. I've seen a few who look like them at Double Take, but that's not nearly enough. And I did see one of those armoured-car Hummer things like Arnie drives, but it could have been anybody driving it, so that doesn't really count either. Now I'm going to be knee-deep in them!

I have a sudden attack of the wobbles and grab Tavis's hand. 'Come in with me.'

'I can't.' He looks at the state of himself.

I look down too. Possibly worse. 'We could get thrown out together.'

He looks very doubtful.

'Don't leave me alone,' I say. 'Supposing Gil's got fed up and buggered off. I'd be stranded then.'

He's caving.

'Five minutes,' he says, and instead of jumping over the side of his car, he gets out of the door. That's how intimidated Tavis feels. 'I'll get your bag,' he says and scuttles round to the back of the car.

He swings my bag over his shoulder and the valet parker makes a lunge for his car keys, clearly relieved that he's going to be able to spirit it away and hide it behind a bush so that it doesn't spoil the view.

Our courage departs as we head into the reception area, which does manage to make us look unutterably scruffy. The pink theme has gone into overdrive – carpet, ceiling, chairs, cushions – they're all pink. I'll swear that everything has been modelled on the colour of candyfloss. I can just imagine Elton John staying here. Faded denim and combat pants look completely out of place.

As we approach the main desk, Gil rushes towards us.

'Sadie,' he shouts across the quiet expanse. His face brightens and then dulls again as he catches sight of Tavis.

'Hi.' He embraces me and kisses me on the cheek, but it's a bit half-hearted and his eyes don't leave Tavis. My friend shuffles uncomfortably.

'I'm sorry I'm late,' I say. I'm not actually late and I'm not sorry at all as I had no idea when Gil might deign to come back from San Francisco, but I thought it might help to get off on a conciliatory note.

'That's okay,' Gil says, looking at me for the first time. 'You're here. Now.'

The 'now' is slightly loaded, but I let it pass.

'What happened to you?' Gil looks askance at my char-grilled proboscis and medium rare face.

'Sunburn,' I provide limply. What did he think had happened? Did he think I'd been trying a bit of self-barbecuing for sadists?

'I'll delay dinner so that you can clean up.'

He clearly thinks I need to. I wonder how I'm going to eat when I'm already stuffed full of pasta. Maybe if he delayed it until tomorrow I might be able to find a little space.

Tavis drops my bag to the floor. 'I'll be going,' he says.

I think it would be nice to invite him to stay, but I'd probably be the only one.

I plant a kiss of Tavis's cheek. 'Thanks,' I say. 'I really appreciate it. You've been great.'

'Any time,' he says and kisses me back. 'It was fun.'

Out of the corner of my eye I see Gil tap his foot.

'I'll catch up with you in the week,' I add as I pick up my bag. 'Thanks again.'

'No worries,' Tavis says and he waves to me and then Gil and walks away.

Gil and I stare at each other for a minute. It's like one of those moments when you get in a lift with someone who looks a bit dodgy and you don't know quite what to do.

'Could you do me a favour?' Gil says. 'Speak to the desk clerk. Delay dinner. I just want to catch Tavis.'

'Why?'

'I want to thank him personally,' Gil says. 'I didn't say the right things. I was a bit taken aback.'

Oh. Phew. And I thought things were going to be tricky.

'Is half an hour okay?'

'Fine,' Gil says. 'Are you hungry?'

I do my best seductive smile. 'Ravishing.'

Gil grins at my joke. 'Give me a minute.'

I make myself a promise that I will give him my

undivided attention for the rest of the evening.

Gil caught up with Tavis as he waited for his car to be returned. If there was anything Gil hated more in the world than men who wore embroidered combat pants it was good-looking guys in embroidered combat pants who had been entertaining his girlfriend for the weekend.

'Hey,' Gil shouted after Tavis. 'Hey, you!'

Tavis spun round.

'I want you to stay as far away from Sadie as you possibly can,' Gil snarled. 'If I hear that you've been breathing in the same air space I will make it my personal business to ensure that you never breathe again!'

To Gil's utter annoyance, Tavis merely burst out laughing. 'Hey, man,' Tavis said. 'She's acting as my agent. I'm going to be seeing her.'

'Not if I can help it.'

Tavis snorted with disbelief. 'If you're so paranoid about what your lady's up to, spend a little more time with her.'

'What I do is none of your business!'

'Hey.' Tavis's smile had disappeared. 'You made it my business. It was Sadie's first weekend in LA. You were planning to leave her all alone. You should be pleased that I stepped in. I was trying to help out.'

'Well don't,' Gil said. 'Don't help out. Butt out.'

'You don't know how lucky you are, man,' Tavis said. His car arrived and he tipped the valet and jumped over the side into the driver's seat. 'She's come a long way to be with you. The least you can do is make sure you pay her some attention. Otherwise someone else just might.'

'Don't you threaten me.'

'It's not a threat, it's advice,' Tavis said. 'I'm not interested in taking your lady. Next time you might not be so fortunate.' He revved the engine and it coughed, spluttered and backfired into life.

Gil eyed the car critically. 'I see that you and Sadie have a lot in common.'

'More than you think,' Tavis said.

Gil pulled out his wallet and peeled off a fifty-dollar bill. 'Here.' He threw it into Tavis's car. 'For your trouble.'

'It was no trouble,' Tavis said tightly. 'It was fun.' He picked up the money and tossed it onto the sidewalk. 'And I don't need your money.'

Then Tavis drove away, leaving a stream of noxious smoke in his wake and the resonant sound of pistons begging for oil.

Gil was determined that he wouldn't bend down and pick up the money, so he turned on his heel and headed back into the hotel, leaving in his wake a fifty-dollar bill fluttering in the breeze and a broadly smiling parking valet.

Chapter Fifty-Six

Gil marches back into the reception area looking a little more purple than when he left.

'Everything okay?' I ask.

'Fine,' Gil says, smoothing down his hair which is standing up like the back of a cat's neck when its hackles are raised.

'Sure?'

He nods tightly. 'I just wanted to straighten up a few things.'

'Tavis is a good bloke,' I say. 'He's got a really nice boyfriend too.'

I wait for the reaction, which seems to be different in every recipient. Except for females over the age of consent who generally seem to view it as a tragic waste – me included. A small but noticeable gulp travels along Gil's throat. 'Boyfriend?'

'Mm. Lovely couple,' I add to load it.

Another gulp follows.

'I went with him to a job yesterday at Universal. Botty double. And he could tell I was really miserable. You were away. Daniella and Alexis were away. I was going to be all by myself.'

A flush of embarrassment rushes to Gil's cheeks.

'His boyfriend was busy too, so he whipped me to his parents' house up the coast for some R & R.'

'His parents' house?'

'Yeah.' Gil is clearly in some discomfort about this. 'They're really nice too. I feel so much more refreshed.' And stuffed like a little pig. 'How did your business go?'

Gil has sagged a little. 'It was fine,' he says.

'You managed to get everything sorted?'

'I'll take you with me next time.'

'There's no need. Really.'

Gil gives me his I'm-a-complete-heel look. 'I promise.'

We're starting to attract attention in the Reception area and I remember my earlier promise to him. 'Come on,' I murmur. 'You can take me to your room and show me your etchings, while you tell me exactly what you're doing here.'

'Hey! Hey! Gil!' The shrill sound of a woman's voice carries across the area.

Both of our heads snap up simultaneously and in time to see the young and lovely author Elise Neils, curls and bosoms bouncing as she dashes headlong towards us.

I hear Gil groan and hope that she hasn't.

'Hi!' She rushes up and kisses Gil full on the lips. He manages to prise her off and sneak a look at her. I think he can tell that I'm less than pleased.

'I didn't know you were in town,' Gil says.

'I've been trying to call you.' Her eyes widen. 'You never reply to your voicemail.'

'Sorry,' Gil mumbles. 'I've been away. Fighting fires. It's good to see you.'

'I just arrived,' she gushes. 'I'm staying here. My publishers dragged me out here for another book fair.' She treats us to a pained expression. Dirty job, but someone's got to do it. As Alexis would say – yeah, right. She is definitely the sort of person who couldn't be dragged anywhere that she didn't want to be. 'I'm sure I told you I'd be flying out here.'

Gil slaps his palm against his forehead. 'I forgot all about it,' he admits. 'I've got a lot of things on my mind.'

'I hope I'm one of them.' Her eyelashes could beat a man to death at ten paces.

'*The One That Got Away* is coming along fine.' Gil sounds very assured now he's on firmer ground.

'Are you staying here?' Elise takes in the opulence of her surroundings and is obvious in her appreciation.

'Yes,' Gil says, but he looks as if he was thinking he might deny it. 'Temporarily.'

I wonder how long that means in Gil's dictionary.

'This is Sadie.' He sort of yanks me forward.

Elise frowns and it is the cutest thing you ever did see. 'Don't I know you?'

'We met at the London Book Fair.' I sound as sheepish as I feel.

'I remember. You had your photograph taken with me. Are you here for the Fair too?'

'Err . . .' I look to Gil for an adequate description of what I'm here for.

'Er . . .' He seems at a loss to describe it too.

'Oh,' she says. 'I didn't know you two were . . .'

I'm not sure that we're . . . either.

'Let's catch up while you're here,' Gil says and starts to steer me away from her.

'Yes, let's.'

'I'll get my office to call you.'

Elise screws up her tiny little nose. 'Do you have anything planned for tonight?'

'Well . . .' Gil says, giving a delicate cough that might as well be a shout across the room that he's planning to shag his girlfriend.

'I'm only here for a few days.' Elise has gone all girly. 'My diary is pretty full. Tonight would be great.'

'Well . . .' Gil gives a sideways glance at me. He might as well wave my knickers in front of her nose.

'I'm sure, er . . .'

'Sadie,' I provide.

'Sadie wouldn't mind.'

I do mind, desperately. 'No. Not at all.' I even do a broad grin to enforce it.

Gil looks at me as if I have just rolled all of my marbles across the floor. 'That's settled then,' my involuntarily celibate boyfriend says tightly. 'Dinner it is.'

'I changed it to nine o'clock.' Which is just as well because we've frittered half an hour away standing here.

'Ooo. That's lovely,' Elise says. 'Just time to change.'

She already looks as if she just came off a catwalk. Or is that me being catty? She takes in my outfit and tiger-stripe sunburn and makes no audible comment.

'Nine,' Gil says and takes me by the elbow and walks me towards the door. 'Why did we just agree to that?' he mutters under his breath.

I have absolutely no idea. But if this were a game of tennis, I'm pretty sure it would be game, set and match to Miss Smiley Author.

Chapter Fifty-Seven

We are on a lovely private terrace behind Gil's bungalow, seated at a candlelit table which is now set for three. The candles are hardly even flickering in the balmy evening and there is barely an undercurrent of breeze. There are, however, plenty of other undercurrents. The smiley author doesn't realise that she's supposed to be the gooseberry here and instead is making the unsmiling girlfriend feel like one.

My head and my sunburn are throbbing in equal measure. Every one of Elise's giggles is high-pitched enough to shatter the crystal glasses and my brain. I'm not sure which is going to give first. She hasn't mentioned that the end of my nose looks as if it's had an unfortunate coming together with a barbecue, but she keeps looking at it.

Gil is treating me coolly and I'm trying to work out why this is my fault. I've always had this feeling that everything is my fault and I sort of assumed that I'd grow out of it, but I've not. All of my boyfriends have left me for other women and I've never hesitated to find some reason in myself for this betrayal rather than the fact they were feckless, faithless bastards. I wonder if I will ever have a man all to my little self.

Gil says that he moved into this hotel to get away from Gina, but we seem to have acquired a replacement in the blink of an eye. Elise, like Gina, is clearly used to having men fall at her feet. I'm not. The only thing that falls at my feet is my face. My relationships are always fraught and complex and I always love him more than he loves me. I've never been pursued wildly by someone who I didn't give a jot about, but I never give up hope.

Elise has all the right poses and postures at her finger-tips – which, naturally, are beautifully manicured. She has the hands of a writer and she flutters them over the conversation like pretty little butterflies. She's very nice and I detest her. I try to entertain myself with visions of her in years to come with a great fat bottom because of all the hours she's spent sitting at a computer.

Gil's watching me toying with my food and it's not because I'm sulking – which I admit I am – but is more to do with the fact that Tavis's mother decided that I was about four stone underweight and set about correcting that deficiency with a vengeance. I have a raft of pasta in my stomach that will probably take about two weeks to digest.

Our tiresome threesome is onto dessert and heading rapidly towards coffee, for which I'm eternally grateful. I just hope Elise doesn't invite herself to spend the night. My boyfriend and my new enemy are having an in-depth discussion about film, having moved on from an in-depth discussion about books.

I know nothing about books. I have never read Joyce, Tolstoy or Dostoevsky. I'm definitely in the minority here. They both like Trollope. As soon as I chipped in, 'So do I,' I realised they meant Anthony. I meant Joanna. It's not that I've deliberately neglected my literary educational advancement, it's just that I'm too bloody busy. By the time I've arrived home from yet another crummy job, I'm too tired to think about mind-enhancing pursuits – *Brook-side* is about my limit. It doesn't mean that I'm a bad person. It just means that my knowledge of literature extends to books that you don't mind getting suntan oil on and those that you can buy at three for a pound on the market.

When we studied meaningful books at school, I wasn't the slightest bit interested. I didn't care if this was a dagger, et cetera. I wasn't bothered who wandered lonely as a cloud. I preferred Domestic Science, because you could eat the fruits of your labours (mostly) and PE and rolling my skirt up as short as I could get it to try and snare

Ian Phillips. I appreciate, now, that I wasted a lot of valuable time – even though the skirt thing worked for Ian Phillips. I'll just about be ready to dip into the classics when I retire.

I thought I was on safer ground when we moved onto films. But no. Despite the fact that Gil is producing a romantic comedy and Miss Literary Knickers is writing them, they both prefer 'art house' films. I'm not sure what constitutes an art house film, but I'm pretty sure Bruce Willis isn't in any one of them. Me? I like anything with Hugh Grant. I like it even better if he gets his kit off.

I'm an ignorant bystander in a world which I'll never be a part of. I don't need to say this out loud. Both of them have stopped talking to me and, instead, are engaged in mutual ooo-ing and aah-ing, while I sit here trying not to go to sleep. I'm bored to tears and am thinking about getting rat-arsed drunk just to annoy Gil. The God of Love is sitting up in the heavens peeing on my party. I can't see Gina putting up with any of this and I wonder if this is why she left Gil in the first place.

I miss Tavis. Even when we're not talking we have a laugh. He doesn't have any intellectual muscles to flex. He's just quietly knowledgeable about nothing in particular – pizza toppings, the best place to park for which beach, the sharpest beer, all the lyrics to Madonna songs. Normal stuff.

I can raise important issues with Tavis, without feeling like an idiot – such as why was the first *Star Wars* film not the first episode. Why is the first one now the third one – or is it the fourth? And if George Lucas knew all along that there were going to be loads of them, why didn't he just start at the beginning of the story and work his way forwards? Then he might have realised that Ja Ja Binks was a crap character too. I have no idea how wimpy Anakin Skywalker is going to become dastardly Darth Vader in the space of one film. This is what real people think about films. They don't care who the director is, or that it was great cinematography, or that it has a meaningful message. *Die Hard* has a meaningful message – don't get stuck in an office building with a bunch of mad-arsed terrorists unless you've got a man in a ripped vest handy. The general public want action and car chases and a few laughs along the way. Why don't Gil and Smiley Author know this?

When Elise giggles again I wonder how much more of this I can tolerate. Not much, is the answer. I catch Gil's eye and even in the candlelight it looks flat. There's a dead spot where the pupil should be and I can tell that he's not enjoying this as much as he's making out. Behind that intelligent glaze there beats the heart of a man who cares about the Ewoks too. I smile at him and we both light up again. He squeezes my knee under the table. Elise is expounding the virtues of some arty-farty French film I've never heard of and I look away so she can't see me grinning.

And as I do, who do I see crossing in front of the luscious pool area but my luscious friend, Daniella. I nearly call out, but something about her demeanour tells me not to. She's being furtive and I know enough about furtive to last me a lifetime. Her handbag is clutched to her chest and her eyes dart left and right, but in the shadows and the soft candlelight, she can't see me. However, I see *her* and I wonder what the hell she's doing here. Whatever it is, it doesn't involve writers or convention.

Chapter Fifty-Eight

'I thought she'd never go,' I say to Gil.

He sighs and flops down on the bed, massaging his hands over his face. 'Me neither,' he agrees. Then he looks at me and twitches his eyebrows with evil intent. 'Alone at last.'

'I feel like Princess Diana,' I say. 'Didn't she say something about threesomes being vastly overrated?'

I think of Daniella again and can't wait until I see her to find out why she told me she was on a writing course when she's clearly been on a sneaky, secret assignation. I smell the scent of a Mad Movie Mogul in the air.

'Come here,' Gil says and I go and sit down next to him. He wraps his arms round me. 'Sorry about all this.' His look tries to encompass the past week, the hotel suite, the ex-wife, the trip to San Francisco and the smiley author. And it very nearly works – until he squeezes me tightly.

'Arrgh! Ouch!'

'What? What?'

'Sunburn.' It feels like being rubbed with a cheese grater or being caressed with a Morphy Richards steam iron. I think I've got whatever degree of burns is the worst – is it first or third? I can never remember. 'I fried myself in Tavis's parents' yard.'

'Is it that bad?'

'Excruciating.' I lift my top up, baring my midriff.

'Medium-rare,' Gil says.

I nod.

Reluctantly, he eases my T-shirt back into place. 'Let's go onto the terrace and have a drink,' suggests the man who could be the love of my life if only we didn't keep making such a bollocks of it.

I nod again. Champagne is as good a painkiller as any.

We take up our places on the terrace and pull our chairs together and face the sky. Gil pours us two glasses of fizz and we sip them in a silence that may be contemplative or not. I don't know if there's an atmosphere – despite all that has happened, I still don't know Gil well enough to tell.

'I thought there was something going on between you and Tavis,' he says candidly.

'He's gay.'

'I know.' Gil stares at where the stars would be if there wasn't too much competition from the twinkling, artificial lights of LA. 'He just doesn't look gay.'

I'm not sure that it's politically correct, but he does have a point.

'He looks like a movie star,' Gil says, and there's a certain amount of envy in his tone.

I snuggle closer to him. 'Let's not talk about Tavis,' I say. There are already too many people in this relationship; I don't want Tavis to crowd it too. Not now.

Gil strokes my hair. He looks as if he might be going to say he loves me, but doesn't. His lips find mine. First lightly, tentatively, then deeper, searching.

'Arrgh!'

'What?'

'My nose. My bloody nose! Ow. Ow. *Ow!*' Gil's stubble has scratched all the fried skin off it. I'm clutching it and I think it might be bleeding. Oh, God. Oh, God. There's only one thing I can do. I stick my nose in my ice-cold glass of Dom Perignon and whimper with relief.

Gil sighs and slumps back in his chair. I have a feeling the moment is broken. He hands me a napkin without taking his gaze from the heavens, for which I am grateful.

Sunburn, I think, is going to be as good a contraceptive as Gina the Coil.

Chapter Fifty-Nine

'You look like you had a wild night,' Steve said, nodding towards Gil's bleary eyes.

'No,' Gil said. 'I spent all night trying not to touch Sadie's sunburn.'

Steve's fork paused on its way to his mouth. 'Is that a code word?'

'Yes,' Gil said. 'For sunburn.'

'Oh.'

He and Sadie had managed to share the same bed, but that in reality was as close as they got. Every time he moved anywhere near her, Sadie whimpered, whined and wailed.

'I like these Hollywood power breakfasts, don't you?' Steve asked in the middle of his ruminations. He was tucking into a mammoth plate of potato pancakes and scrambled eggs with something approaching ecstasy.

'Yes,' Gil said. 'They're lovely.' He looked at his strawberries and granola without enthusiasm. They were at Nate and Al's, a Jewish deli that had been an industry hangout for the fifty years it had been in business. A place that's so unglamorous it's glamorous. Though the days when you could catch Doris Day having breakfast here in her bathrobe had long since passed.

'It's the only time I don't end up wearing mine,' Steve said, admiring his stain-free polo shirt proudly. 'My kids could grow up to be champion cereal throwers.'

Gil didn't want to have breakfast with Steve. He wanted to have breakfast with Sadie. Preferably after waking up in bed with her. Preferably after waking up in bed with her after a wild night of mutually satisfying sex. He sighed into his freshly squeezed orange juice.

'It's not going well is it, mate?'

'No.' Gil indulged in more sighing at the British propensity to understate everything.

'Are you still hiding behind the mad poodle fluffer?'

'Gina?'

'Is there any other?'

'No,' Gil said. 'I don't think so. I've moved out of the house.'

Steve raised a quizzical eyebrow. 'Where to?'

'The Beverly Hills Hotel.'

Steve's fork ground to a halt. 'That is an expensive way to make a point.'

'It was the only way.'

'I suppose a two-room rental apartment in Santa Monica isn't your style?'

'This is an emergency measure,' Gil assured him.

'It sounds a bit Looney Tune to me. What does Gina say?'

'Nothing,' Gil admired. 'I haven't heard from her.' He laughed to himself. 'In a bizarre way, I kinda miss her.'

'That *is* bizarre,' Steve said.

'But it's not that.' Gil tutted impatiently. 'It's everything. I've had two divorces already.'

'Not quite two,' Steve pointed out. 'And that's mere piffle for this town. When you're approaching double figures, that's the time to worry.'

'I wanted everything to go smoothly this time. Instead it's all going wrong.'

'Are you deliberately sabotaging your relationship?'

'Like hell I am.' Gil snapped his head up. 'What makes you say that?'

Steve shrugged. 'Christ knows. Maybe I've been in SoCal for too long.'

'When I went away this weekend, Sadie spent it hanging out with a hunky young actor,' Gil complained. 'I hate actors.'

'You're feeling marginalised and jealous.'

257

'Have you been watching *Oprah*?'

'Mate, you lot agonise about this sort of stuff far too much. At home, you meet a girl, have a shag, get married and have a couple of kids. You worry about the details later. By that time the kids have worn you down and you're too bloody knackered to think about getting divorced.'

'You make it all sound so easy,' Gil said sarcastically.

'It's the same as happy ever after but without the Hollywood gloss.'

'Sadie wants commitment. Suppose that involves children – one of the scariest "c" things you can think of?'

'Children are great.'

'Why?'

'Because they are.' Steve spread his hands expansively. 'It's like looking at a miniature version of yourself – before the hairy nostrils kick in, of course.'

'I don't want to see a miniature version of myself.'

'They're fun.'

Gil looked disbelievingly at his friend.

'The things they can do with Jell-O are unspeakable. And you can teach them things.'

'If I wanted to teach I'd get a job at UCLA.'

'They look up to you. Respect you.'

'Kids do?'

Steve shrugged. 'Well, maybe that's stretching it.'

'And the down side?'

'They don't let you paint them like poodles do.'

'My parents were divorced,' Gil said. 'I've been through it from the other side. I couldn't do that to anyone else. I have to be sure.' He rested his head in his hands. 'I'm scared that I'll do this and then I won't want it any more.'

Steve looked at him sympathetically. Or as sympathetically as someone could with scrambled egg on their lip.

'What if Sadie puts on weight? What if she gets ill? What if she loses her looks?'

'That's what you sign up for.'

'And that's what I'm not sure I can do.'

'Gina's an alcoholic and a drug abuser and a general pain in the arse, yet you can't kick her.'

258

Gil wished his friend wasn't watching so much self-help television. He kept quiet.

'She's your habit,' Steve said. 'And you've only just managed to break it.'

'So why would I want to be responsible for someone else's heart again?'

'Sadie is a different kettle of fish. This is because you were traumatised by your parents' multiple divorces,' Steve said. 'It doesn't have to keep happening to you. It can stop.'

'How?'

'Don't marry madwomen,' Steve said.

'It could be a congenital disorder.'

'You can go to a clinic for that, man.'

'Hilarious,' Gil said. 'Gee, I love your British sense of humour.' He drained his coffee. 'My father married a string of madwomen, each one of them more loony than the last. Most of my mother's husbands haven't been old enough to buy their own liquor. I could have inherited it.'

'Your parents were actors. That's why you hate them all – including this hunky young one, no doubt. They're all weird. If you spent your entire working day making out with Cameron Diaz and getting paid for it, you'd be weird too.'

'Just because there's some sort of irrational explanation for it all, it doesn't mean that it will all just go away.'

'You have too much history,' Steve said. 'You need to forget it. Move on.'

'I don't know how to.'

'Take Sadie to the Oscars.'

'That's moving on? It's four hours of boredom and being trapped in a seat so that you can't even go to the bathroom. How is this going to further my relationship?'

'You only feel like that because you've been a million times. Sadie will love it. It's not every day you get an invitation to the Oscars. It will blow her away.'

Gil remained unconvinced.

'Trust me, I'm a married man with loads of experience with women.'

259

'I didn't think the two went hand-in-hand?'

'You need to get her a great dress.'

'A great dress?' Gill shook his head. 'Sadie isn't that shallow. She hates me buying her things.'

'She's a woman.'

'Yeah, but she's different. A dress won't make the slightest bit of difference.'

'It will,' his friend insisted. 'They go all gooey. Women love that sort of surprise.'

'Surprise? How the hell do you buy a dress as a surprise? That way spells danger. What if I get the wrong size? If it's too big it'll be because *I* think she's too fat. If it's too small, *she'll* think she's too fat. No, no, no. I can't do this.'

'It's simple, mate. You steal some clothes from her wardrobe. Make sure you get ones that fit.'

'She doesn't live with me.' Gil was already beginning to spot flaws in the plan. 'How do I get access to her wardrobe?'

Steve brushed his objections aside with a wave of his hand. 'You're a Hollywood producer – a good one. It's your job to fix things. You'll think of something.'

'I'm glad you have such confidence in me.'

'Then all you have to do is take the stolen frock to a boutique. A nice one. Choose another dress. A class one. Find an assistant who fits Sadie's stolen frock. Get said assistant to model same size classy dress. Buy it. Gift-wrap it.'

Gil frowned. 'It can't be as simple as that?'

'She'll love you forever,' Steve said. 'And forever can be a very good thing.'

'This is Hollywood,' Gil reminded him. 'Forever lasts around five minutes.'

Chapter Sixty

This is just *so* LA! I'm doing a lunchtime Pilates class with Daniella because she's worried that I'm turning into a couch potato after a whole week of no workouts. The fact that I've walked further than she does in an entire year doesn't seem to figure in the equation. Walking only counts if it's done on a treadmill, not on honest-to-goodness pavements. I have driven over in Delores to get here and exercise for half an hour. I haven't pointed out that I could have spent my lunchtime power-walking round Larchmont instead as that is obviously not the ticket.

That apart, this place is fabulous. Daniella is paying for us both, which means I have no idea how much it costs and she has clearly deemed it beyond my meagre means. It's all very understated in a glitzy way with uninterrupted white walls, chrome downlighters and Lycra-clad personal trainers. Its atmosphere shouts *relaxation*! There are auto-graphed pictures of stars all over the walls in the reception area and I can't believe I'm going to exercise in the same place as Samuel L. Jackson. Of course, at the moment Mr Jackson is nowhere in sight.

The equipment looks as if it came straight from a medieval torture-chamber. Daniella is lying on The Reformer – yes, it really *is* called that – a long low bench to which she appears to be shackled. My friend is being 'reformed' by Kerry-Emma who is wearing a leopardskin all-in-one jumpsuit in the style of the late Elvis Presley and still managing to look fantastic. She also disappears when she turns sideways. If this is what Pilates can do for you, then let it do its worst! Kerry-Emma puts Daniella's legs behind her head and pulls on a variety of straps and pulleys. Daniella groans. That looks pretty bad.

I'm right next to her on The Cadillac. If the name suggests a degree of comfort, then it is misleading. The Cadillac comprises of a big metal frame, like a four-poster bed but without the drapes or the mattress and with what appear to be manacles. I'm being hung, drawn and quartered by Monica – a small Chinese woman with a wide cruel streak. There are pinging noises coming from inside my body from things that I don't think should go ping. My sunburned skin is trying to tear itself apart and even a vision of Tavis soothing me with calamine lotion isn't enough to stop me from wanting to scream. Whatever we are paying for this, it's too much.

If the Spanish Inquisition had invented this stuff, it wouldn't have gone on for half as long. After ten minutes, I'm ready to confess to anything. I'm hoping Daniella feels the same.

'How was the convention?' I ask, absorbing my pain silently as Monica hoists my legs up and out of their sockets.

'Fine.' I can tell that Daniella's teeth are gritted in agony.

'Worthwhile?' I gasp.

'I think so.'

'Where was it held?' I'm going to pass out in a minute.

'A seedy hotel out of town,' Daniella says, puffing effusively.

'Not at the Beverly Hills Hotel then?'

A sharp intake of breath. Daniella turns to look at me and something in her neck goes ping. I think she is ready to crack. 'What were you doing there?'

'Probably not as much as you,' I manage.

Daniella lets out an unhappy groan.

'3Ms?'

'Who else?' she says miserably.

'Would you still class it as worthwhile?'

'I don't know,' Daniella says. 'I can't think straight any more.'

I know that feeling only too well. Kerry-Emma and Monica continue to tear us limb-from-limb whether they have our full participation or not.

It's not a good time to tell Daniella that Gil has finally left Gina. It may be rubbing salt into wounds that are very raw. I could tell her that I spent the weekend with Tavis, but somehow that won't come out either. Alexis will probably spill the beans for me on that one. I have spent most of the morning staring out of the window at Double Take and trying not to think about Gil or Tavis.

'Why do women want unavailable men?' Daniella huffs.

'Perhaps because the available ones are available for a reason. Arrgh!'

'True,' my friend agrees.

'What a pair we are,' I say. The pain now is excruciating.

Kerry-Emma and Monica exchange a look that says they indeed think we're a pair of idiots, but then I'm sure they hear this same conversation a dozen times a day. I can think of a few people I'd like to put on this rack and interrogate.

'We have to do something about it,' Daniella says decisively.

'We do,' I agree. 'What?'

'I don't know.'

We both moan simultaneously and not with pleasure. I'm sure all this stretching is making my stomach grow bigger. For some reason I'm absolutely starving and can't wait to get back to the office and eat my sandwich. I've a busy afternoon of bums to book out.

Daniella's mobile phone rings. I don't know how she manages it, but she ferrets it from somewhere in her shorts and answers. Her face goes pale. Despite what Kerry-Emma has done to induce redness of the complexion, all the blood has suddenly drained away. 'Yes,' she says tightly. And that's all she says before she hangs up.

We do some more enforced acrobatics before she speaks. 'It was 3Ms' wife,' she says. 'She wants to meet me.'

My eyes widen, but this is partly because my knees are touching my ears and I had no idea I could do that. 'And you said yes?' I ask when I can eventually breathe again.

'I did,' Daniella says. 'Do you think that was wise?'

I try to shrug, but Monica is manhandling my arms. 'Probably not.'

'I need to confront this situation.' She sounds very convinced.

I hate confronting situations. I think situations are usually best avoided. I don't like the idea of Daniella confronting her situation because it makes me think that I should confront my situation. And I'm not sure which part of my situation needs the most confronting.

Just then, Monica does something hideous with one of the pulleys. All my vertebrae snap into line. Four gallons of blood sprint to my brain. I get up feeling all giddy and light-headed and as if I'm floating about a foot off the floor. This is such a fabulous rush. If I could do Pilates like this on a daily basis I'd never need to trouble myself with men ever again.

Chapter Sixty-One

One of Sadie's dresses had been secured via the services of a well-versed miniature exponent of espionage. But not without coercion. Alexis – his small but effective partner in crime – had driven a hard bargain. The price had been one Kennel Care Barbie. As Gil paid the shop assistant for it, he studied the grinning doll carefully. It came with its own fluffy poodle, a work station and a tray full of stuff to manicure dogs with. It bore an uncanny resemblance to Gina – with the notable exception that Kennel Care Barbie didn't have a bottle of vodka stashed in her grooming kit. He stowed the doll in the carrier bag along with Sadie's stolen dress and headed down towards Rodeo Drive for some serious shopping.

Gil knew nothing about women's shopping – which was a terrible admission after two wives. Maybe that's where he'd gone wrong. Steve seemed to think that the way to a woman's heart was through a series of well-timed dresses. In affairs of the heart, Gil himself had always found things a lot more complicated. He'd phoned one of Gina's more rational friends and had solicited some advice. She'd recommended a one-off boutique run by a hip Californian designer hidden away among the less radical Chanel and Prada. The sort of place where you'd pay twice as much for half the amount of material. Definitely the place to buy a dress to impress.

Gil found the boutique and sidled inside. There was a dazzling array of merchandise within that almost took his breath away – and his courage. Guys had it easy. You couldn't really go wrong with pants and shirts. Shirts conveniently came in a small selection of styles not too confusing for the average male brain – long sleeves, short sleeves, dressy, casual. Some patterned, but often not. Pants weren't too taxing either – black, blue, brown or maybe, if you were feeling reckless, beige. They didn't come in backless, sleeveless, flared, fluted, gipsy, girly, sophisticated, sexy, saint or slut. Or in such an awesome range of colours that would make any self-respecting rainbow feel depressed. Gil looked at the racks and felt a burgeoning headache. This was a minefield.

'Can I help you, sir?' a pretty blonde assistant asked.

'I sincerely hope so,' Gil replied, presenting his carrier bag. Never in his life had he felt more like he needed help.

One hour and several outfits later, Chloë the blonde assistant emerged from the dressing-room in a long white dress that literally did take Gil's breath away.

'Wow!' he gasped.

Chloë twirled. 'You like it?'

Gil thought there was a note of relief in her voice.

'I *love* it.'

The dress was covered in tiny crystals that caught the light and sparkled with rainbow colours. This was a head-turning dress. An Oscars Night dress. A dress that would make Sadie feel like a million dollars. He had a feeling it was going to cost him a good proportion of that, but she was worth it.

He'd like to say he'd chosen it, but he'd left all the hard work to Chloë. And she seemed to have come up trumps.

'Would you like it if someone bought you this dress?' Gil asked tentatively.

'Are you kidding me?'

He could never quite tell how Sadie would react – but wasn't that part of the attraction?

'It's fabulous,' Chloë assured him as he sat and nervously chewed at his fingers. 'Whoever this is for is a very lucky woman.'

'And it will fit like that?'

Chloë twirled again. 'I don't see any reason why not.'

'I'll take it,' Gil said.

And before he changed his mind, he rushed to the cash desk to pay for it.

Five minutes later, Chloë was back in her own clothes and bearing a large white carrier bag containing a gift-wrapped box and the sparkly dress. Gil and his credit card were on the verge of a nervous breakdown.

'Enjoy,' Chloë said and handed over the carrier.

'Thanks.' Gil clutched his purchase to his chest. If dollars could be directly related to happiness, this dress should make Sadie absolutely delirious. If only he could be sure he was doing the right thing. 'Thanks for your assistance.' He pressed a large tip into Chloë's hand and rushed towards the door. He needed strong coffee. Strong, black, reviving caffeine. Lots of it.

He waved his thanks again and pulled open the door. As he did, he ran headlong into Gina. He wasn't sure which of them was the most startled.

His wife recovered first. 'Hey,' she said.

'Hey,' Gil responded, realising that he sounded cagey.

'No kiss?' Gina said with a pout.

If there was one thing he could say about her, it was that she didn't bear grudges.

Gil dutifully kissed her cheeks. Her eyes travelled to his carrier bag. 'I hope that's not for you,' she said.

'No.' Gil felt very self-conscious. 'It's for Sadie.'

He thought he saw a dark cloud flit across Gina's brow, but her wide smile stayed in place.

'Oscars Night?' Gina tilted her head.

'Hmm, hmm.'

'She'll love it,' Gina said. 'Noah and I may be there too.'

'How are things with you and Noah?'

Gina tossed her blonde hair. 'Oh, you know.' She flicked her eyes heavenwards. 'Life is never easy with a rock star.'

Gil had decided it wasn't easy whoever you were with – there were just different types of struggle. Some people were too poor, some were too rich, some were too unfaithful, some were too dependent. The perfect partner seemed

267

to be someone whom you could rub along with most of the time – if you were lucky.

'Come for a coffee,' Gil said impulsively. 'I was just going across the street.'

'Okay.' Gina beamed as she took his arm. 'You can buy me a late lunch. I had to skip mine. As you would say – I had a dog to do.' She giggled and led him out into the street.

Gil thought guiltily of Kennel Care Barbie in his other carrier bag and hoped that Gina didn't notice that too. When she was like this – sober, sweet and not playing the seductress – there were times when he wondered if they could have made it work between them. He glanced at Gina as they waited at the cross-walk. There was too much water under the bridge. Too much sadness and far too much instability. Gina could stay like this for a week, a day, an hour, a minute – brief respites of calm before the inevitable storms. In the end, it was all too wearing.

He hadn't called Sadie today – which was stupid and crass. As soon as he'd finished with Gina, he'd call over. Maybe if he dropped by Daniella's house, he could deliver Alexis's fee and return Sadie's clothes to her closet before she missed them.

They went to the nearest restaurant and the hostess showed them to a booth. As they passed other diners, the men turned their heads to watch Gina, admiring her catwalk sashay. She sat down opposite Gil and tucked her hair behind her ears, grinning coyly. Several men in the vicinity had stopped eating. But there was no stirring in his heart or in his loins. At that moment, Gil realised that for him it was over. He was moving on.

Chapter Sixty-Two

Tavis's abs are as bankable as his bum. I've booked them out on a martial-arts shoot for a *Matrix*-style film without the budget to benefit from Keanu Reeves. The middle-aged male star is, by all accounts, a bit flabby round the midriff. Tavis is very definitely not.

My friend is on his way over to collect the details and Bay and Min can hardly contain their joy. I hate to admit this, but I'm having a bit of a struggle with mine.

I love working here and feel like I've been here a lifetime already. I'm as much a part of the furniture as the knackered spider plant.

Gil hasn't phoned me all day, but that's hardly surprising as we're not exactly love's young dream at the moment. I'm still miffed about the smiley author muscling in on our smoochy dinner and he's obviously still miffed about the sunburn thing. They both seem so petty in the cold light of day, but at three o'clock this morning I was pretty pissed off. If I give myself a bit of leeway, I couldn't help the sunburn thing, but he should have been able to find a way to scare off Elise Neils.

While I'm mulling over the ebbs and flows of my love life, Tavis turns up and reduces my colleagues to giggly, girly messes.

'Hi,' he says and kisses my cheek. Bay and Min swoon. I give them both a superior grin.

I hand him the job sheet which he quickly scans. 'This is great,' he says.

It isn't great, but it's a job. I wish I could do something to make him a star, but I'm having enough trouble making my own dreams come true, let alone someone else's.

'Hey,' Tavis observes as he points at my nose. 'You can hardly notice the burn.'

'Thank you for that.'

'What did Gil say?'

'Nothing very complimentary.' I have spent the afternoon discussing my celibate state with my colleagues, who agree with me that it's a crying shame. Next time, I will use a higher sun protection factor.

'Did you have a good dinner?'

'You could have stayed and joined us,' I say. 'We had company.'

'Oh.' Tavis seems at a loss for words. 'Are you seeing Gil tonight?'

'No,' I say. 'Not that I know.'

'Come to my acting class,' he suggests. 'Joe will be there and he's been beating up on me to see you again.'

'What time?'

'Now,' he says and looks hopefully at Bay. She nods graciously. Well, it would be gracious if she didn't have her tongue lolling out of her head. 'It's in Burbank. We need to get a move on to jump the traffic.'

'I'll get my coat.' Which is a joke because I haven't worn a coat since I got here.

This part of Burbank doesn't look too salubrious and I'm glad I'm not on my own here at night. We skirted round the huge complex of the Warner Brothers Studios on Hollywood Way and out towards a residential area that's looking a little rickety round the edges. I've driven us out here in Delores because Tavis says the classes go on for hours and hours and I'll probably be bored to death; this way I can just go home when I've had enough and he'll catch a ride with Joe. He seems quite nervous to have me with him. Although I'm supposed to be concentrating on the road, I can see that he keeps giving me surreptitious little glances.

Tavis tells me where to go as I head out into uncharted territory for me and eventually I pull up outside an inconspicuous and anonymous door opposite a run-down pool hall and we get out. I feel like clinging on to his arm, but don't.

I think everyone takes acting class in LA. Min does them. Bay does them. Daniella doesn't do them now, but she has done in the past. No one ever seems to be just pumping gas, waiting table, valet parking, driving cabs – everyone is an actor waiting to be discovered. Some must wait a lot longer than others. I feel like an innocent abroad, because I've no idea what to expect.

Inside, there is one large room that looks like a theatre. There's a makeshift stage and rows of beaten-up crimson velour seats in which rows of brow-beaten, would-be actors lounge. Joe is there already. He has his feet hooked over the seat in front and is reading his lines. We go over to him and Joe kisses me on both cheeks. He holds me away from him, beaming widely. 'Good to see you again, Sadie.'

'Good to see you.'

'Okay, people!' An older, handsome man comes out to the front of the stage. 'Our leading man is in the building!'

There is a chorus of decisive hoots and hollers and Tavis takes a mock bow.

'Thank you for joining us, Mr Jones. Shall we begin now?'

'Hey,' Tavis says. 'Take it easy. I have a guest.'

More hoots and hollers and I feel my cheeks flush and hurriedly sit down next to Joe. 'Take no notice of them,' Joe advises. 'They're uncultured animals.'

'I hope I'm exempt from that,' the man says.

'This is Jake Le Fevre, my acting coach,' Tavis says.

'Pleased to meet you.' Jake shakes my hand. 'You'll have to choose another leading lady,' he tells Tavis as he nods towards the entirely male motley crew assembled in the makeshift theatre. 'Jackie called in with a head cold.'

'Great,' Tavis says as he eyes his choices.

'Want to run through it with Joe?'

'Not particularly. He thinks I'm in love with him already.'

More jeering.

'You should be so lucky,' Joe chips in.

'Take Mohammed.' There's a seventeen-stone, bearded man squeezed into a seat at one end. 'It'll be a great test of your acting skills.'

'It'll be a test of my sanity,' Tavis says. 'Sadie'll do it.'

I suddenly become alert at the mention of my name.

Tavis turns to me. 'Won't you?'

'Do what?'

'Read these sides with me.'

In front of all these people. These proper actors! You must be having a laugh! 'Well, I'm not . . .'

'Great.' Tavis pulls me onto the stage and Jake thrusts a bunch of papers at me which I try to get the right way up.

Oh my good God. I'm Juliet and Tavis is Romeo. Bollocks. *Bollocks*. Thank heavens I read this for GCSE so I'm not completely at sea. I always knew that some day, in some very special way, my Shakespearean set text would come in useful. Unfortunately, I haven't read it again in the intervening seventeen or more years. How didst this cruel and damnèd situation befall me most unhaply? In sooth my teeth do perform their uncontrollèd chattering most verily. I'm trying to get into the mood. Method panicking.

The last time I was on a stage I was the Virgin Mary in St Stephen's nativity play, and that's longer ago than I care to remember. I wasn't a willing victim even then. But it was in the days when Catholics still believed that Jesus and His undoubtedly Jewish family were all blue-eyed blonds with button noses. I was chosen because I was the blondest Mary they could find. That is the sum total of my acting experience and very traumatic it was. Timothy Harrison, the most stupid of the Three Wise Men, tripped over the donkey borrowed from the local farm who was joyfully eating the Christmas tree, and dropped the myrrh on Baby Jesus's head while Joseph spent his entire time trying to look up the angel's skirts.

'Don't worry about this,' Jake tells me. Huh! It's easy for him to say that when he's the boss and tells other actors what to do. 'Just read it straight to feed your lover the lines.'

'Right,' I say, and I'm not sure my voice is even audible

or what reading it straight entails. There's a cloudy mist swirling in front of my eyes and I'm pretty convinced I'm experiencing my first anxiety attack.

'Let's take it from . . .' Jake flicks through the sides. My knees are trying to do the steps to the cha-cha all by themselves. . . .'*But soft! What light through yonder window breaks?*'

I look at the sheets which are blurring merrily in front of me and am relieved to see that Tavis is on first and his part is much bigger than mine – if you'll pardon the expression. A hush falls over the audience. I don't think they're going to be able to hear Tavis over the sound of my laboured breathing. Good Lord, *Romeo and Juliet*! Why couldn't we be doing a bit from *King Lear* or *Hamlet* or anything that's not as lovey-dovey as this. I'm going to feel like a right Charlie.

My friend winks at me and helps me to stand up on a box that forms my balcony. 'You'll be fine,' he whispers in my ear. He can't possibly know that. I rustle my pages into order. '*But soft!*' he says, sounding exactly like Romeo should, '*what light through yonder window breaks? It is the east, and Juliet is the sun!*'

My tongue has turned into a Ryvita. I listen to Tavis, the musical lilt of his voice, and for the first time the words of William Shakespeare are making absolute sense. Passion is pouring out of his pores. I'm sure it was never like this in Mrs Gregory's English lessons. He's so intense, it's making all the little hairs stand up on the back of my neck. If Juliet was faced with even half of this, no wonder she was lost.

When it comes to my bit, I take a deep breath and launch forth. '*O Romeo, Romeo! Wherefore art thou Romeo? Deny thy father, and refuse thy name . . .*' Personally, I always thought that '*Romeo, Romeo*' bit was rather naff, but I'm amazed at the strength with which I project it, and I can sense the audience sit up in their seats as I suddenly turn into Helena Bonham-Carter – before she started dressing up as a monkey. We carry on with the rest of the scene, moved by the emotion of the words and the hopelessness of the lovers' plight.

Tavis climbs up onto my box with me, which I'm sure isn't in the script, and he sweeps me into his arms and kisses me long and hard, his body pressed the length of mine. And I'm like a bar of Cadbury's Dairy Milk beneath a radiator – soft, squidgy and melting at an alarming rate.

'*Sleep dwell upon thine eyes, peace in thy breast!*' he continues. '*Would I were sleep and peace, so sweet to rest!*'

His breath is hot and hard against my cheek. I'm glad I'm not wearing one of those pointy wimple hats that everyone wears in Shakespeare plays because he would have knocked it off. I'm sure that Mrs Gregory didn't explain that Romeo was a hot-to-trot sex machine. This must be the X-rated version. I feel like I've been kissed from the inside out. All my fluttery bits are all a-flutter. For someone who is gay, Tavis does a very good impression of enthusiastically snogging a woman. I can't ever recall being snogged so thoroughly. He must be a bloody good actor. It takes me a moment to remember that there are about thirty people watching us. Tavis is clearly less daunted than I am. He is still gazing at me intently. I'm trying to get my eyeballs to stop rotating. Any minute now they're going to rack up three lemons and ping loudly when I've hit the jackpot.

'Thank you, Mr Jones,' Jake say wryly. 'Wonderful improvisation. How could Juliet fail to fall in love with you?'

I'm wondering that myself. Tavis stands me upright again and I adjust my clothing until I look less like I've just been ravished by a rampant Montague.

'Move to Romeo's death scene,' Jake instructs. 'Let's see what you can do with that.'

Tavis and I shuffle our pages.

'Juliet, you're assumed dead and in your tomb,' Jake tells me.

'Lie down.' Tavis lowers me gently and I lie prostrate on the floor, glad that I'm not having to stand upright for too much longer. My heart is beating very loudly for a dead woman.

'Take it from *dear Juliet. . .*'

'*Ah, dear Juliet . . .*' Tavis kneels beside me and takes my hand. He starts his speech while I try to make myself behave dead. Do the deceased normally blush?

'*Eyes, look your last!*' Tavis intones. '*Arms, take your last embrace!*' When I've just about got myself together again, Tavis takes his last embrace and I collapse to a splot of goo. '*And, lips, Oh you . . .*'

Oh no!

'*The doors of breath, seal with a righteous kiss . . .*'

And he does seal my lips with a righteous kiss. Well, not so much righteous as searing and lingering. Romeo's heart is going at a fair old pace too.

'*A dateless bargain to engrossing death? Come, bitter conduct, come unsavoury guide! Thou desperate pilot, now at once run on the dashing rocks thy sea-sick weary bark!*'

I'm feeling decidedly sea-sick.

'*Here's to my love. O true apothecary! Thy drugs are quick. Thus with a kiss . . .*'

Oh no! Not another one! Tavis smothers me with another heart-melting kiss. Our hearts pulsate together. This could well have killed Juliet if she'd been a bit of a shrinking violet. I don't remember there being so much snogging in *Romeo and Juliet* either.

'*. . . I die.*'

Tavis utters Romeo's last words, and as he releases me from his kiss and his embrace, I try not to gasp out loud, which I still have the sense to realise isn't entirely befitting for a corpse. I fall back and Tavis slumps over me. Oh my God!

Tears fill Tavis's eyes, whereas my tears are stuck firmly in my throat. The theatre is absolutely hushed and then the motley crew break into rapturous applause and whistling. A few, including seventeen-stone Mohammed, wipe tears away with their sleeves and then they all spontaneously rise to their feet and give Tavis a standing ovation. Joe is blubbing openly into his handkerchief.

Tavis helps me to my feet and takes a bow. Then he clasps my hand and makes me bow with him. My heart is pounding and I want to cry and laugh simultaneously. For the first time I can see the attraction of doing this for a living. Jake is clapping hard too.

It seems to take forever for the noise to die down.

'Gentlemen, that's the way to do it,' Jake says with an appreciative tilt of his head towards Tavis. 'If anyone can make it in this town, it should be you.'

Tavis's colleagues hoot their agreement. Jake's eyes twinkle. 'Try sleeping with the right people?'

Tavis shakes his head. 'I'm not sleeping with anyone.'

I'm sure Jake's eyes flick over me, but I can't be certain. 'Maybe you should.' Then the coach claps his hands. 'We've work to do, people! It's a tough act to follow. Who wants to be next up?'

Two guys from the end of the row shuffle forward. Tavis is still holding my hand and he leads me outside. The air is cool on my brow and I suddenly feel drained as if all my emotion has poured out of me.

My Romeo takes both of my hands and squeezes them. 'That was great,' he says.

'I don't think so.' I shake my head. 'It's you they were cheering.'

'Those guys are easily pleased. If only casting directors were the same.'

'You *will* make it,' I say. 'You won't be doing botty doubles for long.'

'Thanks.' Tavis smiles shyly. I think he is looking a little wobbly too. 'Sadie, I'm really glad that you came along.'

'I enjoyed it.' In a strange way.

'You should think about taking an acting class.'

I laugh. 'I enjoyed it, but I'm not in a rush to do it again. I'll leave it to the professionals.'

Tavis nods back at the door. 'This will go on forever,' he says. 'But you're more than welcome to stay.'

'I'd better be getting back.'

'You know your way?'

I nod. I haven't a clue, but I'm sure Delores won't let me down.

'Sadie . . .' Tavis leans against the wall. 'All that stuff in there,' he says. 'It's pretty powerful. I wouldn't want you to think . . .'

'Oh, of course not.' I giggle wildly as if it's the last thing that would cross my mind.

'I know what your situation is with Gil.'

Gil? What has Gil got to do with this?

'It was an act,' I say brightly. 'Acting. Very good acting.'

'Yes,' Tavis says. 'Acting. I just didn't want you to think . . .'

'No,' I agree, despite the fact that I don't know what I'm agreeing with. I look at my watch but still have no idea what the time is. 'I'd better go.'

'Me too,' Tavis says and he pecks me tenderly on the cheek. His face is burning.

I strike up a jokey Juliet pose. '*A thousand times good night!*'

Tavis's eyes meet mine and the shabbiness and the noise of the street fade away. '*A thousand times the worse, to want thy light.*'

And with that he rushes back into the building.

The door closes behind him and I'm left alone. I dampen my parched lips and whisper into the night: '*Parting is such sweet sorrow that I shall say good-night, till it be morrow.*'

I get into Delores and sit and hold the steering-wheel for a bit. My hands are trembling and I can't make myself do the driving thing. No wonder leading ladies and men always fall in love with each other. Tavis is a marvellous actor, there's no doubt. For a minute there, he had me absolutely convinced that he was in love with me.

Chapter Sixty-Three

Tavis and Joe were sitting in Mel's Diner on Highland Avenue – a traditional twenty-four-hour, seven-day-a-week establishment that sold burgers and fries with everything. All the waitresses wore short black skirts, cute aprons and pencils tucked behind their eats that made them look like they were straight out of *Happy Days*. It was the early hours of the morning and the only people in there apart from the two of them looked highly undesirable.

Joe had expended all his energy on being Daddy Capulet for the night and was slumped back in his seat being less theatrical than normal. He slurped noisily on a chocolate shake. This had become their post-acting class routine – a way to wind down from the emotion and recover from the constructive abuse that Jake normally doled out to them, although he had been kind to them tonight. They would give a data download on each other's performance, rebuild their shattered confidence, smooth over any insecurities that had surfaced and generally indulge in some brotherly back-patting.

Tavis's burger lay untouched on his plate. Tonight, it wasn't good old American fast food that would sate his hunger.

Joe picked at his burger with his fingers and studied Tavis intently. 'You looked like you were getting well into your role back there.'

'Thanks. I felt it went well.' He could still feel his hands shaking.

'Hm. Great acting.'

Tavis nodded.

Joe pursed his lips. 'If that's what it was.'

'Oh man.' Tavis closed his weary eyes, momentarily blocking out the glare of the hard white light.

'I thought you'd given all that girl stuff up?'

Tavis blew a steady stream of air through his nose which was a completely inadequate way to encompass fifteen years of love gone wrong. 'So did I.'

'Maybe it was just the emotion. You were pretty good,' Joe said. '*Romeo and Juliet.*' He shrugged. 'It doesn't come much stronger than that.'

'I think it was maybe more than that.'

'How long is it since you kissed a woman?'

Tavis dredged his mind back. 'So long ago, I'd forgotten how fabulous it can taste.'

'Better than chocolate milkshake?'

'Beyond compare.'

'Mmm,' Joe said, puckering his lips in disgust. 'I wouldn't know.'

'You've never tried it?'

Joe shook his head vehemently. 'For me this is genetic, not a statement.'

Tavis couldn't believe how weary he felt. He should be pleased with his performance, except that in his heart he knew it wasn't the skill of his acting that had moved him to such dizzy heights. All those things about Juliet being the moon and the stars, they'd flowed out of him with such passion that he felt as if he was the first person who'd ever spoken them.

'Maybe you should have taken Mohammed as your leading lady after all,' Joe suggested.

'I certainly wouldn't be feeling like this now,' Tavis agreed.

'So what are you going to do about it?'

'Nothing.'

'Because she's already with someone else or because of your pact with the devil?'

'I don't know,' Tavis said. 'I've given up women. They're too much hard work.'

'That didn't look like too much hard work back there.'

'That was acting.'

'Of course,' Joe said. 'I forgot.'

Tavis studied his burger. The colder and more congealed it became, the less appealing it looked. What good was love, if even the merest hint of it could put you off your food?

'I have something to tell you.' Joe leaned back in his seat, his loud Hawaiian shirt perfectly at home in this place. 'I've met someone too.'

Tavis sat up.

'He could be important to me,' Joe said.

'Wow,' Tavis said. 'This is news.'

'We've been seeing each other for a few weeks,' Joe went on. 'He's cute. Even better, he thinks I'm cute.'

'He has good taste,' Tavis said with a smile. 'I think you're cute too.'

'Ah,' Joe said. 'But the difference is, you could never love me as I want to be loved.'

'No,' Tavis admitted sadly.

Joe shrugged. 'I'd long since resigned myself to that.'

'So,' Tavis asked, 'where does that leave us?'

'I love you,' Joe assured him. 'Like a brother. I always will. Nothing changes that.'

'Do you want me to move out?'

'No.' Joe shook his head. 'But I guess Saul may be around a little.'

'Saul? Is he in the industry?'

'Hmm, hmm. Producer. Part of the Pink Power.'

'Maybe he'll get you a job.'

'Maybe he'll get us both jobs!'

'Hey,' Tavis said. 'I'm pleased for you. Really pleased.'

'I never want you to stop being a part of my life,' Joe said. 'A big part of it.'

'We're family.' Tavis punched his arm affectionately. 'Almost.'

'We would be if you could get it together with my daughter,' his friend said, resuming his role as father of Juliet.

'That's only make-believe,' Tavis pointed out. 'Real life is a lot more complicated.'

'She's a fantastic woman,' Joe said.

'Aren't they all when you first start out.'

'This one could be different.'

'I don't want any distractions. Two years ago, I very nearly gave all this up for a woman – you know that. You were the one who had to scrape what was left of me off the ground. She loved me, but hated my job. It was the hardest choice I ever had to make, but to give up my dreams would have been the biggest mistake of my life. I'm nothing if I can't act. I vowed then I'd never let anything – *anyone* – take me away from what I love most.' Tavis held up his hands. 'My heart is on ice.'

'Oh really?' Joe said. 'Seems like there's been a slight thaw to me.'

Tavis hung his head. 'I know. And that's what worries me.'

His friend looked at him earnestly. 'It doesn't matter about past mistakes. It doesn't matter what you've promised yourself. If this is really what you want, don't let her slip away.'

'What I really want is to become the best actor I can be.'

Joe took his hand and patted it. 'Make sure that you don't become the loneliest one along the way too.'

Chapter Sixty-Four

I'm on the verge of tears. It isn't 'that time of the month'.
I don't *get* a 'that time of the month'. My mood swings are
purely arbitrary and have no bearing on my menstrual
cycle whatsoever – would they were as scarce as every
twenty-eight days! But my hormones are definitely on
overdrive at the moment and there's nothing I can do to
convince them to calm down.

'It's fabulous.' The dress is covered in tiny crystals and
it glitters manically, grabbing at every ounce of sunlight
coming through the window and turning into a million
miniature rainbows. 'Just fabulous.' I've never seen anything quite so beautiful. This is a movie star's dress, not a
dress for a displaced, dysfunctional dipstick with a South
London accent. I want to be cheerful, but my body is
telling me to weep and I don't know why.

'Is it?' Gil looks terrified, and if I'm not mistaken there
are tiny bears of perspiration on his forehead. 'You don't
look happy,' he says nervously.

'I am,' I weep. 'I am.'

'Do you think it will fit?'

'I don't know,' I sniff. It does look like a skinny person's
dress. 'But I do hope so.'

We're in my bedroom at Daniella's house. Gil called
me a dozen times today to declare undying love and I
finally feel like we're getting back on track. And it has
helped me to rationalise my performance as Juliet – a
passionate but misguided woman in love with an unattain-
able and highly unsuitable man. Tavis and I will never be
anything but good friends, despite the fact that he could

beat all his opposition hands down in a Kisser of the Century competition, if there were such a thing.

'When can I wear it?' I hold this creation against me. 'Isn't it a little dressy for the office?'

Gil clears his throat. 'I thought we'd go to the Oscars Ceremony tomorrow night,' he says cautiously. 'If you'd like to.'

I nearly drop the dress on the floor. 'If I'd *like* to?'

'It can be really boring,' Gil says.

'Boring?' This man has no idea of boring. Queuing up for a takeaway from the Wing-Wah Chinese in Battersea is boring. Sitting in every Saturday night watching Ant and Dec doing something utterly vacuous is boring. Having to Immac your legs every week is boring. Giving leaflets out at the book fair is boring. A night at the Oscars is a long, long way from my idea of boring. 'I could live with boring,' I say.

'Great.'

Cinderella is going to the ball! I can't wait to ring someone and tell them about this. Anyone. 'Shall I try it on?'

'Maybe you'd better,' Gil says, sounding somewhat reluctant.

'Wait there!' I rush off into the adjoining bathroom, I whip off my Cinders rags – in this case Armani jeans and T-shirt – and slide into the dress. I pile my hair up and clip it with the nearest hair grip I can find and then look in the full-length mirror by the shower.

Oh my God! Even without my full war paint or co-ordinating Jimmy Choo accessories, I look like a million dollars. I can't believe this is me. I'd only ever expected to look as fabulous as this on my wedding day. The dress hugs every curve and even manages to give me some that I didn't know I had. The lobster red of my skin is fading fast and with a judicious application of St Tropez cream, I should be able to pass muster as a naturally bronzed beauty. Thank God for the person who invented fake tan! In this mood, I have every reason to believe that by this time tomorrow, my fried nose will have faded enough to resemble rather fetching freckles.

I take a deep breath and prepare to present myself.

'Da! Da!' I say as I emerge into the bedroom.

Gil's eyes widen with surprise and stay fixed and dilated as his brain clearly tries to assimilate this vision he sees before him with the dishevelled old duck who normally frequents his life. His mouth opens but words fail to come out.

'Do you like it?' I ask, and I don't sound nearly as confident as I feel.

Before he has a chance to answer, Alexis sidles into the room. 'Wow,' she says, jaw dropping in awe. At ten years old she's not had time to develop the same inhibitions as a thirty-eight-year-old man. 'Aunty Sadie,' she breathes in open admiration, 'you look like Princess Sparkle Barbie.'

'Do I?' That's a good thing, isn't it?

'Alexis helped me out with your dress size,' Gil admits as soon as his brain can form words again. 'She does great rates for espionage.'

'Good girl,' I say.

'Are you going to dress up like Prince Sparkle Ken?' Alexis enquires of my boyfriend.

'I hope so,' Gil says with a grin.

I sincerely hope not! Have you seen Prince Ken? He looks like a cross between a left-over Glam Rocker and Liberace without the piano. But then anyone who thought Ken was the ideal name for Barbie's prince really didn't have their finger on the button, did they?

'I'm going to go and find him,' Alexis says and marches out of the room, leaving us looking at each other in a slightly dazed way.

'You look stunning,' Gil says with something approaching wonderment. I certainly don't think I've scrubbed up too badly.

'There are a few more bits and pieces,' he says and pulls out another carrier bag from behind the bed. 'I had to take a runner on the shoe size, but we can change them easy enough.'

He unwraps a pair of Jimmy Choo's from the neatest

284

little box you ever did see. They match the dress exactly and I hope to God that they fit. Gil kneels down and offers up the shoe. My foot slides in, nestling perfectly in the soft satin. The slipper fits. I am indeed Cinderella.

Gil stands and hands me a small clutch bag. He has thought of everything and I want to wipe out all the previous bad things I thought about him. It doesn't matter what the dress has cost – although it's clearly a substantial sum. For all I care it could have been from a charity shop, it's the fact that he's taken so much trouble over getting it right that is moving me so deeply. I don't think anyone has ever gone to so much effort on my behalf. If I'm not careful, I'll start myself off blubbing again. Perhaps Gil is my Prince Charming after all. And I thought this kind of thing only happened in the movies.

'One more thing,' Gil says and he produces from his jacket pocket an elaborately padded jewel case. My mouth goes dry. 'These were my mother's,' he says cautiously. 'I hope that isn't too corny.'

'It's not corny,' I say. 'But it's too much, Gil.'

He opens the box and a beautiful diamond necklace glints back at me. I bet Princess Sparkle Barbie doesn't come complete with these otherwise she'd need her own bank vault.

'I can't wear that.'

'Don't you like it?'

'Gil, it's fabulous. But the cost . . .' You could probably buy a house with the proceeds. Two, probably. 'I don't think I can do them justice.'

'You'd make me very proud.'

He takes the necklace out of the box and tenderly clips it round my neck. 'You look lovely.'

I study my reflection again. I don't look lovely – lovely is the sort of word my mum uses to describe a pleasant outing to the garden centre or a cup of tea from a seaside café. I look stupendous, sensational and sizzle-your-socks-off sexy. The sort of bird worthy of taking to an Oscars Ceremony.

'I don't know what to say.'

Gil comes towards me. 'Don't say anything.' He takes my hair clip and throws it to the floor, letting my hair fall round my shoulders. 'You are a very beautiful and desirable woman,' he breathes against my neck. 'I haven't had the opportunity to show you how much I need you.'

I'm feeling a bit needy too. 'Help me unzip the dress,' I murmur as Gil covers me with insistent kisses.

Without a word, he unzips the back and eases the teensy, weensy, oh so insubstantial straps from my shoulders. I'm having the Cadbury's chocolate and radiator sensation again.

The door flies open. 'I found him,' Alexis announces and marches in clutching Prince Sparkle Ken in a vice-like grip with one hand and Princess Sparkle Barbie in full regalia in the other. 'You can play with him now.'

'Maybe not right now, Alexis,' I say, sounding a bit more breathy than I would like.

'Gil would like to,' she says without doubt as she plonks herself down on the bed and affects a pose that indicates she's there for the duration. 'Wouldn't you, Gil?'

And despite the stricken look on his face, Gil still has the good grace to laugh.

Chapter Sixty-Five

Joe was working in Book Fever – his work on the soap was drying up and he'd taken some extra shifts to ease the pain of rejection and increase his chances of bumping into Spielberg over a copy of *Adventures in the Screen Trade*. He'd left a message for Tavis to call him, but it was just as easy for Tavis to swing by as he'd nothing else on the agenda. Maybe his friend would have some time for lunch at Clafouti's or one of the other coffee-shops on Sunset Plaza.

It was Tavis's day off – from everything. A rare occurrence. No shift at Zorba's, no sides to learn that couldn't wait a day or two, no auditions, no buttwork, no housework. Nada. A blissfully unencumbered day stretched ahead of him and he thought, like a true Californian, he might take a ride out to the beach.

Book Fever was a proper bookstore. A series of small rooms with the feel of a private library, it was rather wonkily stacked to the roof with a jumble of eclectic new releases that jostled for space against rare out-of-print books and second-hand gems. All the staff were mad about books and it was a great place to find forgotten tomes about the film industry and, more importantly, the movers and shakers of the industry browsing through them. Tavis often wondered with the amount of books that Joe brought home whether he paid out more to Book Fever than he earned from it. It was probably a close run thing.

The door bell announced Tavis's arrival. Joe was behind the nearest cash desk wrapping a coffee-table book for a long-haired woman with a top that plunged to her navel and low, low rider jeans whose belt-buckle jutted seductively from her pubic bone. She pouted at Tavis – but probably because she hoped he might be a movie producer rather than another out-of-work actor. Everyone in this town was desperate to be noticed which was sometimes a sickening thought. Was this what he was turning into? Tavis fiddled with a rack of modern art postcards while he waited.

'Have a nice day,' Joe said chirpily and then turned his attention to Tavis.

'Hi, bro,' Joe said, high-fiving him.

'So where's the fire?' Tavis asked.

'No fire, but how would you like to go to the Oscars party?'

'You're kidding me!'

'Would I joke about something like that?'

'How did you swing it? Was this your new producer friend?'

Joe looked shady. 'Not exactly.'

'Wait,' Tavis said, holding up his hand. 'There's a catch to this, right?'

'Isn't there always?'

'With you? Yes.'

'What is the worst possible job at the Oscars party?'

'You got us a job? Oh man, why do you do this to me?'

'You need the money.'

'Don't I need my dignity more?'

'No,' Joe said. 'So what's the worst job?'

'Valet parker.'

'We don't have to go that low,' Joe assured him.

'Waiter. Waiting table.'

Joe clicked his teeth. 'Got it in two!'

'That would kill me.'

'Prepare to die.'

'No way, man!'

'Come on, it will be fun. It'll give us something to aspire to. What else were you going to do tonight?'

'I don't know. Watch TV. Wash my hair. Wash someone else's hair.'

'You are very ungrateful, my friend.'

'Aw, come on, Joe,' Tavis begged. 'Don't lay that on me.'

'What other way are you going to get to go to the Oscars party?'

'I'm going to become a movie star, remember?'

'Yes, and back in real life at least this way we can go to our graves saying that we were there.'

'I don't think being hired help is the same as being there.'

'Now you're getting picky. Just think of the stories you'll be able to tell your grandchildren.'

'Are we ever likely to have grandchildren? Look at us,' Tavis said. 'You're a raging old queen and I'm a . . . I don't know what I am.'

'A freak of nature,' Joe obliged.

'Thank you.'

'Just think of the *Movie Premier* magazine headlines. "Waiter to Winner!" Wouldn't that make an interesting piece? I can see it now.'

Strangely enough Tavis could see it too. He held up his hands. 'I'll do it,' he said. 'But only because you're my best friend and because it beats watching it on TV.'

'You'll enjoy it,' Joe assured him. 'It'll be a blast!'

No, Tavis thought. A blast would be *winning* an Oscar – and one day he was going to make sure that he did.

Chapter Sixty-Six

Daniella was waiting in LA Farm, a trendy restaurant on West Olympic Boulevard way out past the high-rise office blocks of Century City that was once upon a time a thriving movie backlot. Mrs Mad Movie Mogul was fashionably late and now Daniella was as nervous as hell.

LA Farm was low-key, light, airy and the converted barn effect was softened by hints of delicate chintz. Daniella had spent a ridiculous amount of time choosing her outfit. It was as if she were going on an important date rather than facing up to the wife of her long-term lover. She'd settled on a black shirt and trousers – understated and slimming. Something that didn't scream 'mistress'. Despite the conviviality of the surroundings and the pleasant hum of chatter it was doing nothing to help her feel calm. She'd tried deep breathing. She'd tried rehearsing a conciliatory speech. She'd tried avoiding alcohol so that her head would be clear. All had failed. When Mrs 3Ms finally arrived she could be sure that there would be at least one table that wouldn't be humming with pleasant chatter.

When she eventually crossed the restaurant towards her, Mrs 3Ms's outfit screamed Mad Movie Mogul's wife. She was a vision of power-dressing in powder-blue Prada, small, slender, nipped-in waist, Ivana Trump hair and heels. Daniella stood awkwardly to greet her, extending her hand. Extending her hand in what – friendship?

Mrs 3Ms's cool, dry palm took it briefly and she allowed herself to be seated opposite Daniella.

'Hi,' Daniella said as she sat down again.

'Hello,' Mrs 3Ms said in an accent that was more expensive and polished.

His wife was younger-looking than Daniella had imagined, and she'd spent a lot of time imagining her over the years. It was clear she'd benefited from the services of a skilful cosmetic surgeon, but she looked refined and rejuvenated rather than resembling a Picasso painting where the eyes, the nose and the mouth were not necessarily in exactly the places they should be. Daniella felt drab in comparison.

'Shall we order?' Mrs 3Ms said and rattled off a list of what she wanted without glancing at the menu.

Daniella fumbled to catch up. 'I'll have the same.'

Mrs Mad Movie Mogul gave her a secret smile showing that the irony wasn't lost on her.

The waiter came to fill their glasses and Mrs 3Ms drew him to her with her blue eyes that had surely been chosen specifically to match her suit. She'd become the only person in the room for him and Daniella was convinced he was about to spill the mineral water.

The waiter, with one last attempt at a killer smile, reluctantly departed. Mrs 3Ms turned her attention back to Daniella, fixing her with a steady gaze.

'Does he know that you're meeting me?' the Mad Movie Mogul's wife said as her opening gambit.

'No,' Daniella said.

'That was wise,' his wife said. 'He'd have tried to talk you out of it.'

That was exactly what Daniella had feared. And, for some inexplicable reason, she desperately wanted to hear what this woman had to say.

3Ms' wife slowly scanned her. 'There've been others,' she said. 'Many of them. But I expect you know that.'

Daniella put her glass down with an unsteady hand and a giveaway little rattle against her cutlery. Of course she knew, but it felt very different to have one's suspicions so boldly confirmed. She was clammy in places that she shouldn't be, despite the restaurant being chilled to arctic conditions.

'I grew not to mind after the first few. I *learned* not to mind,' the older woman corrected herself with a dismissive wave of the hand. 'It goes with the industry, doesn't it? Impressionable starlets. Obliging models. They're queuing up. You have to live with that.'

Daniella studied the woman opposite her. This was the woman she had loathed with a vengeance for the last decade. She had loathed her without even knowing her, knowing only *of* her. The waiter appeared again. And now she was sitting opposite her number one adversary with only seared salmon and a plate of asparagus risotto between them.

The Mad Movie Mogul's wife was beautiful. Stunningly beautiful. This was not a woman who had over the years 'let herself go' as her husband had so often claimed. If this was a woman who had let herself go, Daniella thought, then God only knows what she must have looked like before. She was more serene than Daniella expected too. More serene, but with a hint of mischief and fire behind her compelling eyes. Daniella felt pale and washed out by comparison, a cheap imitation, a wannabe but lacking the style, taste and money to compete. The only thing she could fight Mrs 3Ms on was her youth, and in a town where youth was everything that wasn't to be sniffed at. But soon enough everyone grew old – even the beautiful people. Even Hollywood hadn't managed to find a way to reverse aging.

The Mad Movie Mogul's wife dabbed delicately at her pink butterfly mouth with her napkin and fluttered her eyelashes winningly. 'This is wonderful.'

Daniella assumed she meant the asparagus, but she could have meant watching her love rival squirm. Daniella wasn't sure whether she'd eaten any of her salmon or not. If she had, she hadn't tasted it. Why did 3Ms come to me, she wondered – a mere hamburger lover – when he clearly had châteaubriand waiting at home all the time?

'No one said life would be easy, did they, Daniella?' Her lover's wife leaned forward conspiratorially.

Daniella. It seemed funny to hear the other speak her

name. The way she said it made it sound insubstantial, bouncy and cheap like the name in a teen magazine or a trashy novel. Daniella knew the woman's name – it was as glossy and expensive as she was – but they never spoke it. She was always 'his wife'.

'I bet you wanted to be an actress or a writer?' His wife looked at her without rancour. 'I bet you never imagined in your wildest dreams that you'd turn out to be the single mother of an illegitimate child waiting around for someone to leave his wife.'

'No,' Daniella said softly. That certainly wasn't what she had imagined for herself.

'I, on the other hand, can't complain,' 3Ms' wife continued. 'No matter what else my husband has done, he has always seen to that. I have wanted for nothing. Not even love,' she said. 'In his own way.' She picked at her asparagus. 'You and I are in the same line, Daniella. I've just always been at the head.'

It was true. Daniella realised that she had spent her time with the Mad Movie Mogul waiting in line. Waiting and waiting. Waiting for phone calls. Waiting for snatched dinners. Waiting for hurried sex. Waiting for the time when he would leave this woman sitting opposite her who looked as happy as Larry. Whoever Larry is. This woman was not the tear-stained clinging drab whom she had been told about that kept her lover from her. This was not a woman who would crumble the minute he found the courage to walk out of the door. Even the exquisitely tailored suit and her fragile frame couldn't conceal the fact that this woman had a steel girder running through her. She was no helpless dependent, blown by the winds of emotion. No way. This was a woman who was in control of her destiny. A woman who had known all along what she wanted and how to hold on to it. Any fool could see that. And it came as a shock to Daniella to realise that for the first time she was seeing this woman through her own eyes, not her lover's.

'How did you know where to find me?' Daniella said.

The other woman gave a small laugh but there was no

bitterness in it. 'I've always known,' she replied. 'I know your cell-phone number. I know where your house is. I know about Alexis. She must be ten now.'

'Yes,' Daniella said quietly. 'She's ten.'

'And Molly is seven. Imani is coming up to five.'

Daniella felt all the hairs stand up on the back of her neck.

'His other children,' Mrs 3Ms informed her coolly. 'I know where their mothers live too.'

'Why now?' Daniella mumbled. 'Why now, after all this time?'

The Mad Movie Mogul's wife looked as if she was about to cover Daniella's hand with her own, but then thought better of it. Instead she examined her immaculately manicured nails. 'Life shouldn't be about standing in a long line waiting for your turn on a thrilling rollercoaster ride. It should be about walking arm-in-arm along the beach.'

Does she not realise that I know that? Daniella thought. I've known that all along.

'If you're on a rollercoaster long enough,' the other continued, 'it loses its thrill. Believe me.'

Suddenly Daniella did want to believe her.

'Are you meeting the others too?'

'No.' 3Ms' wife shook her head. 'You're the only one I've ever been concerned about. You're the only one he truly loved, the only one who was ever a threat. The others were takers. You've a giver.' She paused. 'My husband is a taker too. He loves to be worshipped.' An elegant shrug of her shoulders. 'And I became indifferent to him a long time ago. I didn't have to learn that – it just happened. Powerful men don't know how to cope with that.'

Daniella had never been indifferent to the Mad Movie Mogul. She'd always been there waiting – faithfully – if that wasn't a weird choice of word. It was she who had known *his* indifference. She was the one who had lost all her friends because they'd grown tired of her putting them to one side to grab hungrily at a few precious moments with her married lover. She thought she could learn a lot from the Mad Movie Mogul's wife and wondered if she would have liked this woman if they had met before she loved her husband.

'I left him,' his wife sighed contentedly, 'for a man who likes a walk on the beach. Three months ago.'

Daniella dropped her fork. It clattered to the floor making heads turn in the cheerful atmosphere of the LA Farm. She bumped the table as she scrabbled to pick it up and noticed that the waiter didn't rush to her aid. She realised she was making a fuss as she tried to marshal her scattered composure and her cutlery back from the four corners of the restaurant. The Mad Movie Mogul's wife waited patiently, methodically tasting her risotto until she had finished her meal.

'He's free to come to you,' she said, and her eyes were full of pity. 'He has been for a long time.'

Daniella felt that her face was as white as the over-starched tablecloth.

'I'll get the check,' 3Ms' wife insisted and she stood, ready to leave.

'Why are you telling me this?' Daniella wanted to reach out and grasp her arm. She couldn't go like this. But her limbs were numb and frozen.

'I don't really know,' she said. 'Perhaps because in twenty years you'll be just like me and I wouldn't want you to waste your life. You've already wasted enough.' She looked sadly at Daniella. 'Give your love to someone who will cherish it.'

And at that, the sane, sensible and serene woman who used to be the Mad Movie Mogul's wife smiled happily and calmly walked out.

Chapter Sixty-Seven

This is my big night. I've taken the day off from Double Take especially to prepare myself. There isn't going to be one single bit of my body that hasn't been puffed, plucked, polished, painted, preened and pampered in the line of duty. By the time I've finished, it will be impossible to tell where I finish and Gwyneth Paltrow begins. Bay and Min could hardly contain their excitement and I'll never dare show my face in the office again unless I take several thousand compromising photographs of the stars.

I am back at Daniella's watching some hideous daytime quiz show and having a quick tuna sandwich before the serious work of my makeover commences when the door bell rings. I peep through the curtain and my heart does a funny little lurch when I see Tavis standing there. Off I trot to let him in.

'What are you doing here?'

'That's a nice welcome.'

I stand aside and let him in. 'We're friends,' I say. 'We don't need pleasantries. How did you know I'd be here?'

'I used all of my potent psychic powers to detect where your aura was in the universe.'

'Only Brits do irony,' I inform him.

'I swung by the office and they told me you had the afternoon off.'

'Guess where I'm going?'

'To the beach with me.'

'No.'

'Ah, come on. I have the afternoon off too. Joe can't play, he's working at Book Fever.'

'Take another friend.'

'I don't have any other friends.' Tavis turns puppy eyes on me. 'You're my only friend in the world.'

'That's because you work too hard.'

'So where are you going?'

'To the Oscars Ceremony!' I can hear myself squeaking with delight.

'Oh.' Tavis doesn't look quite as thrilled as I do. 'With Gil?'

'Who else?'

'And to the party afterwards?'

'Of course.'

Tavis picks up the Prince Sparkle Ken that Alexis has abandoned on the sofa and flops down. He purses his lips and quietly says, 'I'll be there too.'

'Fantastic!'

'Not so fantastic.' He looks up at me, wrenching Ken's arm backwards with a certain degree of brute force. 'I'll be on the other side of the fence.'

'I don't understand.'

'While you're having fun, moving and grooving with the stars, I'll be waiting table.'

I sink down on the sofa next to him. Now I feel like smashing Ken's face in too. 'Oh, Tavis.'

'It may be the only way I ever get to go there.'

I put my arms round him and give him a big hug. 'Don't talk like that. You're brilliant. A fantastic actor.'

He smiles reluctantly. 'You're just saying that.'

'No, I mean it. Last night was . . .' What was it? Unnerving, that's what. 'It was superb. You're very talented.'

I fall silent.

Tavis grins at me. 'Keep going.'

I tut. 'You know I'd do anything to help.'

'Come to the beach with me,' Tavis begs. 'That would make me feel a lot better.'

'I can't.' I try an Alexis-style whine. She seems to win every argument with it. 'I have to get ready for tonight.'

'How long will that take?' Tavis says. 'You already look fabulous.'

'I don't,' I protest. 'I'm a mess. I have to do hundreds of girl things before six o'clock.' This is the designated hour of white stretch limo arrival! 'It's nearly twelve now. That is six short hours away.'

'What are you going to do in six hours?' Tavis is aghast. 'You could repaint a street of houses in that time, not a few toenails.'

'I'm a high maintenance babe.'

'You are not,' Tavis snorts. 'The natural look is very fashionable. Come with me,' he pleads pathetically. 'I have to go to work early too. Before then I can show you some good old-fashioned Californian entertainment.'

'Like what?'

'Rollerblading.' He looks pleased with the idea.

Somewhere inside me a little bit of resolve weakens. 'I've never been rollerblading.'

Tavis is already on his feet. 'You'll love it,' he says. 'How can you come to California and not rollerblade?'

'Gil will go bonkers if I'm not back on time.' Worse still he'd probably go without me.

'We'll be back in plenty of time. Joe will go *bonkers* if I'm late for work.'

'It's not difficult, is it?'

Tavis takes my hand. He fixes me with those damned Romeo eyes and my last inch of willpower crumbles to dust. 'It's a piece of cake,' he assures me. 'Would I lie to you?'

I feel my insides sigh. Last night this man was willing to lay down his life for me. You don't forget that sort of thing too easily. I feel that I owe him.

'Rollerblading it is,' I say. I hate myself for it, but I've always been a pushover when it comes to doe-eyed men.

298

Chapter Sixty-Eight

Venice Beach is packed with hippies who came in the 1960s, tuned in, turned on, dropped out, chilled out and never went away again. There is an extraordinarily large population of sixty-year-old men wearing long ponytails and tie-dyed vests. This clearly is where the laid-back citizens of California's Derby and Joan Club hang out.

A woman who is possibly ten years older than my nan whizzes past on silver rollerblades in minuscule Nike shorts beneath a cropped top and nearly takes me out at my knees. She is the only eighty year old I've seen with thighs of steel. But then she's also the only eighty year old I've ever seen on skates. It can't be that difficult then, can it?

I've got my skates on – ha, ha! Ten slithering wheels that are determined to have a life of their own beneath something that has all the comfort of a hard plastic wellyboot. And I'm clinging onto Tavis for grim death.

He tries to prise me off him. 'We'll rent them for just an hour,' he promises.

That sounds like more than long enough for me. I reaffirm my limpet grip.

'Okay?' my personal trainer says.

'Fine,' I mutter through clamped teeth.

'Take it easy to start with,' Tavis urges.

I don't think I could take it any other way. Does he think I'm going to go whizzing down Venice boardwalk at ninety miles an hour after Grandma Roller Queen on my first outing?

'One foot in front of the other.'

Advice like this, I really need!

We set off. Gingerly.

Oh fuck! The minute I move, all the wheels charge off in different directions. I wave my arms around in an attempt to retain my balance and lose my dignity. I must look like one of the Muppets.

Tavis is trying not to laugh.

'Don't laugh,' I warn him.

'I'm not laughing!' He bloody well is!

The legendary LA smog doesn't become troublesome until late in the summer, so the unhindered sun is intent on baking all the visitors to the beach. I have already been deceived by the strength of its rays and have smeared on an inch-thick coating of sunblock. I'm not taking any chances. I want to look *perfecto mundo* for tonight's shindig. You wouldn't catch J-Lo turning up with a fried proboscis – she's probably having her St Tropez air-brushed on at this very moment.

The sun also seems to have brought out all the nutcases. Whatever you've heard about Venice Beach is true – that and a little bit more. There is a wide variety of cranks who inhabit these shores and this area in particular. Many of them make a living – of sorts – by selling arts and crafts down here. The Ocean Front Walk is an open market for the alternative. It offers everything from Chinese massage, henna tattoos, sand sculptures, Tarot readings, original paintings by ponytailed and tie-dyed-vested artists, tacky T-shirt shops and the biggest selection of cheap, rip-off designer sunglasses in the Western world.

The pavement is lined with street performers. Because it's the 'off-season', the entertainers outnumber their audience by about three to one. A bare-footed man plays the ukulele with considerably less flair than George Formby – and that's saying something. Another man is juggling chainsaws for our entertainment. There's a pint-sized pop star being filmed for a music video who seems extremely reluctant to pose with his guitar, which is more than can be said for the man dressed as an incarnation of Jimi Hendrix who is playing his electric guitar louder than is strictly necessary whilst rollerblading aimlessly in amongst the grannies.

Normally, I could stay and watch this spectacle all day, cough up a few dollars and go home happy, but at the moment my entire concentration is centred on keeping my feet moving. Which they are doing, but an inch at a time. The boardwalk – which follows Santa Monica Bay – is twenty-five miles long. At this rate it could take some time. I'm going to be due back home to begin my Oscars Ceremony preparations before we've got to the end of the next block. Once upon a time I used to be able to ice-skate. I was quite good at it, in fact – not in a Torvill and Dean sort of way, but I could go backwards for a few steps and do a bit of a twirl. Let me assure you, it isn't like riding a bike, you do forget.

Tavis is being very patient, but my lack of co-ordination is obviously amusing him more than these whacko street performers.

'Don't laugh! I'm concentrating.' Tavis is doing it backwards, forwards, inside out, everything. All with an amazing grace and fluidity. I hate this man. He must be crap at something.

'You're doing fine.'

I'm not. I can categorically state, I'm not.

We head up towards Muscle Beach, the open-air gym that gave Arnold Schwarzenegger his start in life. Currently it is populated not by men resembling the Incredible Hulk, but by dear old things with chicken legs in brief checked shorts and lurid bandannas to hide their bald pates who have coughed up their five dollars to pump their withered, walnut-brown pectorals in front of a small but faintly revolted crowd of observers. This place is too weird. Why can't pensioners here behave like they do at home and sit indoors and watch telly all day?

'You're doing great,' Tavis says with an encouraging grin.

I'm not doing great. I look like one of those little five year olds you see hanging onto their father's hands and tiptoeing along on their rollerblades to the sound of parental cooing.

'Try to get a bit more rhythm going.'

It's all right for him to say that. I would love to get a rhythm going. My brain is doing all it can to get a rhythm going, but it doesn't seem to be passing the right messages to my legs.

'That's it!' Tavis shouts, shimmying backwards and away from me. He draws his hand away until we are only touching by our fingertips. A little confidence is pushing down towards my toes. I'm starting to enjoy this. 'Faster,' Tavis says. 'Feel the wheels. Good. That's good.'

It's not bad. I'm picking up a bit of speed now. I can feel a cooling breeze on my face and in my hair. Ha, ha! Watch out, Granny! A few people notice the grim determination etched on my face and wisely move out of my way. We head away from the stalls and the hawkers and wind our way on the ribbon of path threaded through the sand and the palm trees, passing the fabulous, boxy beach houses of steel and glass that face off against the ocean.

'You're a natural,' Tavis says.

And you know, I'm starting to feel the wheels. I'm doing more skating than slithering and it feels good – really good. This is what life should be for – sun, shorts and skates.

At that moment an octogenarian wearing a gold Lurex thong and very little else skates by, overtaking me on the inside. And I don't know what distracts me the most – the fact that I can see most of his wrinkly little hazelnut of a bottom or the fact that he's smoking a pipe – when absolutely *no one* in California smokes. Whatever it is, I'm suddenly aware that we're heading down a slope, a tiny incline to all those who aren't wearing rollerblades – but something approaching Kilimanjaro to me. I'm gathering speed at an alarming rate, catching the old boy up quicker than I'd like to.

'Shitshitshit!' I can feel my arms flailing, but they are not helping to halt my progress.

Bloody hell! I'm heading towards some sort of contemporary artwork – a graffiti-sprayed wall which several youths are working on. They're lounging around admiring their work, aerosol cans in hand.

'Stop!' Tavis shouts.

Which is really helpful. I would if I could, but he seems to have left out one vital part of my instruction. He didn't tell me *how* to STOP! 'I don't know how!'

The youths turn in my direction and a look of terror spreads across their collective faces.

'Don't these bloody things have brakes?'

'No.'

'No?' Now I'm really worried.

'Make a "T"!' Tavis is belting after me.

'Make tea?' What?

'*A* "T"! With your feet!'

Oh! Why didn't he say so earlier?

'Get out of the way!' I shout at the hardened graffiti-sprayers.

They scatter on command, dropping their cans of spray paint and diving behind palm trees and I'm heading – no steaming – towards their wall.

Fuck. I'm running out of time.

'Do a "T"! *Now!*' Tavis sounds very panicked. 'One foot behind the other.'

A 'T'. I try to lift one foot to put it behind the other, but something suddenly is not quite right. My universe is inverted. The pavement is where the sky should be and vice versa. The sound 'Aarrgh!' comes involuntarily from my throat. And after a pleasant flight through the air, I land in an ungainly heap, a tangle of arms and legs, splayed out on the boardwalk.

Tavis comes up behind me, breathless. 'Are you all right?'

I want to say 'do I look all right?' – but all the breath has departed from my body.

To make matters worse, the man in his glittery G-string, still puffing serenely on his pipe, skates gracefully by.

Chapter Sixty-Nine

'Are you feeling better now?' Tavis is looking very chastened.

'Hmm, hmm.' I nod, but I'm not entirely convinced and neither is Tavis. After he'd scraped me off the boardwalk, he examined all my limbs – rather thoroughly, I thought, for one who has only been a TV doctor – and then, having pronounced none of them to be broken, returned the offending and rather scratched rollerblades to the rental hut and loaded me into his car.

It's not only me who's looking shaken either. 'You had me worried for a minute there,' he says as we head back toward Larchmont.

'Only for a minute,' I say. 'I must try harder next time.'

He smiles at me. 'I'm not too sure about your style, but I'd give you ten out of ten for artistic interpretation.'

'Yeah, very funny.' The graffiti boys, when they had eventually deemed it safe to come out from behind their palm trees, had given me deep respect and were spraypainting my name on their wall in honour. Upside down.

Tavis squeezes my hand. 'You had a lucky escape.'

I know. It was a stupid thing to do. Everyone else prepares for weeks for Oscars Night – and not by going rollerblading. Most take the more obvious route of the beauty parlour. My hands are trembling and my eyes feel all teary. And although I don't appear to have come to any physical harm, I feel sort of sore all over.

'Gil would have killed me,' Tavis says with a rueful shake of his head. 'I don't know what I was thinking of.'

'No harm done,' I say. I try one of my most winning

smiles, but it feels a bit feeble. 'I'm fine. Really.'

'Sure?'

'All in the world is well.'

He sighs, deeply, and I see a little tension seep out of his body. We stop at a red light and he turns to me. 'It was fun though.'

'Yes.'

He grins at me as he pulls away. 'I think you've done it before.'

'Yeah,' I say. 'Maybe I was a roller-disco queen in a former life.'

We laugh and a little of my wobbliness vanishes and I relax back in my seat, eyes closed, enjoying Tavis's driving until he pulls up outside Daniella's house.

'There you go,' he says. 'Safe and sound.'

'Yeah.' Not for the want of trying.

Tavis twitches round in his seat and faces me. 'Have a great time tonight,' he says, sounding serious. There's a little shadow of sadness around his eyes. 'Spare a wink for a friendly waiter.'

'I will.' I lean over and kiss him lightly on the cheek. His skin feels warm from the sun and tastes of the sea. 'Next year you'll have a proper bona fide invitation – I'm sure of it.'

'Get outta here,' Tavis says. 'Or you'll be late.'

I risk another kiss. 'And thanks for today. It was fun.'

But as I go to get out of the car door, it jams. I give it a hefty push, but no good. 'It's stuck.' I have another push and shove.

'There's a knack to it,' Tavis says. 'Wiggle it around.'

Wiggle. Push. Shove. 'No. It doesn't want to know.'

'Here,' Tavis says and makes to get out of the car. 'I'll get it.'

'Don't worry.' I dismiss him with a wave of my hand. 'I can manage.' And I spring up in my seat, deciding to vault over the top of the door as I've seen Tavis do a dozen times.

'Wait!'

I turn back to Tavis as I start my jump and following the

horror-struck look on his face, I see that the seatbelt is wrapped around my foot. But too late – *Houston we have lift-off* – I'm launched. 'Ooohhhh!'

In a scene reminiscent of the recent rollerblading incident – there is far too much air between my feet and terra firma. 'Aarrgh!'

When Tavis does this he always manages to look cool. It's not something I'm achieving. I can feel myself doing a cartoon scramble to try and turn myself the right way up, but whatever I was in a former life, it wasn't a cat and I don't land gracefully on my feet, but straight on my face. My knees and elbows aren't far behind.

And neither is Tavis. He's out of the car and crouching beside me before you can say that-was-a-stupid-thing-to-do. He is ashen. 'Are you hurt?'

'Yes.' All over. And there's blood. Coming from my nose and possibly my lip. I'm not crying, but only because I'm too shocked.

'Can you stand up?'

Only if they rebuild me using metal pins and bionic technology. I will never again think that *The Six-Million-Dollar Man* was a load of old codswallop.

I ease my face from the pavement, leaving what look like vital bits of skin behind. 'What do you think Gil will say?'

Tavis shakes his head. 'I don't know,' he admits. 'But I bet it won't be nice.'

Chapter Seventy

The white stretch limo pulls up outside Daniella's house.

I glance nervously at my friend. 'He's here.'

'You look fine,' Daniella reassures me. 'No one will be able to tell.'

I touch my lip with a tentative finger. 'Ow!'

Daniella winces.

'Sure?'

'Well,' she says, 'not many people.'

I catch my reflection in the mirror. 'Especially if they've got a squint or a glass eye?'

'Don't touch it,' she says, looking worried. 'Or it will bleed again.'

'Bollocks.' It's the only comment that's appropriate.

The door bell rings. I push Daniella towards the door. 'You go.'

She ducks behind me and pushes me forward instead. 'You're going to have to face him sometime.'

'Tell him I've died.'

Her eyes light up. 'You can tell him you've had a car crash.'

'I can't do that!'

'It would at least buy you some sympathy.'

She has a point. The door bell rings again and I take a deep breath and open it. Gil's smile freezes. 'What the hell happened to you?'

The imaginary car crash option pauses in my brain for consideration. 'I had an accident.'

'You sure did,' he says. Concern furrows his brow. 'Are you okay?'

'Well . . .' I'm not sure what qualifies as okay. I have a black eye, a livid red graze on my cheek and a split lip. I've chipped a tooth and although it feels like I've had a razor inserted in my mouth, I don't think you can actually notice that. I may well have bust my ribs, I have no skin on either elbow or knee and one of my ankles is the same size as both of them put together. An awful lot of me is turning a deep navy-blue colour. 'Well,' I say brightly, 'I'm still ready to party!'

A look crosses Gil's face. It's no longer concern. It's a look that says, 'You cannot go out like that!'

Daniella has put a pound of foundation on my face and force-fed me Extra Strength Tylenol. She's lent me a white gauzy stole which will disguise the worst of my elbows. The fabulous, fabulous dress that I wanted to look so wonderful in covers my knees and so long as I don't try to eat, walk or generally have too good a time, I should be okay.

Despite the fact that I'm laden down with his mother's diamonds and am wearing this killer movie-star dress, Gil can't tear his eyes away from my split lip.

'Are you in pain?' he says. He still hasn't moved towards me.

Fucking loads of it. 'Only when I laugh.' I try to smile without making my lip bleed.

'Are you sure you want to go?' He does look concerned again – in a sort of hypnotised way. 'We can give it a miss.'

Give it a miss? Miss the Oscars? Is he mad? If I was on a stretcher I'd still want to go. And believe me, it was a close run thing.

'I'd like to go,' I say, sounding feeble. 'But only if you don't mind me looking like this.'

I can see the decision cross his mind. 'You look fine,' he says, but there's no depth to the words. 'You always look beautiful.'

I risk a wider smile and feel my lip tear slightly.

'You'd better go,' Daniella urges anxiously.

'Yes,' Gil says. 'Yes.'

I set off and limp towards him. He takes my arm and I try not to complain as my raw elbow brushes against his jacket. Aaahhh! I want to cry. I've ruined everything. This was going to be perfect and I've cocked it up completely. And I'd like to be able to say this is all Tavis's bloody, bollocky fault, but it isn't, it's mine. All mine.

Hobbling towards the limo, I wonder if Gil thought to get all my labels removed. I have a mental fear of leaving home with the price tags attached to my clothes. It used to be because they were too cheap. Now it's because they're too expensive. But then I think that someone catching a glimpse of my labels is the least of my worries.

'How did you do this?' Gil says as he eases me towards the open door. I look at Delores, but she is standing in the drive rusty and relatively unharmed and, as such, would be a useless alibi. The chauffeur looks at me and flinches as he sees my face.

Gil is still looking at me in mesmerised horror and waiting for detail.

'I fell,' I explain.

'From the top of a ten-storey building?'

'I tripped over. Onto the pavement,' I mumble, thinking it's probably wise to miss out the vaulting from the car episode.

'Poor you.' Gil awkwardly tries to cuddle me and I wince. Shaking his head with bemusement, he helps to lower me into the car. 'Did someone come to help you?'

'Yes,' I say, without trying to incriminate myself further. I daren't tell him that it was my unreliable actor friend who helped me, otherwise I think his face would turn as black as his tuxedo.

Chapter Seventy-One

Hollywood, as I understand it, had become a bit of a dump. The Tinsel Town had lost its shimmer and was showing its rather seedy underside far too often – like a battered old Christmas tree that had seen far too many festive celebrations to be capable of glitz. The grim reality of today's down-and-out littered Hollywood had digressed a heck of a long way from the glittering, celebrity-studded Hollywood of legend. It's hard to believe that this notoriously decadent place originally started life as a quiet suburb for a Christian community – a sort of Utopia, blissfully free of saloons and gambling halls. My, how things change!

In the last few years there has been a huge attempt to perk it all up again; it's been dusted down, spruced up and given a sugar-coated frosting and a billion-dollar facelift that must go down as one of the town's most expensive exercises in cosmetic surgery. (Cher's bills don't even come close.) And while it may not quite have recaptured its former glory, it's having a damn good go at it. The eyebags have gone, the cheeks are full and high, the chin set at a jaunty angle.

Gil has been telling me all this on the limo trip, whilst trying to avoid looking at me. I wanted so much to enjoy this and it's all turning very horrid. This could be a once-in-a-lifetime experience and I didn't want to experience it with navy-blue knees.

I get a thrill as we crawl up in the lavish, limo traffic of Highland Avenue and we see the gigantic, glamorous Hollywood sign hanging on the hill.

Gil points to it. 'That started out as an advertisement for

a real-estate development,' he says. 'People liked it and it sort of stayed.'

And I don't know how I thought it got there, but I had expected it to be far more significant than a housing-estate accident.

'It was originally going to be called Figwood,' Gil adds.

Figwood? Making it as a movie star in Figwood? It just doesn't have the same ring, does it? No one would clamour after the glamour of Figwood, would they?

'So it was just a happy mistake that the movie centre of the world wasn't called Figwood?'

Gil nods. 'The developer's wife overheard the name Hollywood on a train journey and liked it better.'

Trust a bloke to think Figwood was a catchy name. Somewhere inside me, another one of my illusions is softly crushed. This whole place is just one lie stacked precariously on top of another like a house of cards.

I think we were supposed to get here early before the crowds, but it hasn't worked out like that. When we arrive we're knee-deep in starlets working the heaving throng of the great, unwashed public – who have camped out for days on a square inch of sidewalk just to get a fleeting glimpse of their favourite stars. There's an equally great and unwashed crowd of paparazzi.

'Ready?' Gil says and he squeezes my hand. I realise it's the one bit of me that doesn't ache.

'Let's try to enjoy this,' I say nervously, and I see his shoulders relax a little.

'You're right,' he says. 'I just hope no one thinks I did this to you.'

And I can tell that he's only half-joking.

We step out onto the red carpet – which is actually burgundy – the crowd starts screaming and we're blinded by the lights of a thousand camera flashes. Maybe Gil is sufficiently well-known to warrant a photograph, I don't know – but I'm certainly not. That doesn't stop the paparazzi though. They're calling at me to stand this way and that, just in case they discover later that I might have been important.

The carpet, dotted with larger-than-life replicas of the Oscars Statuette, stretches for miles and we form a slow procession towards the rinky-dinky theatre that's been purpose-built for the Oscars Ceremony as part of the regeneration of the area. My heart is pounding as much as my head and I can't believe that I'm really here.

I've been in the town for weeks now – movie-star headquarters of the world – and I haven't seen a single celeb so far. Not one. Not even some measly TV soap celeb out of *ER* or *West Wing* or *The Sopranos* – never mind a bona fide film star. Unless, of course, you count Noah Bender in his knickers in Gil's lounge. Now I'm in star heaven – they're running amok, twinkling brightly. They're all here – Nicole Kidman, Tom Cruise (though obviously not together), Sharon Stone, Dustin Hoffman, the dashing Denzel Washington, Russell Crowe (I'm trying not to faint), Robert 'Bob' Redford, the beautiful Ben Affleck and the perma-tanned Sylvester Stallone whose mother reads bottoms. The atmosphere is super-charged. There are more teeth and diamonds on show than I've ever seen in my life. How am I ever going to get them to believe this down at the Wing-Wah Chinese Takeaway?

I'm so glad that Gil has gone out of his way to make sure that I'm properly attired. I lean against him and gave him a little squeeze. A dozen flashbulbs record it.

'This is a feeding frenzy,' I whisper.

'Welcome to LA,' he says with a sardonic smile. We stop amidst the furore and he fixes me with his soft blue eyes. 'Are you feeling okay?'

Just when I think we're going nowhere with this relationship, that we're never going to manage to get it right, I suddenly fall in love with him all over again. 'Yes,' I say. 'I'm feeling fine.'

We finally reach the entrance and join the crowd in the theatre foyer, waiting for the ushers to show us to our seats in the Orchestra level. I'm sure it's really nice in here, but I can't see anything for wall-to-wall people. It's hot and squashed and even though I'm fizzing with excitement, I can't wait to sit down again.

A young guy in a trendy tuxedo with a dragon embroidered down one sleeve comes towards us. He shakes Gil by the hand and I recognise him as the fourteen-year-old director with whom Tavis had worked on the botty double shoot.

'Hey,' he says to Gil. 'I thought you avoided these like the plague.'

'I have to come out every so often,' Gil responds, 'just to let them know I'm still around.' Gil turns to me and so does the ridiculously youthful director. 'This is Toby Portman. He's going to direct *The One That Got Away*.'

'Can't wait, man.' The Boy Wonder director claps his hands together. 'We are going to put a boot to the butt!'

'We start casting in a couple of days,' Gil informs me.

This is news to me. I know so little about Gil and his life. That's not good, is it?

'I have to go,' Toby says. 'I'll catch you later.' He shakes my hand. 'Nice to meet you.'

'He's a hot shot,' Gil says as soon as he's a discreet distance away. 'I'm lucky to get him.'

'He looks very young,' I remark. Is it the same here as it is everywhere else with policemen? You know you're getting old in Hollywood because all the directors look like they're straight out of high school.

Gil shrugs. 'It's Hollywood. You're over the hill by the time you're thirty. Maybe not even that old.'

What a depressing thought. I feel like I haven't even begun the climb yet.

A slim, dark-haired woman heads towards us. She's wearing a full-length silk gown the colour of emeralds. 'Gil!' she says, and kisses my rather surprised-looking date.

'Katherine.'

'I didn't expect to see you here,' she says.

'No, no . . .' Gil stammers. 'Me neither.'

And I don't know whether he means he didn't expect to see her here or he didn't expect to be here himself.

'You look great,' she says.

Gil's eyes take in her dress and everything else about her. 'So do you.'

'It's been so long.'

'I didn't know you were back in town.'

'The East Coast is too cold in winter,' Katherine says with a mock shiver.

Hello! I'm still here! 'Hi,' I say, feeling like I could give her a mock punch on the nose. And not for the first time in Hollywood, I wonder whether it's her own.

The woman smiles serenely at me. 'You must be Gina.'

I flick a glance towards Gil, who has definitely blanched.

'No,' Gil says, jumping to my rescue. 'Gina and I split too.'

Too?

'You did?' Now it's Katherine's turn to look shocked. 'I hadn't heard. I'm so sorry. You were a great couple.'

I feel like throwing up in my cute little handbag.

'This is Sadie,' Gil says. 'She's English.'

She's English? Is that all the description I warrant?

'Oh my,' Katherine says just as a younger, handsome man comes to take her arm.

'We need to take our seats, honey,' he says, nodding curtly at Gil.

'You remember David, don't you?'

'How could I forget,' Gil says.

I have the impression I'm missing a vital piece of information.

'We must meet up,' Katherine says. 'Have lunch sometime.'

'Definitely.'

The fragrant cloud of Katherine and her toy boy leave us.

I look at Gil for an explanation. 'That was Katherine,' he says.

'I gather.' Nothing else is forthcoming. 'Lunch?'

' "Let's have lunch" in this town means "I hope we never meet again as long as I live".'

'She's an old girlfriend, right?'

Gil shakes his head. His lips are pinched and white. 'No,' he says. 'She's an old wife.'

'Another one?' I need to sit down. 'You've been married twice?'

'Does it make a difference?'

'I think so.' I'm not sure why just at the moment. 'Why didn't you tell me?'

'Sadie,' Gil says, and he sounds more exasperated with me than he should, given the situation. 'Since you got here we've hardly had five minutes to ourselves. You don't even know what brand of cereal I prefer, let alone my past relationship history.'

'Well,' I say, 'I happen to think one is a lot more relevant than the other!'

'We were married straight out of college. For two years. It was a sort of starter marriage.'

'Thanks for telling me.'

'And I like Cheerios. Although I do eat Golden Grahams on occasion.'

I would have had Gil down as a Kashi GoLean man – but that is the least of my troubles now. Through the crowd I see another face – a more familiar one. Gina has spotted us and she and Noah are threading their way through the bodies towards us. I have a heart-sink moment. If Katherine was the starter marriage, this one is very definitely the main course. Everything might not have been going along swimmingly, but we certainly don't need Gil's current wife to come wading in with her five-inch stilettos.

'Oh no.' Gil is obviously having his own heart-sink moment.

I see a gulp travel down his throat and his face turns even more white if possible. I tug at his sleeve. 'Gil? What is it?'

'You'll see,' he says tightly.

The crowd parts and Gina is standing slap-bang in front of us. Noah is stage-right, like some aging lackey. And now I know why Gil's face looks like one of those carved out of stone on Mount Rushmore. This is my worst nightmare come true. What a cruel coincidence. The female *faux pas* to beat all *faux pas*. Unlike me, Gina seems unperturbed. She's wearing my dress, my lovely

315

sparkly dress and, for the record, she fills it out in places I could never hope to. Daniella told me that the only way you can truly tell if boobs are made of silicone is to shine a torch on them in the dark – apparently the silicone glows. I wish we'd have a power cut and I was carrying a Pen-lite All Purpose torch with extra-strength Duracell batteries and then she'd feel like a fool too.

'Hi,' she says brightly, all teeth and tonsils on show.

'What do you think you're playing at?' Gil mutters through his white lips.

'Oh!' she says, looking down at her dress for the first time. Her hand goes up to stifle a giggle. 'Snap!'

I'd like to go snap too. Preferably to Gina's neck.

'You knew I'd chosen this dress for Sadie,' Gil says tightly.

Does she? I wonder how. And then I realise this isn't a coincidence, it's Gina being spiteful and petty, and whatever her motive behind it, I don't want to get dragged into it.

'So I did,' Gina admits with a roll of her eyes. 'I must have forgotten.'

'You look lovely,' I say quietly.

'And so do you,' Gina agrees. 'You're even wearing Gil's mother's diamonds.' She emphasises her bare décolletage and heaving cleavage. 'I used to love wearing those,' she continues. 'Even though they are a little outmoded.'

My cleavage – what little there is of it – is heaving too. With rage.

We all stand there exchanging meaningful silences.

'You *both* look fantastic!' Noah chips in. 'Like twins.'

Gina's jaw drops and she gives him a withering glare.

Noah shrinks but doesn't seem to know why. He holds his hands out. 'I don't see what the problem is.'

'She looks like she's been used as a punchbag!'

'I think it gives her face character,' Noah says thoughtfully. 'No one else has gone for that look.'

'You're an idiot.' Gina pushes away into the crowd with a loud and obscene expletive.

316

Noah shrugs. 'I'd be pleased that someone else liked my dress enough to buy it too.'

If it wasn't for my split lip, I'd risk a smile. 'Thanks, Noah,' I say. He's a truly nice man, despite his dependence on strong substances and his penchant for women's pants. 'It's a bit of a girl thing.'

The world famous, aging rock star sidles up closer to me and whispers softly in my ear. 'Do you think I could maybe borrow it sometime?'

I try very hard to see him in the same way that his legions of adoring fans do. 'Can I get back to you on that, Noah?'

'Sure thing, doll,' he says and wiggles away.

Chapter Seventy-Two

Tavis tugged uncomfortably at his bow tie. He was wearing a wing-collared shirt which was a size too small and it felt like it was strangling him.

The main party of Oscars Night is the Governor's Ball which is hosted by the Academy. Everyone who is anyone goes and very few who are no one. The Ballroom is a shrine to glitz, hung with sparkling chandeliers the size of space stations.

'Are we ready, people?' the head waiter asked. 'Do we have our hors d'oeuvres?'

Tavis looked at the silver tray before him. He certainly did have his hors d'oeuvres – so did the army of servers lined up in ranks behind him. It looked like the feeding of the five thousand – except that in Hollywood, no one was going to rely on a few fish and a loaf of bread to do the job. The Tinsel Town version involved tuna tartare, Maryland crab cakes, miniature hamburgers with Roquefort cheese, delicate blinis with the finest caviar, shrimp tempura and a dozen other dishes, the names of which they'd all had to memorise. Each tray would be presented as if they were doing an audition for a major role, because tonight people who could make or break futures were the revered guests and you never knew just when you might be spotted and catapulted into stardom.

The room was filling up, the first of the lucky partygoers drifting in, the champagne starting to flow. The battalions of waiters were mobilised. Everything glittered suitably to reflect a glittering occasion – there were more flowers and silverware in view than an episode of *Dynasty*, and above each table was a tank of exotic fish balanced precariously on stilts complete with a notice urging each guest not to eat the fish – and Tavis couldn't help wondering why they would want to.

Tavis straightened his posture. If Brad Pitt could start out in Hollywood dressed as a chicken, parading up and down Sunset Boulevard to advertise El Pollo Loco restaurant, then there was no reason why he couldn't wait table for the extraordinarily rich and the stellar famous.

'See you back at the ranch,' Joe said and winked at him. 'Happy hunting. Wait table like you've never waited table before.'

Tavis set off through the crowd of shrieking and hugging ecstatic winners and the tight-lipped and resolutely stoic losers. Out of the corner of his eye, he spotted Gil McGann standing alone. He quickly scouted the room for Sadie, but couldn't see her. He hoped to God that she'd managed to get here. He felt terrible. She'd protested that she was okay, but she'd looked in a pretty bad way when he'd left her at Daniella's and he felt that it was all his fault. He had to know whether she was still in one piece, so he worked his way towards her boyfriend.

With a few detours en route, Tavis eventually offered his hors d'oeuvres to Gil, who availed himself of a miniature hamburger. Tavis cleared his throat, but Gil's eyes were too busy working the room to notice him.

'Hi,' Tavis said.

A shadow of recognition crossed Gil's face. 'Hi there.' A quick glance took in the waiter's starched white uniform.

'Is Sadie here?' Tavis asked.

Gil's eyebrows shot up in surprise and he fixed Tavis with a stare.

'I wanted to check that she was okay,' Tavis said, aware that he was in danger of babbling. 'She did get here?'

'She did,' Gil said slowly.

Tavis felt his heart lift. 'Wow,' he said. 'That's great. I was really worried about her. It was all my fault, man. My stupid car door . . .'

'Your car door?'

319

'I keep meaning to get it fixed.' Tavis looked anguished. 'If I had, she wouldn't have had to jump out.'

'She jumped out of your car?' Gil said. 'That's how she fell?'

'Yeah.' Tavis was having a flashback. 'I think she must have been more shaken than she thought.'

'From what?'

Tavis paused briefly, but it was too late. He bit his lip. 'From her rollerblading accident.'

'Rollerblading?'

'Yeah. It was a stupid, stupid idea. I'm sorry, man.'

'You took her rollerblading?'

'She was good at it . . . briefly,' Tavis added.

'Briefly?'

'It was the guy with the thong and the pipe,' Tavis explained. 'I think it put her off.'

Gil's face darkened. 'The thong and the pipe?'

At that moment Sadie appeared. She was such a vision of loveliness in the most fabulous creation that Tavis nearly gasped. He checked himself in time. Even surrounded by some of Hollywood's finest, she still managed to create a little buzz as she approached. He could see heads turning, people commenting as she passed. When she came to Gil's side he could see why. She still looked stunning, but close up you could see that she was battered and bruised. Her split lip was crusted with blood and she had a great shiner that nearly closed her eye. When she tried to smile, her face creased in pain.

'Oh shit,' Tavis said.

'Thanks,' Sadie remarked.

Gil turned to her and there was no hint of a smile on his face. 'You didn't tell me that Tavis had taken you rollerblading.'

'Didn't I?' Sadie's voice came out like a squeak.

'No,' her boyfriend said.

Sadie pressed her lips together. 'I'm trying to blank out the whole experience.'

They both looked at Tavis.

'I'd better move on,' he said. 'So many people, so many

hors d'oeuvres. The shrimp tempura are wonderful.'

'Really,' Gil said.

He offered his tray, but Gil remained impassive. Sadie gave a barely perceptible tilt of her head, but it was patently clear that she was saying, 'Move on.'

Tavis put on his most cheerful look. 'Can't tempt you?'

'I'm very tempted,' Gil said flatly. 'But not by the hors d'oeuvres.'

If Gil had his way, Tavis thought, he was certain to be catapulted somewhere tonight – but it certainly wouldn't be towards stardom.

Chapter Seventy-Three

This is just getting worse. What was supposed to be the best night of my life is turning into *Scary Movie*. Tavis looked so depressed, I thought he was going to fling himself into his tray of hors d'oeuvres and commit the culinary version of hara-kiri.

Gil, who wasn't very impressed with my cuts and bruises to start with, is even more unhappy now that he knows who the chief instigator of my injuries was, even though I can't lay the blame squarely at Tavis's feet. I look to Gil for support, but I get a tired, forced smile in return. I've never seen him look more cheesed off – or, while I'm at such a swanky bash, perhaps I should say *Roquefort*-ed off.

I feel that I don't belong here – not in this town, not in this room, not in this stupendous dress and not by Gil's side. For one wild moment, I'm wishing I was back home with my dull little job and my dull little life. I shouldn't be here amongst the Hollywood aristocracy. I'm an impostor, an interloper, a fake. I'm not part of this world.

To make matters worse, the other stupendous dress is heading towards me; Gina's threading her way through the crowd with a confidence that has always eluded me. The dress is filled out admirably by the smiling Gina, pneumatic assets fully pumped and on red alert. She's turning heads with her sheer beauty and not because she looks like she's been recently mugged. I can't handle this, not now and probably not ever. I'm feeling besieged by ex-wives who are more beautiful than me. My head hurts, but not as much as my feet and nowhere near as much as my heart.

I tug at Gil's sleeve. 'I have to nip to the loo.'

He turns to me. 'You just came back,' he says. 'Are you okay?'

No, I'm not okay. I'm miserable. I want you to love me. I don't want to be in competition with your wives – ex or otherwise – because I can never win. I want to spend some time alone, just you and I, getting to know each other. I don't want to be in this room full of people I don't know and never will, making small talk about things I don't understand. And I don't want to eat goldfish in the tanks and I can't believe that anyone would think I would want to. And it all makes me realise that I really don't belong here. I belong in rainy Britain with its cold weather and its hot tea, doing dodgy jobs for piffling amounts of money but with a great bunch of supportive mates, none of whom have pretend breasts or would think of eating goldfish either. 'Yes,' I say, returning Gil's tired smile. 'I'm fine.'

And before Gina can blast her way into my universe and my self-esteem again, I slope off before sprinting for the loos like a greyhound out of the traps at White City.

Chapter Seventy-Four

'I saw Sadie rush off,' Gina said. 'What's the matter with her?'

'She's not feeling too well,' Gil said. 'The bruises she has are from falling out of a car after a rollerblading accident this afternoon – I think. She's a bit shaken.'

'Rollerblading?' Gina queried. 'This afternoon? Before Oscars Night? What was she thinking? She should have been at the salon.'

And suddenly Gil realised why Sadie had rushed off. He was so stupid. This was all getting too much for her. One ex-wife that she didn't know about popping up out of the blue, another soon-to-be-ex-wife turning up in the same outfit. Of course she didn't want to see Gina wearing the same dress – the dress which had been ruined for her just as his wife had planned. And he cursed himself for being so uncaring. He looked at Gina and his heart went out to his funny, feisty English girlfriend and he knew that one of the main reasons he loved Sadie was that she was the sort of person who would spend the afternoon rollerblading with a friend – albeit a threateningly handsome one – rather than sitting for hours on end getting whatever it was women got done in beauty parlours.

'You spoiled her night turning up in that,' Gil said. 'It was a spiteful thing to do.'

Gina looked as if she was about to protest and then changed her mind.

'It's over between us, Gina. I've moved on. None of this hurts me. It just makes you look petty.'

Gina opened and closed her mouth again.

'Why can't you be pleased for us? I don't love you any more,' Gil said, 'and if you carry on behaving like this, I won't even like you.'

Gina sighed. 'Have you finished?'

'Yes,' Gil said.

'I'm sorry,' Gina admired. 'It was a stupid thing to do. Sadie's nice. I shouldn't have done it.'

'Then go after her,' Gil said, indicating the direction in which Sadie had so hastily departed. 'Apologise. Make it up to her. You know, she could be a very good friend to you if only you'd let her.'

'Let's take it one step at a time, Gil,' Gina warned.

'You could do with a good friend,' Gil said. 'One with her feet on the ground.'

'I'll find her and apologise about the dress,' Gina conceded. 'I still care for you, Gil.'

'Then make it up to Sadie,' he said.

Gina looked contrite. 'I will.'

And as she disappeared into the crowd again, he realised he was a fine one to talk. If anyone needed to make it up to Sadie, he did.

Chapter Seventy-Five

I'm at the mirror in the ladies' powder room and I can't believe how terrible I look. I've had a good cry and emotionally I'm feeling a lot better. I'm trying to repair the ravages of my make-up and hoping that, physically, I can at least patch myself up ready to re-enter the fray. I try to think back to a time when I had no extraneous wives to contend with and now find that I have not only one but two. I'm trying to convince myself that being divorced twice isn't a bad thing – but I'm failing. Doesn't it indicate a certain flaw in the personality somewhere? A certain lack of staying power? And why did Gil have to be hitched to two such stunning women? Doesn't anyone in Hollywood have ugly exes?

I wave my lipstick as near to my split lip as I can cope with.

'Hey.' One of Hollywood's triple A-list actresses comes to stand next to me. 'Could I steal your lipstick? I don't know where mine went.'

I think I might hyperventilate. 'Sure.'

Taking my Top Shop lippy, she runs it round her trademark full lips. 'Great colour.' She's won an Oscar tonight and is clearly feeling mellow.

'Thanks.'

She glances at my bruises. 'What happened to you?'

'I fell out of a car,' I say. Deciding not to mention the rollerblading accident.

'Poor you,' the star of a dozen hit movies says. 'I live in mortal fear of anything like that happening. I wrap myself in cotton wool for months before Oscars Night.'

'I'm not an actress,' I say. 'It doesn't really matter what I look like.' And as I say it, I realise that it doesn't matter at all. Not one jot. It doesn't matter if Gil has a dozen exes, because he's chosen to be here with me and he's chosen my fabulous dress and it's not his fault his wife is an old cow who decided to copy it. I'm here to have fun and somehow in the stress of it all, I'd forgotten that.

'Lucky you,' she says. 'You can probably eat all that wonderful food too. They waft it all in front of us, but I'm not allowed any of it.' She pats her washboard stomach ruefully. 'If it isn't made out of egg white I can't touch it. I'm having to survive by trying to inhale the vapours.'

I do my restricted version of a smile and notice that she is trapped in her dress by bones and fabulous corsetry that probably makes breathing, let alone eating, an art.

'It's nice to see someone looking natural,' she says, and I don't think she's being facetious.

'I think I look rather more natural than I would have liked.'

She grins and hands my lipstick back. 'Thanks.'

'You're welcome.'

'Nice meeting you.' She heads towards the door. 'Have some of those cute little burgers for me,' she says over her shoulder.

And, do you know, I think I just might.

Oh no. Oh no. As I swing out of the ladies' loo with renewed confidence, I see Gina heading towards me. And I really don't want her to burst my bubble so soon after I've managed to inflate it again. I'm feeling all floaty and buoyant and she looks suspiciously like she's brandishing a pin. I watch my arch enemy – it looks like she's searching for someone and I hope I'll go undetected, but she's definitely heading towards me. Oh bollocks. I look round for a means of escape, but I think there's only one corridor heading back to the main reception area and we're both on it. We're heading for collision course whether we like it or not.

Huddling behind a group of dinner-suited men, I have a

quick look round and see an anonymous-looking door. The sort of door you wouldn't notice unless you were on the hunt for somewhere to escape from the love-of-your-life's wife. The sort of door behind which a superhero would strip off to his tights and undies undetected. Gina is bearing down on me, but hasn't spotted me yet. Like a flash of lightning, I whip inside and close the door behind me.

It's some sort of store cupboard. I stand there, frozen to the spot and, for some strange reason, holding my breath. Mentally, I'm trying to work out where Gina would be now. She could be standing right outside. I press my ear against the door, but can't hear anything. In films when people hide in cupboards like this to escape the baddie, there's always a hard floor so that you can hear their footsteps or there's a conveniently large gap under the door so that you can see their shoes as the baddies conduct their futile search, or a strategically placed keyhole through which you can watch their progress. Here it's all plush shag-pile and tightly fitting doors with no keyholes, so that I can't see or hear a bloody thing – just my luck.

I think I'll sit here for a while, take the weight off my poor old puffed-up ankle and bide my time until I can be sure she's gone. I fumble around and find the light and click it on. A low-watt bulb shows me that my cupboard is stacked with champagne. There could be infinitely worse places to hide! Although I daren't risk popping a cork in case it gives me away.

It's cool in here and I sit back on a convenient crate of fizz and rest my weary bones. I could, without too much prompting, lie down and have a lovely little sleep. It must be all the painkillers I've munched. I resolve to try harder with Gil. I can't let this clinging woman and a spurious ex-wife ruin a potentially wonderful relationship. I press my ear to the door again, but it's hopeless. All I can hear is the tinkling of a distant piano and a general hubbub of animated conversation. I can't hear any heavy breathing from my love rival so I guess I'm safe. It's time to face the music and dance again.

I stand up and stretch. If I had a big enough handbag, I could help myself to one of these bottles of fizz for posterity, but of course, I don't. I've got one of those useless little evening purses that's only big enough for holding a lipstick fit for lending to a movie star. With a little smile to myself, I prepare to depart.

I go to turn the door handle, but in the place where a door handle might be useful is just smooth, polished wood exactly the same as the rest of the door. Oh. Just in case I'm going mad, I check again. No. Still no door handle. Bugger. There must be some way out of here. I lean against the door. It's absolutely and very firmly closed. This is ridiculous. It can't be closed. What good is a cupboard if you can't get out of it from the inside? I lean against the door again, this time with a bit of judicious shoulder pressure in the style of Eddie Murphy in *Beverly Hills Cop* movies. All it does is remind me that I have more than my fair share of pavement-eating disabilities.

Oh man! How can this be happening? I'm locked in a cupboard while all manner of wondrous things are going on around me. There's only one thing for it. A bit of pride swallowing and some well-aimed fists. I bang on the door and shout, 'Help!' I might be a bit tentative, because no one comes. And now I wish Gina was lurking round outside, because she might at least let me out.

'Help!' This time I'm definitely louder and more desperate-sounding. 'Helphelphelp!'

Nothing.

'Help! Let me out!'

But there's no one to let me out. Not Gina. Not Katherine. Not even the friendly A-list actress. No one.

'Help!' This is pathetic. There's a party with thousands of people going on just down the hall. If only they'd shut up for a minute, someone might hear me. What about Gil? Surely he must be missing me by now. 'Helphelphelp!'

There's only one thing for it. I must try not to panic, conserve my energy and then try again in a little while. I hope that they all drink like fish and that someone has to come and get these reserve supplies. Ooo. That reminds me. If I'm going to be locked in a cupboard for the entire duration of the Oscars Party then I might as well be comfortable.

Choosing myself a bottle of champagne, I then pop the cork – as close to the door as I can manage, but not close enough to put my own eye out. That really would put the top hat on the evening. I treat myself to a good long swig and position my crate so that if I swing my leg, I repeatedly kick the door with my good foot. Someone is bound to hear this soon. And I settle down, bottle in hand, to wait.

Chapter Seventy-Six

'I don't know where she is,' Gina said wearily. 'I've looked everywhere.'

'She must be here somewhere,' Gil said. The party was getting louder and louder and it was giving him a headache.

'Why? She could have gone home in a huff.'

'Sadie doesn't do that sort of thing.'

'How do you know?' Gina said. It was true, he didn't know. It just didn't seem like the sort of thing Sadie would do. Perhaps she was more upset than he realised. He'd have to explain the Katherine thing to her. He genuinely hadn't seen or heard from her in years. She wasn't another Gina – but Sadie wasn't to know that. He and Katherine had parted reasonably amicably when, tiring of living with a young, hungry producer who was a workaholic, she discovered she had a penchant for a young, hungry actor who was permanently unemployed. She moved out and, such is the way of the world, the young, hungry actor made it big on Broadway and they relocated to the East Coast so that he could work more. Gil wondered, with the benefit of hindsight, if that was when his phobia of actors had started.

Gil hadn't seen Katherine again until tonight. It was disconcerting, but his first wife was a balanced, independently minded woman – she could take care of herself. He wasn't sure that he'd ever been deeply in love with her and she certainly didn't have the power to tug on his heart and his conscience like Gina did.

'Let's do one last circuit,' Gil suggested. 'Can you check the bathroom again?'

'Come on, Gil,' Gina whined. 'My feet hurt. I need more champagne. This is supposed to be a party. Face it, Sadie's gone.'

'Do you really think so?'

'Of course. I wouldn't hang around if you treated me like you do her,' she said.

'That's not what I needed to hear.'

Tavis was doing another round of dishing out hors d'oeuvres. When he saw Gil and Gina, he went to give them a wide berth with the shrimp tempura. 'Hey, Tavis!' Gil shouted and, very warily, Tavis approached them. Gil noted that he took in Gina and the dress. 'Have you seen Sadie anywhere?'

'No,' Tavis said, shaking his head. 'Is she all right?'

'I don't know,' Gil admitted. 'She shot off.' Gil flicked his eyes towards the dress in the hope that Tavis might catch his poorly concealed message. Tavis acknowledged it with a blink. 'Any idea where she might have gone?'

Tavis shook his head. 'No, man, but I'll have a look around. Leave it to me. I owe you one.'

Yes, you do, Gil thought. 'Thanks,' he said and a relieved Tavis hot-footed it out of the reception.

'So now what?' Gil said. 'Do we stand and wait?'

'No way,' Gina said. 'I have an invitation to the *Vanity Fair* party at Morton's.'

'You do?'

Gina shrugged dismissively. 'Well, Noah does. But he went home ages ago. He hates other people's parties.'

Gil couldn't say that he blamed him.

'Take me,' Gina pleaded. 'Take me in your limo. It's the most chic party in town.'

'I don't want to go to another party.'

'You do,' Gina said. 'It's Oscars Night. No one goes home before dawn.'

'Except aging rock stars.'

'And disgruntled girlfriends.'

'Touché.' Gil smiled.

'Come on. Let Sadie cool off. She'll be fine in the morning.'

Gil bit his lip. 'I don't know . . .'

Gina linked her arm through his. 'I'll apologise to her – really I will. Take me to the party. I promise I won't drink too much.'

'You won't?'

'Just a lickle-ickle champagne to relax.'

Gil thought Gina was quite relaxed enough. 'Okay,' he sighed. 'We can go. But just for a short while.'

'I still love you,' Gina said and kissed him softly on the cheek.

'Yeah? Well, let's hope Sadie does too,' he said wryly.

He put his arm round Gina and escorted her towards the door, failing to notice that Tavis was watching them as he did.

Chapter Seventy-Seven

'I can't understand that man,' Tavis said, loading a blini with a precarious heap of caviar. He wasn't even sure he liked caviar, but it was a taste he hoped to acquire in the future. He licked the fishy eggs, grimacing as he did so. 'He's got someone like Sadie in love with him and yet he still seems to be sleazing around with a woman who's supposed to be his ex-wife.'

Tavis and Joe were both relaxing amidst the debris of the grand ballroom and it was the first time they'd seen each other all night. They'd kicked back and loosened off their bow ties and waiter's coats and were now sitting on the floor, backs against the wall, sharing the remains of a bottle of champagne, the leftover canapés and a joint.

'It's no good asking me,' Joe said. 'Heterosexual relationships are a complete mystery to me.'

'And to me.' Tavis shook his head. 'I just don't want to see Sadie get hurt.'

'It may be too late for that.'

'Did you see Saul tonight?' Tavis asked.

'Hmm, hmm,' Joe nodded. 'I wanted to introduce you to him, but he was with his industry cronies and was acting very cool towards me. I don't think he wanted to associate with a lowly waiter. I had such high hopes for this guy, but maybe it won't last.'

'Don't worry.' Tavis punched him playfully. 'You've always got me.'

Joe clapped him on the back. 'What would I do without you, my friend?'

'Get a room-mate who could always pay his rent on time?'

'Think how dull my life would be if I always knew where my next meal was coming from.'

Tavis laughed. 'Come on, buddy. Let's hit the dirt.'

The cleaners had arrived and were starting to make a move towards returning the room to normality.

'I'll walk you to your car,' Joe said.

'I need to go to the bathroom, man,' Tavis said. 'I'll see you back at the apartment.'

'Okay. I'll fix us a nightcap.' Joe waved goodbye.

'Hey, Joe!' Tavis called after him. 'Thanks for making me do this. It was fun.' Though Tavis had begun to realise that anything that involved seeing Sadie, however briefly, could be classed as fun. He wondered where on earth she'd disappeared to as there had been no sign of her for the rest of the night.

'Yeah?' Joe shouted back. 'So is getting a Brazilian wax.' He disappeared through the kitchens towards the service elevator.

Tavis wandered down the corridor. Apart from the steady, quiet movements of the cleaners, there was no one around, which was markedly different from earlier on, when it had resembled feeding time at the zoo.

As he walked towards the men's room, he heard a thumping noise that stopped him in his tracks. It was coming from a nearby door. There it was again! Tavis tip-toed over and heard movement again. Perhaps it was one of the cleaners getting some stock or something. He decided to leave them to it. He'd done enough work for one night and his feet were killing him. Turning away, he headed off down the corridor. *Thump*. The noise came again. He couldn't ignore it. No way.

He marched back towards the door, listening to the thumping again and then turned the handle. As soon as he opened the door, he was met by a terrible scream. The shock made Tavis think he was having a heart attack and there was nothing for it but to scream back.

Sadie was first to stop screaming. She looked at him

335

through wildly blinking eyes. 'What are you doing here?' she said.

'Shouldn't I be the one to ask that?' Tavis said, heart still pounding. 'You're the one in the broom cupboard.'

'You nearly scared me half to death,' she said, and slumped back on a crate of champagne from where it seemed she had just risen.

'How long have you been in here?'

Sadie rubbed her face. 'Too long.' She hiccuped. 'I dodged in here to avoid Gina, one of Gil's wives.'

'He has more than one?'

'Loads,' Sadie said. 'It seemed like a good idea, but then I couldn't get out.'

'He was looking everywhere for you.'

'He was?' She sounded genuinely surprised. 'Is he still here?'

'No,' Tavis said. 'Everyone's gone. I think he thought you'd run out on him.'

'I must go to him,' Sadie said, and when she stood up Tavis realised how much she was swaying. There was one empty bottle of champagne on the floor and another one clutched tightly in Sadie's hand.

'I can see what you've been doing to entertain yourself.'

Sadie stared sightlessly at her bottle. 'I was thirsty.'

'I bet you were,' Tavis said. 'I searched the place,' he admitted, 'but I didn't even see this cupboard.'

'*You* searched the place?'

'Yeah,' Tavis said. 'After Gil left.' He smiled at her. 'I didn't think you were a quitter.' He took the bottle of champagne from her. 'But then again, I didn't think you were dumb enough to get yourself locked in a cupboard.'

'Well, now you know,' Sadie slurred. 'If I'm dumb enough to give up *everything* to come out here after a man who's still in love with his mad wife and has another one that he conveniently forgot to mention, then I'm certainly dumb enough to have a little trouble getting out of a closet.'

'I'll take you home,' Tavis said. 'You need to sleep this off.'

Sadie staggered out of the cupboard and he took her arm as they tottered down the hall. Sadie was limping badly and every few steps she managed to fall off her shoes.

'You're going to hurt yourself,' Tavis said. Besides, it was going to take all night to get out of here if they went at this pace. He bent down. 'Jump on.'

'You are *not* giving me a piggy back,' Sadie said, horrified.

'Jump on,' Tavis instructed again. 'No arguing. I'm your knight in shining armour. I just rescued you from eternity in a dungeon. My trusty steed is in the parking lot. Jump on.'

'You're very stupid,' Sadie said. 'I'm very heavy.'

'I lift weights,' Tavis assured her.

Sadie hitched her skirt and took a run at him, but cannoned into him instead and fell down giggling onto her bruised knees. Champagne was a wonderful anaesthetic, she'd discovered.

'Sadie, you'll have us both on the floor.' Tavis tried to be stern. 'Do it properly. Just a little jump.'

'Hold my bag.' She gave Tavis her little clutch purse, hitched up her skirt again and with an indelicate 'ouff' jumped on his back.

'Jeeze, Sadie,' Tavis puffed. 'You must have heavy bones.'

'I have childbearing hips.'

'Well, some guy will be glad of it one day,' he said, panting heavily. 'Let's go.'

Sadie smacked his rump. 'Giddy up, horsey.'

'You can quit that right now, madam,' Tavis wheezed.

And then he plodded off down the hall, Sadie slumped against his back.

'I don't want to go home,' she said sleepily. 'Take me somewhere, Tavis.'

'I'm taking you home before you do me an injury,' he grunted.

'Take me to the beach. Or to a party,' she said. 'I want to go to a party.'

'You've been to a party.'

'I spent it all stuck in a cupboard, so that doesn't count.'

'I don't have any invitations. I'm the wrong guy.' And that hurt more than he liked to admit. 'You need your A-list boyfriend for that. I'm not even on the list. I'm a wannabe *E*-list.'

'I don't care,' Sadie mumbled. 'I like being with you.'

Tavis was aware that his heart had stopped beating and he didn't think it was because carrying Sadie was like having Dumbo on his back. He swallowed hard. 'I like being with you too,' he said softly.

She leaned her head against his shoulder. 'I wish . . . I wish . . .'

'What do you wish?'

'Oh, I don't know,' Sadie sighed. 'I just wish things were different.'

Tavis wished with all his heart that things were different too. He wished that he were rich. He wished that he were famous. He wished that Sadie was in love with him. And he wished wholeheartedly that he was the sort of man who could fall head over heels in love with her.

Chapter Seventy-Eight

Daniella is sitting on the terrace in her garden. She's wearing sunglasses and crunching Kashi GoLean and looking as if she's regretting that it's so loud.

I pad out to join her.

'Ooo,' she says, lifting her head gingerly. 'Are we the colour of Spackle because we have a hangover?'

'We are,' I say, sitting down next to her and trying to minimise the scrape of chair on paving stones. 'Are we wincing at our breakfast cereal because we have a hangover too?'

'We are,' Daniella says and abandons her spoon which clunks on the table and we both shudder in unison.

'So what did you get up to last night?' I ask. 'And with whom?'

'I stayed at home and got drunk,' she says. 'Alone. At least you had fun getting wasted.'

'No,' I say. 'I sat in a cupboard alone – except for several crates of champagne.'

'Which you felt moved to sample?'

I shrug. 'I had nothing else to do.'

We watch the sun shine for a bit, which sort of hurts and we watch some birds being relentlessly chirpy. A few butterflies flit dizzily among the flowers. I cover my sunglasses with my hands. There are times when you can really grow to dislike wildlife.

'Why did you spend Oscars Night in a cupboard?'

'I was avoiding Gina.'

'With a certain degree of success by the sound of it,' my friend notes.

'With a little too much success,' I agree. 'Tavis had to rescue me.'

'Tavis? What was he doing there?'

'He was a waiter at the party.'

'That guy's becoming a regular feature.'

'Isn't he.'

'And where was Gil at this point?'

'I don't know,' I say. I can't cope with revealing to Daniella that Gil seems to have a short memory when it comes to marriages. I need to get my own head round it first. 'I tried to call him this morning but his phone goes straight to voicemail.'

'They're never around when you need them.' Daniella's moan sounds particularly heartfelt.

'If it wasn't for Tavis, I could have spent my entire life in that cupboard.'

'Then it is your duty to show him that you're eternally grateful.'

I shudder again when I think of Tavis lugging me through the maze of corridors on his back until we reached his car. 'I tried to,' I say.

Daniella lowers her sunglasses. 'Really?'

'He wasn't interested.'

'Did you get your baps out?'

I lower my own sunglasses. 'What sort of a question is that?'

'A very valid one.'

'No,' I say, trying to sound indignant. But I'm mainly miffed because I didn't think of it. After the 'Katherine' revelation, I don't think a revenge shag would have been completely beyond the pale. I had a lucky escape because my chosen target deemed it out of the question. In the cold light of day, I'm rather relieved that Tavis is gay. 'I might have been drunk, but I was a bit more subtle than that.'

'And?'

'Tavis doesn't do girl, remember?'

'Do you think you're in love with him?'

'I don't know,' I say, trying to avoid shaking my head.

'I'm very confused. I love Gil – really I do, but Tavis makes me feel . . .'

'Horny?'

I tut. 'Special.'

'Horny's the same as special.'

I sip my freshly squeezed orange juice and all my taste buds curl up in horror. 'It doesn't even come close.'

'Wow,' she says thoughtfully. 'One woman in love with two men. Isn't *that* the sweetest taboo?'

'Yes,' I say. 'It's a lovely idea and would certainly make a change from the usual arrangement, but the truth of the matter is that I'm currently struggling to hold onto one in the face of mounting competition, and the other one isn't interested in women at all.'

'*Mounting* competition?' Daniella quizzes me. 'Is that an English joke?'

'No,' I admit. 'Gil has two ex-wives.'

'Just two?' Daniella says. 'I'd say that was a miracle in this town.'

'Well, it's more than enough for me to contend with.'

Daniella sighs wearily. 'I hate men,' she says. 'All of them. Short ones, fat ones, tall ones, slim ones, rich ones, poor ones. I even hate gay ones.'

'This has something to do with the Mad Movie Mogul?'

'I met his wife yesterday.'

'God, Daniella, I'm sorry. I complete forgot to ask about it.'

'You did have more pressing problems.' My friend waves away my concern.

'It went badly?'

'In a way,' Daniella says. 'She is a very nice woman. I liked her.'

'But she didn't like you?'

'I don't know. She was fine – very civil. I don't know if I could have done that in her position.' Daniella fiddles with her nails and stares off into the garden. 'She told me a lot of home truths, Sadie. Things that I didn't want to hear.'

I sigh. Why are relationships always so complicated? I

341

think I'm going to get a cat and possibly a budgie and grow old and mad alone.

'She left him,' Daniella continues. 'Months ago – for someone else. And he never said a word. He just carried on letting me think they were just still playing Happy Families.'

'Perhaps he's keeping his options open.'

'I think he's been doing that for a long time.' She looks at me ruefully. 'There are several other "Daniellas" dotted around the place.'

'His wife told you?'

Daniella nods.

'She could be lying.'

'I don't think so.' Daniella puts her head in her hands. 'I feel such a fool. Why did I think if he was being unfaithful to his wife, he would ever be faithful to me?'

I'm afraid that I don't have an answer for that. If he's been stringing her along for ten years then I'm not sure that a few more months makes a lot of difference. 'What are you going to do?'

'I'm not sure yet,' she says. 'He called me several times last night and left messages, but I didn't answer.'

'I guess if he's just got rid of one wife, he won't be in a tearing hurry to take another.'

Despite the perfect Californian climate, I feel a little chill trickle through my blood. I wonder what lessons I can learn from this for my own relationship.

'In my next life,' Daniella announces, 'I'm going to come back as a man – preferably a stinking rich, extremely handsome and well-hung one – and wreak havoc on the female population.'

At the moment, I think that sounds like a damn fine idea.

Chapter Seventy-Nine

Tavis's agent never called him. He never returned his calls either. Which was pretty much par for the course for struggling actors in this town. It was what he had come to expect.

Now this was very mystifying. Not only had his agent called, but he'd gone as far as inviting Tavis into his office – for a discussion. Tavis hadn't been into his agent's office in two years, maybe more. They'd never exchanged more than three sentences. They'd certainly never had a 'discussion'. He was probably going to get fired. Now that Doctor Robert was dead and buried and wasn't imminently looking like he was going to be – by some miracle of TV – resurrected and there was nothing else looming on the horizon, it could well be that he had become surplus to the agency's requirements. He was about to find out.

The offices were plush – all palm trees in chrome pots and leather sofas – and were halfway up a high-show, high-rise building on Wilshire Boulevard. Tavis was glad he'd spruced up. His agent's assistant had offered him coffee and he'd accepted, but he was now too nervous to drink it and every time he picked the cup up it rattled in the saucer. Tavis decided to abandon the coffee and pretend to read the trades instead. He picked up the *Hollywood Reporter* and flicked through the pages as if he was riveted by the snippets of industry news inside, even though he'd read them all before. He was glad that he'd had a distraction this morning; it had prevented him from thinking about Sadie and how cute she looked when she was drunk.

'Hey, Tavis!' His agent bowled out of his office. He was a short, fat Jewish man in his late fifties sporting more gold than Tiffany's window. Taking Tavis's hand, he pumped it until all his fingers had gone numb. 'I haven't seen you in a long time,' his agent growled. 'You're always too busy to come and see me.'

Tavis didn't like to point out that he hadn't ever been asked.

'You're like a fine wine,' the agent continued to bark. 'You get better-looking every year.'

Tavis wasn't sure that he was even talking to the right person.

'I won't beat about the bush . . .' the agent said next.

That was it. He was going to be fired. He knew it.

'Toby Portman called.'

The Toby Portman?

'He said you did some good work for him.'

I got my ass out for him, Tavis wanted to say. And wiggled it about a bit. I was a butt double in a sex scene. It wasn't good work. 'Yeah?' he said aloud.

'Good work, bad fee. I got my cut.' The agent shrugged at the infinitesimal amount. It had paid Tavis's rent for a month. 'He liked you.'

'He did?'

'He's casting for a new movie. Big budget. Great story. He wants you to read for the lead.'

Tavis wanted to lie on the floor and kiss his agent's feet. 'Gimme the script,' the man said to his assistant. She handed it over and the agent slapped it into Tavis's hand.

'Do good and the part's yours,' he said brusquely.

Tavis was speechless. He knew he ought to say something, but he didn't know what.

The agent smiled. His teeth were like little razors. 'You're on your way, kid.' He slapped him on the back as if they were long-lost friends. 'This is the big break I've been waiting for.'

You've been waiting for? Tavis managed to find his

breath long enough to speak. 'Do you have any advice for me?'

'Yeah,' the agent said. He was already walking away. 'Don't fuck up.'

Chapter Eighty

Gil and I aren't talking. Well, not really. I'm still nursing my wounds – emotional and physical – and we've driven out to Marina del Rey for a barbecue at his friend Steve Bernard's house in a sort of strained silence. He is mad at me for getting locked in a cupboard, I think. I'm mad at him for having more than one wife and because he went off to another swanky party with Gina – the second Mrs McGann – leaving me to a fate that could have been worse than death – or even death. How long could you survive in a cupboard without air or food and only champagne for sustenance? It was a good job that Tavis came along when he did. I don't think the fact that I've mentioned this several times has gone down too well either. When I stopped saying 'Tavis this . . .' and 'Tavis that . . .' at the beginning of every sentence, the conversation sort of petered out.

Marina del Rey is a calm, suburban version of LA just south of Venice Beach and as far away from the wackiness of it as humanly possible. In Marina del Rey there are fewer people with collagen-enhanced lips or pneumatic chests and more families in evidence – every driveway has a basketball hoop and an obligatory abandoned bike or skateboard. It's generally cooler, but not in the trendy sense of the word. There's a lovely harbour chockful of bobbing yachts and ostentatious motor cruisers, with areas named to evoke the romanticism of the South Seas – Tahiti Way, Bora Bora Way, et cetera – and why not? It has a jaunty seaside air about it, rather like Bournemouth, but without the chip shops and pensioners.

Steve lives in a large white detached house close to the marina, but not right on it. I'm in the kitchen with Sarah, Steve's lovely wife, preparing salad. She's a good old-fashioned English girl – straight-talking, down-to-earth and I can't help wondering how she copes with some of the worst excesses of LA. By not getting involved in them, I suspect.

'Gil's nice,' Sarah says nonchalantly, confirming my suspicion that this is intended as some sort of peace summit with the idyll of family life on full display. I don't need convincing of this, but I rather think that Gil does. 'There aren't many men like him in this town.'

'I don't think there are many men like him anywhere,' I agree. And I guess that was part of the attraction, no matter how many wives he's had or how terrified he is of further commitment. I look out of the window and I still get a rush when I see him. But is a rush enough? Is love when someone makes you go all giddy every time you see them, or is love when you have common ground and aims in life and the ability to make each other laugh and not too many ex-wives running around?

Outside, the children are creating havoc and Sarah's not the slightest bit concerned. And this is what I want. I want cosy domesticity. I want my own backyard to barbecue in. I want a few freckle-faced kids to nag and a good solid and steady husband to provide for me while I spend my days giving my children quality time and passing off shop-bought cakes as my own. I am not living the life that I want – my enforced career break has made me realise that this is not what I'm destined to do. I want babies – not desperately, not urgently and not with the wrong man. My biological clock isn't battering my door down, but I know that this is definitely on my agenda and I appreciate this is not a fashionable thing to say unless, of course, you are Victoria Beckham, Kate Moss or Liz Hurley.

Gil and Steve are outside too. They're doing men things with raw steak and the barbecue, which is good because it means that I can avoid having to not talk to Gil for a bit longer. I look at Gil, trying to see him objectively, and wonder if he might be The One.

'She's lovely,' Steve said in a conspiratorial whisper. 'Why haven't you got down on one knee and proposed before now?'

Steve's children Leila and Tom were digging in the borders with their bare hands. 'Don't pull up the flowers,' Steve instructed.

'They're not flowers, Daddy. They're weeds,' came the reply.

'Well, ask your mother then.' Steve slurped his beer.

'I don't know her well enough yet,' Gil said.

'To do what?' Why was it impossible to hold parents' attention when their offspring were around.

'Marry her!' Gil spun round towards the kitchen, checking that he hadn't spoken too loudly, but Sadie and Sarah were engrossed in conversation. Probably ripping men as well as the lettuce to shreds. 'To marry her,' he repeated more quietly.

'What do you need to know?' Steve prodded the coals with something approaching proficiency. 'Look at her. She's gorgeous. She's got curves everywhere.'

'I'm fully aware where she's got curves.' It was just that he hadn't been able to get his hands on them yet.

'I don't think you are, my friend,' Steve said. 'You're too used to seeing these child-women movie stars with the bodies of thirteen-year-old girls. Sadie is all woman.'

Did his friend think he hadn't noticed that? 'I don't think she'd have me even if I did propose,' Gil said mournfully.

Steve looked up for an explanation.

'She met Katherine yesterday,' he said.

'Who is?'

'The first Mrs McGann.'

'And this was a problem?'

'Only because Sadie didn't know there were multiple Mrs McGanns.'

'Ah.'

Gil shook his head. 'I can't seem to get anything right with Sadie.'

'Not mentioning previous wives is a bit remiss.'

'I'm fully aware of that too.' Steve stared at him. 'Now,' Gil admitted.

'Tom, don't throw charcoal briquettes at your sister. Mummy will be cross.'

'How do you do this?' Gil said.

'A few minutes either side,' Steve said. 'Maybe a little piquant sauce.'

'Not the steak,' Gil sighed. 'This.' He looked at the kids, the house, the garden. 'The whole domestic thing. I can't even get the wife part right. And if Sadie and I get together she'll want the whole nine yards.'

'And what do you want?'

'I don't know,' Gil said. 'An uncomplicated life.'

'Hey,' Steve said. 'Let's introduce a little realism here.' He brandished his barbecue fork in Gil's direction. 'I want a Ferrari Testarossa and fifty million dollars in the bank, but it doesn't mean I'll get it. I drive an SUV on the weekends because I can fit four bikes on the back, and eat Big Macs more frequently than I'd like. We all have to compromise. There are benefits.'

'Like what?'

'Man, you'll never know till you have your own kids. Everyone else's kids look like monsters.' Steve was certainly right there. Only a few of his friends had kids and Gil was terrified of them all. 'When they're your own, you think it's cute. Ever got a bogie out of a kid's nose?'

'Strangely enough . . . no.'

'It seems such a gross thing to do when you watch some other parent doing it. When it's your own kid, you just get right in there and root around. I can't explain that. It defies logic. It must be a biological thing.'

'And this is what I have to look forward to?'

'You'll love it. Believe me.'

Gil lowered his voice. 'I'm frightened of it, Steve. Of the whole thing. Suppose I mess up?'

'That's the fun of it. No handbook. No shooting script.

You just make it up as you go along. There's no right or wrong. You just do your best.'

'I know how I felt when my parents split,' Gil said. 'I couldn't do that to anyone else.'

'That's why you need a sensible wife and not one of the Hollywood flakes that you like to date. You spend too much of your life in La-La Land – you need to get a grip on a real woman. Real life doesn't begin until you become a family man; everything else until then is just play-acting.'

Gil's gaze wandered over to the two children. The thought of parental responsibilities looming large on his horizon made him want to shudder.

'Don't you look at those two and think how adorable they are?' Steve asked.

'Er . . .' Tom had hold of his sister by the throat. 'I have no idea what to do with children.'

'You're a natural,' Steve assured him. 'You just need to practise.'

'Don't make me do bogies!'

'Quit worrying. Hey, kids!' Steve shouted. 'Come and talk to Uncle Gil.' Tom, quite sensibly Gil thought, made a run for it. Leila wasn't quick enough and Steve grabbed her, pushing his reluctant daughter towards an equally reluctant Gil.

'Hi,' Gil said.

'Hi,' Leila replied and sat down next to him.

'Tell Uncle Gil how old you are,' Steve encouraged her.

'Twenty-seven,' Leila said.

'No, honey,' Steve said. 'How old you *are*. Not how old you'd like to be.'

'I'm six,' Leila said. 'Do you want to play with My Pretty Pony?' She shoved a manky, moth-eaten pink horse towards him.

'No,' Gil said.

Leila looked desperately at her father. 'Do I have to do this?'

'Honey-kinney. You've been looking forward to seeing Uncle Gil all day.'

Leila huffed. 'What do you know about Glitter Girls?'

'Nothing,' Gil said. 'What do you know about producing a movie?'

'Nothing.'

Gil looked at his friend for help.

'Gil, you're just not trying,' Steve said with an exasperated puff.

'Can I go now?' Leila said.

'Sure.' Steve waved her away with his barbecue fork.

Leila wandered off, looking for some torture to inflict on her brother. 'Just don't maim your brother,' he shouted after her. 'There.' Steve grinned at Gil. 'That wasn't so bad, was it?'

'Isn't that steak ready yet?' Gil said.

I read in the *National Enquirer* that Kylie Minogue has been dumped again. If Kylie can't keep a boyfriend then what hope is there for me? She is rich, famous, stunningly beautiful and has one of the most desirable posteriors in the world – none of which can be said for me. I have other assets, it's true – but they are more subtly appreciated.

Why is it that some women get men running after them and others, despite their best efforts, just don't? I'm always astounded at these stories of married men from Basingstoke leaving their comfortable lives and their comfortable wives and children to travel across the world and set up home with dumpy blondes from Kansas who've beguiled them over the Internet. I once had trouble getting a bloke to come three stops on the Tube for a free meal and the promise of an exotic dessert. I'm going wrong somewhere. Perhaps Kylie and I just keep picking the wrong guys.

We're heading for home after a rather subdued barbecue which ended abruptly when Steve's children set fire to the pergola in the garden. When we'd helped reduce the flames to a mere smoulder and both of the children had been sent to bed, we thought it best to leave. If Sarah and Steve were hoping to give us a display of how idyllic family life could be in order to convince us to settle down together then it failed miserably. Gil is wearing more ketchup than is desirable in someone over five years old and I can tell that he's not comfortable with it. He was terrified of the children and it wasn't simply to do with their proficiency with barbecue lighter fuel. Perhaps this whole thing with Gina is merely a way of avoiding getting his hands dirty in real life. It was as if a little cupboard door opened inside of him, and I got a brief glimpse of what really might be hidden there.

I look over at him and think that I love him, but I don't know if love is just another illusion. I remember the summers at home being long and hot, but the meteorologists insist that it's all just an illusion – a false belief, a misconstrued hope that we might one day return to that Utopian state. According to records, the summers were always cold and damp and we always wore jumpers in July.

If life is like a movie, then I want to be in a better one than this. I want one where the gal gets her guy, and there's a great tune and they gallop off into the sunset. But they don't make 'em like that any more, do they? The Golden Age of cinema has long gone. And it makes me think that the Golden Age of everything else has disappeared too – including relationships.

I wish things were like they were in the 1950s when you married the first bloke you snogged, worked in a shop until you got pregnant and then gave up work and looked after children and cooked roast dinners and apple pies for the rest of your life. There was no choice about whether to have children or not, or whether you wanted a career and family. The rules were laid down and you just accepted them. You didn't consider juggling a dozen different men and they didn't juggle you.

I've decided that too much choice can be a very dangerous thing – and Americans thrive on choice. I'm back to the beverage thing again – if there are forty-two different choices, you end up completely bemused and can never decide quite what you want. You spend the entire time you're drinking it feeling dissatisfied and wishing you'd got what your neighbour picked. It's the same with men.

By the time you've dated loads of men, you realise that none of them are perfect and end up wanting the best bit of each one all lumped together. Or wanting what your neighbour has. Perhaps they feel the same about women too.

'What?' Gil says even though I haven't spoken.

'This isn't going anywhere, is it?'

'What do you mean?'

'Our relationship. It's a non-starter.'

Gil takes my hand. 'We've had some problems,' he says. 'Nothing we can't get over.' He looks at me with pleading eyes. 'I'm getting it all sorted. With Gina, and everything. Don't give up on us now.'

But I can't help but wonder whether it's all the drama that's keeping us together. If that were to end, wouldn't we then have to face the real differences in our lives, our aspirations and our desires for the future?

'Come and stay with me tonight.' Gil softly squeezes my fingers.

And I think of his pink room and his pink silk sofa and his pink sheets and I can't face it. I think of him staying in a hotel room that looks like the inside of a carton of strawberry ice cream because he cannot cut the ties to his wife. 'Not tonight,' I say.

'Can I ask you something, Sadie?' Gil says.

I turn to him and his face is grim. 'Anything.'

'I need to know this.' His expression is bleak. 'Is there something going on between you and Tavis?'

'Tavis?' I say in a soap opera-style shriek. This is beyond belief. Instead of being pleased that my friend was there to get me out of the cupboard of death, Gil is putting two and two together and coming up with several more than it should be. If he thinks he's found the moral high ground in this situation, then he's reading from the wrong map! 'I don't think you're in a position to ask that, Mr *Two Wives* McGann.'

Gil's lips tighten and he descends into a sulking silence. He turns his concentration back to the road and raises the volume on his CD player.

I, in the meantime, am whatever the female equivalent is of impotent with rage. Infertile with rage. If Gil is disgruntled then I think I'm entitled to be not very gruntled either.

I can't believe this. Despite my patience while Gil tries to disentangle himself emotionally and physically from his second wife, he's now pushing our problems on to me by accusing me of having an affair with a gay man. If this was a film, the audience would be guffawing by now. But I'm not. I'm slap bang in the middle of it and can't see the funny side at all. I don't do make-believe. Despite my dreams of happy ever after, I am firmly placed in the real world. And I cannot in the face of all the evidence to the contrary convince myself that this relationship is working.

Chapter Eighty-One

Even the ratty old spider plant seems to have perked up. Bay and Min certainly have. And all this, of course, is due to the appearance of Tavis.

He's lounging on the edge of my desk, looking all sort of tousled in a way that says he spent hours getting like that. 'I called you last night,' he says.

'I know.' I'm tired. Bone tired. And I can't seem to perk up even though my favourite friend and rescuer has bowled up unexpectedly in my office. I say 'my' office with a certain amount of largesse. Bay announced this morning that the IRS had phoned to ask about her employing illegal aliens and seeing as I am one and she is employing me, she's feeling very jittery. She says she doesn't want to let me go, but may have to before she has a visit from the men in black – the IRS ones, not the Will Smith ones.

To add to it, Delores steadfastly refused to budge out of Daniella's drive this morning for reasons best known to herself. If there's something seriously wrong with her, other than a severe case of lassitude, I might not be able to afford to fix her. I can tell already that this is not going to count as one of my better days. I don't think I can cope if both the men and the machinery in my life are going to give me grief. I want to lay my head down on my desk and pretend that none of it is really happening. If I'm soon to be without a man, without a job and without a car, what is there to keep me here? I've already discounted the wall-to-wall warm weather. 'I got your message,' I say to Tavis. 'So what's the good news?'

He's clearly beside himself with glee. 'Sadie.' He lowers

his voice. I don't know why because both Bay and Min have ultra-sensitive listening devices where their ears should be and don't miss a trick. 'I have an audition,' he says. 'A great one. This could be my big break. My agent says if I don't fuck it up, the lead could be mine.'

'Fantastic,' I say, but Tavis can tell that it's not coming from my heart but from a much more shallow and forced place just under my skin.

'This is what I've waited for, Sadie,' he continues, trying to elicit some enthusiasm from me. 'One day all of my body could be famous – not just my butt.'

'I'm pleased for you,' I say. 'Really I am.'

'But?'

'There aren't any buts, Tavis. I'm delighted.'

'You don't look delighted.'

'I am. I just haven't the energy to jump up and down for you.'

'Have you fully recovered from your cupboard experience?'

I can feel myself flush a fetching shade of beetroot. 'Yes,' I say. 'Thanks again for coming to my rescue. This role isn't for a superhero, is it? You'd be perfect.'

'No, it isn't. It's for a sexy, romantic heart-throb.'

He'd still be perfect, but I don't tell him that. Bay and Min slaver onto the carpet.

'So what's wrong?'

'Man trouble,' I say. Bay and Min turn away – I've been bending their ears all morning about my relationship with Gil and at a guess I'd say they'd heard enough.

'Oh, Sadie . . .' Tavis's smile fades.

'It's nothing.' I can feel myself filling up. 'I'm just not sure that Gil and I are destined to be together.' I wave his concern away.

'He doesn't treat you right,' my friend says.

'Well . . .' I force a smile. 'That's a man's prerogative, isn't it?'

'I'd like to give that guy a piece of my mind,' Tavis says darkly.

I can't help but smile, and this time there's nothing

forced about it. Tavis will make a lovely romantic hero. I do hope he gets the part.

Tavis glances at the clock on the wall. 'I'd better go,' he says, swinging his long legs off my desk and making Bay and Min go all unnecessary again. 'Don't want to keep them waiting.'

'Good luck or break a leg,' I offer. 'Whatever it is you actor-types say.'

'Good luck is fine,' Tavis says.

'Call me later,' I instruct. 'Tell me how it went.'

'I will,' he promises as he heads out of the door.

I watch his retreating back and my heart goes out to him. Funny. I feel very protective of him and I wish that it was me suffering under pressure rather than him.

'Hey!' I shout after him. 'I'll be thinking of you.'

Tavis smiles bashfully and my insides melt. If he does that in the audition they'll hand over the contract there and then. 'Thanks.'

He goes to leave again and suddenly I can't bear to watch him walk away. I'm feeling very emotional and I want this to be his big breakthrough. He deserves to do well and I truly wish him all the luck in the world.

'Hey!' I yell. 'You didn't tell me what the film was called!'

My handsome friend turns and gives me a wave. '*The One That Got Away*,' he calls out.

And as my heart sinks to my boots I realise that he is, indeed, going to need all the luck in the world.

Chapter Eighty-Two

Tavis was sitting in a small reception area in the Cecil B. De Mille Building, one of the famous office blocks at Paramount Studios. It was halfway down Paramount Plaza, an immaculate palm-tree-lined boulevard that sliced through the tall, pale pink administration buildings.

It was making all the hairs on the back of his neck stand up just being here. How could anyone not get a buzz out of being on a movie lot? The closest he'd come to the inside of these hallowed halls so far was picking up free tickets for the recording of sitcoms from the famous Bronson Gate.

Paramount was the first studio in Hollywood and the only one left today after all the others had fled to the outer reaches of Burbank and Culver City. Its list of films read like the complete history of Hollywood – from the days of classic silent films, through to *Sunset Boulevard* and *Star Trek – Nemesis*. All had started life on this sprawling lot. Paramount was the place where you could still smell the glory days of cinema, feel the history in its walls, walk the sidewalks that had been trodden before by Rudolph Valentino, Mae West, Marlene Dietrich, Gloria Swanson, Gary Cooper, Cary Grant – the list was endless. And it was still the place where wannabe movie stars flocked today. Tavis worried at his lip and wondered was it possible to die of anticipation, longing and ambition. He was sure if they kept him waiting for too long he'd have a heart attack.

Despite the icy blast of air-conditioning his palms were damp with perspiration. He'd heard that on an average day an average man secreted – on average – two and a half quarts of sweat. But this wasn't an average day and, at the moment, he didn't feel like an average man. He felt like a star waiting for his supernova. This was the stuff that dreams were made of and it had been his dream for as long as he could remember. Success was so close that he could taste it, smell it, feel it. It was an inch beyond his grasp.

Tavis wasn't entirely sure where the acting bug had come from, but it had bitten him hard and wouldn't let go. If anyone asked him to explain the need it created inside him, he couldn't. It was something that only other actors could understand. If he wasn't acting, he wasn't living. Without a role to run with, he felt as if he was only half existing.

It had been a long and bumpy road, but when everyone else had doubted him, he'd hung in there. Now he, out of all the struggling and equally talented actors in this town, had his big chance waiting just behind that very plain and innocuous-looking door ahead of him.

He'd never really discussed it with Sadie, but he felt that she understood. She, above anyone, seemed to know where he was coming from. And if the truth was known, he was starting to feel that he was only half existing when he was away from her too. For someone like him, this was a terrifying thought. It was good to know that there was someone waiting for him, back in the real world, someone who was a good friend, someone who was rooting for him, someone who loved him unconditionally. *Loved?* Tavis halted on the word. *Loved!* Whoa!

Just then, the plain and innocuous-looking door opened and Tavis found himself staring at a familiar face.

'Hi.'

'Hi,' Tavis said. It was Toby Portman, the director who'd recommended him for the role. Tavis was tongue-tied and it wasn't a great time to be tongue-tied.

Toby clasped his hand, grinning broadly. 'How are you doing?'

'Fine,' Tavis breathed. 'Just fine.'

'This is going to be a great movie,' Toby said effusively. 'You've had time to look at the script?'

'Yeah,' Tavis said. 'I loved it.' That wasn't strictly true. It was a bit sugar schmaltzy for his taste, but it was destined to be a big box-office blockbuster and that was all that mattered.

'Come on in,' the director said. 'Meet the producer. I don't think you know him, but he's followed your work closely and he's a big fan of yours.'

'All right,' Tavis said. That couldn't hurt. He just hoped it wasn't the usual Hollywood bullshit.

Tavis followed the director through the door. The door that could lead to stardom. The door that could change his life.

As he entered the office, he did a wide-eyed blink as a feeling of horror flooded through him.

'Hi,' the producer said calmly.

Not only did Tavis know him, he also realised a big, steaming load had just been dumped on him.

'Gil,' Tavis said with a nod and sat down opposite him. The atmosphere in the room grew decidedly chilly.

'You two guys know each other?' Toby said, mildly perplexed.

'Yes,' Gil said. 'We have a mutual acquaintance.' The subtext was obvious. What Gil really meant was, this guy wants to get jiggy with my girlfriend.

Tavis could almost smile – so *that's* what this was about. Gil viewed him as competition. Gil, the hot-shot producer, was jealous of him – the out-of-work actor. If he wasn't just about to be auditioned by him for the role of his life, this would have been laughable. Didn't he realise that Sadie had eyes for one man only? This guy might be a whizz at putting a movie together, but he was a non-starter when it came to women. Tavis grinned to himself. Like he'd know!

'Is something amusing you, Mr Jones?' Gil said frostily.

'No.' That sure wiped the smile off his face. Gil had clearly got him here just to exact some kind of sadistic revenge. Dangle the juicy carrot and then snatch it away. 'I'm sorry.'

'Perhaps you'd like to read for us.'

Tavis nodded. His mouth was as dry as the Mojave Desert. His agent's words reverberated in his head. *Don't fuck up! Don't fuck up! Don't fuck up!*

'I'll feed you the lines,' Toby Portman said, his glance shifting from man to man. 'We'll take it from page one hundred. The restaurant scene.'

'I got it,' Tavis said, flicking through the script and sounding a lot more nervous than he would have liked.

Gil made a steeple with his hands and leaned on his desk, staring at Tavis.

'I'll take it from the top.' Toby Portman started to read. *'I know that you love her. Do you think I'm blind?'*

Oh no. This was a great way to start. Tavis glanced nervously at Gil. Maybe he should ask for another section; this just seemed too loaded. But then that would be unprofessional and he was here to show that he was up to the job. Gil would know that. He was professional too. Wasn't he? The producer's face was impassive as he watched and listened. *'No. You should know better.'*

'You're always there for her. Just at the right time.'

'Maybe you should try it yourself.'

'Or maybe you should try butting out.'

'S . . . Christie and I go back a long way.' My God, he'd nearly said Sadie. Tavis licked his lips. *'We're friends, man. Nothing more. Romantically, she doesn't know I exist.'* The words were starting to stick in his throat. *'Maybe you should look after her better.'*

'Or what?'

Gil's face was darkening by the minute, but his expression remained unmoved. Tavis hesitated.

Toby glanced up. 'You okay?'

Tavis nodded.

'I'll take over,' Gil said and he slowly turned the pages until he reached the appropriate scene. He looked levelly at Tavis. *'I want you out of her life. I don't care how you do it. I never want **Christie** to see you again.'*

Tavis could hear his own heartbeat. 'I can't do that,' he said evenly.

Toby Portman flicked frantically through his pages. 'Is that in the script?'

Gil tossed his script to one side. 'I've heard enough,' he said. 'Thanks for coming.' He stood up to indicate that the reading was over.

Toby Portman glanced at the producer, surprised. 'We're finished?'

'I think so,' Gil said firmly.

It was clear to Tavis that he was being dismissed. This was so unfair. It was so unfair as to be cruel. Gil had to know the situation between him and Sadie. He couldn't take that out on him in an audition. This was his life. His one big chance. He'd played it nothing but straight with Sadie while Gil had been stringing her along since the moment she'd landed in LA.

Tavis stood up. Bile was rising in his throat. He should be able to take this – he'd stood in enough lines for hours on end at open castings that had ended in abrupt dismissal because his eyes were the wrong colour or he was an inch too short. He should be able to take it. Rejection was a part of the job. If you can't take the heat, he told himself, you shouldn't be in the goddamn kitchen. He could feel his hands bunching into fists. He tried to take his mind back to his acting classes, get his breath and his temper under control. The difference was, this time the rejection wasn't because he was the wrong shape, size or colour – it was personal. It was because this man suspected, quite wrongly, that he was in love with Sadie.

'This is unprofessional, man,' Tavis said to Gil, despite all his best instincts telling him not to.

'Thank you for your opinion, Mr Jones,' Gil said coolly. 'Now get out.'

Toby Portman was searching furiously through his script. Tavis walked towards the door and then thought better of it. He wheeled on Gil.

'You treat her like shit,' he said. 'You don't deserve her. What the hell are you playing at?'

'That is none of your business!'

'You've made it my business,' Tavis said.

'Get out of here,' Gil repeated. 'Then get out of my life and out of Sadie's life.'

Tavis squared up to the producer. 'Make me!'

Toby Portman scratched his head. 'What page are we on?'

Gil lunged towards Tavis and grabbed him by the shirt.

'She is one hell of a woman,' Tavis said. 'And if you can't see that, I certainly can.' Gil was shaking him.

'Improvisation,' the director shouted. 'This is great. Keep going!'

Tavis swung Gil round by the lapels of his jacket while the producer flailed at him. Tavis drew back his arm. He hadn't punched anyone since kindergarten and it wasn't a great idea to resume his pugilist career on movie producers, but he was too far in now. 'What are you afraid of, Gil? You're hanging onto that drunken wife of yours like a security blanket. Keep doing that and you'll lose her anyway.'

Gil stopped in his tracks. 'You're right.'

Tavis dropped his arm.

Gil leaned back on his desk, breathing heavily. 'You're right.' He put his head in his hands. 'You're absolutely right,' he said, looking directly at Tavis. He wiped his hand across his mouth. 'But I'll still make sure that you never work in this town again.'

Tavis threw down his script and headed for the door.

As he reached it, Gil shouted to him. 'Tavis,' he said, 'I'm not an idiot. I can tell that you love Sadie too. I might be hiding behind my wife, but what's your excuse?'

Without answering Tavis marched out of the door and slammed it behind him. The row of assistants stared up as he stomped out of the office.

Gil was still leaning against the desk, but his composure was slowly returning.

'That wasn't improvisation, was it?' Toby Portman asked tentatively.

'No,' Gil said. 'It wasn't.'

'He's damn good though.'

363

'Yes.'

'He would have been perfect for the part,' Toby said.

'Yes,' Gil said with a humourless laugh. 'He would have been.'

Outside in the sunshine, Tavis leaned against the wall of the Cecil B. De Mille building, panting and snorting like some knackered old bull. The sun was still shining. The palm trees were still waving in the breeze, but something inside him somewhere had shifted. Jeeze, what was he thinking of? He'd nearly punched a Hollywood producer. A man who had the power to make the rest of his life a misery. If that wasn't a fuck-up, he didn't know what was.

Tavis shook his head, trying to dislodge the images replaying in his brain. It was only sheer willpower that kept him from falling to his knees in despair. What on earth was he thinking of? He put his hands over his eyes. Sadie. Quite simply, Sadie.

Chapter Eighty-Three

Gil waited in the porch outside Daniella's house. He hoped Sadie had forgiven him, because he felt he'd done enough fighting for today. Maybe he should go and get a vitamin shot to give him a much-needed boost of energy.

Just as he was thinking of ringing the bell again, Daniella opened the door.

'Hey, Daniella,' Gil said.

'Gil – hi. Come on in.' Daniella stood aside while he went into her home.

There was a mess of papers strewn all over the kitchen table, almost obliterating a well-worn laptop. 'I'm interrupting your work,' Gil said.

'No, not at all.' Daniella shook her head. 'I'm glad of the break. I have writer's block,' she explained. 'I get it at least five times a day and it can only be cured by an excess of coffee and calories. Want some?'

'Sure.' Gil nodded and wandered over to the table. He liked Daniella. She seemed sweet and uncomplicated – but then he was also the worst judge of women he knew.

The pages of a script with scribbles all over them were piled high. He slipped into her seat.

Daniella poured the coffee. 'Cream and sugar?'

'Black's good,' he said distractedly as, out of habit, he scanned the pages.

'You look like you need this,' Sadie's friend remarked as she passed him the coffee.

'I'm not having a great day,' Gil said. He didn't feel like going into the details of his fight with Sadie and his subsequent fight with Tavis.

'Sadie said you guys had a fight,' Daniella said.

Gil's head snapped up to look at her.

'Hey,' Daniella said. 'We're buddies. She tells me everything.'

'Everything?'

'Well, almost everything.'

'I came to see if I can make it up to her,' he admitted sheepishly.

'Sadie's not home right now.'

'Oh. I saw Delores parked outside.'

'She was misbehaving this morning. Sadie said she couldn't persuade her to start, so she walked to the office.' They both exchanged a horrified look. 'We'll never make a Californian of her.'

'I hope we will,' Gil said.

'You need to tell *her* that,' Daniella suggested. 'Not me.'

Gil's eyes made another involuntary scan over the script. Mmm. It wasn't bad. He flicked over a few more pages. 'This is interesting,' he said.

Daniella pulled up another chair. 'You think so?'

'Mmm. How far have you got with it?'

Daniella inched closer to him. 'I've finished the first draft and now I'm agonising over the second.'

Gil sipped his coffee without taking his eyes off the script.

'We need cookies,' Daniella said. 'Lots of them.'

'Daniella,' Gil said with a sigh, 'you're a woman.' That much he could work out. 'You know about these things. Why can't I get it right with her?'

'You really wanna know?'

Gil nodded and helped himself to a cookie.

'There are too many women in your life, Gil. Ditch a couple. One in particular would be a good start.'

'But I only love Sadie.'

'Maybe it doesn't feel like that from her side.'

'Gina needs me.' Gil puffed out a breath. 'I can't abandon her.'

'Sometimes you have to be cruel to be kind,' Daniella said. 'Gina has to learn to stand on her own two feet.'

'This is good,' he said.

'The cookie, the script or the advice?'

'All of them,' he answered with a smile. He spread the pages out before him. 'Can I take it?'

'Only if you take the advice too.'

'What about the cookies?'

'Get your own,' Daniella said with a grin.

'I'll read this as soon as I can,' Gil said. 'I think you have something here.'

'Really? You're not bullshitting me?'

'Why would I?'

'Because you're a male of the species and a movie producer. I'm naturally suspicious of both.'

Gil held up his hands. 'No strings, I promise,' he said. 'I'll take a look and if I like the rest of it as much as I like the first few pages we'll go from there.'

'Thanks, Gil,' Daniella said, suddenly looking shy. 'I appreciate it. This means a lot to me.'

He walked towards the door. 'Tell Sadie I came over. Maybe she could drop by tonight – if she doesn't have another engagement.'

'How can she drop by? She doesn't have a car,' Daniella reminded him.

'I could get Delores fixed up for her,' Gil said, a spark of excitement in his eyes. 'She'd like that.'

'She'd love it,' Daniella agreed.

'I'll do that,' he said. 'I'll get the garage to come and collect it – *her* – later.'

'Don't mess this up, Gil,' Daniella warned.

'I won't,' he assured her. 'I'll make sure they do a great job.'

'I wasn't talking about the car,' Daniella said with a shake of her head. 'I wasn't talking about the car.'

Chapter Eighty-Four

I'm in a quandary – but then that's nothing new. I'm in my bedroom at Daniella's house lying flat out on the bed and Alice, my lovely, longlost friend from London, is on the other end of the phone. I love our girly chats and I realise just how much I've missed her. I feel as if I've been away for yonks.

Britain has gone to pot since I've been gone – quite literally. Cannabis is about to be decriminalised and Alice tells me Hyde Park looks like some sort of hippie love-in from the 1960s, with everyone passing round joints while the policemen look the other way. I'm chewing my nails.

'They want me back?' It bears repeating. And I have done so. Several times.

'I think you'd be mad to consider it,' Alice says. She's not to know that my sanity has definitely been skewed since I got here.

'I don't know.' I sound so pathetic.

'You don't know?' she echoes incredulously. 'Why would you want to swap sun-kissed California for soggy old London?'

'Ooo, I don't know.' I think it's just the fact that someone – *anyone* – wants me that's turning my head.

'Don't even think about it,' my friend instructs.

'If you don't want me to think about it, why did you ring me up and tell me they want me back?'

'Because I thought you'd go "Ha!" and tell them to shove it where it didn't shine.'

'Ooo,' I say again. 'I don't know.'

'Has all that Californian sun shrunk your brain?' my friend wants to know.

I think it probably has, but not for the same reasons that Alice may think. The job she's talking about is my 'real' job. My real job back in the City with stocks and shares and all the other things I used to know about, with real money and real long hours. Not a job that involves giving out leaflets or serving drinks to drunken teenagers or trying to make actors' bottoms famous. I'd get a real salary – a big one. Even more if I play hard to get. Hard to get? Who am I kidding? I've always been too biddable. But it would mean that I could stop living a hand-to-mouth existence and shop again. I have another nail nibble. 'How much do they want me back?'

'They're begging you to go back,' she says.

'That's nice.'

'Nice?' I hear her tut. Loudly. 'You seem to forget these are the same people who sacked you without a second thought.'

'They're obviously regretting it,' I suggest.

'Let them,' Alice advises. 'I hope they can't get anyone decent to work for them and that the whole company collapses.'

I felt like too when I left – was forcibly ejected – but it never happens, does it? Life trundles on as it always does with the bad guys winning and the good dying young.

I feel tired of California, tired of Gil, tired of everyone being married loads of times except me who hasn't been hitched a measly once, tired of having a nice day, tired of doing the 'hey' thing, tired of rollerblading pensioners, tired of not being able to compete with people who are more famous and have bigger chests, tired of everyone saying 'excuse me?' when I call something 'wicked', tired of people who have so many riches and yet are somehow so poor. I suddenly get an overwhelming urge for piping hot tea with proper tea bags and weather that doesn't involve wall-to-wall sun and unbroken blue skies. This place definitely isn't real – it doesn't rain between May and October. How weird is that? I miss daffodils and the

Daily Mail and squashing through Soho on a Saturday afternoon and eating picnics while it's pissing down and food that you don't need a linguistic degree for and litter and foul-tempered bank cashiers and most of all I miss *Steve Wright in the Afternoon* on Radio 2.

'I'm missing London,' I say. I can feel tears welling up inside me. 'I'm missing everyone.'

'No you're not,' Alice says in her sternest voice. 'And no one's missing you. Li in the Chinese takeaway never asks about you. They all forgot about you the minute you'd gone.' She's about to start crying too. 'I'll come out on holiday for a few weeks,' she offers. 'That'll make you feel better.'

'You haven't got any money.'

'I'll sacrifice my lounge carpet for you.'

That is a true sign of friendship. I know how long Alice has been saving up for her lounge carpet and it makes me wail more.

'Don't do this, Sadie,' she says. 'I wish I'd never phoned. Stay and make it work.'

'You're right,' I say. 'I know you're right.'

'You could have a really good life out there.' She's talking to me like I'm a clingy toddler. 'Don't throw it away.'

'No.'

'How's Gil?' she says when I've stopped sniffling.

Not talking to me. 'He's fine.'

I'm not sure whether I'm pleased that he's taken Delores to get fixed as Daniella said or whether, as I suspect, he's actually repossessed her as he's technically the owner. Daniella thinks Gil is a warm and deeply desirable man, but I think that might have more to do with the fact that he thinks she could be the next hot-shot screenwriter than anything remotely objective about his suitability for me as a life partner. And, anyway, she's been hanging on for some crusty old Mad Movie Mogul for the past decade so I'm not sure that I trust her judgement either. She struggles with the fact that her man had one wife while glibly overlooking the fact that mine has had *two*.

'Look, there you are,' Alice says encouragingly. 'You've got a lovely man and a lovely life.'

I've not. My life is like a broken vending machine – I keep pushing money in, but nothing comes out at the other end.

'Promise me you won't do anything silly?'

'Like flinging myself off the Hollywood sign?'

'No, like rushing back to take this crap job just because they've clicked their fingers.'

I wipe my nose on my sleeve. 'I wouldn't dream of it.'

Chapter Eighty-Five

'I'm going home,' I say to Bay.

'Home?' she echoes. 'I take it you mean London home and not round-the-corner-to-Larchmont home.'

I shake my head – or should I nod? 'I've got a great job offer back in London,' I say. 'A *fabulous* job offer.' I sound as if I'm saying this to convince myself rather than Bay. 'I'd be a fool to turn it down.'

'You'd be a fool to go back,' Bay says, bosom heaving beneath her snakeskin Lycra.

'I don't want to get you into trouble with the IRS,' I say. 'I have to go.'

'What about Gil?' Bay says.

'What about Tavis?' Min says.

'What about me?' I say.

Bay flounces about the office. 'We can't allow this,' she says. 'You've only just got here. You're one of the family. I'll give you a pay rise.'

'I don't want a pay rise.'

'I do,' Min says.

'This is a great opportunity,' I say.

'What?' Bay snorts. 'Working in some sweatshop office in the City? A crap Labour government, high taxes, dirty streets, getting mugged for a mobile phone, NHS hospitals where you're more likely to come out dead than cured?'

'I think that's a slightly biased view.'

'You have a great opportunity here,' Bay insists. 'I'll retire,' she offers. 'You can run the office. Can't she, Min?'

'Okay by me,' Min says graciously.

'You can't do that,' I say. 'You don't want to retire.'

'Honey,' she says in her best West Coast accent, 'I have a toy boy fifteen years my junior. I can find *plenty* to fill my days.'

I get a vision of Bay in her lurid Lycra ensemble in years to come as a rollerblading geriatric.

'I can't stay here.' I can hear myself weakening. 'I keep forgetting to put sun cream on. My face will turn into a raisin.'

'Get Botoxed,' Bay says.

'A major earthquake is overdue by about forty years,' I point out. 'It could happen any day.'

'And you could get hit by a London bus crossing the road in Kensington,' Bay counters.

'Oh, that old chestnut.' I admit that I always wear nice underwear in case I get hit by a bus, but how do you prepare for a disaster on the scale of an earthquake? I have no idea. Clearly I'm not meant to live here.

'You have two men in love with you,' Min says. 'That must be more than at home.'

'Two men in love with me?' I'm struggling to think of one.

They both look at me open-mouthed.

'What?'

'Tavis is besotted with you,' they say in unison.

'Tavis?' I can't help but laugh. 'Tavis is gay.'

'If Tavis is gay then I'm Danny La Rue,' Bay says decisively.

I always wondered who she reminded me of. 'My mind's made up,' I say. 'Nothing can persuade me otherwise.' I bite my lips in case they foolishly think about quivering again. 'London here I come.'

Chapter Eighty-Six

'I'm going home,' I tell Daniella.

'You are insanity itself,' Daniella declares. She looks like she's about to stamp her foot.

'Don't go, Aunt Sadie.' Alexis's chin is trembling.

'I have to, sweetheart.' She starts to cry into Princess Sparkle Barbie's nylon hair and I feel like the biggest heel in the world.

'Now look what you're doing,' Daniella says, cuddling her daughter. 'You're breaking all of our hearts.'

'I've booked my ticket,' I say lamely.

'Fine,' Daniella says. 'Then there's no talking to you.'

The last time I felt like this I'd been caught behind the bike sheds with Jeremy Dickinson sporting a hickey on my neck and clutching a packet of ten Number 6 ciggies. 'I'm sorry.'

'What does Gil say?'

'Nothing.' I wrap my arms round myself.

'*Nothing?*'

I can feel myself cringing. 'I haven't told him yet.'

'And are you planning to?'

'Eventually.'

'And when is this ticket booked for?'

'Tomorrow.'

'So "eventually" will be when?'

'I think I might just leave him a note,' I mumble.

'What has he done to deserve that?'

'Had more wives than he admitted to. Left me in a cupboard at the Oscars Party.'

'I think you're focusing on the negatives in this situation,' Daniella says in a very Californian way. 'These are very small misdemeanours in the scheme of things.'

They may seem like small misdemeanours to Daniella, but to me the whole thing just feels like bloody hard work. Should love be like that?

And I guess if I was being truthful it's starting to niggle at me that I have a much better time with Tavis than I do with Gil. We don't fight, we don't fall out, we don't have to creep round other people's feelings all the time. And he's a very good snogger – even if it was acting. Surely there must be straight men out there like that? Just one would do.

'You know that this is running away, don't you?'

'Of course I do.'

'It will be raining in London.'

'It always is.'

'Stay and sort this out with Gil,' Daniella begs. 'He adores you. Just because he's a jackass who can't get his act together doesn't mean that he doesn't love you.'

'Thank you for those encouraging words.' I smile when I want to cry. 'I need to go for a walk.'

'You'll get mugged.'

Right now the thought of getting hit on the head with a hammer by someone doesn't seem like such an unpleasant prospect – it might even do me some good. 'I'm going to tell Tavis.'

Daniella's eyebrows rise. 'Tavis – but not Gil. You don't think this might be significant?'

'I don't have a car,' I point out, 'and Tavis is working just around the corner. I can walk to Tavis.'

'You're conveniently forgetting the miracle of telephone communication,' Daniella says.

'Yes.'

'I like Tavis a lot,' Alexis pipes up. She is sucking Princess Sparkle Barbie's foot in contemplation.

'So do I,' I say.

'But I like Gil a lot too.'

'I think Alexis might have summed up the problem,' Daniella suggests.

And although it pains me to admit it, I think she might have too.

Chapter Eighty-Seven

Zorba's is packed to the rafters. I can tell as I approach the restaurant that Tavis isn't going to have a lot of time for meaningful conversation. And sure enough he's whizzing out of the door, arms stacked with plates of salad and grilled lamb and all things Greek. He distributes his dishes with a smile and a cheery comment for everyone and my heart goes out to him because I know that he is destined for so much more than this. I stand and watch him unobserved and I can't begin to articulate how I feel about him. Oh bollocks, is how I feel.

As he turns to head back towards the kitchen, he catches my eye. 'Hey,' he says. 'What are you doing here?'

'I came to find out how the audition went.'

His mouth twists into a bad shape.

'Not good?'

'I'm trying to remain positive about the experience,' Tavis says.

'Which means?'

'That I didn't actually punch Gil.'

'Oh dear.'

'Oh dear indeed,' Tavis says, mimicking my accent.

'I was worried to death for you,' I say. 'When I realised that your audition was with Gil, I didn't know what to say. I guess he's not your number one fan.'

'I don't know why that is,' Tavis says.

There's a moment when all the restaurant disappears, all the chatter stops, the stream of traffic looking for parking meters on Larchmont fades away and there is just Tavis and me. 'Maybe it's because I am.'

We both look at each other. The moon is hanging high over the Hollywood sign. This is a Romeo and Juliet moment. I'm dying inside and I don't know why. Tavis takes a step towards me.

'Sadie . . .'

'Waiter!'

The noise comes back. 'Right with you,' Tavis says brightly. 'We can't talk now,' he says to me.

'I just have one more thing to say,' I tell Tavis.

He looks like he really doesn't want to hear it.

'It's important,' I add. I can feel that I'm shuffling my feet. 'I've decided to go home.'

'Hey, waiter!'

'Home?'

'To London,' I clarify. 'Real home. Tomorrow.'

'You can't do this,' Tavis says.

'There's nothing here for me,' I say sadly.

'That's not true!' Tavis looks panic-stricken.

'I can't live on dreams and make-believe, Tavis. I need stability and commitment – all those things. I can't go where the wind blows me. I can't do one thing while dreaming about another. I'm too earthed.'

'What does a fella have to do to get some more wine?' Tavis's customer yells.

'I have to go,' Tavis says. 'We need to talk about this. I'll come by the house when I finish my shift. It'll be late.'

I shake my head. 'I have too much to do, Tavis. I have to pack.'

'We can't say goodbye like this,' he pleads. 'Let me take you to the airport.'

'I don't know . . .' I've never been one for goodbyes.

'There are things I want to say.' Tavis looks distraught.

'Like what?'

He rakes his hair. 'I don't know,' he says. 'I need time to think about them.'

'I have to leave the house around noon,' I say. 'Don't be late.'

'I won't,' he promises.

I turn to leave and give him a wave.

'Sadie . . .' Tavis's shoulders sag. 'Think very carefully about this.'

'I've been thinking about nothing else,' I say – and I'm going to be thinking about it for the rest of the night too.

Chapter Eighty-Eight

Delores was barely recognisable. Gil stood in awe looking at her sleek, shining curves. 'Wow,' was all he could manage to say.

The garage had worked flat out on her through the night. She'd been stripped down, sorted out and spruced up to the nth degree. The rust was gone, the chrome sparkled and all of the mechanics were in working order. Even he had to admit that it was a far cry from the car he'd brought in. Gil winced as he handed over his credit card. The labour charges alone would have paid for a new Mercedes. But what the hell, this former heap of junk was Sadie's baby and if it made her happy then it was money well spent.

'I appreciate it,' Gil said to the garage-owner.

'No trouble, Mr McGann. Anytime.'

This was the same body-shop that had repaired Gina's crumpled cars times too numerous to count. Gil's custom had probably gone a long way to providing the man's pool home in the Hollywood Hills, so it was no wonder that they'd managed to pull out all the stops for Delores.

Gil checked his watch. It was nearly lunchtime and too late to take the car to Daniella's house, but he could call by Double Take and maybe let Sadie take her out for a spin in her lunch-hour. He jumped in the car and headed off through the bustling traffic towards Wilshire Boulevard. He'd spent a long and sleepless night worrying about Sadie, Delores, Gina and Katherine. In the end he'd got up and read Daniella's script. Maybe Sadie's friend was right – there were too many women in his life. Even if one of

379

them was a car. By the time dawn struggled through the curtains, he'd decided what he was going to do. One was to buy Daniella's script. The second was to ask Sadie to marry him.

Bay and Min exchanged nervous glances. 'She's left,' Bay said, licking her lips nervously.

'What do you mean, "she's left"?' Gil said. 'Did you fire her?'

'Of course not, you stupid man,' Bay barked – the Essex girl fighting her way through the polite Californian polish. 'I wanted her to stay. It's a shame *you* didn't.'

'Stay?'

'She's going back to London.'

Gil felt as if he was in one of those horror films where suddenly all the world goes fractured and out of focus. 'Sadie is?'

'This *is* who we're talking about?'

'When?'

'You're supposed to be her boyfriend,' Bay said. 'Shouldn't you know these things?'

'She's said nothing.' Gil could feel himself going hollow.

'She's leaving today.'

'I've got to stop her,' he said.

'Good luck,' Bay said. 'We both had a go and failed.'

Gil headed towards the door. It was as if he was drunk and stumbling. Out on the pavement, the world was still the same. The car drivers were still impatient, the sun was still golden, the sky was still blue. But inside everything had changed. Gil could feel himself sweating. He fumbled for his cell phone and, pulling it from his pocket, he punched in Sadie's number. It went straight to voicemail. He'd go over to Daniella's right now. She must be still there. He didn't often pray to God, but he was prepared to give it a chance and pray that she hadn't left yet.

380

He jumped into Delores and eased her smooth, new, non-clonking transmission into gear. Before he could pull away from the parking lot, his cell phone rang. Maybe it was Sadie returning his call.

'Sadie!' Gil said as he snatched it up and answered the phone.

'No.' The voice was slurred and he knew instantly who it was. 'It's me.'

'Gina,' Gil said. 'Not now. I've something very important to do.'

'Noah has left me,' Gina sobbed. 'He threw my clothes in the pool. All my favourite clothes.'

'No, Gina,' Gil said. 'I can't buy this now. Take a cab to the house. Get Maria to make you some coffee – strong coffee – and maybe a little something to eat . . .'

'I need you, Gil.' Her voice veered between hysterical and sleepy. 'I've only ever needed you.'

'Go to the house. Do some yoga. I'll be back later.'

'No one loves me,' Gina wailed.

'They do,' Gil said. 'We all love you.' One-handed he managed to pull out into the traffic. 'I'll talk to Noah later. I'll talk to you both.'

'I'm feeling all funny, Gil.'

'Oh no!' Gil slammed the steering-wheel. 'Don't do this to me!'

'I'm so sleepy.'

'Gina,' Gil tried to stay calm. 'What have you taken?'

'I don't know.' She was sounding fuzzy round the edges.

'Have you taken something? Gina! Have you taken something?'

'Hmm, hmm,' Gina sighed.

'Oh shit,' Gil said. 'Where are you? Gina! Where are you?' There was no reply from his wife bar weary sighs travelling down the phone line. 'Are you at Noah's?'

'Hmm, hmm,' Gina murmured. 'Pool house . . .' And the line went dead.

Gil threw the phone on the passenger seat, floored

Delores's throttle and headed up towards Beverly Hills and Noah's house. He patted Delores's steering-wheel. 'Come on, old girl. Show me what you can do,' he said. 'This is an emergency.'

Chapter Eighty-Nine

Tavis paced up and down on the roof terrace of their apartment. Joe, resplendent in an open Hawaiian shirt and reclining on a sun-lounger, lifted one slice of cucumber from his eye.

'So what are you going to do?'

'I don't know,' Tavis said, trying to control his breathing. 'I'm thinking.'

'Well, think quicker,' Joe advised. 'You're running out of time.'

'Don't you think I know that?' Tavis snapped.

'Hey,' Joe said, peeling off both slices of cucumber. 'There's no need to lose it just because I'm stating the obvious.'

'I don't know what to do,' Tavis repeated. 'I don't know what to say.' He looked at Joe, stricken. 'What shall I do?'

'Man,' Joe said with a sigh, 'I am the last person to ask.'

The phone rang. Tavis and Joe stared at it. 'Maybe she's changed her mind,' Tavis said hopefully.

'Yeah,' Joe agreed. 'And maybe Steven Spielberg wants you to replace Harrison Ford as the next Indiana Jones.' Joe eased himself from the sun-lounger, picking up the script which had fallen to the ground as he did so. 'I'll answer in case it is Steven. You sound too hysterical.'

'Hi, Tavis Jones's residence.'

Tavis made a face.

Joe covered the mouthpiece. 'Next best thing,' he whispered. 'It's Toby Portman for you.'

Tavis smoothed his hair and took the phone. 'Hi.'

Joe wrapped his arms round Tavis and pressed his ear to

the phone too. Tavis tried without success to shoo him away.

'Hi, Tavis,' Toby said. 'Can you come down to my office?'

'Sure.' Tavis could hear his heart beating. This couldn't be bad news. If Toby Portman even wanted to be in the same room with him again, this had to be good.

'Within the hour?'

'Oh man,' Tavis said as a sinking feeling hit his stomach. He was due to go and take Sadie to the airport. He'd promised her he would. There was no way he could let her down now. He had a vision of Sadie standing waiting for him with packed luggage. He saw his final chance to say the things he thought he needed to say but which wouldn't formulate in his brain. 'I can't be there. I have something really important to do.'

There was a pause at the end of the line. Toby Portman clearly wasn't a man who was used to struggling actors saying no to him. 'More important than kick-starting your movie career?'

'More important to me than anything,' Tavis said.

'Then I'll get my office to call you with a more convenient appointment,' Toby Portman said. But as Tavis hung up the phone he guessed that he probably wouldn't hear from Toby Portman again. It was one thing being marked down as difficult if you were Russell Crowe or Jack Nicholson, but who'd want to start out with a difficult Tavis Jones?

'More important than *anything*?' Joe said incredulously. 'That's quite a statement.'

'I guess it is,' Tavis sighed.

'You realise you just turned down a meeting with Toby Portman for a woman?'

'I do,' Tavis said.

'Are you insane?'

'Yes,' Tavis said. 'Or in love.'

'It's the same thing,' Joe said dismissively. He started fanning himself with the pages of his script. 'You should be the one having an attack of the vapours.'

'I'm fine. I'm cool,' Tavis said. 'There'll be other movies.'

'There'll be other movies!' Joe fell back on his sun-lounger, overcome with hysteria. 'There'll be other movies!'

The sinking feeling wasn't about to leave Tavis's digestive system alone. 'It's no big deal.'

'No big deal!' Joe was squealing. 'You've waited years for this! Years! Didn't you give women up because of this? What happened to single-minded Mr Single?'

Tavis was beginning to wonder that himself.

'Jeeze,' Joe said, loosening his shirt even more so that the air could get to him. 'You've lost your mind.'

But Tavis knew that it wasn't his mind he'd lost, it was his heart – altogether a much more delicate organ.

Joe was prostrate with emotion. 'I hope she's worth it.'

'So do I,' Tavis said, trying to ignore the flicker of doubt that was ready to spontaneously combust in his brain. 'So do I.'

Chapter Ninety

Daniella is standing at my bedroom door. Her arms are folded and her lip is wobbling. 'You've got everything?'

'Yeah.' I glance towards the suitcase I've had to borrow from my friend, because – what seems like a million years ago now – my own was stolen the night I first arrived. 'Daniella . . .'

'Don't get all sentimental,' she says. 'I'm going to cry.'

'I just wanted to say—'

'Stop it,' she instructs. 'Stop it right now. We've had a fabulous time. We've become great friends. My child and my mother adore you. You've been a marvellous house-mate – except for your annoying habit of being able to eat whatever you like and not put on weight. And now you're going to spoil it all by going home.'

I cross the room and give her a big hug. 'That's exactly what I was going to say.'

'I hate the English,' Daniella says with enthusiasm, 'with your stiff upper lip and your "jolly good, old sport". You're so unemotional.'

'I'm not unemotional,' I say. 'I'm trying to hold it all in.'

'Why?' Daniella wants to know. 'It's much better out all over the carpet. In ten years' time you'll get cancer or arthritis from holding all that pain inside.'

'That's a very comforting thought.'

'Haven't you read Louise Hay?'

I can quite honestly say that I have no idea who Louise Hay is, but I feel that's probably to my detriment. I'd take a wild guess at her being of Californian extract.

'Let's change the subject,' Daniella suggests. 'I can't deal with this.'

I hand an envelope to her. 'I've written a letter to Gil,' I say. 'Will you give it to him for me?'

'This is exactly what I mean,' she rails. 'You should have called him. What does the letter say? *Terribly sorry, old sport. Have fucked off home to Blighty. Bad luck, what?*'

'That's unfair.'

'Running out on Gil is unfair.'

'I've tried his cell phone,' I say. 'Several times. There's no reply.'

That leaves Daniella at a loss for words.

'I've put the spare set of keys for Delores in with it.'

'Great,' Daniella says. 'That should double her value.'

My eyes start to well up with tears and I press my lips together until I can feel them going numb. Daniella crumbles. 'I don't want to fight.'

'I'm not fighting,' I point out. 'You're saying mean things to provoke me into caving in and staying.'

'Is that such a bad idea?' Daniella asks.

At this moment I don't know. I have no idea what the hell I'm doing or why, in fact, I'm doing it.

'Tavis should be here soon,' I say.

'Good,' Daniella says and she lifts my case and carries it into the sitting room while I trail obediently behind her. 'I'll tell you something to cheer you up while you wait.'

I sit next to her on the sofa and she squeezes my hand. 'I'm thinking of having my butt enhanced.' There is the squeal of excitement in her voice.

'What with?'

'What with?' Daniella looks perplexed. 'Implants.'

'Why?'

'Why not?' she says. 'If Gil likes this script as much as he says then I'm on my way. I'm going to be a famous Hollywood scriptwriter and a woman of independent means. I will be free of the Mad Movie Mogul. I think it will be a statement of my new status. It's all the rage. Everyone's having them.'

'No, they're not.' Even though my friend is deadly

serious, I can't help but laugh. ' "Everyone" is just a very few madwomen in Hollywood. It's a bum. There's nothing wrong with it.'

'It could be better.'

'How? Is it comfortable to sit on?'

'Yes.'

'Then it does its job perfectly well.'

Daniella pouts. 'You just don't get it, do you?'

I shake my head. 'Obviously not. But I am glad to hear that you may be on your way to financial independence. You've worked hard for it and I really, really hope that you succeed.'

'Then I can give 3Ms the flick and find a nice man. Preferably much younger.'

'That's all the rage too, isn't it?' I ask.

'Of course,' she says. 'And I promise I'll bring him to visit you in London. I've never been to Europe.'

'Well,' I say, 'it's about time that you did.'

A car pulls up outside and we both crane our necks. 'Tavis,' Daniella says. And sure enough my Romeo is leaping out of his car and sprinting up the path to Daniella's door. My heart does a very strange little twist at the thought that this might be the last time I see him.

'Let's hit the grit, sister,' my friend says and heaves my case up. She opens the door to Tavis and dumps my case at his feet. He looks at it with a hint of disappointment in his eyes.

'Hi,' he says. Tavis looks very scrubbed and polished and vaguely smart. I wonder if he's going somewhere important after he's dropped me at the airport. 'I thought you might have changed your mind.'

'No.'

The disappointment spread to the rest of his face and I can't believe I'm doing this to my friends. Friends who looked after me so readily when I landed here as an orphan.

Just then, another car pulls up outside Daniella's home – a huge black beast of a Mercedes that's probably a top-of-the-range one, stretched way beyond its normal measurements and fit for Mafia dons or First Division footballers. For one mad moment everything inside me surges as I think it might just be Gil. But it isn't. Out of the titanic car gets a short, fat, bald man. Despite the brain-scorching heat he's wearing a black rollneck sweater and a fluffy wool jacket with white loafers. In the middle of his chest hangs a gold medallion – the like of which I haven't seen since the 1980s.

'Good Lord,' I breathe as recognition hits in. He's much older than I imagined, and I can't begin to think what Daniella sees in him. But then money and power are potent aphrodisiacs and beauty is only a light switch away. I turn to my friend who has gone into a state of suspended animation. So this is the Mad Movie Mogul.

'What's he doing here?' Daniella hisses at me.

How should I know? 'Maybe he's come to see if you've got a future together now that you know he's free,' I suggest.

'I've longed for this moment, Sadie,' she says under her breath. 'And now that it's here, I don't know what to do.' She looks at me with wide eyes that say 'help me.'

'You said you wanted to be free of him, Daniella.'

'I did, didn't I?' she says.

This is not the time to tell her that she could do a lot better.

Tavis's jaw is trailing on the floor as he clearly recognises who the Mad Movie Mogul is. He looks like he might throw himself prostrate at his feet.

'I'll have to get rid of him,' Daniella mutters.

'Look,' I say, 'I hate goodbyes. Let Tavis take me to the airport. You stay here and sort out your future.'

The Mad Movie Mogul arrives in front of us. 'Hi,' he says. 'Daniella.'

Daniella nods.

'You must be Sadie,' he says and takes my hand. 'I hope we'll be seeing a lot more of each other.'

'Sadie's going home,' Daniella says. 'Tavis is just taking her to the airport.'

The Mad Movie Mogul runs a critical eye over Tavis.

'You're a fine-looking young man,' he concludes. 'You an actor?'

Tavis, still rendered speechless, nods.

3Ms hands Tavis a gold-edged card. 'Call my office,' he says.

Tavis nearly faints.

Now the Mad Movie Mogul is standing in front of Daniella. Despite his advancing years, charisma emanates from him. 'I've been calling you,' he says.

'And I've not been returning them,' Daniella says.

As much as I'd like to be a fly on the wall for this conversation, time is marching on. 'I have to go,' I say to Daniella.

She gives me a hug. 'I love you,' she says. 'You are completely and utterly wrong to leave. Isn't she, Tavis?'

'Yes,' Tavis says with what sounds like a heartfelt sigh.

Daniella lets go of me and we exchange a kiss. 'Keep in touch,' she says, wiping away a tear.

'Come and see me soon.'

'I will,' she sniffs.

A taxi pulls up behind the Mad Movie Mogul's Mercedes with a screech of brakes and for a brief moment I wonder whether it might be Gil, without wondering what he'd be doing in a taxi. The driver gets out and it's my Armenian robber who stole my suitcase on the first night. He walks towards us with it in his meaty hand, rendering me speechless. The case is dumped at my feet. 'Mistake,' he mutters in a thick accent. 'I find you.'

'You didn't rob me,' I say. 'You drove away with my case by mistake? And now you've tracked me down?'

The driver looks blank. 'Armenian,' he says.

I fumble in my purse for the biggest tip I can manage and hand it over. 'Thanks. Thank you,' I mumble.

With a curt nod, the Armenian cab-driver pockets it and marches off.

'So this is closure,' Daniella says with another sniff.

'I guess so.' My manky clothes have come back so that I can restart my manky life. What comes around goes around. 'Have these,' I say to Daniella and push the case I borrowed from her filled with my designer clothes towards her. 'I'm not going to need strappy tops in London.'

'I'll keep them,' she says, 'but only in the hope that one day you'll come back for them.'

I kiss Daniella again. 'I'd better get going.'

'Ready then?' Tavis says to me.

'As I'll ever be.'

He picks up my battered old case. 'Your chariot awaits.'

'Thanks.' Tavis and I exchange a rather sad, sickly grin and he throws my luggage into the back of his car. I'm really looking forward to going back to London and I'm sure that this is absolutely the right decision. Isn't it?

Chapter Ninety-One

Gina's eyes rolled back into her head. She was limp in Gil's arms and he shook her gently. He'd found her in Noah's pool-house as she had said, slumped half-on, half-off one of the sun-loungers. Her forehead was soaked with sweat and she was as white as a sheet. 'Stay with me,' he said, forcing her to look at him. 'Open your eyes.'

Gina struggled to comply.

'Come on, baby,' he urged. 'Don't go to sleep. Help is on its way.'

He'd called the paramedics from the car and he was sure they'd be here any minute. All Gina had to do was hang on. She'd be fine. He was sure she'd be fine. His wife had gone this far before and she'd always pulled through. He just hoped that this time she hadn't pushed her luck once too often.

Gil glanced round the magnificent pool-house and out towards the palatial mansion that had belonged to a string of beleaguered film stars. The sun sparkled on the still blue water of the pool that Noah had recently refurbished with a mosaic of *Born to party* on the bottom. The palm trees swayed in the breeze, parakeets chattered in the trees, thousands of dollars' worth of red geraniums were grouped in ancient Turkish oil jars. It was an idyllic location, but it wouldn't be the first time someone had overdosed in this place. If anyone questioned the old adage that money couldn't buy you happiness they only had to come to Hollywood and look at the track record of the fabulously wealthy and famous. Of Noah there was no sign.

The siren of the paramedics' ambulance announced their

arrival and seconds later Gil heard their feet pounding across the handmade Italian terracotta tiles that bounded the pool area.

'They're here, baby,' Gil murmured softly, stroking her hair. 'Hang on. Just a little while longer.'

'I'm sorry, Gil,' she gasped.

The paramedics ran into the pool house and took Gina from his arms.

'Do you know what she's taken?'

Gil handed over the empty plastic pill container. It was white – the same flat colour of Gina's skin. 'And some booze too.' He flicked his gaze towards a discarded bottle of vodka.

'We're gonna take you to the hospital, ma'am,' the man said. They put an oxygen mask over Gina's face and loaded her onto a stretcher while Gil stood and looked on helplessly.

Gina reached for his hand and squeezed it with the strength of a child. 'I won't do it again,' she whispered. 'Not ever.'

As they wheeled her towards the waiting ambulance, he hoped that they'd be able to get her to the hospital in time and that those words wouldn't come back to haunt him.

Chapter Ninety-Two

The journey to LAX is interminable. Tavis is driving so slowly that I'm not sure we'll ever get there at all. All the other traffic on La Cienega is whizzing gaily past us. We've hardly spoken a word and Tavis seems fixated by the tarmac. I just want to get there as I'm actually feeling physical pain at doing this.

As we get to the airport and the soaring concrete archway at the front of the terminal becomes visible, Tavis suddenly blurts out, 'I wish you weren't going home.'

I don't want to admit that I feel the same way too. 'I have to,' I say. 'My relationship with Gil isn't going anywhere. I need to get out. This is the only way.'

Tavis clears his throat. 'There are other men in LA,' he says. 'Not many of them who aren't gay or mad,' he continues, 'but there are some.'

'I only need one.'

'Sadie . . .' 'Tavis . . .' we say together and both stop.

'You first,' Tavis says.

'I think you're a wonderful bloke.' I'm stammering and it isn't particularly attractive. I don't know where the eloquence of my Juliet performance has gone. 'A really wonderful bloke.'

Tavis looks bashful.

'And I did wonder . . . for a time . . . if I had feelings . . .' I glance over at him and his knuckles have tightened on the steering wheel. 'I did wonder . . . if I had feelings for you.'

'Sadie . . .'

I put my hand up to stop him. 'I know what you're going to say.'

'Do you?'

'Yes,' I say firmly. 'And I know that it's stupid to feel like that. I understand completely where you're coming from. I'm fine with that. Really. It's ridiculous to think that we could ever have had a . . . a . . .'

'Relationship?'

'A relationship,' I confirm. 'I know that you and I could never be anything more than just good friends.'

'We couldn't?'

'No.' I'm very clear about that now. I just wish it didn't hurt so much. 'You're a very good friend,' I say. 'One of the best. And if you're ever in London I want you to ring me and we'll meet up and have dinner.'

Tavis turns to me, despite the fact that we're swinging into the parking lot. 'Have *dinner*?'

'Or something.'

Tavis pulls into a parking space and he sits there for a moment staring out of the window. He takes a deep breath and turns to look at me. His eyes are so beautiful they'd make your heart stop.

'Sadie . . . Sadie . . .' then he reaches into the back seat for my case. 'Let's go,' he says, 'before you miss your plane.'

Chapter Ninety-Three

Gina had tubes everywhere and a monitor that sounded every beat of her heart with an irritating, tinny beep. Gil had never been so glad to hear anything so annoying in all his life.

The hospital room was white, stark and sterile. The shade was pulled down to block out the sun. It was like the hospital room in a movie. A nurse bustled round checking charts and drips and that Gina was comfortable.

His wife lay motionless on the bed, an oxygen mask covering her mouth. Her eyes were closed and her skin had gone from white to a pasty green.

'Is she going to be okay?' Gil said to the nurse.

'We're going to monitor her for a couple of days,' she replied in a kindly voice that was perfect for a nurse. 'She's a very lucky woman.'

Lucky, Gil thought. Was Gina lucky? It was an odd choice of word to describe someone who had come back from the brink of death. And Gil wondered for the thousandth time why someone who could have so much and give so much would want to play Russian roulette with their life.

'She's out of danger?'

'We think so. Doctor will be in to see her later,' the nurse said. 'We're going to let her sleep for now. She'll be fine.'

'She looks so pale.'

'You don't look so hot yourself,' the nurse said, offering him a gentle smile. 'Why don't you go home and get some rest too?'

'I have things to do,' Gil said.

'I'm sure they can wait,' the nurse said.

'No,' he said. 'They can't.'

'She doesn't know that you're here. Your wife will sleep for a while yet,' she assured him. 'You can slip away if you need to. I'll contact you as soon as she wakes.'

'You promise?' Gil said. 'The minute she opens her eyes?'

'I'll get right on the phone.'

Gil scribbled down his cell-phone number and handed it to the nurse. 'Go on, now,' she said. 'Don't you worry.'

He looked at Gina's face. She looked like the Sleeping Beauty. Fragile and vulnerable. What was he going to do with her?

'I don't like to leave her,' he said, and the sentence pulled him upright. Somehow it was always the same story.

Chapter Ninety-Four

'Ooo,' I say. 'That was quick.'

Mercifully, there was no queue and I'm all checked in. We took so long getting here, that now I'm very nearly late. My bag has gone off down the little chute, hopefully to reappear out of a similar one in London, Heathrow a few cramped hours hence and I'm clutching my boarding card.

Tavis still hasn't spoken.

'I'd better go through to the departure gate,' I say.

He takes my arm and we walk towards the passport control desk. This is torture.

'I guess this is it,' Tavis says.

I reach up and kiss him on the cheek. 'I'm going to miss you,' I say. And from nowhere, absolutely nowhere, tears spring to my eyes.

'Oh Sadie,' Tavis says, and he folds me into his arms and pulls me against his chest. His lips are feathering my hair with kisses and as I look up to him, he kisses me full on the lips. A long, lingering kiss that brings the sensations of our steamy rendition of *Romeo and Juliet* come flooding back. Again, if I'd been wearing a hat he'd have definitely knocked it off.

'If things had been different,' Tavis says as he holds me, 'if *I'd* been different, I could have loved you, Sadie. I want you to know that.'

I'm not sure if this makes me feel better or worse. I sniff my tears away. 'I've got to go.'

I ease myself away from Tavis's warm embrace. I think it's airports that engender this type of super-charged emotion. We hold hands as I walk away from my dear, dear friend, our palms sliding away from each other until only our fingertips are touching.

Tavis is crying too. 'I could have loved you very much.'

I walk to the passport gate. 'I could have loved you too.'

I blow a kiss to Tavis and he stands looking so forlorn my heart is tearing in two. 'Joe is a very lucky man,' I say.

Tavis's eyes widen. The man glances at my passport and waves me through. Tavis rushes after me and we're separated by a panel of glass at head height.

Tavis jumps up. 'Joe?' he says. 'What's Joe got to do with this?'

I carry on walking towards the departure gate and Tavis keeps pace on the other side of the glass. We stop and stare at each other.

'What's Joe got to do with it?' he says again.

'Do I have to spell it out?'

'I think so,' Tavis says.

'I hope that one day,' I say, 'I can find someone to love who's just like you.'

Tavis still looks blank.

'Someone who's just like you – but who isn't . . .' How do you do 'gay' with your hands?

'Who isn't . . .?'

'Involved with someone else.'

'Someone else?' Tavis says rather too loudly for my liking. Either side of our glass partition we seem to be gathering a crowd. 'You think I'm involved with someone else?'

I lower my voice. 'Someone else who isn't a man.'

'A man?' Tavis says. 'You think I'm involved with a man?' His eyes widen a bit more. There is the sound of a penny dropping from a great height. 'You think I'm involved with *Joe*?'

The crowd are very interested by now.

'Yes,' I say weakly.

'You think I'm gay!' Tavis is bellowing. 'Oh my God! You think I'm gay!'

'Aren't you?' I wish there was a big hole that would

swallow me up, but even though we're on a major earthquake fault and it had previously been my biggest terror, nothing seems to be so obliging.

'You think I'm Joe's *boyfriend*?' Tavis is pacing up and down tearing his hair. I think he's about to go into full rant mode.

'Yes.' There doesn't seem much else to say.

'Don't you think if I was gay, I'd have better taste in men than Joe?'

'I'd never thought about it,' I admit. 'Joe's nice.'

'Joe's nice!' Tavis shrieks. 'I share his apartment, not his bed.'

'How am I to know that?' I say in my defence. 'You never said.'

'You never asked!' Tavis pulls at his hair. 'What makes you think I'm gay?'

I'm not altogether sure where this misapprehension came from. 'Er . . .' I say. 'You're an actor.'

'I'm an actor!' he shouts. 'And that's it? Not all actors are gay! Mel Gibson has seven children!'

He could be the exception that proves the rule. I don't voice this.

'You and Joe seemed very *happy* together.'

'Of course we were happy. We've been through so much together. He's like my brother.'

Ooo. 'I told Alexis you had a boyfriend – right in front of you – and you didn't correct me.'

'I thought that was your weird English sense of humour.'

'I told Gil you were gay.'

'Well, *he* clearly didn't believe you. Our fight was over you.'

'You fought over me?'

'Oh, Sadie.' Tavis looks as if he wants to pass out. 'SadieSadieSadie.'

'Oh.' They had a fight over *me*!

'Jeeze.' Tavis paces up and down again. 'Do I look gay?'

'If you mean do you dress like one of the Village People,

400

no,' I say snippily. 'Look, Tavis, I'm not prejudiced. I don't mind. Really. It's your life.'

'It's not my life,' he says. 'It *is not* my life! It could have been *our* life.'

Now I don't know what to think. The audience around us are muttering.

'I'm not gay,' Tavis shouts. The crowd behind him jump. He turns on them. '*I* am *not* gay!'

'Shame,' one very butch-looking man says and minces off.

'I can't believe this,' Tavis says. 'What do you think all that kissing was about?'

'You said it was acting.'

Tavis sags.

'You said it was acting and that I shouldn't read anything into it.'

'Goddamn it,' Tavis says. 'So I did.'

This can hardly be blamed entirely on me.

'I was frightened of commitment,' Tavis says. 'I didn't want anything to get in the way of my career. That's why I don't get involved with women. Or men!'

I've definitely got the wrong end of the stick on this one.

As an afterthought, Tavis adds, 'And you were in love with Gil.'

An announcement comes over the Tannoy system. 'This is the last call for passenger Sadie Nelson flying to London, Heathrow. Your flight is now boarding.'

'My flight's now boarding,' I say.

'I'll call you,' Tavis says. 'I'll come to London.'

I'm rushing away and Tavis is following me, leaving the crowd behind. 'I'm sorry,' I say.

'I'm sorry too,' he says.

We stop and touch our fingers together either side of the glass. I rest my cheek against the pane. 'One day you'll be a big movie star and forget all about me,' I say with a laugh. 'You'll meet someone wonderful who isn't an idiot.'

'I take it you mean a woman,' Tavis says. He's trying to

smile but it's forced. 'I can't believe we got this so wrong.' He moves away from the glass. 'Take care.'

I stand rooted to the spot as I watch him walk out of my life.

Chapter Ninety-Five

The lunchtime diners had drifted back to work and the afternoon was quiet. A few people sat out under the umbrellas on the sidewalk sipping coffee or beer. Tavis leaned on the bar and contemplated the mess that was his life.

Not only had he managed to lose the movie part, he'd also lost the girl and he wondered if that counted as some sort of record. How could he have messed up so badly with Sadie? In trying to keep his heart intact and sending out 'unavailable' signals, he'd somehow contrived to convince her that he wasn't even interested in women. Joe would think it was a hoot. Tavis was less sure. He was going to have to get his own apartment and start doing 'guy' type things.

'Oh, Jeeze,' he said out loud to no one in particular.

As he looked up, Gil McGann walked into the bar. The producer sat down on the stool opposite Tavis. 'Hey,' Gil said.

'Hey.' Tavis couldn't help but sound wary.

Gil sighed heavily before he spoke. 'I take it Sadie's gone?'

'Yeah,' Tavis said, wishing he didn't sound quite so miserable.

'Did she get away okay?'

'Yeah,' Tavis said with a half-laugh. 'She got away okay.'

Gil leaned on the counter. He looked like a man who'd had all the stuffing ripped out of him. 'Daniella told me that you'd taken her to the airport.'

'Yeah,' Tavis said, unsure whether Gil might want to punch him.

'That's nice,' Gil said. 'I should have done it.'

'Well,' Tavis said. 'Yeah. Maybe you should have.'

'Do you think she would have stayed?'

'Man,' Tavis said, 'I know nothing about how women's minds work.'

'Me neither,' Gil conceded. 'I had Delores all spruced up for her.' He flicked a thumb towards the door.

Tavis looked out. At the kerbside, right by the restaurant, Delores sat in full glory.

'Wow,' Tavis said in admiration.

'She drives nicely.' Gil nodded towards the car. 'Now.'

'Sadie would have loved her,' Tavis said.

'She loved her anyway,' Gil said. 'With all her flaws.'

'Yeah,' Tavis agreed. There was an uncomfortable pause. 'Wanna beer?'

Gil nodded.

'Look,' Tavis said. 'I'm real sorry about the other day. I didn't mean—'

'No,' Gil interrupted. 'You were right. Absolutely right.'

Tavis pulled his beer and put it down on the counter.

'You were only on the list because I wanted to see what you were made of. But Toby was right,' Gil continued. 'You're perfect for *The One That Got Away*.'

'Yeah, well . . .'

'You've got the part,' Gil said. 'If you think you can work with me.'

'I've got the part?' Tavis was incredulous.

'Toby Portman wants to see you to firm up the details.'

'I've got the part?' Tavis was in danger of hyperventilating. All his dreams were coming true at once. Well, most of them.

'It was unprofessional of me to let personal feelings get in the way,' Gil said. 'Let's shake on a new start.'

Tavis grasped Gil's hand. 'Thanks,' he said. 'You won't regret it.'

'I hope not,' Gil said.

'This calls for a celebration.' Tavis poured himself a

beer and the two men toasted each other.

'To *The One That Got Away*,' Gil said.

'*The One That Got Away*,' Tavis echoed.

They both downed their beers. 'I was right about Sadie though,' Gil said. 'You loved her too.'

'Yeah, well. She's gone now,' Tavis said with a shrug. 'Man, we were both dumb enough to lose her.'

'I'm not so sure about that.' I'm standing at the doorway, suitcase in hand. Both men turn to look at me. And I don't know who is more surprised.

'Sadie!' Tavis and Gil turn to each other.

When it came to it, my legs couldn't make me get on the plane. And despite the fact that I brought the entire wrath of the British Airways ground crew down on my head when I insisted on staying on this side of the Atlantic and they had to unload my manky luggage, I knew it was absolutely the right thing to do. I don't know what life holds for me, but I know that going back won't take me forwards – if you know what I mean.

'What do we do now?' Tavis asks.

As I walk towards them, I'm thinking exactly the same thing. Daniella's right. This is the sweetest taboo. The sweetest, most exquisitely painful taboo. I look at Gil and Tavis and love them both.

When I finally find my voice, I say, 'I couldn't leave.'

'I tried to find you,' Gil says. He jumps down from his stool and comes to me, taking me in his arms. It feels as if he could hug the life out of me. 'Gina had an emergency. I had to take her to the hospital. But she's OK. I think she's going to be OK. I did try to find you. I tried everything.'

I give a tearful smile. This is the hardest thing I've ever had to do. How do I choose between them?

'And I've had Delores cleaned up for you,' he says excitedly. 'She runs like a dream.'

'You are a wonderful man.' I stroke his cheek. 'A beautiful, kind and wonderful man.'

Tavis is fading into the background. His eyes are dark and clouded and I can't tell what he's thinking.

Gil's phone rings and he lets his arms drop from mine to

answer it. 'It's the hospital,' he says. 'They said they'd phone as soon as Gina woke up.'

I can feel my throat closing. Tavis and I exchange a glance.

Gil pockets his phone and looks at me. The expression on his face is bleak. 'She needs me,' he says plainly.

'She always has,' I tell him softly. And she always will.

I take the keys for Delores from the bar and hand them to him. 'Take my lovely car,' I say and kiss him on the cheek. 'Go to her.'

Gil hugs me to him and I wonder if he will ever be able to let me go.

'I still love you,' he whispers in my ear and before I can reply, he tears himself away and heads out of the restaurant.

I stand there and watch him leave, wondering what on earth I've done.

Tavis jumps over the bar and lands just in front of me. For the first time, he looks shy and unsure. 'I got the movie part,' he says, with an effort at a careless shrug that can't disguise his true feelings.

'And the girl,' I add with a tearful smile. 'If you want her.'

He takes me in his arms and holds me tight. 'Things don't get any better than this.'

'Oh, I think they will,' I say, resting my head against his chest. 'This is Hollywood – and they just love a happy ending.'

A Compromising Position

Carole Matthews

Emily Miller has been betrayed. When her boy-friend posts compromising photos of her on the internet, her life goes into sharp decline. Emily is about to lose everything – including the man she thought she loved.

Her best friend, Cara, is determined to mend Emily's broken heart and she believes that a little magic is all that's required. But will Cara cast the right spell to get Emily out of her current position? Or will it go horribly wrong when they both fall in love with the same man?

'A feel-good tale . . . fun and thoroughly escapist' *Marie Claire*

'Will have you giggling from the start . . . hilarious' *OK!* magazine

Praise for Carole Matthews' previous bestsellers:

'Warmly written' *Express*

'You'll love this!' *Essentials*

0 7472 6769 3

headline

A Minor Indiscretion

Carole Matthews

A Minor Indiscretion is about to turn major . . .

Happily married with three children, Ali Kingston can't believe that a quick cappuccino in Covent Garden will turn her life upside down. But then it isn't every day that a gorgeous street artist, fifteen years her junior, falls at her feet.

When Ali's husband, Ed, finds out that she's spent time with another man, he's sure there's more to it than meets the eye. In a moment of madness he kicks her out and what started as a minor indiscretion soon turns into a major affair.

Despite intervention from family and friends, the chances of a reconciliation between Ali and Ed seem pretty slim. It's time for fate to play its part . . .

Don't miss Carole Matthews's previous bestsellers also available from Headline.

'Warmly written' *Express*

'You'll love this!' *Essentials*

'An amusing romantic romp' *Books* magazine

'An easy, amusing read' *Family Circle*

'She's good' *Bookseller*

0 7472 6768 5

headline

Now you can buy any of these other bestselling books by **Carole Matthews** from your bookshop or *direct from her publisher*.

FREE P&P AND UK DELIVERY
(Overseas and Ireland £3.50 per book)

A Compromising Position	£6.99
A Minor Indiscretion	£5.99
For Better, For Worse	£5.99
More to Life than This	£6.99
A Whiff of Scandal	£6.99
Let's Meet On Platform 8	£5.99

TO ORDER SIMPLY CALL THIS NUMBER

01235 400 414

or visit our website: www.madaboutbooks.com

Prices and availability subject to change without notice.